COONTINUUM . .

When Sophia Delaney returns to her earthly life following a near-death experience in a car accident, her awareness instantly expands far beyond the three-dimensional world. She soon discovers innate intuitive abilities, enabling her to tap into countless historic events through dreams of past lives, which over time expands her soul's journey.

As Sophia weighs her new awareness against the life she once knew, a mystical Lakota shaman introduces her to a conclave of people from around the world, called the Order of Apeiros, a culturally diverse collection of intuitive sages, seers, and shamans, whose spiritually gifted sensitivities, sacred talismans, and enlightened wisdom raise their vibrational energies in service of the earth and all her inhabitants. They invite Sophia to join them, for they are aware that she has returned to this lifetime as the most powerful oracle the world has ever known. Overnight, Sophia shifts from her everyday mundane existence to many lives of mystic wonder.

Ardyce West's Continuum Series weaves numerous interlinking stories through each book, blending a bit of self-help with metaphysical historical fiction about unsung heroes and sensitive souls from the present day and the past. The task of her dynamic and engaging characters is simple - to shift the consciousness of the world - one thought, one word, one act of love at a time. Their seemingly ordinary lives are, at times, quite astonishing through the mystery and intrigue of their mystical experiences, with interwoven stories and tales told with humor, romance, suspense, intrigue, and timeless universal wisdom.

AETERNALIS
COONTINUUM BOOK TWO

Sophia's metaphysical journey through her many past lives leads to the startling revelation of a family she never knew existed. Empowered by her newfound ability to pull back the veils of time and space, Sophia learns the truth about the mother she never knew, and the dark secret her enigmatic father took to his grave.

Sophia embarks on a quest for understanding and forgiveness as the Order of Apeiros unites in Colorado, introducing her to widely diverse and delightful people who share a common purpose. As Sophia learns more about her mysterious past, a persistent vision transports her to the fateful maiden voyage of the RMS *Titanic*, where she found true love and spiritual calling on a passage into destiny.

SÍORAÍ

CONTINUUM BOOK THREE

Sophia's metaphysical awakening leads to a family she never knew existed, but she must confront a demon from the past before she may fully embrace the future. Her journeys lead her and Michael to Ireland, where they discover ancestral roots that impel Sophia to continue her recall of a past life aboard the RMS *Titanic*.

 In the meantime, members of Apeiros reunite to embrace beloved White Buffalo, who shares his noble legacy that foretells an eternal life.

FROM THE PUBLISHER

This rich and captivating story draws elements from Ardyce West's previous two Continuum novels, blending them into a compelling new slant on the metaphysical themes of spirituality, reincarnation, and eternal life. West's dynamic storytelling further fleshes out the core characters of the previous two books, Apeiros and Aeternalis, starring Continuum's heroine everywoman, Sophia Delaney, a seemingly ordinary, middle-aged American artist whose life was upended after a car accident thrust her into the ethers of eternality in a near-death experience.

Siorai – Continuum Book Three picks up in the aftermath of the tragic RMS Titanic disaster, where Sophia recalls her past-life aboard the doomed ship. Lost and cast adrift in a lifeboat, she watches the horrific demise of the great ship, which carried over 1500 souls to their icy doom, among them the man with whom she fell in love on what they believed was a voyage to a new life of hope and redemption. The story further develops Sophia's journey of reawakening as she and her beloved Michael tour Ireland and explore their ancient ancestry, while back at home Sophia's spirit guide and mentor, White Buffalo, must face his own destiny in the circle of life.

APEIROS

APEIROS

απειροσ

ARDYCE WEST

COONTINUUM BOOK ONE

LoneWolf

Published in the United States of America
First edition published 11.20.2015 by KC LoneWolf
admin@kclonewolf.com
Littleton, CO

ISBN-13: 978-0-9969544-0-2
ISBN-10: 0996954406

EBook edition also available on Kindle and other devices

Author contact information: admin@ardyce.org

This book is dedicated to all who have gone on before me. I stand upon their mighty shoulders. Their wisdom lives, as me, in ways they were unable to realize. May I continue to write about that of which they only dreamed, knowing the continuum of the eternal never ceases.

Prologue

*Apeiros (ah'-pay-ros) (Greek) - eternal,
boundless, infinite, endless expansion.*

The cause of all unity and measure of all things.

There are healers that have a medical degree, wear a
clerical collar, or are intuitive healers. They come through
the ranks among colleagues within their community,
oftentimes greatly misunderstood by the masses. They
learned the tricks of the trade frequently through trial
and error. Some are mystics, seers, and sorcerers who
have healing magic in their blood, having learned from
their ancestral line. They are devoted to their calling.

There are healers, and then, in this lifetime,
there is Sophia Delaney.

CHAPTER
One

Sophia abandoned the mundane for the numinous dimension of worlds without end. Far beyond the average belief that the mystic life was solely a story of fantasy, one of solitude and obscurity, she lived within the authority of her own mind and heart. She celebrated her liberation as she voyaged along the eternal unbounded timelessness - that of *apeiros*.

The journey of her soul was comprised of her lineage, both of her bloodline, and her past lives as well. She was left to live in the present time, influenced by all she had ever been and would yet become, perpetually returning unto herself, revitalized in every sense of the word.

There is nothing like a car accident to alter one's trajectory. Sophia did not believe in coincidence or happenstance, but as she reflected back on the event, she found herself questioning if it was an "accident" at all, for afterward she catapulted into an amazing life she never envisioned for herself. Until death makes itself known, the mystic realm of existence is rarely revealed. Most people are not aware that such dimensions exist, thinking that they are the fantasy of books and movies.

However, such was the life of Sophia.

Before the impact, her life was rather ordinary. Nothing too exciting ever happened. Rutted in her stuckness, Sophia lived in the day-to-day humdrum of habitual repetitive cycles, doing the same thing in the same way, for the same reasons. However, the doldrums were about to shift, which meant transformative changes were on the horizon, and Sophia recognized them as a mere point along the journey of what was yet to come. To live such a life in the obscure mystery of constant personal renewal was to exist eternally in the continuum of timeless exchange.

Early summer brought thick layers of Payne's Gray-darkened skies that poured heavy sheets of rain upon the earth. Driving down the highway in her Mazda at sixty-five miles per hour, Sophia hit a large watery pool gathered at the base of a hill. She slammed on the brakes, but nothing could prevent the car from hydroplaning to the left and madly swerving toward the cement median. Frightened for her life, she frantically gripped the steering wheel, certain she was about to die. Without thinking, she instantly cried out from the depths of her soul, "God, I am yours! I surrender!"

Dimensions beyond her earthly existence instantaneously opened to the nothingness, where time and space no longer existed. Sophia drifted outside her awareness of the material realm far beyond what her present lifetime had in the offering. In that instant, everything went into slow motion as the car inexorably inched toward the concrete divider. Although her eyes were open, she saw only a vision of her present life flashing through her mind's eye, reminiscent of a movie on fast-forward. Each image held a significant moment spent with someone she loved, beginning with her earliest childhood memories, and ending with visions of the people she held most dear.

Amazed at how easy it was to leave her body and bypass time and space, Sophia immediately transported to a brilliant atmosphere of pure golden-white light. There was no tunnel - no brilliant light beckoning her toward its radiance - just absolute golden-white light instantly permeating her awareness. Suspended in mid air were miniscule living energies, dazzling sparks of light that surrounded her in warm welcome, akin to the magic of fireflies on a warm summer's eve. Sophia perceived no visible shadows, nor darkness, only light and color.

Luminous, benevolent beings gathered in celebration of Sophia's arrival, each a unique translucent color, ever changing shape and evolving in individual form. She stood at the center, awestruck by what she witnessed. The more she opened her awareness to their presence, the more they revealed themselves as she eventually found herself surrounded by thousands, perhaps millions of beings standing on layers of hillsides that faded into the surrounding distant horizon.

No single being was recognizable, yet all were familiar energetic entities known to her from some connection to the past or other dimensional field. Some of them were human at one time, others were animals, and some were unknown, leaving Sophia to question the origin of her association with them. She felt an extraordinary sense that she once knew every soul in some form or another.

They celebrated Sophia's arrival with a vibrant joyful energy that rose to its heights in harmonious frequency, far beyond what her ears could possibly hear. Each and every one present in that moment was there to commemorate Sophia's arrival. Never as a human had she experienced such acceptance. She was awestruck by the grace of love's presence, with overflowing feelings of peace, harmony, and abundant blissful joy. Pain and illness did not exist, leaving her to know only perfect health and well-being.

She no longer possessed a body, or the emotions that came with the human form. She sensed neither judgment nor condemnation for any of her prior human decisions or actions. Instead, she experienced an opulent, energetic magnitude of abundance far beyond plenty, with an increasing awareness that life was ever expanding and eternal, never to end. Sophia was instantly aware that she knew all there was to know, for there was no doubt that she was a part of the universal field of the Infinite Mind.

What she knew for herself, she also knew for everyone. Truth was all-inclusive. Every occurrence and circumstance happened on purpose for the greater design of life. She knew it well, in the way that her intuition let her know of all truths as an expansive association with everyone and everything in existence, from the past, as well as the present, with the same all-knowing awareness of the beckoning future. In this realization, she fully became herself within her own mysticism as the Divine Feminine.

She felt an awareness of pure love, a love that both included and extended far beyond who she knew herself to be, as a universal presence larger than her imagining. Yet, that presence was not so vast that she could not comprehend love's tenderness, from love's compassion and mercy, to its magnificent power of evolutionary, expansive grace. Because time and space did not exist in that realm, everything made perfect sense to Sophia. She knew she was an integral part of pure awareness, like a single drop of water in the ocean's infinite expanse. Sophia was that drop of water, as well as the ocean itself.

Her preconception of what she thought was God only moments before was minute compared to the instantaneous, immense nature of this new experience. Her extraordinary amazement by it all opened Sophia beyond comprehension. No restrictions applied, with every need fulfilled. The truth was she no longer had any needs, for she was now in the state of absolute pure fulfillment. What came to her mind was a simple truth - *All Is Well.*

Sophia had read several books about near-death experiences, in which some people recalled facing a deity that commanded them to return to their human life to rectify some wrong they had done, but she experienced nothing of the like. In that moment, what she then knew to be true transcended far beyond any form of study, unparalleled by anything obtained through her research. In fact, the opposite was true. With the recognition of truly having done no wrong, she realized that her life experience was for the greater good of her own advancement, and for the progression of the universe itself. She discovered that she was an integral piece in the grand puzzle of life's design, just as she knew this to be true for everyone and everything. It was no different in her perception of the next dimensional field - the beings of varied colors and shapes were of equal status, and yet, all were one entity - all One.

As she basked in the wonderment of it all, Sophia suddenly heard a voice speak into her left ear, although she was not aware of anyone next to her in bodily form. From her perspective, it was the voice of the Divine speaking to her as the still small voice of the all-existent wisdom coming from within. From that point on, there would be no doubt - she would know that voice as her spiritual guide. She heard it before, but now she *knew* it was hers. She would know it as well as she knew herself, with wisdom beyond her immediate comprehension coming to, and through her, as that of her all-knowing intuition.

She was given a choice. The voice simply asked, "Do you want to stay, or go back?"

Sophia instantly became aware that she knew everything there was to know, with all power and knowledge being hers *before* she made the choice. Life would be extraordinary with such awareness, but that was not what came to mind when she made her decision. Without hesitation, Sophia immediately responded with absolution.

"I must go back! I have too much to do!"

Upon this declaration, she immediately returned to the precise point in time of her car accident, before she surrendered. She was back in her body - back inside the car, hurtling into the highway median in the middle of a torrential deluge. Sophia briefly lingered in the residual feelings of the timeless domain, taking notice of the details and colors that were dim compared to what she had just experienced. The pure light reduced to muted shadows as the pelting rain washed her new reality into varied shades of gray.

Her car hit the cement median with an enormous jolt. The impact violently spun the car in the opposite direction. As her front wheels dug into the pavement, the back end of the car rose up, scraped along the chain-link fence on top of the median, and slammed back down in a heap. The crash left no doubt in Sophia's mind that she had returned to the world with her personal version of the Big Bang.

Her mind reeled *I'm alive! I didn't die...how could that be?* She had to think quickly and leave the philosophical meaning of her near-death experience behind to ponder for a later time. In that moment, she needed to process the facts. Her car stalled out, and its color was light blue, not one that showed up well in a cloudburst. She would not be able to remain in the fast lane facing oncoming traffic much longer without a disastrous result.

Sophia just made a life-giving choice to return to life on earth. It was clear that, in every moment, each choice was just that - either one that was life-giving and revitalizing, or one of death and damaging destruction, no matter how big or small the choice. To remain among the living, Sophia had to take immediate action. *I must get myself out of the way!* she thought.

That very thought would turn out to be one of Sophia's mantras to liberate her from the life she knew just minutes before the accident. No longer would she be able to live her life in the same way. Everything had instantaneously changed - a cosmic paradigm shift had just taken place.

Suddenly, a pickup truck crested the hill and quickly approached through the downpour. Sophia flashed her headlights, praying they still worked. The truck swerved into the middle lane just in time to avoid catastrophe. She took a deep breath, surprisingly calm, and anxiously turned the key, fearing the car would not start. To her great joy and relief, the engine sputtered to life.

Before another vehicle approached her in the fast lane, she carefully turned the car around, drove off the next exit ramp, and found a safe place to park to regain her wits. Several ribs were out of place, and judging by the severe neck pain and throbbing headache, Sophia was certain she suffered a whiplash and most likely a concussion. Shock set in from both the physical and emotional trauma. *What just occurred?* she wondered.

Fully back into her humanity, she knew this was more than a car accident. She had just returned from the realm of infinite possibilities - back into the confinement of earthly limitation - all in what could not have been more than a few seconds of measured time. How was she going to integrate this new knowledge into her life?

In the long run, the dying process was not what challenged her most. That part was surprisingly easy, never again to worry her about what death may bring. The bigger problem was processing her return to earthly life with such an instantaneous expansion of knowledge. It was similar to inflating a hot air balloon while attempting to stuff it back into the original crate. Something would have to change, otherwise fully comprehending what just happened was not possible.

Her expanded awareness did not fit into the world she had previously known only moments before. In her experience of the next dimension, there was only love made up of love's unconditional qualities with feelings of the heart's blissful joy, beauty, peace, harmony, abundant prosperity, and well-being. There was no earthly reference to the restricted human feelings and emotions. Judgment did not exist, nor did envy, jealousy, shame, or guilt. There was neither physical nor figurative darkness, for she knew that darkness was simply the absence of light - being nothing in and of itself. Fear was non-existent for the same reason, for fear was the retraction of love. Instead, everything was known, all was well, and nothing was out of place.

Upon her return, she was able to compare the pure light of the ethereal plane against what seemed to be earth's darkened shadows. The absolute nature of the heavens and the limitation of the human dimension seemed to contradict each other. In appearance, they were opposites, but in reality, they were interconnected.

With such enlightened information, Sophia realized she could enjoy the same quality of life on earth that she had just experienced in the next dimension. It had ever been available to her in the same way it was obtainable to everyone. Because the earthly realm was a part of the ethereal plane, all that was love and its qualities were already in existence. Within the human experience was the perfection of the spiritual being. One could not be without the other.

Once Sophia let go of the false beliefs that made her feel small, her spiritual nature automatically appeared. In reality, it never left, being that her spiritual nature was a part of her infinite soul's journey. The absolute awareness of the entirety of love's wholeness existed at all times, in every experience, and in full force. It was that simple and easy. All she had to do was get her small self out of the way

- to be willing to receive and recognize that all-knowing existence was already within her. Trusting that simple truth would lead her to the answers for every question. The key was to remain open and receptive, with a mindset of the expectancy of good, and the absolute knowing that it was already hers.

Sophia realized, to live the life of her deepest desires, she had to get out of her own way. Her choices would determine from what level she could achieve love's presence. Realizing there was truly no death, Sophia could live in the fullness of life's offerings. She discovered the key to living well was to utilize every minute fully, being in gratitude for that opportunity, knowing that she had the power and presence within her to live in joyful purpose, one moment at a time. It was up to her to come from the love she experienced in the next dimension. By utilizing her gifts and talents, she would be in service to herself and others. Most importantly, she was to make the life-giving choice to first love herself.

In order to put all the new information into action, Sophia had some major changes to make. They were not voluntary changes, but more so out of necessity. Originally, she thought she could easily slip back into her life as she knew it, but nothing in her consciousness remained the same. Therefore, most everything in her world had to change, too. It took time to adjust to the changes, and it was not an easy transition.

The transformation started with a shift in awareness in her heart and in her mind. Sophia felt as if she was left wide open, feeling tremendously vulnerable to all the adjustments. She had no choice but to release her false expectations of the past to make room for something greater to occur. Even though it had not yet happened, she sensed something amazing was about to transpire. Old habits died out automatically from the lack of attention given to them. Friendships and relationships that were no longer healthy faded away, and the natural response to grief took over from the many losses she endured. She wondered if her visitation to that higher domain was truly phenomenal after all. Everything she knew had changed.

Eventually, patience was her watchword. Meditation and a prayerful mindset - asking for wisdom and grace in all things - became the practice of her daily walk. The shift occurred out of the dark night into the light of day. She began to realize a sense of liberation from her life before the accident.

Her near-death experience presented her with a simple formula for living well, but it was far beyond living a life in the mundane. That life was over. What she attained were simple principles for living an inspired life beyond anything she previously imagined, but living simply in the world was sometimes not easy.

Coming from all the necessary changes were what she called "dream-visions." Sophia's dream-state permitted her access to otherworldly dimensions. She developed the ability to travel into different dimensional fields, beginning with past lives that revealed clues to her present life, and subsequently, her future.

Her soul was awakening - again. Sophia found herself constantly remaining in the question, which instead of leading to solid answers led to even more questions: *What have I returned to do? How do I best come from love in all that I am becoming?*

CHAPTER
TWO

Winter's crisp night was welcomed by heaven's infinite expanse, wrapped in a star-studded canopy of deep indigo. Temperatures registered well below zero, while silver moonlight softly bathed the snow's crystalline layers. Sophia's part of the world was asleep, but the angels were ever awake, as were all the ancestors beyond the veils of time. The darkest hour of night brought with it the expectancy of dawn's first glimmer.

Even though the outside temperature was frigid, Sophia unknowingly kicked off the duvet with unsettling dreams of sweltering heat. She observed herself standing at the village center, envisioning her life from centuries before. Overhead, the sun at its zenith radiated blazing sunrays, penetrating through the thin cloud cover and scorching the island.

She looked down at her feet wrapped in handcrafted leather sandals, the straps crossed and tied at the ankle. On the sleeves and ankle-length hem of her loose fitting saffron *peplos* were elaborately embroidered, interwoven wine and Tyrian purple spiral designs. Tied around her waist was a garnet colored *zonai*, accentuated by the same embroidery of Tyrian purple, the color of royalty and imperial station, indicating her distinguished ancestral lineage. The exclusively rare color came from the city of Tyre, located in Phoenicia - meaning *land of purple* - where the milking of thousands of mollusks from the eastern Mediterranean Sea yielded just enough dye for the thread that decorated her garments.

She stood at a stone fountain of natural spring waters. The pool reflected her light olive skin, accentuating her striking dark eyes like polished bronze. She proudly wore gold hoop earrings and bracelets made of lapis and gold beads, another demonstration of her family's wealth and high standing within the social order. She was an extraordinary young woman in her prime, with the promise of life offering anything and everything she could possibly desire.

Sophia recognized every notion that went through the young woman's mind as her own thoughts. Words flowed from her lips in an ancient language unfamiliar to her ears, yet there was no need for translation. She understood what she was communicating as an energetic awareness and perfect discernment of her life and surroundings from 3600 years before.

Suddenly, violent tremors shook the ground beneath her feet. She grabbed the stone fountain's edge to keep from falling. Toxic fumes from volcanic vents melded with the sizzling summer heat, making it difficult to breathe. There was increasing cause for concern among the elders for the well-being of the island's inhabitants - the quakes were not only increasing in frequency, but also in magnitude.

The tremors suddenly ceased for the time being.

Because earthquakes were a common occurrence, the young woman quickly steadied herself. She straightened her clothes, then twisted her fallen, waist-length curls into a loose knot at the nape of her neck and anchored it in place with a long gold hairpin as if nothing out of the ordinary had happened. At the same time, however, she sensed an escalating apprehension among the island's people, along with her own increasing anxiety over the imminent danger of the island's volatility. She knew the day was soon coming when all of the island's inhabitants would have no choice but to leave their homes. She and all those she knew and loved needed to prepare for the day when their lives would dramatically change.

She took another lasting gaze into the fountain pool, marveling at the image of her eternal soul in a different body.

"Roxana! Roxana! You look into the spring water as if you have ascended into the heavens! Come back down to earth!"

The young woman raised her eyes from her reflection and turned to see who was speaking with such authority. Standing before her was a tall, beautiful woman who appeared to be an older version of herself. The woman wore a red sash with the same purple spiral design embroidered into the fabric.

She then heard herself say, "Yes, mother," processing in her mind that her name in that particular timeline was Roxana. *That's a good name. Okay! I'll accept that.*

Although asleep, Sophia realized she was consciously participating in what she referred to as an extraordinary dream-vision, much more than lucid dreaming. She had shifted from Sophia of the 21st century, to Roxana of around 1630 B.C.E. She was fully engaged in her recall of a life she once lived in the village known as Akrotiri, located on the far southern edge of Thera, an island in the southern Aegean Sea.

In Sophia's waking hours, she knew this was the Greek island of Santorini. Her cognitive mind filled in the gaps with her understanding of history. Because there was no technology of accurate calculation in Roxana's era, all references to time were approximate in relation to the rising and setting of the sun and the ever-changing starlit skies.

The Minoan culture of Akrotiri was a far more advanced civilization than other societies of its day. Craftsmen constructed multiple-story buildings, uncommon in that time. Most societies had only one-story structures with a much smaller makeshift loft on the top, thus calling it a two-story building. However, Akrotiri had architecturally sound, multiple-story, earthquake-resistant buildings constructed of wood and masonry, with some walls twenty-six feet high. The outside walls were painted cinnabar, ochre, and umber. Columns made of porphyry, the prized reddish-purple igneous rock - the hardest stone known in antiquity - supported some of the rooflines in Minoan construction for religious or royal purposes. An organized grid of cobblestone streets interconnected the village structures.

Akrotiri's modern conveniences were the envy of other societies. Twelve hundred years later, Plato would speak philosophically of tales passed down from bard to storyteller about the demise of an advanced civilization, suggesting Thera was the ancient lost city of Atlantis.

Thera boasted fine artworks among other superior trades. Exports included woven rugs and beautifully embroidered woolen and linen fabrics dyed in brilliant colors. Akrotiri's master potters created stunning ceramic arts, both of functional design and aesthetics. They made large clay amphorae - tall bottles lined with pitch, some with an eight-gallon capacity - for shipping olive oil and wine. Like most islands in the Aegean, Thera thrived on the fishing trade, conducting business as far as Anatolia and Rhodes to the east, Sparta and Athens to the northwest, and Crete to the south. Crete was the middle ground between Thera and the coast of North Africa. Only on rare occasions would Therans sail the distance to such faraway ports to barter with Egypt and the Phoenician colonies.

Thera's topography was the result of three volcanic eruptions dating back two million years. Yet again, out of the center of the island's caldera, a new volcano arose. The rising peak vastly increased in diameter and elevation with each passing year. Two rivers flowed around the volcano, one consisting of seawater fed by a perpendicular canal engineered from the Aegean Sea to the south, the second generated from fresh water springs flowing from underground thermal sources.

The volcano was active again, spewing gas and steam high into the heavens. Increased earthquake activity indicated the impending doom of a volcanic eruption. There was no doubt that the island was alive. The volcano's mountainous crest had risen above the interior cliffs of the caldera, originally formed by prior eruptions.

Many people living in communities along the rim of

the caldera had no choice but to leave their homes as the volcano's rapid growth changed the topography and rendered their cave dwellings uninhabitable. Subsequent earthquakes distorted much of the land, destroying many of the town's structures. The gods were clearly exhibiting their anger, their vaporous breath spitting sulfur and other toxins. Ominous rumbling deep beneath the earth created profound concern among the island's people, who were no strangers to the peril of living on the volcano. Twice before, the enraged mountain had driven their ancestors away from Thera. History was again about to show the world the fractal nature of repetitive cycles.

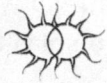

CHAPTER
Three

*U*pon awakening from her dream of Thera, vivid colors of ancient images faded from Sophia's immediate memory as nighttime's grey solitude filled the void. With a flip of the switch on her bedside lamp, light filled the darkness and she returned to present time. She arose and stretched her arms above her head as she slowly walked to the bathroom to splash cold water on her face. Staring at her reflection in the mirror, she noticed her nest of long blonde hair in complete disarray. Her deep teal-blue eyes revealed not sleepiness, but instead wide-eyed wonderment. The images of her dreams were beginning to come together. Waking moments were joining with the once unrecognizable landscape of images from her dream-state.

Typically, she embarked upon her voyage into the unknown at the fertile time of morning's early hours when the dark mystery of nighttime met the promise of the awakening dawn. A distant, yet increasingly familiar journey revealed vivid images that arose from her subconscious mind, more like a grand vision from the unknown, rather than the murky past.

Each night she pulled back a multitude of veils,

revealing her re-awakening soul. She was just beginning to build a scaffold of ancient memories of her distant past lives. Her dreams remained etched in her subconscious memory as she expectantly sought them out each night, hoping to return to a world she only knew when in her deepest sleep. It was there where complex details filled in the distant and unclear reminiscences of her many lives, some from long ago.

Her artistic creativity helped her bridge the gaps between her ancient lives and the present. In those early hours of the new day, when most people in her part of the world were not yet awake, she took the opportunity to work on her latest book or painting without distraction.

First, she needed some tea to warm her. Earl Grey was her choice, in the tradition of her English ancestry. After the tea steeped long enough, she arranged the china teapot on a silver tray, with a porcelain teacup cradled in a matching saucer, all hand-painted in delicate violets. She added a linen napkin, a sterling silver spoon, and a small plate with a cranberry muffin and lemon slices for her tea. Sophia was big into ceremony, and it all began with food.

At the top of the stairs, just outside the loft that doubled as her art studio, sat an antique walnut table upon which she placed the silver tray. She developed the ritual use of family heirlooms to honor her ancestors with the intention of bringing a bit of their legacy into most everything she did. Sophia had an affinity for fine art and antiques, most of them handed down for generations. Some were surprising finds from garage sales or estate auctions.

In each room was a remarkable chair or divan next to an exquisitely detailed end table, topped by an unusual lamp accompanied by plants, books, candles, collectables, and art. Adorned on the walls were original paintings and prints, some Sophia's own work, but mostly of other artists of her liking. Deep Persian rugs added elegance to the hardwood floors, accentuating the eclectic assortment of antique pieces among the comfort of contemporary seating.

Her home was a warm invitation to all who entered. Whatever imaginative endeavor she took on, whether it was a dinner party for her closest friends, or her weekly book study group, Sophia created a fine ritual utilizing every bit of mystique she could muster to make the occasion one of inspiration.

In the same way, Sophia readied herself to paint. She donned her oversized, well-used overalls, splattered with every possible paint color, over a long-sleeved t-shirt, topped with an old oversized cardigan sweater to keep her warm. She looked like a painted vagabond. Throughout the studio, she strategically placed lamps to illuminate even light onto her canvas.

Like so many artists, she dabbled in many crafts and art media, using watercolor, pen and ink, pastels, and acrylics. She painted furniture with mosaic surfaces, and dabbled in photography. Sophia used her photos of scenic beauty to inspire her abstract paintings with an ever-changing combination of color and texture, but her current work consisted of emotive art stirred by her dreams.

Well-chosen music streamed through her sound system. She listened to many forms of music from classical to contemporary instrumentals and synchronized her painting style accordingly. With music playing, along with strategic lighting and the scent of bergamot in the air, she was ready to paint. Before she began, she gave thanks for what would transpire, knowing that whatever she was about create would be even more inspired when she opened up to the Infinite Field that generated her creative impulse.

With her palette filled and brush loaded, paint strokes flowed onto the canvas as if they came from an untamed source. Images bypassed her thoughts and exposed feelings evoked by her dreams. Her latest paintings were powerfully explosive, with an exhibition of vibrant, searing tones and textures, contrasted by darkened shadowy recesses. Her work was fiery, explosive, edgy, and evolutionary, revealing images of her dreams of dynamic change brought on by the earth's fractal patterns of growth.

Sophia painted until the sun rose substantially above the horizon, pleased with the results of her work that morning. The colors came alive on the canvas. Layers of textures married deep, varied shades, invoking unfathomable emotion.

Remembering that she had not eaten since she awoke around 3:00 a.m., she made herself a couple of soft-boiled eggs, fresh tomato, and avocado slices, with buttered multigrain toast and more tea. She curled up with her breakfast in the oversized chair facing the hearth, already lit with a blazing fire. Digit, her elegant black cat, circled and weaved through the chair legs before perching on Sophia's lap. Digit always seemed to know just when Sophia was about to sit in front of the fire, waiting to snuggle on her human pillow for her own comfort. Sophia was without a doubt Digit's human, or more likely her servant.

By that time in the morning, most of the neighbors already left for work. She could hear children laughing as they played on the snowy pathway along the edge of her property. All were on their way to primary school located just around the bend. When finished with her breakfast, she returned to the loft for the final touches on the painting.

Sophia could not help but reflect upon how each night's dreams gave her explicit details about the life she once led, leaving her with a grand vision of how history changed at the earth's behest. Her paintings illustrated life in its depth of spirituality, tempered by the human condition, all with powerful feelings in vivid tones and textures.

Uncovering some of the mysteries of her dreams gave her greater insights to unexplained attractions for specific cultures and periods of history. She began to understand her affinity for animals and nature. Her likes and dislikes in the human realm also began to make sense. Sometimes her immediate connection with a complete stranger found her sensing the possibility that they might know each other from another time and place.

Her near-death experience had also created challenges, because nothing following her trip to the other side was the same since she returned. It took some time to adjust. She became automatically accountable for every decision she made. No longer could she carry on with unconscious actions or words toward another without feeling the immediate effect of her choices.

What she learned in next dimension was just the beginning of that which would eventually come into her full awareness. Sophia learned to become still, to meditate and contemplate in order to take in the continuous changes that never ceased. Karma came to camp on her doorstep, and it was not about to leave. Everything she did from that point forward was purposeful, or soon would be by default.

It was not long before she realized that the ancient, unhealed traumas from her past lives left a residual imprint that carried out from one lifetime to the next. Those challenges continued to carry forward and replicate as personal issues in each lifetime until she faced them head-on, sometimes with boxing gloves. If she was courageous enough to come to terms with what challenged her, healing occurred immediately, resulting in the freedom from their effects. The recall of her dreams revealed just enough memories from her ancient uncertainties, assisting her to release primal fears that left their impress from successive lifetimes. Her dreams also revealed the magnitude of strengths she carried forth to her present life.

Sophia discovered that every moment had within it the opportunity for healing and wholeness, by making conscious choices and viewing circumstances with a renewed perspective. Every situation had within it numerous occasions to heal current disputes, challenges, and ancient hurts that repeated themselves in varied forms awaiting acknowledgement. By dealing with the issues of the present time, the past then healed, altered, and re-shaped. Sophia's willingness to forgive released and set free the traumas carried from many lifetimes. She altered the future with life-giving energy that enhanced and liberated all that held her back through her practice of forgiveness and letting go.

What once felt like deep and unforgiving wounds had no authority, because they no longer existed in her mind. She was just beginning to understand that the conscious actions to forgive freed her from the grip of the past. They also energetically liberated others who knowingly or unknowingly shared in her story. Sophia healed her field of awareness by liberating unhealed moments of the past lifetimes she recalled. She released circumstances of ancient pain, thus altering the past and healing its wounds, incrementally breaking through the obscurity of primordial memories from lives lived in another dimension. Sophia consciously called to herself the grand adventure of her soul's enfoldment.

However, some of Sophia's concerns remained. One was the fact that she remembered very little of her mother, Elizabeth, who died when Sophia was only three years old. Numerous unanswered questions remained about her mother's existence, and subsequently her own life. Someday Sophia would come to know about the woman who for most of her life was a stranger. Sophia's father rarely spoke of Elizabeth, leaving her mother even more shrouded in mystery. She could only speculate that his grief prevented him from speaking about Elizabeth. Perhaps, just maybe, something would come to Sophia's dreams to help her understand the loss that she suffered at such a young age. For that very reason, she held out great hope.

CHAPTER
Four

Sophia's vivid dreams held key components that empowered her waking moments, occasionally leaving her with transparent messages not difficult to decipher. However, her dream-visions transported her to other dimensions of time and space, somewhat like astral travel. Oftentimes, she found herself, in her dreams, helping others in ways that were impossible in the tangible earthly realm.

Her dreams evolved from one night to the next, and were similar to reading a novel. She entered her past as images reappeared from one dream to the next until she understood the totality of their importance. Sometimes it was a message from the depth of her soul's evolution. Oftentimes she returned to heal a harrowing memory, or to recall a current lifetime's traumatic death to reconcile grief and reach a level of peace and acceptance. Only then did she complete her journey within a given time and place.

Sophia could easily interpret the dreams of others, but when it came to her own experience, she needed help. She was unable to be objective enough to deduce her own dream's messages. For her own spiritual challenges, Sophia called on cherished friend, White Buffalo, her spiritual leader and counselor of many years. The venerable Lakota chief was a well-known author, psychologist, shaman, and Native American medicine man and dream interpreter proficient in many spiritual modalities.

Sophia invited him to her home, but before he arrived, she contemplated the first time she met White Buffalo. He was a keynote speaker at a healing conference she attended years before, lecturing on the topic of applying one's intuitive gifts to bring healing to the world. Rarely did Sophia ever stay for the question and answer period following a talk, but White Buffalo had so inspired her that she eagerly awaited a chance to engage him. When it was her turn, she asked, "When I am in large crowds, specifically parties, I feel drained. Typically, everyone is having a good time, but I cannot wait to leave. Why does that happen?"

White Buffalo's eyes sparkled, and he gave her a warm smile as if he knew her. "May I ask your name?"

"My name is Sophia."

"Ah! Your name is Greek - meaning wisdom."

"Yes, it is."

"There is such love in your voice, Sophia. The aura about you is golden - this is good. You are a healer, aren't you?"

"I have been told that."

"You have a pure nature. Loud, vexing people are a challenge to you, yes? When in a large crowd, do you quickly feel anxious and compelled to go outside to get grounded again?"

"Oh, yes! Sometimes I feel like running away!" The audience laughed with her.

White Buffalo nodded. "And when you are alone, that is when you get your batteries charged. Am I right?"

"Yes, you are right about all of this."

"You are often intuitively aware of things about others before they know it themselves," he said, becoming stoic.

Sophia felt a chill in her spine as the audience grew still.

White Buffalo's eyes penetrated her. "At one time you thought that everyone had these abilities, but you are now aware that not everyone can do this as easily as you."

Sophia felt a thousand eyes on her. "Yes."

"You love nature. Mountains and trees inspire you, yes? But water calls to you more than anything - mountain streams, rivers, spending time in contemplation on a remote beach at the ocean's edge." She just smiled and nodded her head. "You deeply connect with small children and animals, don't you? They immediately trust and approach you, sometimes as if they are in awe of you?"

"Yes, it's true."

"Do colors and textures jump out at you?"

"Well, I'm an artist. I suppose that is natural for me."

"Yes, but for you, colors and textures and details of the physical plane are much more intense. You are also sensitive to loud noises and bright lights." He looked deeply into her eyes. "Tell me Sophia, do you often get strong intuitive hits? Some people call it 'the still small voice within.'"

Sophia nodded.

"You simply know things, sometimes hearing needed wisdom - like an ethereal voice speaking to you... or perhaps you are able to see the future with a vision of what it would look like, knowing ahead of time just what to do because you are aware of the outcome. Are you able to collapse time, accomplishing so much more in much less time than what seems physically possible?"

Sophia smiled and shrugged her shoulders. "Yes, to all of those."

White Buffalo's eyes met her gaze. "Sometimes you are intuitively aware of disturbing events on the other side of the world. You often wake up in the middle of the night, knowing something happened. Yes?"

"Yes!" Sophia excitedly said. She felt as if White Buffalo could look into her soul. "On the morning of 9/11, I dreamt of explosive fires, which are not typical for me. I rarely have dreams of any form of violence, but on that horrible morning, I was jolted out of bed from a dream of a massive explosion! I remember looking at the clock. It was 7:05 a.m. here in Colorado. Twenty minutes later, I received a phone call from a friend who told me to turn on the news - the second plane had just hit the south tower at 9:05 a.m., New York time. I just couldn't believe it."

Sophia shifted her feet, suddenly feeling uncomfortable at the audible whispers in the audience. She was an introvert. Typically, she was the one who helped others understand and interpret such astounding revelations, but now she was in the spotlight. White Buffalo walked down from the stage and stood directly in front of her.

Looking calmly into her eyes, he said, "Have you been told that you are too sensitive?"

"Yes," she sighed, "all the time."

"Sophia, do you sometimes think you are crazy?"

Sophia shrugged with a nervous laugh. "Yes. Well, not *all* the time!" The audience laughed with her, but White Buffalo remained compassionately still with the slight hint of a fatherly smile.

He stood directly in front of her, grounded and strong. "You are not crazy. Instead, you are very tapped in, as a highly attuned intuitive, and your empathic sensitivity is a gift. These gifts enable you to read others and to sense deeper levels of awareness with intensity. Unknowingly, you probably slip into other dimensions." Sophia nodded. White Buffalo continued, "You are also considered a master healer/teacher, and have been for many lifetimes, but what makes you a master is that you have mastered the ability to be a student, knowing that you are ever learning and will never cease in your growth and expansion.

"Your ability to heal is quite advanced. You probably would not refer to yourself as such, but you are a seer and a miracle worker. You're certainly in a higher connection with Great Spirit, as the Infinite Intelligence operates through you, and as you, allowing you to open up as a healer."

Sophia took a step back and felt like she needed to catch her breath. This was not at all what she had expected to hear during a simple Q&A session at a lecture.

"You happen to be gifted with what are referred to as the spiritual gifts of prophecy, healing, clairvoyance, and clairaudience. Your primary gift is prophecy, which is inclusive of the others." He now smiled, knowing Sophia was not going to find words to respond. With a gentle wink, he said, "Prophecy is intuition on steroids." The audience laughed, which helped ease Sophia's discomfort.

She was stunned by White Buffalo's words, as he had just answered a myriad of questions that she didn't even know were issues in the first place. She felt deep peace course through her body, feeling refreshed and renewed. "I didn't expect all this!"

"You didn't?" White Buffalo said with that infectious smile. He turned to the audience. "Well, never mind then!" The audience burst into laughter and applause as Sophia took her seat.

White Buffalo returned to the stage, still addressing Sophia, "Come and speak with me afterwards. I have more to tell you." He returned his attention to the audience and said, "You all need to know this - I do not tell people what I know about them until I have first asked Great Spirit, through my heart, if it is alright. If I receive the wisdom that it is okay, I will tell them what I see.

"Not long ago, I sat next to a man on a plane, and I was overcome, knowing that he would soon die. I could see and sense that his life force had nearly run out even though he was probably only in his mid-thirties. I simply said a silent prayer to bless him for a peaceful transition. This is important information for you to know. If you *see* or *know* something on behalf of another, it is most likely not your business to tell them. Each of us must make our own discoveries. For those of you who master the ability to 'tap in,' it is as if you have found a private file on someone's life. Only if you feel truly guided do you say anything. Even then, approach them with extreme care, for you would not want to invade another's privacy. Besides, most people will not believe you. The majority of what you tap into is really none of your business. These gifts assist you in helping people heal themselves, and they facilitate you to raise your awareness to be of greater service to others. It is a gift that we all have, but it must be used mindfully."

After the workshop, White Buffalo autographed his books and CDs. Sophia bought two books. He was aware of her the entire time she stood in line waiting to chat with him again. When she approached, he said without hesitation, "You must go to Delphi, Greece. That is where the Oracle lived."

"What is the Oracle?"

"The Oracle was a person in ancient Greece who gave prophetic readings. She lived in the village of Delphi, where people came from hundreds of miles to seek her guidance and counsel."

Interestingly enough, this advice did not sound odd to Sophia, so she asked, "When would you advise me to go?"

"October, March or April," White Buffalo said.

Sophia smiled. "I'll look into it. I want to thank you so very much for the clarity you have given me. It is as if you pulled back the veils, revealing who I truly am. I suddenly feel I have a deeper sense of purpose." There was a new radiance in her being, a buoyancy and effervescence.

"You are most welcome." White Buffalo signed Sophia's books and offered his business card. "I do not typically do this, but I have more insight to share with you that will take more time than we have today. Please call me at your convenience."

She felt a certainty about what he had already said to her, and she agreed to call him the following week. When she reached out to shake his hand, he held it warmly with both hands, and upon their touch, there was a palpable energy exchange. The room lit up with golden light. Those nearby were taken aback, as they could see the energy filling the room.

Following the workshop, Sophia decided to do very little research on Delphi and the Oracle, because she did not want to obtain any pre-conceived ideas. If it was the right place for her to visit, her intuitive guidance would give her a nudge to go, and all would fall into place to make it easy for her. Then she would know for herself why White Buffalo encouraged her to go to Delphi.

CHAPTER
Five

When White Buffalo arrived at Sophia's home, he addressed her as "Baby Sister." Such a sweet relationship had developed between them, one of deep mutual respect and reverence. He brought several items with him, including an unusual leather satchel.

His full head of hair was pristine white, with eyes of vibrant blue accentuated by his deeply tanned skin. Only the crinkles at the edges of his eyes and smile lines were evidence of any sign of his reputed age. Instead, his calm, grounded demeanor was proof of his ever-present wisdom. She had heard rumors of his age, but paid them no attention. Often, she heard him say, "Aging is an attitude, not a way of life. Besides I'm not old - just experienced!"

"Follow me. We'll meet upstairs in the library," Sophia said. The drawn tapestry drapes created an atmosphere of sacred space. There was a glow in the room from several white candles already lit. In the corner, flanked by two walls of bookshelves filled with hundreds of books, art, family treasures and collections from Sophia's travels, sat two overstuffed easy chairs facing each other. Sophia invited White Buffalo to sit wherever he felt most comfortable.

Rarely did White Buffalo look directly into another's eyes, except when giving a lecture. In his culture, to hold another's gaze was disrespectful. He calmly sat and methodically placed his belongings on the floor, with the exception of the leather satchel, which he carefully placed on the end table next to the chair where she sat. He briefly looked into Sophia's eyes and nodded toward the satchel. Sophia couldn't help but feel a powerful, radiant heat coming from inside the leather carrier, which obviously piqued her curiosity.

"My friend, what have you brought me?" she asked.

"The Grandfathers told me it is time to give to you what has always been yours."

Sophia looked at him quizzically and smiled. "You never fail to surprise me."

White Buffalo nodded with a knowing, yet humble smile indicative of his nature. "Before you open this, you must know what is written will be for you to later understand. Then, and only then, what you need to translate these writings will come to you." Sophia knew enough not to question White Buffalo's mystical powers and words of wisdom, yet she was left to wonder.

Anxiously, she opened the leather carrier like a small child anticipating a surprise inside, yet she was cautious because of its heat. She discovered an elaborate eight-inch diameter octagonal metal box, with cut designs on the lid for heat to escape. The box was obviously centuries old and perfectly crafted. Sophia had done enough silversmithing to understand some of the intricacies in making such a work of art, but nothing would prepare her for what was inside the box.

To unlock it, she pulled the pin from the lid's hinge, leaving it to dangle by its chain. As she lifted the lid, all eight sides of the box automatically fell away, revealing exquisite etchings of an unknown source inside each of the metal panels. She caught her breath, not only impressed by the craftsmanship of the box and its beautiful calligraphic inscriptions, but mostly by the gift inside - a brilliant golden chalice filled with burning oil, which explained the source of the heat.

Sophia was stunned by the simplistic beauty of the piece, polished to perfection, and was mesmerized by the dancing flame on the oil. The chalice's golden surface seemed to reflect not only a mirror image, but also a radiant light of its own. Sophia's mind took over as she pondered why not one drop of oil had spilled from the chalice during its transportation, nor was the leather carrier burned. She lifted the chalice and noticed the etchings along the top rim. They were definitely not of the earth, as she knew it - at least, not yet.

Sophia sat silently for a few moments and then shifted her gaze from the chalice's ethereal beauty to White Buffalo. He sat observing her obvious admiration of not only the unique work of art, but of a powerful new awareness opening before her.

"Now you understand why I brought this to you," White Buffalo said. "You are the rightful keeper of the eternal flame."

This was a lot of information for Sophia to take in. Something told her this was just the beginning of what had already begun the tremendous changes since her near-death experience. The quantum shift to a new paradigm was always a challenge, instantaneously leaving behind what once was, while embracing a new archetypal understanding. Her mind was moving at rapid speed, and so were her questions.

"I don't understand," she finally said. "What do you mean eternal flame? How can you possibly know this is an *eternal* flame? You also said it has always been mine. Help me out here!" She sat back in her chair, attempting to take it all in.

"Okay, let's slow down." White Buffalo realized she was overwhelmed. "The flame cannot be extinguished. Its power is perpetual, undying and timeless. As you can see, the oil will not spill, nor does it burn away. The Ancients tell us the chalice's oil and flame is older than mankind."

Intuitively, Sophia knew what he was saying was true, although it was difficult to fathom the age of the chalice, or the fire burning from the same oil for hundreds of thousands of years.

"So many questions," she whispered as she examined the chalice. "Where did you get it?"

"Its origin and how it came to me is unimportant for now," White Buffalo said. "You'll learn the answers on your journey. The flame, now in your possession, represents the universal light - the Creator - Great Spirit. Fire is energy. It represents power, and authority on many levels. It also is associated with creativity, passion, and sexuality. In sacred ceremony, fire like water cleanses and purifies, so as you look into the flame with intention and purpose of mind, cleansing and purification takes place as old ideas and unhealthy thoughts burn away. Simultaneously, fire's universal power fills the void, but only if that is what you believe to be true.

"The chalice is a vessel, in the same way you are a sacred feminine vessel of strength and influence. When using the chalice in ritual, ask Great Spirit for support, humbly trusting the fulfillment of your intention. Then, look intently into the fire, and wisdom will come to you in ways you cannot imagine. Even though the fire is eternal, the chalice and flame must be well tended and cared for, and kept in a safe and sacred place. If you are away for long periods, unable to take the chalice with you, have someone you trust watch over it. I will take care of it, if I'm available."

Sophia shook her head. "But…why me?"

"In time, that answer will come, for it is now your journey to find who you are in the world. The chalice will take on new meaning for you. Today, you will come to some answers, but the pot will be stirred, and more questions will arise for you to later seek understanding."

Sophia felt a deep sense of humility and had little to say in response. After she took several moments to examine the chalice, she said, "I am deeply honored." She stood up and leaned over to kiss him on the cheek. She reassembled the box and placed both it and the chalice next to the water fountain on her altar.

White Buffalo rose to his feet and pulled out a small shell filled with sage from his breast pocket. He lit a match from the eternal flame and then lit the herb. Using eagle feathers, he fanned the smoking sage over her, cleansing her as she turned her body around in a circle. She did the same for him. Both were prepared for the ritual ceremony that was about to commence.

Sophia had no idea what was to happen next. She simply trusted him. It was a good thing that she had an open mind and heart, for she was about to go on another journey.

White Buffalo prayed, speaking in Lakota to call in the Grandfathers. He prayed for their wisdom and presence on behalf of Sophia. She recognized a few of the words, but sat back, just feeling the power of the prayer. He gave thanks in Lakota to the Grandfathers, to Grandmother Earth, and to Great Spirit, and then said to Sophia, "I am going to take you on a journey into your own mind. I want you to tell the Grandfathers about the dreams you have. Tell them and Great Spirit of your heart's concerns."

She briefly spoke of what she could remember. "In my dreams, I see myself, except in a different time and place. Sometimes, I am a seer and a healer, always doing similar work, but with centuries of time in between each dream's portrayal of my life. It is as if I stepped through a portal into another dimensional field. It caused me to open up to something I never was able to understand before the car accident. However, I am not yet sure what it all means now.

"When I was in the next dimension, I decided to return, because I have too much to do, but now that I'm here, I'm not sure what that is, for my life has changed so much. Quite honestly, with your gift of this chalice, I have the feeling I am going to need to adapt to more changes. Can the Grandfathers help me?"

"They are always with you," White Buffalo said, "but you must ask more often for their help, Sophia. During this journey today, the Grandfathers will speak through me to interpret what your dreams are telling you. Now sit back in your chair, get comfortable, and gently close your eyes."

She eased back into the pillows of the large chair that cushioned and enveloped her in safety and security. She could smell the scent of the sage hanging in the air. The heat from the chalice seemed to emit an energy that permeated her being. She closed her eyes and heard nothing other than White Buffalo's voice. Stillness reigned within their shared sanctuary.

"Take a deep breath through your nose and let it out through your mouth." He paused. "Take another deep breath, and this time, as you let it out, let go of all the stress and tension you feel in your body. Inhale the four directions. Breathe in peace, and the knowing that all your angels and the Grandfathers are here to protect you. Feel the sensation of tranquility as you breathe in deep peace and harmony, feeling more and more relaxed.

"Focus on relaxing every part of your body. Starting with the top of your head - feel the warmth settle into your scalp and through your mind. Relax your forehead, your eyes and facial muscles. Allow your jaw to drop and release your tongue from the roof of your mouth - relaxing and releasing all tension. Let the warmth move down your head into your neck muscles. Drop your shoulders - release the weight of the world from them. Feel the warm relaxation move down your arms, past your elbows, and into your wrists, into the tips of your fingers. Feel your hands tingle. From your shoulders, sense peace seeping into your upper body, down your back and throughout your torso.

"Feel the beat of your heart. Sense the love of Great Spirit coming through your heart, pouring its love into every cell of your being. Let go of all the tension in this part of your body, knowing that all is well. Release all the stress down into your belly, through your abdomen and lower back, through your hips and down your thighs. Keep releasing and relaxing your knees and calves, feeling the sensation of peace and harmony. Serenity and tranquility move into the soles of your feet. Your toes relax. Now, your body feels like it is blanketed in the arms of Great Spirit - like a cocoon protecting you and shielding you. Allow yourself to move more deeply into this space of serenity.

"Now see yourself walking along the upper northwest Pacific Coastline. You are on a cliff, high above the sea as you observe the serene aqua tones along the shoreline. You hear the surf's continual, never-ending ebb and flow along the ocean's edge. The brilliant white clouds overhead are the backdrop for soaring seagulls catching the updraft of the summer breeze. Now you hear a waterfall nearby, calling you to its cleansing waters. The path you are following leads you down toward the deep aquamarine pool at its base. You are standing at its edge. Remain there for a few minutes to feel the light mist of the waterfall moisten your skin. You will return to the warm waters following your journey.

"Flowers grow around the pool and hang from the side of the cliff. They fill the air with clean, fresh scents. Many species of birds, butterflies and dragonflies are among the sights and sounds, too many to identify. The animal life is harmoniously engaged in this Garden of Eden, of which you are now a part. You are feeling vitalized and invigorated. The sun shines upon your skin, warming you in the midst of the cool, gentle breeze. Now unified with

All That Is, in this sacred space, you realize it *is* you, as the trees, flowers, fields, and lovely waters.

"To your right, notice an ivy-covered canopy of trees. It is a natural sanctuary inviting you to enter. As you walk through the natural arch to the canopy's end, you come to an ancient granite building with a beautifully hand-carved, rounded door. The finely engraved woodworks on the door are of intertwining designs, making it difficult to imagine the skill to carve such an exquisite piece. Even the hinges are a work of art, in hammered iron twists and curves, accentuating the artistry of the woodwork.

"As you draw closer, you realize the carving itself is lit up with golden light with your name engraved in the middle of the design. You take the wrought iron handle and turn it downward. The latch releases, and the door opens to a sanctuary with walls of beautifully veined cream marble. Individually carved marble columns, each thirty feet high, support the ancient vaulted ceiling. There are lofty, arched windows letting in sunlight, but filling the room is an ethereal golden-white light that is a part of the presence of the room with tiny gold sparkles floating through the air, alive with energy. Each sparkle is an angel who has come to welcome you.

"Anchored high on the marble walls are bronze torches of firelight. As you follow each light, you are lead to the edge of the wrought iron balcony. From the edge of the railing, right where you stand, you see a beautiful marble spiral staircase descending gently to the next level. Over the center of the staircase is a magnificent chandelier with crystals that appear like starbursts. You will begin your journey down the spiral staircase, aware that each step takes you deeper and deeper into relaxation. You welcome each stage of deepening.

"From the platform, you are on step twelve. You step down to eleven, ten, and then nine. Deeper you go - eight, seven, six, and five. Further down the steps you go - four, three, two, and one. You have reached the bottom level. You feel peaceful, tranquil, and harmonious. You then notice more torches flanking a wide hallway, leading you along the parquet floor to another carved doorway at the end, its frame surrounded in glowing light. You turn the handle on the door until you hear a click. The door easily opens.

"On the other side of the threshold, you see very different surroundings of a different time and place. You are perfectly safe to enter. The angels surround you, and Great Spirit protects your every step. It is an adventure to visit another time, graced by your soul's journey.

"Now, step over the threshold and stand on the other side. Take in the atmosphere of these surroundings. What do you see?" He paused as he asked each question, giving her the needed time to process what she was envisioning. "Look at your feet, body, and hands. What type of shoes and clothes are you wearing? Are you wearing any kind of adornments like jewelry? Is there a large basin of water near you? Look into it. See your reflection. What do you look like? Are you a man or a woman? Are you able to tell the time-period? Is it the past or the future? All this is easily known to you, instantly."

White Buffalo waited for her to recognize her surroundings and herself.

"Now rise above the scene. See yourself from a higher

perspective. Move either forward or backward in time. What are you doing? Are there any others with you? Do you recognize anyone who resembles someone from your current lifetime? Look deeply into their eyes - who are they? What is your purpose in that time and place?

"You may ask Great Spirit any questions pertaining to the life you are now witnessing. Listen for the answers. Take it in. The information you receive will be instantaneous. The meaning will sink in and make sense to you as your days progress. Know that you will continue to receive clarity when you leave this vision, so you do not need to feel rushed or hurried. You may stay in this place as long as needed."

He paused to give Sophia time to take it all in. "Now step away from this scene. Allow yourself to be clear of it. You are now in a state of great union with the Creator, Great Spirit, the Grandfathers, and all your angels and guides. Every time you return to the memory of this meditation, you can recall this vision of your life to journey further, if you so desire. More important is your awareness of being able to communicate with Great Spirit, for it is ever available to you. Great Spirit is always present in all you do, ever ready to serve you. Again, all you have to do is ask.

"Now, it is time to return to the outside. Turn around and go back through the lighted doorway, down the hall along the parquet floor that leads to the spiral staircase. With each step, you will return to greater awareness. Now take your first step back up the stairway - one, two, three - higher and higher, four, five, six, you are nearly there, seven, eight, nine - you can see the landing at the top - ten, eleven, and now twelve - you have arrived. Now walk toward the carved, arched doorway. Open the door to view what is outside the sanctuary. Step onto the path that will lead you through the trees with the ivy-covered canopy as you approach the edge of the aquamarine pool. You can feel the cool mist of the waterfall beckoning you to the pool's warm waters.

"Now you may step into the sacred pool. With each step, the cleansing waters wash every cell of your body and each thought in your mind. Gently swim from the edge of the pool to the waterfall. Stand under its flowing waters and wash away all that you no longer desire in your life. You are cleansed and purified. Hold out your hands and feel the force of the water flow through your fingers. You are never to forget how very powerful you are. Feel the water's energy, knowing that you are the water - the healing authority of water.

"When you are ready to leave, you will notice flagstone steps leading you safely from the pool. Climb the path that takes you to the cliff overlooking the Pacific Ocean, where you will notice a bench facing the sea. Sit and contemplate what came through for you during the guided meditation. When I count down from five, you will open your eyes and feel completely awake and refreshed. Five, four, three, two, and one. How do you feel, Sophia?"

Sophia took a deep breath. "Amazing!"

"Now, tell me about the person you saw as yourself."

She leaned forward in her chair and began describing what she saw. "Both my dreams of my past lives and this vision seem to be related by a common theme." She began to tell him what she saw in her vision, as if she was presently there, "My name is Laurinda - coming from the laurel plant, meaning honor, victory and fame. I am the youngest of the Druid High Priestesses from the island of Hibernia. Fields of green grass cover the land, bordered by thick forests in the distance, farther down in the valley. I am standing on the edge of the high cliffs overlooking the blue seas that turn to white foamy waters at the rocky shoreline. It is around the year 300 A.D."

Sophia shifted to a different scene, as Laurinda, in the same timeframe. "A primordial anger exists among the people of the island. It has emerged with a power all its own, enveloping the island's communities in hatred and greed. For many seasons, I have tried to reason with the people, to bring them back to a state of harmony, but they want only to be at war. They refuse to listen. They hate me for trying to reason with them. I am in great danger."

Sophia was in a trancelike state as she related what she recalled. She paused before continuing. "Now I see another time and place. I am inside a white stucco building with windows to the north and west. In the back of the room, several people are dining at a rectangular table, unaware of what I see outside the window. To the north, in the far distance, I see an immense black tornado increasing in power and approaching in our direction. Its vortex takes in everything in its path, turning it to dust. Nothing remains in its wake except a twisted scar upon the earth's surface, like a twisting half-mile-wide python.

"This massive tornado seems to deliberately come my way, directly to the windows where I stand, and then it changes direction, veering west and hovering beyond the end of the building. The tornado's churning darkness blocks the light of the sun. Black swirling masses of dust and debris coil in the destructive spiral expanse far into the heavens. Even though it is mid-day, it seems more like twilight. I stand inside the doorframe and watch in awe the tornado's writhing, twisting power and violent force. Briefly lifted off my feet, my hair and clothes are blowing parallel to the floor directly behind me. The tornado, an entity entirely unto itself, seems to be waiting. Then it quickly swells toward me, as if it pulsates a warning for me to get out of the way, and so, I do.

"I run to my right and hide in the northwest corner of the room, covering my ears with my hands and burying my face to the wall. No one at the table behind me seems to notice the storm. They remain seated at the back of the room. Just then, the windows violently implode. The sound is deafening. I turn to see glass daggers flying parallel to the floor in slow motion toward the people seated at the back of the room. The glass transforms into crystal shards, flying like deathly projectiles that will cut through and annihilate anything in their path. They stop just short of the people seated at the table. The shards fall to the floor with the sound of a multitude of crystal tones, and the storm immediately ceases. The heavy black dust spirals swirl into the heavens and disappear as the sun emerges, again radiating its warmth and brilliance which was temporarily blocked by the tornado's chaotic wrath."

Sophia sat back in her chair and smiled in astonishment.

White Buffalo smoked the pipe and spoke again to the Grandfathers in the language of the Lakota. He waited a few moments and opened his brilliant blue eyes, looking directly at her. Sophia thought looking into his eyes was like venturing into the abyss of the ocean's depths. She saw in them worlds beyond her reckoning.

"The Grandfathers want you to know that you are very sacred among women. You have the gift of great seeing, hearing, and feeling - helping you to see with your heart, beyond the conditions of humankind. These gifts immerse your soul, deep in your DNA, but it also comes to you from lifetimes of being a mystic seer and prophet.

"What you see in your dreams is one of your previous lives as Laurinda. She was a powerful force, and her energy has never left you. She comes back to teach you what you need to know for this time in history. Even though she died a tragic death, it is important for you to know that no one is ever lost. Their essence lives on. You are here, Sophia, to be what she and all your ancestors could not be. Over time, you will come to understand the layers of this truth. You will soon remember Laurinda through your dreams, as she awaits the opportunity to pass on to you what she knows.

"The tornado vision is a metaphor of extremely turbulent times to come. It clearly indicates that you will survive by being the observer - not caught in the storm's wrath. Instead, you see the beauty and the message of the storm, while the majority, represented by those seated at the table, sit back unaware. Even though the others in your dream were not injured, they did not bother to get out of the way to save themselves. The aftermath of the storm will affect them, because they are not prepared. You, however, will remain as one who sees with the connection of the mind and heart, leaving you to help lead the masses in ways you cannot envision at this time. That wisdom will come to you when you need it.

"As for the future, you must be prepared, Sophia. A devastating storm is coming. You must listen with both ears, and see with both eyes before you speak with your mouth, of which you have only one. In other words, the Grandfathers always want us to notice and listen twice as much as we speak. This will allow you to take in the guidance needed to fulfill your task here on earth.

"But know this: from the impending storm are crystal images, clear, pure and untouched. Great Spirit is ever-present, even in the midst of the storm, which is, by comparison, temporary and fleeting. You are guided to prepare, so you can help bring the world out of the devastation of the storm."

He closed his eyes again in contemplation. After several minutes, he continued, except his voice changed, not seeming to be that of White Buffalo. "The Grandfathers want you to know that you are now ready. Because of this, sages and wisdom keepers from all over the world are making themselves available, passing on to you their knowledge and wisdom. It is time. Many other shamans and spiritual leaders, like me, have been waiting for you. We knew you would soon make yourself known. For generations we have waited for the ancient soul of the yellow-haired woman, blessed by the Anointed One.

"The Wisdom Keepers have been waiting for the woman who thinks with her heart, has the soul's artistry, and speaks only truth. You, Sophia, are that woman. Your calling is to meet with these sages, so they can impart the wisdom of their grandfathers and grandmothers.

"Over the next several years, you will be honored when

they want to be known by you. Make yourself ready to meet each one. This is your task. This is the reason for your dramatic dreams - for you to realize who you are, how you are empowered beyond the masses of humankind, and how you will help bring healing to the earth and for those who will continue to dwell here. Great and powerful events are coming - some unlike anything of human history. Sophia, you must be prepared to be of service to the earth and her inhabitants during these times of change. You will be serving the universe as a whole.

"Some guides will come to you through your dreams to endow you with their wisdom. They are not of this world, yet they have knowledge to impart to you. Others you will meet in your travels. Great Spirit - the Creator - and all the Grandmothers and Grandfathers, including Grandpa Napayshni are always with you. They want you to ask for support more often because it is always available. They want you to know that the greatest wisdom is in simplicity. It is not elaborate or difficult. Real knowledge is free - it is within you, within everyone. When you find your heart, Sophia, you will find your way. Are you willing to live and love from your heart, Sophia? Are you willing to receive these gifts?"

She humbly nodded, looking deep into his eyes. Tears flowed down her cheeks. Oddly, none of this sounded unusual to her. It was as if she had already known, and so it was that her soul knew all along. "Yes, I will accept. However, I have no idea how to go about this. I have so many questions."

"You do not need to know how," White Buffalo said. "All you must do is keep your focus on the direction of your intentions - of that which you love. Your willingness will be your guide, as answers will easily come from the questions you pose. The guidance may not make logical sense sometimes, but your strong intuitive nature will sense the clarity of the guidance you receive. From this you will take action, and you will instinctively know what to do and when, being ever guided and sourced.

"When we are in alignment, Sophia, we bypass strife and challenges that otherwise affect most people. What is considered as evil cannot reside in company of one who is awakened and aligned. That evil simply passes by, as if it is unaware of the higher presence with which you reside. It cannot see you, because it only seeks lower frequencies that take advantage of vulnerability. By your staying in union with the Divine, you will instinctively know what to do when the time comes.

"This is a great responsibility, Sophia. As the wisdom keepers pass their knowledge on to you, you are to write and speak of it in a way that future generations will understand. This will be part of your task, to chronicle what they have known from all their ancestors. You are to record this knowledge in a way that will be best understood to serve the masses. It must encompass all the perpetual wisdom passed down through the ages.

"You will soon be known. The word of your knowledge will spread like the wings of eagles through the United States, on this hemisphere, and before long, all over the world with writings translated into many languages. This is ancient, yet timeless wisdom, not only of our world, but also of many worlds throughout the universe. At a time, which will be soon, we will openly commune with other worlds. The chronicles that you record will act as a bridge between worlds - between dimensions. Do you understand the depths of how important all this is, Sophia?"

"I understand what you are saying. I accept that it is mine to do, but what I do not understand is why I have been selected to accomplish such a task?"

"One reason is because you *do not* understand. Your gifts are beyond the cognitive mindset. It is not just who you are in this lifetime - but the collective whole of your soul's journey, being varied incarnations for many millennia. You are not just you, but the united collaborative of every being of your experience, bringing you to this point in history. This is why we must all live conscious lives, because our choices not only affect us now, but who we will be, and with whom we will commune, ad infinitum. Does this make sense to you, Sophia?"

"Yes."

"Furthermore, there will be many attempts to exploit you and your powers, as has been done before in your lifetime."

Sophia was not certain to what he was referring. She had no recollection of any such abuse.

"You are not to become involved in corporate strategies, religious hierarchies, or the dangling carrot of fame." White Buffalo continued. "Stay clear. Stay pure and you will not suffer any ill effects, no matter the efforts of many who will desire to take advantage of you.

"Have your writings published by only the most trusted individuals. When you ask Great Spirit for guidance, the answers will appear to you as if by a miracle.

Some publishers will offer you more money than you can possibly imagine, but you are not to accept the offer for the sake of money.

"Never make a decision based on money alone. You will be tempted. Remember to be in the world and not of the world. If you do take worldly advantage of these gifts you now possess, you will be in servitude to the madness that seems to rule the world. In that mindset, you cannot know joy or peace, and you cannot return home, because you are ever seeking something outside yourself - something you will continue to chase and never be able to grasp. If you choose this worldly path, these precious gifts will vanish from your possession, hidden again, possibly for many centuries before the next deliverer will bestow them to the planet.

"Always remember, you are constantly provided for, greatly sourced with all you need, and ever protected and guided. You will continue to live in great abundance and in wealth as long as you circulate your prosperity, for it is energy. Only in its mindful application will it return to you multiplied. Never will you want for anything, for it will be given to you freely from sources beyond your imagining."

"It is time for humanity to become aware on a deeper level. Most have been asleep for many millennia, and only a handful have any knowledge of these deeper insights in this time and place. It will be necessary to protect your writings. Keep them to yourself until you are guided to publish and speak of these great wisdoms."

Sophia was aware of the source of her power. It was not of her, but through her, and she knew it was not for her alone. Many great teachers had expounded insights that came from the same source. Thousands of years before, Jesus gave us all a promise. He said, "He who believes in me, the works that I do, he will do also, and even greater works than these he will do." The promise remained. Anyone who believed was as able as Sophia was, but only a handful of people had ever acquired that magnitude of faith and conviction. It was the knowledge that they were truly one with the Divine - that there is no other - only the One. She knew that everyone was of this magnificent, all encompassing energy, but most were not yet able to utilize its power and strength, because they were not yet aware of their own potential. Her dreams and visions were evidence of this.

White Buffalo continued. "Night after night, transmitted through your dreams, the Grandfathers will teach you of your soul's next journey. My guides tell me that you are one of the gifted ones, as you are also now realizing you are the Sacred Feminine. Successive lifetimes will be revealed to you, solidifying the gifts you have carried for millennia."

White Buffalo advised Sophia to alter her diet so her body and mind would be receptive. Moderation was the key. He advised her to eat mostly fresh vegetables and fruits, nuts and seeds, with occasional fish and seafood, and to stay well hydrated with water. More importantly, he invited her to remember always to give thanks, in advance, for everything that nourished her mind, body, and soul.

"The Grandfathers want you to know that you will be more receptive to the guidance of Great Spirit if you meditate. You will understand why over time." They exchanged silence, but she was more fully aware of the volumes of information that transferred to her from the Grandfathers... most of it unspoken.

"I will conclude now. The Ancestors and Great Spirit are now finished relaying, through me, their messages to you. Remember, all you need to do is ask. They are ever with you." White Buffalo sang a prayer in Lakota. No other song, or sound for that matter, had greater effect on her. It touched her soul. She was certain that all the people and beings she had ever known could hear the prayer of White Buffalo. The tone and vibration of his delivery extended far beyond time.

Sophia had much to consider following the evening's events. She catapulted even more deeply into the mystic realm, with no earthly idea of how she would find her way back from White Buffalo's directions. She was beginning to trust both her dreams and intuition. Her inner guidance always knew, and her greatest task was in trusting her own inner wisdom.

Time and space had little dominion in her world. She had become an adventurer. She certainly traveled the world from city to city, but in her case, she voyaged from one lifetime to the next. Her mode of transportation, for now, was through the mystery of her dreams, activating her life in various dimensions.

CHAPTER
Six

*T*hat night, Sophia returned to Akrotiri in her dreams. It was not long before she realized that she was once again Roxana. Her blonde hair had become dark ebony, and her teal blue eyes were again bronze. Roxana's thoughts melded with those of Sophia.

The sun moved past the center of the sky overhead. Roxana was soon to join her mother and grandmother for her daily lessons. She began her ascension to the mountaintop along the familiar stone pathway that zigzagged up the hillside. She could feel change in the air. Along the way, Roxana greeted many of the villagers who knew she would be passing by. Some of them gave her a basket of fresh flowers, and others an offering of bread for the temple altar. They all knew the importance of her studies and rarely detained her.

Roxana's mother, Althaia, stood on the temple plaza overlooking the volcano rising from the heart of the caldera. The mountainous volcano was growing so high it blocked her view of the north end of the island. She needed to put her worries about the volcano aside, for Roxana would soon arrive for her daily lessons.

She watched her daughter walk up the sacred way

toward the summit. Althaia's mother, Elene, joined her on the temple plaza. Elene was the previous High Priestess before Althaia, a role passed down the ancestral line from mother to daughter for a millennium.

The High Priestess usually bore at least one female child in each generation. If more than one female was born, the daughter with a propensity toward spiritual leadership ascended into the role. If she had only sons, the eldest assumed the role of High Priest. Women of the Minoan culture carried as much power as any man. The ineffable supremacy of the High Priestess reigned as the healer and spiritual leader. She also held a position on the High Council, the governmental authority.

For the next several months, Roxana's education would be essential to carry on the tradition of the High Priestess. Both Althaia and Elene felt a sense of urgency to finish her training, and to initiate Roxana quickly. Month by month, they grew more aware of emerging crucial circumstances with respect to the volcano and related earthquakes that would bring drastic change to all life on their island home. Roxana was an only child, prepared since birth to carry on the sacred call of High Priestess. Her father, Nikolas, also took part in her training. He was a member of the High Council of Akrotiri and was a shrewd tradesman of olive oil, textiles, and wine in the South Aegean shipping trade. They were among the wealthiest families on the island.

Roxana was a well-rounded, intelligent, and insightful young woman. She was educated in the healing arts, spiritual pursuits, and leadership, along with the business of trade with surrounding countries and cultures. The tremendous privilege of her birthright offered her a bright future. She clearly was born an old soul, possessed by the wisdom of the ages. There was a fresh brightness about her - like the dawning of a new day, ever clear with an adventurous determination enabling her to carry out her ideas with courage and resolve. Now approaching adulthood, she showed a strong propensity toward powerful leadership.

Althaia had been the High Priestess since her eighteenth year, having now served for twenty-three. It would not be long before she would step down, for the time had come for her to pass the spiritual leadership role to her daughter. In other shamanic traditions, a chosen successor would not follow until the death of a shaman, priestess or priest. However, in Akrotiri, the current High Priestess offered her successor her lifetime of wisdom while remaining vital.

Roxana approached the temple's east entrance, positioned and precisely aligned with the sun's rising at the Spring Equinox. The west entrance aligned with the setting of the sun of the Autumn Equinox. As with most cultures, Akrotiri's temple was the most exquisitely designed building in the city. Anyone entering the sanctuary for the first time was awestruck, not only by its beauty, but by the ingenuity of its design. The rectangular building housed two adjoining circular rooms that overlapped to create the center, where the circles interlocked.

Minoans believed that the almond-shaped center, revered as a sacred entity, contained infinite wisdom and knowledge - the center from which all creation emanated as the divine source of all things. The basic shapes of the triangle and square later evolved from the union of circles, as sacred geometry. These shapes made up the sophisticated architecture of the temple. Yet, another thousand years would pass before Pythagoras' mathematical theorems were widely known, indicating the complexity and brilliant mindset of the Minoan people.

The interior center contained a sunken bath, where one was required to bathe before entering the temple. Both cold and hot water flowed from the mouth of an exquisitely carved stone dolphin perched over the upper edge of the limestone bath, creating a waterfall to the pool below. Suspended overhead, flaming crystal oil lamps resembled starlit skies against the ceiling's backdrop painted in deep indigo. Torchlight from wall sconces illuminated the room between the massive plum-colored porphyry columns that supported the temple's vaulted ceiling.

Roxana sat on a stone bench at the edge of the bath, untied her sandals, and removed the sash from her waist. She pulled her peplos over her head, baring herself as she stepped down into the warm water. This was one of her most cherished moments of each day. She lay back in the warm water and gazed into the lighted crystal lamps overhead. The waterfall poured over her, while she imagined the water cleansing and purifying her body, mind, and spirit. After bathing for several minutes, she emerged from the pool and dried off with a cloth. She rubbed balanos oil scented with purifying myrrh over her body and scraped off the excess with a strigil. It left her skin lightly oiled with a rich, smoky scent. Placed on a stool next to the bath was a fresh white floor-length peplos. She wrapped a long red sash around her waist and tied it in a ceremonial knot, leaving the ends to hang over her left hip.

Ritual traditions prepared one before the gods.

She twisted the sections of her waist-length hair to pile loosely on top of her head, and then wrapped a long strand of prized pearls - the most ancient of gemstones - around her head several times to hold her hair in place. Her wavy ebony tendrils naturally spiraled down the back of her neck. She appeared like a goddess as she entered the temple. Her feet were bare in reverence to the gods. Althaia and Elene waited for her as she entered the sanctuary to the left of the bath.

The left circular sanctuary was for instruction, healings, and private ritual ceremonies not intended for public view. The right sanctuary that mirrored the left was for public rites of passage, blessings of newborn babies, marriages, and ceremonies to honor the dead. Both sanctuaries had a triangular altar and several rows of raised stadium seating along the outside circular walls.

The fresh flowers, given to Roxana by the villagers, were in a vase placed at the center of the altar. Flanking the flowers were several rows of clay and bronze oil lamps, each filled with olive oil used for ceremonial ritual. One would light an individual chalice from the large, freestanding urn containing the eternal flame of Akrotiri. The flame had continuously burned since the beginning of humankind. The rich aroma of smoldering incense of cedar, myrrh, and frankincense filled the air. Althaia and Elene, both healers, used these as medicine, along with many other combinations of herbs, spices, and flowers for the cure of many serious ailments.

Roxana was ready for her daily lessons, but this day would prove to be unique. Althaia embraced Roxana and held her steadily by the shoulders, looking deeply into her daughter's eyes. "From this day forward, you will be in meticulous instruction from when the sun reaches its highest point in the sky, to when it disappears beyond the edge of the sea. Every day, you will apply what you learn until you are well trained enough to teach others. Then, and only then, will you be ready to assume the role that your grandmother and I have undertaken, along with all the women of your ancestral heritage. You will be in training at least until the end of the grape harvest, when the sun's heat begins to wane."

To begin each day's lesson, it was typical for Roxana to first light her chalice from the eternal flame that burned in the large, freestanding hammered bronze kettle next to the altar. However, that particular day's lessons commenced in a different way. Her mother took Roxana's elegantly designed, flawless bronze chalice from the altar and handed it to Roxana. She instructed her daughter to stand with her in front of the eternal flame.

"Roxana, you have come here to light your chalice since you were a child. Do you understand why this is so?"

Roxana considered her words carefully before she answered. "The fire is lit to evoke the gods' presence. As I light the oil, I am declaring that I am also a part of the eternal flame, which is of the power of the invisible, eternal gods."

"Yes. By lighting the chalice, we declare to the gods, I Am! I am the light of Gaia - water, fire, earth, and air. I am the stars above and earth below. I am one with all that has ever been and will ever be. Whatever you do, Roxana, remember this as your truth, for you are to believe and know you are greater than all things of the earth. From this wisdom, you will know the same for all you serve. All beings are the I Am, the light of Gaia. In this, you will powerfully serve others with humility and respect, honoring the earth, its inhabitants, and ultimately the gods. Whenever you are in doubt, remember these very words, believing they are true, and the gods will supply, support, and source you with all you need to accomplish any task. It is just that simple.

"And when we do remember who we are, miracles occur, because we are opening up, broadening ourselves to something greater, which is always available to us. Your task, Roxana, is to always remember, and remain in the eternal power generated by your heart and honed by the knowledge of your mind. This is the power of the gods, as wisdom, working through you and as you.

"You are the only One. Never will there be another like you, with the same ideas, intelligence, gifts, and talents. Nowhere is there anyone more important, or less important than you are. This is one of your greatest lessons to remember - always retain your humility. It is one of humanity's greatest strengths. The people that know this have much greater influence than those who live in their illusion of power over others. With humility, you become a listener - an observer - one of great discernment. When you remain humble, you are better able to hear your inner voice - the voice of the gods speaking to you. This is where you gain your greatest strength from your knowing - your insight - that comes when you are in servitude to that which is greater than you, the infinite power of the gods. Contrary to what some believe, the gods are here to support you as you grow and become what you came here to be.

"When you feel challenged, you are stuck somewhere in your mind. Something is not moving forward within you. It is up to you to find that part of yourself that seems to be immovable, to learn from it, to forgive yourself and others, and then let it go. Release it into the river, and let it flow to the sea where it becomes life-giving again. The water will cleanse and transform it. Water is your power, Roxana!

"You reside at the center of your world, which is ever changing in the here and now. That center is between two circles, one of the past and one of the future. Knowing this evolving truth will enable you to know this for all the people you serve along your soul's journey. What you now learn will serve you for many lifetimes to come. What you embody in your heart and soul will remain with you for eternity, which will continue to expand and enhance the lives you touch. However, what you solely retain in your mind that separates you from the gods - attitudes such as jealousy, envy, and hatred - will remain as your experience in future lifetimes until you come to terms with them and understand the lessons."

Roxana stood in front of her mother, unaware of anything else around her in that moment. She looked deeply into her eyes, taking in her words and realizing it was ancient wisdom coming from not only her mother, the High Priestess of Akrotiri, but from the Ancients that had gone on before her.

"Roxana, I now direct you to pour the oil from your chalice directly into the eternal flame. I ask you to trust that you will not be burned."

Roxana followed Althaia's direction. She thought to herself, *I Am! I am the light of Gaia - water, fire, earth, and air.* As she poured the oil from the chalice, the fire shot up in a sudden burst of flame. With the full authority of the High Priestess, Althaia calmly said, "Continue, my daughter. The fire will not bring you injury if you do not believe it will. Nothing can harm you unless you give in to fear that diminishes your heart and mind. All you have to do is hold the truth, without any doubt. Know for yourself, *I am one with all that has ever been and will ever be.* With this conviction, you think with clarity, speak with certainty, and act with confidence, knowing that you are fully empowered by the gods, and nothing of the lesser can touch you. It is entirely up to you."

Infused by the High Priestess' direction, Roxana trusted what she was told and poured in the remaining olive oil. The fire flared, and although her hand was directly in the flames, she was unharmed. Althaia continued, "While holding the chalice by the stem, dip it through the heart of the flames into the oil below the eternal fire."

No longer questioning, Roxana obeyed. She lifted the chalice from the kettle and through the blazing flames, immediately noticing the chalice's bronze had transformed into a gleaming golden metal, already lit with the eternal flame. No oil dripped from the chalice onto the floor at her feet. The metal was not only cool, but was dry to touch, and the vessel itself seemed to obtain a transparent glow as if it had its own energy source far greater than anything she could imagine. There was one more thing that Roxana had never before noticed: exquisite markings that were unrecognizable inscriptions along the outer edge of the chalice.

At that time of Thera's history, the Minoan language was a type of calligraphy developed from earlier hieroglyphics. Hundreds of figures were used, later referred to as Linear A, a written language that later developed into more advanced forms of Greek writing. She was well educated in other written languages, but the inscription matched nothing she knew.

She was awestruck by all that just occurred. She stood very still as she stared into the fire, wondering, *Where did this chalice come from? What just happened is far from the ways of Gaia, far from what I learned from my teachings. It is almost too much to take in.*

Her grandmother took the burning chalice from her hands and placed it on the altar. Althaia took her daughter's hands in hers and said, "What you just witnessed has always been in your power. It is you who transformed, not the chalice. You have stepped out of the realm of whom you have been up to now, and are advancing into the power of the gods, which has ever been within your abilities. It may be difficult to understand in this moment, but you have revealed the golden chalice to yourself. What you now see has always been so.

"The chalice is now in service to you. It will help you view life more clearly beyond the ways of Gaia. The eternal flame will cleanse the clutter of your mind to gain access to your heart's wisdom. You will know how to use it when you need it most. When you are ready, instant knowledge and inner wisdom will be revealed to you.

"Remember, and believe, I Am! I am the light of Gaia -

water, fire, earth, and air. I am the stars above and earth below. I am one with all that has ever been and will ever be. In this awareness, you will serve others with the love and full power of the gods."

Roxana then knelt in front of her mother and bowed her head in reverence to the High Priestess. Althaia anointed Roxana's forehead with sacred rose oil, further sanctifying her for what she was about to receive. Althaia then offered a blessing as she closed her eyes and raised her face to the heavens.

With her palms raised upward, Althaia said, "To the gods of all existence, of all beings and people, to those of the land, sea, earth, and to those of the heaven's sun, moon and stars, we humbly come before you today, offering your daughter, Roxana, to be in service to you. May she be ready to receive all that she is now to become. May she welcome her many gifts and talents, so that she may freely offer them for your glory and for the good of all she serves, and for herself as well. We thank you for everything that you provide, for we are eternally grateful, and we know that we are already greatly blessed. Praise be the gods. So be it!"

Roxana then stood, looked into her mother's eyes, and with a gentle smile bowed her head. She turned to her grandmother who stood next to her mother. Roxana lowered her eyes and bowed her head in recognition and honor of Elene's former status as High Priestess. Elene had lived far beyond the average age, now in her sixty-eighth year. Roxana hoped to live as healthy and well, to be an equally influential presence, as had both her grandmother and her mother.

CHAPTER
Seven

*R*oxana was unprepared for the additional information presented to her that day, as if what she just witnessed was not enough to absorb. Elene took an artfully painted ceramic pitcher and filled it with sacred spring water that flowed from the dolphin's mouth. She poured the water into a golden bowl on the altar.

The bowl, like the chalice, engraved with the same runes along the upper rounded rim, came from another origin beyond the human realm. Neither the chalice nor the bowl was made of gold, but rather a very hard, yet lightweight, richly gold-toned metal impervious to scratches or dents. The artisanship of both items was flawless. The bowl itself was seven inches in diameter, without the appearance of hammered metal. It was smooth and symmetrical with a shine akin to the reflection of a perfectly still pond. Roxana had never seen such fine metalwork. She could not imagine the technique used to achieve the fine engraving on such a hard surface.

"These golden vessels have passed from one generation to the next for millennia," Elene said. "No one has yet interpreted the mysterious writing. Its origin is unknown, but legend says that the lamp and bowl came from the

Ancients, the star people of the heavens who first inhabited the earth.

"The golden bowl, unlike any other vessel used in our sacred ceremonies, emanates great power, especially when filled with the sacred spring waters. One has to be of higher consciousness to evoke its powers during sacred ceremony. The bowl or vessel is not for use by just anyone. Only the initiated can invoke its magic, with the understanding that its authority comes from the invisible - the gods themselves. Therefore, its use is only for private ceremony by the High Priestess. To protect it from those attempting to exploit its use, be very aware of those you allow to witness its power."

Elene took Roxana by the hand and led her to the right side of the altar, where three finely crafted wooden cushioned seats sat in a circle on a colorful hand-woven rug. Tall torchier floor lamps surrounded the area in firelight. All three women took their seats around a small table.

"Together, your grandmother and I share over fifty years of wisdom of the High Priestess, passed down to us from our grandmothers for many generations," Althaia said. "Now, Roxana, your grandmother has something to give you."

Elene removed a golden necklace from around her neck. An amethyst crystal amulet hung from the chain. She placed it over her granddaughter's head. Roxana took the amulet in her hand and noticed etchings on the sides of the crystal.

"The markings are similar to those on the chalice and golden vessel," Roxana curiously said. As she held the crystal in her hand, the normally dark room lit up as if the sun shined directly from the crystal itself. Roxana's ability to make the crystal shine was all Elene needed to affirm her granddaughter's power. She knew Roxana was ready.

"Grandmother, this is your finest piece of jewelry. I cannot accept this."

"I was going to give this amulet to your mother when she was nearly your age, but she was unable to make it shine. However, it is clear that you are the rightful recipient, my granddaughter. As you hold the crystal in your hand, it will illuminate wherever you are in alignment with the gods. The amulet, used as a pendulum, will increase in its power as you become comfortable with it, for it represents air and motion and will permit you to know the appropriate times for future events. You can also ask questions, or make affirmative statements, and the amulet will let you know the truth. It is a very powerful tool that will save you from needless regret, assisting you with decisions of great significance and consequence."

"As time passes, you will receive prophecies that will progressively increase in power," Althaia said. "When given these insights, know that you are joined in union with the gods. What will come to you through their guidance will be beyond your current understanding. Simply trust it. Over time, you will be guided by the gods of their increasing, ceaseless power and knowledge - that which is ever expanding. Last night, I received such a prophecy that came to me in my dreams. Your time of sleeping will develop to become some of your most powerful moments, revealing awareness unavailable from any other source.

"The golden vessel, which we now place in your hands, is a powerful tool of foresight. You must fill it with pure water to access its greatest power. Water, the most powerful force on the earth, represents the gods and their omnipotence. We humans can best use water if it is contained, and so you will use the golden vessel to hold the power of water to access the gods. You will see future events and the truth of the present and the past through the water. All you have to do is ask the gods, or hold a high intention, and the vision will unfold as you look into the bowl.

"As I know you have discerned, the golden vessel has the same origin as the necklace and your golden chalice. The golden metal is identical. There will be a day when you understand the symbols. Until then, the amulet, chalice, and vessel will help you serve the masses for lifetimes to come. Individually, they obtain specific powers. The amulet is of air and motion, representing the ever-present nature of the gods. The chalice is of fire, symbolizing energy and authority - the gods' all-knowing potentiality. The vessel is of water, the most powerful force on earth, which represents the absolute power of the gods.

"Collectively, they will enable you to work miracles - to transcend time and space. The amulet is attuned to them and will help you find them if they are misplaced. It will also indicate when other celestial items of the same type are in your presence, for there are many, although obscure.

"Use the chalice to clear and cleanse. Also, reflect its light into the water of the golden vessel. Gaze into the reflection of the flame upon the water, and your insights will multiply. By wearing the amulet when using the flame and the water, you will surround yourself in a circle of safety. Within this circle, you will be able to travel to other worlds beyond the earth. There are so many other uses not yet discovered, but both your grandmother and I know for you, that you will be the one to do so. We are certain of this. All these will work well for you as you find comfort in their use.

"The golden vessel is sacrosanct, and is not to be used lightly. Only when you are spiritually prepared to receive its powerful gifts will it serve you well. Remember, the key is being receptive and believing that you are worthy of receiving the power that will come to you through its use. Confidence, courage, and strength through humility will help you access the power of these golden tools."

Althaia passed the water-filled golden vessel to Elene, who in turn placed it in her granddaughter's hands. The High Priestess continued, "Now, look into the vessel, through the sacred waters." Roxana bent down and looked directly into the water. She saw her own reflection on the surface. "Look deeply into the water. Your eyes will relax, and the vessel will appear to split into two intersecting circles. The two round shapes will appear to merge in the middle, creating a shape like an almond. This is like the center of the sacred bath here in our temple. Keep your eyes relaxed and look deeply at the inscription at the bottom of the bowl. Contemplate and place your full attention on these ancient, sacred writings."

As Roxana followed her mother's instructions, she could feel a current of energy passing from the bowl into her hands, up her arms, and filling her entire body with what she could only describe as light. The only reference to the power she felt was similar to a summer thunderstorm when lightning passed over the island, except magnified to a higher frequency. She not only felt the electric pulse, but also heard a tone - a wave - a mesmerizing frequency deepening her awareness.

She continued to gaze intently into the bowl. Her mind further opened to a consciousness not yet known until that moment. Flashbacks of memory filled her mind with a review of her life's history, yet she saw a world unfamiliar to her. Roxana was peering through the eyes of her future, beyond her recognition. Simultaneously, intuitive thoughts came through with hypersensitive ability to see, hear, and know beyond the five senses. Roxana saw a blonde woman with teal blue eyes reflected in the water. The woman wore a golden necklace with an aquamarine crystal hanging from it, similar to the one Elene had just given her. Roxana felt a familiar sense about this woman, yet she was clearly not from Thera.

Then, in her mind's eye, Roxana saw herself in the center of her universe, all-powerful, all knowing and everywhere present. She found it oddly humbling to have access to such power, realizing that only in humility would she have the ability to be the conduit of the gods through which these abilities developed. This was only the beginning of what it meant to be the High Priestess. Filled with excitement, Roxana looked up from the vessel, her eyes gleaming. A bright smile formed upon her face. She was radiant, emitting energy unfamiliar to her. Elene nodded at Althaia, acknowledging that her granddaughter was ready to continue.

"Roxana, now I must share with you the dream that

came to me last night," Althaia continued, deliberately leaving the golden vessel in Roxana's hands. "Never before have I foreseen such a clear path for anyone. This indicates the vital importance of what is to come. The mountain is growing every day and is changing our island home. The gods are angry, shaking the earth from deep beneath our feet, bringing formidable change. Soon, we all must leave, for we will no longer be able to live here. We will be forced to sail to other lands to begin our lives again." Roxana's radiance diminished as she shifted her gaze from the golden vessel to her mother and grandmother.

"When that time arrives, you will be the High Priestess," Althaia said. "The time is near, and you must prepare for the vital responsibility that lies before you. Your duties will be even more immense than what has fallen upon your grandmother and me. You must prepare yourself." She paused and took a deep breath. She gently lifted Roxana's chin with her upturned fingers and looked deeply into her daughter's eyes. "You, Roxana, are to be the last High Priestess of Akrotiri."

Shocked at what she heard, Roxana's eyes filled with tears. It was difficult to fathom what her mother had just said. The words echoed, again in her mind, *the last High Priestess of Akrotiri.*

"On rare occasions during history's progression, a few people come along to alter the flow of what has been for centuries. These few have great influence and foresight for humankind's well-being, and for the good of Gaia. Their awareness tips the balance, changing destinies for future generations. That person in this moment is you, Roxana, for the gods have chosen you. I have known this since before your birth, but there is more for you to know. Keep your gaze in the waters of the golden vessel so you can envision the future as I share the remainder of this significant vision with you."

Roxana looked into the water and wiped the tears from her eyes.

"In the months and weeks before you leave Thera, all others from the island will sail to nearby lands of their choice. However, the gods direct you to go to Athens, but you will not stay there for long. You will be the last to take leave of our island home. You are to bless the island in its destruction, setting the future for it to become an even greater home for generations to come. The last ship will await you to take your final steps off the island. You and the remaining members of the High Council will then sail to the mainland north of here. Even though you will no longer live here in Akrotiri, you will develop a new sense of what the high priestess will become."

Roxana could see glimpses of the upcoming events.

"You will not be widely accepted in Athens," her mother continued. "There are those in power who will be threatened by your beauty and what you know. Some will attempt to use you for selfish gains. Women, through their jealousy, will attempt to bring misery to you. Others will seek to destroy you, but some will help you in ways that you will feel forever indebted. The important thing is to trust and allow them to assist you. They will guide you far from Athens, where you will be safe. Eventually, you will arrive at a mountainous valley filled with trees of olive to the north and west of Athens. The location you seek will eventually become a village at the base of Mt. Parnassus, where two faults meet - one traveling from the east to the west, the other from north to south. There, you will be the first of the most powerful of all High Priestesses.

"From your seed, the Oracle tradition will develop eight hundred years into the future and beyond, following Akrotiri's tradition of the High Priestess. She will reign there for another 1200 years. Thousands will travel to that sacred site, from distances afar, to request your counsel. Many will be kings, generals, and heads of state. They will bring much treasure in payment for your insight. You will serve the world using this ancient golden vessel that you now hold in your hands, along with the amulet and the golden chalice that houses the eternal flame. They must remain in your care, for you are now in possession of nothing of greater value. Their use will enable you and your daughter's daughters to direct thousands of people toward their future.

"Your seed will travel the earth as it spreads your power with these elemental tools. I see you far into the future. You will most likely live a life of quiet obscurity, because as the world becomes larger, it will also be a small place filled with fear. Religion will not serve, but control. You are not to involve yourself in its dominion. Instead, you will sometimes live in the shadows, which will enable you to be of greater service to thousands of the spiritually starved.

"The power you possess is not yours, but is of the gods. Knowing this will help you remain humble, to keep yourself from getting in your own way. This is where the power lies, knowing it is not you doing the work. You are a medium and a channel, using the authority of the gods to serve Gaia, the earth and its inhabitants. This, you shall pass on to your daughters and granddaughters in preparation for them to become powerful leaders. The public will know some of them, and others will be even more dynamically influential while working in the shadows.

"In the far future, I see your seed in a seaside town on the west shore of Italia, and also in Hibernia. You will commune with sacred sages. Centuries later, you will cross the great waters to the west. Your influence will affect the world as the Oracle tradition will grow far into the future. You will be the one to set the stage for history. Roxana, there must not be any deviation from my direction, for what you are called to do will change the history of the world."

As her mother described these events and places, Roxana could see the faces of those she would encounter in fine detail through the powerful waters of the golden vessel. Future generations of the Oracle appeared to her at the temple in Delphi. She would be a seer and prophet upon other lands, thousands of years later. She could see herself as the familiar blonde woman with teal blue eyes, far into the future. Roxana had a new sense of confidence, knowing that she would live on. She connected with all that she would ever become, as her soul continued its magnificent journey through time.

The extent of the ancient vessel's energetic frequency then transferred to her. Only Elene, Althaia, and Roxana could invoke its powers using the sacred waters of the spring to magnify its energetic force. She had the inherited authority, as a master healer/teacher, to utilize the power of the vessel to enable her ability to heal, bring transformation, and to tell the future. From that point forward, she could no longer look back.

In mere moments that day, Roxana instantly transformed from a freethinking adolescent, to a responsible adult. She understood the gravity of her appointment to the primary source of leadership and spiritual direction for her people, and eventually for all of Greece and the surrounding lands.

Dawn had broken. The sun shined streaks of golden sunlight through the trees and over the blue shadows of the fresh fallen snow. Sophia awoke with so many unanswered questions. She put on her robe and immediately walked into the library to turn on her computer. Typically, she was not a morning person, but on this particular day, she was fully awake. She even forgot her ritual of a steaming cup of cappuccino or Earl Grey.

The library was her inner sanctum, where she wrote and meditated. Metallic golden walls reflected ambient light from decorative lamps strategically placed on the shelves. Bookshelves flanked three of the walls. The organization of thousands of books according to subject matter represented millennia of recorded wisdom displayed among artwork, photos, paintings, drawings, and memorabilia. Most were gifts, but some were collected treasures from Sophia's travels. There was an African mask, vases of antiquity and value, urns, small statues of the

Buddha, Kwan Yin, and a golden cross left for Sophia when her mother died. Rosary beads, handcrafted boxes, glass globes, and polished gemstones lay among the shelves. A trickling fountain gave her the sensation of sitting by a small creek.

The sound system played a recording of falling rain in the background while she wrote. As she recalled her visitation of her life on Akrotiri, her fingers flew across the keyboard. Sophia spent hours that morning, filling in every detail and nuance. What she remembered most was seeing herself through the eyes of Roxana when their souls melded together, knowing they were one being.

Throughout the day, she found herself feeling anxious, desiring again to return to her dreams. Akrotiri was calling her to fill in the remaining details of her fascinating life as the High Priestess and the eventual Oracle of Delphi.

CHAPTER
Eight

Sophia's ten-year marriage ended the year before her car accident. As sometimes is the case when young people marry, Sophia and her husband, Joe, simply grew apart as they matured and explored new paths for their lives. She was still reeling from the aftermath of the divorce, adjusting to all that came with starting over again, when her elderly father, Patrick Delaney, began the final descent to the end of his life. Sophia decided she would not participate in art shows outside of Denver so she could spend quality time with Patrick at the hospice during his final weeks.

During this trying period, Sophia found herself expressing her grief through her painting. She painted her sorrow at the failure of her marriage - grieving the loss of someone she once loved. She painted about giving up a home of heart and family, but mostly about the disappointment of not reaching the dream of a life once imagined. The losses were difficult to bear. Sometimes it seemed more than she could handle, but from out of the pain came paintings that were a raw, unvarnished, holy work from the deep recesses of the dark night of her soul. They were authentic and true - her best work yet.

While having coffee with a dear and respected friend, she asked him why she was enduring such loss. His response never left her. "I find that the people that have the greatest loss also have the greatest call." Feeling sorry for herself, she thought *it had better be a damn good call!* Over time, she humbly remembered his words, knowing that as she healed, she continued to live an extraordinary life.

Sophia had no choice but to make yet another heartbreaking decision, which was to euthanize three of her animals on the same day due to illness and old age. She had held onto them too long, fearing she could not endure more loss in addition to the failure of her marriage and the inevitable demise of her father. She had done all she could to give her animals a good life, and to bring them to their best health, but for months they showed her they were ready to leave. She was hanging onto them, but they were ready to go.

Miles, her beautiful black Smooth Chow, had been with her for twelve years. Her cats, Zaide and Emmy, were with her for fifteen. When Sophia lived in Michigan for a few years, one of her co-workers had a farm, where a feral cat had kittens in her garage. Five of the kittens survived - three yellow striped, one black, and one white. Her friend's not so subtle ulterior motive was to entice Sophia into taking a few critters home. Sophia wanted them all, but because she already had a cute little Lhasa Apso dog by the name of Rufus, she wisely decided to take just the black and the white.

The two feline sisters could not have been more opposite personalities. Emmy had medium length black fur with emerald green eyes. She would only squeak, chirping like a bird. Zaide was a Lynx Point Himalayan with bright blue eyes, long white fur, and dark chocolate ears, feet, and tail. She had a chocolate stripe down her nose, with a white streak in the middle. In the morning, when Sophia fed them, Zaide would mew like a siren. Conversely, Emmy kept silent. Zaide became an instant lap cat, loving the close attention of Sophia, while the aloof Emmy stayed to herself, remaining a somewhat feral in her nature.

When Sophia moved back to Colorado, of course the animals came with her. Sophia enlisted a friend to help drive the moving van with all of her belongings. Rufus sat at the front of the truck with the humans, while Sophia put both cats in the same cat carrier on the floor between the seats of the van. Everything went smoothly until the van began to move. The cat carrier suddenly twisted and flipped upside-down to a chorus of hissing and shrill yowls. Sophia quickly opened the hinged door, and both cats flew out and fled to the back of the truck, hiding among boxes and furniture for the remainder of the trip. Sophia left them food and water, neither of which disappeared. They stayed hidden, quiet, and separate from each other during their cross-country adventure.

Sophia's return to Denver brought about many changes. She met and married Joe, and shortly thereafter Rufus sadly passed away. But the couple's furry family grew by three more dogs. Each dog came into their lives at six-month intervals, all abandoned in their neighborhood and subsequently rescued by Sophia and Joe. Frankie showed up at the same time they lost Rufus in December, followed by Saxon in June, and Miles came into their lives the following January, during frigidly cold nighttime temperatures well below zero.

That January, Joe came across an injured dog down by the river, five blocks from their house. He had taken Frankie and Saxon for a run in the nearby park, where they first spotted the dog hobbling on three legs near the river. Two weeks later, when Sophia joined them for a winter walk, she saw the majestic black being and immediately fell in love with him. He was very timid and unapproachable, allowing no one but Frankie and Saxon to get close. Sophia sat on a rock at the edge of the riverbed, close to where the dog made his home. Someone had left him a blanket to sleep on, along with some bags of dog food. She felt such joy watching the three dogs play together, but she was concerned for the dog's injury. He walked with a distinct limp, favoring his back left leg.

They came by and visited the dog daily, until he eventually grew comfortable enough to come up and greet Sophia. She looked deeply into his beautiful brown eyes, her hands disappearing into his thick black mane when she scratched his neck. What a beautiful being he was. Reluctantly, she left him by the river, hoping someone would soon claim him. Temperatures plummeted that night, with the wind chill at twenty below. Sophia had difficulty sleeping out of concern for the dog, and for the next several days after work, she visited him, gave him food, and spent time with him.

A few days later, Joe came into the house and said, "Someone is here to see you." Sophia came out of the kitchen and found the beautiful black dog standing in the living room. He had followed Joe and the other dogs home on three legs. Sophia wanted to keep him, but he was quite thin and needed care for his hip. After placing several ads in the papers, they posted flyers around the neighborhood, but no one responded. They finally took him to a no-kill shelter, where a vet treated him for giardia. The people at the shelter identified him as a purebred Smooth Chow, a larger version of the Chow Chow, with a smooth, shiny black coat and the telltale black tongue. One of the veterinarians named him Miles, after his favorite musician, Miles Davis.

During the six months while Miles stayed at the shelter, only one person expressed any interest in adopting him, but he never followed through. Sophia visited Miles a couple of times each month and took him for long walks. The two were deeply connected. A vet who ran the shelter told her, "Some afternoon, just put him in your car and take him home. He acts like he belongs to you already."

Joe did not want another dog, but Sophia thought differently. Miles had been at the shelter far too long, so, while Joe was out of town visiting family, Sophia went down to the shelter and adopted him. She kept his name, because her grandfather's middle name was also Miles. When Joe returned from his trip and drove into the driveway, he found Miles playing with the other two dogs. Tears filled his eyes, and he later admitted he immediately knew that giving Miles a home was the right thing to do. They were then a family of seven - two humans, three dogs, and two cats.

Late one summer night, Sophia and Joe propped open the front screen door to move some furniture out of the house. When they finished, she put food out for the cats.

Zaide came when she heard Sophia tap on the bowl with a spoon - their signal that it was time to eat - but Emmy did not show up. The cats were all housebound, having never spent time outdoors since they came to live with Sophia and Joe.

Emmy had no front claws and therefore no defense against other animals. Each night at 9:00 p.m., and again at midnight, a female fox and her kit made their rounds in front of the house. Cats happen to be a favorite meal for foxes, and Sophia began to panic. It was late, and Sophia could not sense Emmy's presence, concerned that the silky black cat escaped.

Sophia went outside on the front porch with a flashlight in her hand and called her three-dog posse to gather. She spoke to them. "I think Emmy got out of the house. Have you seen her? Can you help me find her?" Miles walked up the porch stairs and looked up at Sophia, and then walked back down, looking back as if to say *follow me*.

Miles took about ten steps, stopped, and looked back at Sophia, making sure she followed. He took her all the way around the house, ten steps at a time, looking back at her until he reached the shed at the back of the house, where he stopped at the door. Miles looked into the dark shed and then up at Sophia. Sophia was still astonished to think that Miles was actually leading her to Emmy. She entered the shed and shined the flashlight under benches, behind flowerpots, and around the garden tools, finally finding the stealthy black cat hunched down at the back corner of the shed. She gently picked Emmy up and took her to Miles, who was still waiting at the shed door.

"Emmy, tell Miles how grateful you are to him for

saving your life."

Emmy hissed at him. For a cat, that was as good a 'thank you' that she had for him, but Sophia later gave Miles a big hug to show how much she loved him. Sophia knew that she and Miles were soul family - deeply connected and attached to each other. She was certain she had known him before, in another life, and would know him again.

When Sophia and Joe divorced, both agreed that she should take all the animals, for they were inseparable. Sophia and her furry family had only lived in their new home for a year when a terrible June thunderstorm raged overhead. Thunderclaps boomed, blinding lightning struck close to the house, and winds raged. A torrential overflow of rain flooded the streets. When the time came to feed the animals, Sophia prepared their food and whistled for the dogs. Frankie and Saxon came running, always hungry, but that afternoon Miles was nowhere to be found. Miles was nearly deaf, but was still able to hear the shrill tone of her whistle. Sophia sensed that something was wrong and rushed into the backyard to find a section of the fence had blown down in the storm. Miles took his exit when he saw the opportunity to roam.

Sophia was especially concerned, because by that time, not only was he nearly deaf, but almost completely blind. He had arthritis in his back hips and had trouble getting around. Sophia was frantic. She lived close to one of Denver's busiest boulevards, and it was rush hour.

She grabbed her keys and headed for the door, but she suddenly stopped and recalled her recent car accident and near-death experience. She instantly calmed herself and prayed, asking for guidance and help to find Miles. Just then, she heard a familiar, still small voice say to her, *Go talk to the guy across the street.* Sophia received this type of guidance in the past, but many times she argued with it, because oftentimes it didn't make sense. Rarely did the still small voice leave a roadmap, but since the accident, she was learning to trust that the guidance would never fail her, providing she was wise enough to follow through.

She contemplated the intuitive guidance, and interestingly, she knew which of her neighbors she was directed to talk to. "I don't even know him," she said, speaking aloud into the room. "I've only seen him once when he drove by the house." She heard again, *Go talk to the guy across the street!*

Her house was located on a corner. Several single men lived around her, but she saw in her mind's eye the specific man to contact. She kept resisting, saying, "What can he possibly do to help me find Miles? We have never met!"

Sophia walked outside and left the gate open, in case Miles returned before she came back home. Her old beat-up Mazda was still at the body shop for repairs, so she had no choice but to drive the cumbersome RV she used for traveling to art shows around the region. When she reached for the door handle, she heard again *Go talk to the guy across the street. Now!*

Whenever she heard the guidance three times, and specifically with a *Now* attached, she listened and followed through, for she had enough experience to know what happened if she didn't. She would certainly regret it. She reluctantly walked across the street in the rain and knocked on the door. Her neighbor answered with a curious stare.

"Hi, my name is Sophia. We haven't yet had a chance to

meet. I'm your neighbor across the street." She pointed to the little green house to the east.

To Sophia's relief, he was a pleasant man in his forties with a nice smile. He opened the screen door, a bit perplexed to see her standing in this downpour. "Oh, hi, I'm Jeff. What can –"

"My fence blew down," Sophia interrupted, "and one of my dogs got out. He's a Smooth Chow – he looks like a big black Akita. I'm really concerned for him because he's nearly deaf and blind. I'm about to take off and look for him. Would you mind keeping an eye out for him? The gate is open in case he comes home on his own!"

Jeff instantly responded with genuine concern. "Oh – well, I'm just about to go to the grocery store, but I'll look for him while I'm out."

"Thank you! If you see him, his name is Miles!" Sophia bounded down the walk, still unsure why Jeff was the only neighbor she was guided by her intuition to contact, but she knew she did the right thing – whatever that was.

She drove up and down the neighborhood, desperately searching for a black body streaking down the street, but Miles was nowhere. She looked for an hour and then decided to return home to get a bite to eat and regroup. When she pulled into the driveway, she noticed the closed gate. She excitedly hopped out of the RV and found Miles, soaking wet, curled up on his soggy dog bed on the deck. His coat was so thick that it took several towels to dry him.

After giving him a big hug, she fed him and made sure he had a warm, dry place inside to lie down. Sophia wrapped her arms around Miles's middle and laid her head on his back. For some reason, she only did this with him. Her hands practically disappeared into his heavy mane. She put a lot of love into her precious dog before she went across the street to thank Jeff.

When Jeff answered the door, he excitedly said, "It was a miracle! I tell you, it was an absolute miracle!" She later found out that Jeff was a computer programmer. He rarely got very excited. He was usually quite calm and showed very little emotion or feeling, but that evening was different. "I drove straight down Harvard to get to Federal," he said, excitedly. "Typically, I turn left onto Federal, but traffic was at a complete standstill. Instead, I turned right to drive a couple of blocks to a stoplight so I could get across the street easier. I drove about a half a block, and I saw what was causing the traffic holdup. Miles was standing in the middle of the street! It was pouring down rain, and the car headlights probably blinded him. Poor guy was soaking wet and confused as cars inched by to avoid hitting him. I slowly drove up next to him and called him by name, and he came right up to the car. I lifted him into the back seat. It was like he knew me!"

"I can't tell you how grateful I am," Sophia said. She told him how she felt guided to talk to him in the first place. Sophia was not only appreciative that Jeff saved Miles, but also she was thankful for being wise enough to listen to her guidance. If not, Miles might no longer be.

Before long, however, Sophia knew that Miles would soon leave her. As she watched her father slowly passing to a new dimension, so too would Miles, Emmy, and Zaide. Although she believed the essence of their lives was eternal, she had no choice but to let them go.

CHAPTER
Nine

The summer season would soon commence, which meant Sophia was busy preparing to sell many original paintings and prints of her drawings. She also created more handcrafted jewelry to sell at various art fairs in town. Many of her smaller paintings sold well. She most enjoyed painting pieces usually 3' x 4' or larger, allowing her to express herself with greater creative artistry, but rarely did they sell, because of the higher price tag.

Sophia had an extraordinarily intriguing life, and because of her increasing reputation as a seer and healer, people sought her out as much for her counsel as for her artwork. The art world in Colorado was beginning to acknowledge her unique talents. Word was spreading about the artistic seer who not only sold beautiful pieces of art, but also counseled her clients with wisdom for the betterment of their lives. For the time being, she only sold her work in the Denver area so she could be with her father.

Selling her art enabled her to work incognito, under the guise of an artist who touched lives along the way. Sophia would naturally strike up a conversation, offering her gifts of healing if needed. She gave greater value from her knowledge and wisdom than what she received in monetary gain for her artwork. Whether the client bought a piece of art or not, most people left her company feeling of sense of increase. Oftentimes, they would later return to buy something.

Some of her paintings were of a realistic subject matter, but others were abstract expressions. Intuition guided her, allowing her the freedom to channel every stroke of color and texture. The white walls of her booth were a clean background to hang her paintings. She exhibited her smaller pieces, framed and placed on easels. Amidst the paintings were large glass vases with fragrant fresh floral bouquets and votive candles. A selection of soft music playing in the background created a calm ambience in her booth. She displayed her jewelry in a glass case on a table close to her chair. Large paintings at the entrance of her booth created an elegant invitation to enter her world of art.

Sophia sat off to the side in her director's chair, observing those perusing through her booth. She typically wore long flowing skirts or dresses in beautiful natural fabrics, along with her handmade jewelry and stylish high heels. She was the topic of many a conversation because of her striking looks and charisma. She looked much younger than she was, drawing in men of varied ages, and women trusted her as well, finding her to be warm, intelligent and honest. Next to her was an empty director's chair, where she welcomed potential clients to sit in conversation. She offered them a small glass of mineral water or wine from her favorite vintner.

Sophia could converse with most anyone. People instantly trusted her, feeling at home in her company. Since childhood, people naturally confided in her, opening up with personal concerns and seeking her reliably sound advice. She might be standing in the grocery line chatting with a perfect stranger, who would suddenly say, "I have never told anyone this before, but..." They shared a dream, a secret desire, or sometimes would tell her of great sorrow, as Sophia elegantly held their confidence. She had a natural gift, but had no idea why.

She used this ability to sell her artwork more easily than her competition, because she was genuinely interested in others. As a result, she created a dynamic network of people who helped her rapidly grow her business. On many occasions, her clients returned just to talk. Sophia read them easily, bypassing needless hours of conversation. They would query her for advice because she saw beyond the problem and directly to the solution, sometimes offering sage wisdom through a story or parable.

Early the afternoon of June 7th, Sophia sat watching people tour through her display. A dark-haired woman in her thirties acknowledged Sophia and struck up a conversation about one of the necklaces in the glass case.

"That's one of my favorites," Sophia said. "You have excellent taste. My name is Sophia Delaney." Smiling, she offered her hand to the woman.

"Hello. I'm Olivia," she said, shaking Sophia's hand. "The necklace is lovely."

Sophia opened the case and offered to put the necklace on her. As Olivia looked at herself in the mirror, Sophia noticed tears welling up in the woman's eyes. Sophia calmly described the alexandrite in the necklace. "This is a stone of restorative powers, enhancing the rebirth of the inner and outer self. It balances one's emotional state, providing confidence and self-esteem, and it produces qualities expanding one's creativity and awareness in the realm of manifestation."

Sophia sensed that the woman was troubled, so she asked if she might like to sit down and have a glass of wine.

Still wearing the necklace, Olivia took the seat next to Sophia. "Thank you. I would appreciate that."

Sophia poured a nice red wine into a stemmed glass and offered it to Olivia. "This is my favorite blend of Syrah, Pinot Noir and Cabernet." Olivia could not stop looking at her reflection, running her hand over the necklace as she tried to hold back her tears. "Would you like to talk about what's bothering you?" Olivia looked into Sophia's teal eyes, noticing the compassion and care in them. "Just take a deep breath and tell me."

Pausing, Olivia again placed her left hand on the necklace. "I'm sorry. It's not like me to cry in public, particularly in front of a stranger."

"You are perfectly safe here. You can tell me what's going on."

"I just got divorced. I came to the art fair today just to get out of the house. My husband - or rather, ex-husband - made most of the decisions. Now that I am on my own, I'm not sure how to move forward. I have great dreams and ambitions, but I feel stuck."

Sophia smiled. "Do you mind if I tell you a story?"

Olivia nodded, sitting back in the chair and taking a sip of wine. She appreciated the kindness.

"I knew a woman by the name of Emma who, while visiting Maui, learned a great lesson from a green sea turtle. It was late in the afternoon when Emma heard a deep moaning outside her condominium, like a cry for help. From her lanai, she spotted an adult green sea turtle three floors below, sitting on a rock on the shoreline.

"Emma had been waiting for a chance to photograph the turtles. They were difficult to see among the reflections in the water. She grabbed her camera and ran down three flights of stairs, around the building, and past the pool to the hill above the turtle. The turtle was high-centered on a rock. He stuck his neck out and attempted to push his way off the rock with his back legs, while his front fins flailed in the air. There was nothing for him to grab onto, and he was unable to budge. So, all he could do was wait.

"Emma kept her distance out of respect for his plight while the turtle awaited liberation from his perch. He knew what to do. For forty-five minutes, Emma kept her vigil, anxiously anticipating his emancipation. The tide rolled in, wave after wave, eventually rising above the rocks and enabling the turtle easily to float off his pedestal. He swam toward the ocean, ready to return to his underwater sanctuary, but yet again, he could not reach the open sea. Held literally at bay by several volcanic boulders - enormous black sentinels clustered together, protecting the shoreline - the turtle waited again, knowing just what to do.

"The tide continued to rise, bringing in greater waves with a surge of enormous force. Suddenly, the immense energy of white frothy foam danced through the boulders. Anticipating the moment, the turtle pushed with his fins and gigantic back legs, turning sideways, and easily slipped between the rocks.

"Emma watched his head bob above the water's surface as he swam out to the open sea. When the turtle emerged, she jumped to her feet and raised her hands to the heavens, crying out, 'Freedom!' From behind, she heard cheering. Surprised, she turned to see at least twenty others, some in groups, who had been watching from their higher vantage point on their lanais. They were people from many countries with the common language of joy, celebrating the turtle's liberation."

Olivia smiled as she sipped her wine. "I guess you're saying I'm that turtle."

"The turtle was not stuck after all," Sophia said. "Yes, he was frustrated - his groan was evidence of that - yet he knew just what to do. The water was his natural environment. The turtle knew the tide would soon rise and take him home. All he had to do was be patient and wait for nature to take its course. He was free again to swim to his safe haven deep beneath the ocean's surface."

Sophia took Olivia's hand. "Olivia, in this time of healing from your divorce, you must prepare for what is on the horizon. You are not stuck. Yes, you are embarking upon a new journey, and it is one in which your soul is deeply familiar. If you relax and trust, your intuition will be your guide to assist you in knowing just what to do when you face an obstacle, for it just might be that you simply turn sideways and slip through to the other side. In fact, when you were married, you could not have taken on what you are about to achieve. You are now far stronger than you have ever been. This is a time for you to spread your wings and live in the anticipation of the journey. If you look at your life as an adventure, you will find the way as one of exploration, leading you to goals that otherwise would not be available to you."

Olivia sat in silence, looking at Sophia in amazement. "I didn't expect to have a conversation like this today."

"Often, enlightened awareness comes when we are in a state of surrender, taking in the present moment and being open to new possibilities. You know, your attraction to the alexandrite stone in that necklace is no coincidence. Its powers are exactly what drew you to it. It might be a gift to yourself to remind you of what you need to move forward."

Taking off the necklace, Olivia asked, "Is there a pair of earrings with the same stone? They may be more in my price range."

Sophia showed her a pair set in gold with a two-inch dangle. "These would be beautiful with your dark hair." Holding them up to Olivia's ear, she told her the price. Olivia was surprised that they were not much less than the necklace. She looked longingly at both. "If you purchase the necklace, I will give you the earrings with my compliments," Sophia said.

Olivia's eyes lit up. "Are you sure?"

"It will be my renewal gift to you!"

"Oh, thank you - it's a deal!"

Sophia wrapped the necklace and earrings in gold tissue and placed them inside a shiny black box. Around it, she tied a gold mesh ribbon in a bow, and then put the box in a black bag. She also placed a card inside describing the metaphysical meanings of the alexandrite for Olivia to read later.

"You don't need to go to all this trouble, Sophia," Olivia said.

"Oh, but I do! This is a significant gift for you. Some of my most meaningful possessions are those I acquired for my benefit alone, because they represented substantial value, for me, beyond their material beauty. You are giving yourself jewelry that possesses powers of creative expansiveness, and each time you wear them you will feel empowered. You are now moving forward into your dreams of becoming the woman you have always known yourself to be."

Olivia paid for the jewelry and gave Sophia a hug. "Thank you for taking the time to listen. You have helped me more than you will ever know. I will wear these and remember you." She smiled with a glow she did not have when she arrived thirty minutes earlier.

Sophia looked into her eyes and said, "Love yourself first, and life will naturally come to you."

They parted ways, and Sophia sat back in her chair, waiting for the next conversation to commence.

CHAPTER
Ten

It was their fourth-first date. Their first-first date occurred early in high school. The second came during their sophomore year in college. The third was as young entrepreneurs in their late twenties, when Sophia left him to marry Joe. This was their fourth. While skillfully practiced at a series of first dates, they were at it again, determined to get it right this time. Sophia and Michael proclaimed they would never again have another first date.

Over the years, Michael was not sure what had become of Sophia, but she remained on his mind, because no one he dated ever seemed to compare to her. None of them, in his mind, were good enough, because they were not Sophia. Following time number three, she married Joe and disappeared with a last name Michael could not recall, leaving him to wonder if he would ever see or hear from her again.

A little more than ten years passed, the last five taking Michael many turns around the bend, to distances of no known destination. Only one month before, he said his final goodbyes to his father. Eight months prior to that, his mother had passed on as well. Michael was present with both of his elderly parents when they died. It was a privilege for him to be with them in their final moments, but more so, Michael's grounded nature - that of being the rock of the family - provided his parents a comfortable environment from which they could easily leave when they were ready.

The privilege had its price, however, for the slow, lengthy journey to their deaths took an enormous emotional toll on Michael. He was an only child and single, left with no one to share the burden of caring for his beloved parents, whose health slowly deteriorated over five long years. There was little life left in him, because he gave all he had to the dignity of their final days.

He felt empty. His life was a blank canvas with no future plans painted into its framework. It was a time of healing and a time for reflection, with Sophia's face fading in from distant memories of when their lives were filled with promise. He believed his purpose could only be fulfilled once Sophia returned to him, and that would happen when she was ready.

Occasionally, he Googled her maiden name, hoping to find some reference to her. Either by coincidence – or divine intervention - Sophia changed her name back to Delaney after her divorce from Joe. Michael's most recent attempt revealed her on Facebook. Social networking was not Michael's thing, but he thought, *what the hell!* The temptation to contact Sophia was too great, so he joined with the sole purpose to reach out to her.

About the same time, Sophia spent six days at a spiritual retreat in Santa Barbara. During the Sunday morning service, she heard her familiar still small voice say to her, *This is to be your husband.* Stunned by the intuitive message, she wondered if her intuition guided her to the man who gave the Sunday talk, because she felt an attraction to him.

She took a few extra days after the retreat to spend time along the Pacific coastline prior to catching her flight home from LAX. Sophia first drove up the Pacific Coast Highway to Carmel. She was never able to spend enough time in nature, so she stopped at a beautiful spot and simply wandered along the water's edge as sundown approached. To her delight, she was one of only a few people on the small beach. She took off her sandals and sat, running her toes through the sand, taking in the magnificent sunset.

Suddenly, an adult seagull landed three feet away. A few minutes later, three more gulls arrived, and before long, a flock of juvenile seagulls gathered close by on her opposite side. Sophia smiled and watched as they moved about the sand, foraging for tasty snacks and dancing around the incoming waves. They seemed perfectly at ease in Sophia's presence. She curiously looked around to see if anyone else on the beach experienced the same thing, but she apparently was the only human of interest to the gulls.

Sophia always knew she was energetically in the right place whenever small children and animals magnetized to her, for they had no filters to block them from what naturally called to them. At these times, she paid attention to what she felt. She noticed her sense of joy and blissful calm. She felt centered and, better yet, aligned, which enabled her to duplicate that feeling every day. That was when she witnessed miracles. In truth, it was more than her being in the right place, for it was how she joined the energy of nature, melding with nature's environment by which all things flow to a rhythm of peaceful serenity, joy, and grace.

Point Lobos State Reserve Park was a short distance from Carmel. She spent the next afternoon walking along the many trails, taking photographs for hours and drinking in the beauty of nature, the animals, and the sea life. She then drove down to Big Sur to spend sundown at Pfeiffer Beach.

On her way back to Carmel, she stopped at a small inn for dinner. She sat at a window overlooking the ocean as darkness approached. She noticed an elderly man sitting by himself at the table next to her. His son had left him there while he searched for a motel room for them to spend the night. Sophia asked the man if he would like some company, and he gratefully accepted her offer.

They placed their order, and Sophia selected a bottle of California pinot noir from the wine list. The man, who introduced himself as Henry Martin, toasted her. "To synchronicity!" he said. "*Slainte!*"

Henry was quite elderly. Sophia guessed he was in his mid-nineties. Their conversation was an exchange of heart. She told him about her writing and artwork. He was also quite interested in her travels. When their dinner arrived, Henry told her about his family. He was of Irish descent, and his wife had come from Italy. They had one son.

"Were you in World War II?" she asked.

"Yes, I was first stationed in France and later in Italy. I was in the Navy. It was my job to transport the troops." Suddenly, his energy shifted. Sadness filled his demeanor. Henry continued, "I was at Normandy, on D-Day." He paused, recalling that fateful day. "Never have I seen so many dead people." Tears rose in his eyes as he recalled the horror. Sophia placed her hand on his arm and just sat with him in silence through his recollection.

Then, he looked into Sophia's eyes. "I was later stationed in Italy, and it was not long before I saw the most beautiful angel I had ever seen. Her name was Sabrina. She was sixteen. When the war was over, I married her and brought her back to the States with me. We lived in San Diego, where we raised our son, Tony. My angel, Sabrina, passed on three years ago. I can't wait to join her. I miss her so."

"You know, Henry, I recently had a near-death experience, and I can tell you that, when it is your time to go, the journey will be a pleasant one. The transition is easy. It's like walking over a threshold from a room of complete familiarity into the great outdoors, with magnificent sights and glorious imaginings, and sounds you could never possibly conceive until that very moment. You will wonder, just for a split second, why you waited so long to move on. There is absolutely nothing to fear. And yes, Henry, I am certain that Sabrina is there waiting to welcome you as are so many others you have known and loved. When you decide to move on, your body will be left behind, but the person you know as yourself - your soul - will easily shift into that next reality."

The light in Henry's eyes was radiant as he listened to her wisdom. She intended to give him hope beyond his current concept of death.

Sophia knew she simply did not *happen to be in the right place at the right time* to meet Henry. There were no coincidences, and Henry must have thought the same, for this indeed was 'synchronicity.' She believed there were endless opportunities to serve and help others along their way, even if their course of action was to leave this life here on earth.

She knew life was eternal. She was certain of that. She knew that was true both from her near-death experience and from the recall of her many past lives. The next opportunity to learn of the soul's direction is in simply waiting for the soul's agreement to embark on a new life journey. It is somewhat like traveling by train. One disembarks to stay at their destination for a while, and when finished with the task, they hop on the train and venture on to the next journey of discovery.

Henry's son, Tony, returned to the restaurant, having found a little cabin down the road to share with his father. They were on a vacation together, driving up the scenic Pacific Coast Highway to visit relatives in Seattle. Sophia thought this was probably their last trip together. Tony thanked her for spending time with his father. When Henry went to leave the restaurant, he paused and returned to the table. Sophia stood. The two embraced, and he looked into her eyes and smiled. He patted her cheek lovingly. "Thank you for your kindness, Sophia."

"I am honored, Henry. May you travel well."

The next day, Sophia awoke at 6:00 a.m. To save time, she packed the car the night before, for her flight from LAX to Denver departed at 4:40 p.m. She took many photographs along the highway and arrived in Santa Barbara around noon. There, she stopped at a state park and walked quite a distance to reach a cliff that overlooked the ocean. She sat for an hour and took in the atmosphere of the surf breaking in timely patterns on the beach below. Suddenly, she realized she had better get back on the road.

She stopped a couple more times before she approached North Hollywood. Her road map, which had the directions to the rental car site, was nowhere to be found. Unable to recognize any of the signs along the highway, she decided to ask, "Spirit, am I too far south?" The answer, which came through as her inner voice that she now knew so well, said *No*.

She continued, but soon she was convinced she was not in the right place. She took the next exit and looked for somewhere where she could stop and ask directions. Time, it seemed, was ticking away, and she knew the airlines waited for no one. She drove into an area of shops in old Hollywood and found a realty office. She greeted an office assistant sitting at her desk inside.

"I am trying to find my way to LAX. Could you help me please?"

The young girl tossed her a great smile. "Sure," she said. "Let me look it up on Google maps and I'll print out a copy of the directions for you."

It just so happened that the highway Sophia needed was just three blocks north of the realty office. Sophia thanked the girl for her kindness and went on her way. It was 3:00 p.m. Time to get antsy.

Traffic on the highway was already bumper-to-bumper. Sophia learned the hard way that rush hour in Los Angeles started long before it did in Denver. In fact, every hour in Los Angeles seemed to be rush hour. After passing several exits, Sophia saw a sign for Century Boulevard, which was not on the directions to her destination, but it seemed familiar, so she took the exit. She drove several blocks and suddenly spotted her rental car lot, right there in front of her, where the shuttle to the airport was just about to leave.

Fortunately, it was Wednesday, and there were fewer people traveling out of the airport that day. The shuttle dropped her at her departure terminal, and she checked her bag at the curbside counter. So far, so good. After going through security, Sophia hustled to her gate, which of course was at the end of the concourse. She breathlessly arrived at the gate, amazed to discover she still had forty-five minutes to spare before her scheduled departure, but how could that possibly be?

Astonished at how quickly she arrived, she silently asked Spirit, Why did you tell me that I was not too far south? The answer that she received was simple - *You were not too far south. You were on the wrong highway. You asked the wrong question.*

Sophia had her answer. She sat down and smiled. Before it was time to board the plane, she took a moment to contemplate the many seemingly miraculous events that occurred in the past few days. She began to notice such things when her intuitive voice spoke to her loud and clear on many occasions. This time her intuition was accompanied by the personal visit by the seagulls on the beach, then dinner with Henry, and being able to enjoy the vast beauty of the California coastline. She was easily able to get to LAX in record time by knowing just what to do at the opportune moment, and all while collapsing time. The consistent synchronicities revealed to her, this was how she wanted to live her life: in alignment with nature, with the earth, and the world in which she lived.

When she returned home and caught up on her emails, she was more than surprised to receive a Facebook "friend request" from Michael O'Hara. It had been over ten years since they last spoke. The message he wrote was sent precisely at the same time as the prior Sunday morning when she heard, *This is to be your husband.*

As in the past, Michael's intelligent sense of humor left her grinning. His Facebook message read:

My Darling Sophia,

The last time I saw you, I was digging a hole in my back yard. I can only assume, since I have not seen nor heard from you now for more than a decade, that:

a. My dirty state of being persuaded you to hold onto the memory of when I was once clean

b. The dirty state of my being included the additional 'smelly'

or

c. You noticed the body I had hidden in the bushes, and you put two-and-two together.

Even if you did do the math, I see no reason why I should be deprived of staying in touch with one of my dearest friends. Therefore, since you chose to put your pretty face on Facebook, I hope you don't mind that found it and decided to end a more than decade-long dearth of updates. In fact, I had to join this Facebook thing just to send you this note, so HOW THE HELL ARE YOU?

Write me back or call, if you're in a chatty mood. –Michael.

He ended the message with a phone number.

Sophia was nervous. It was so long since they last talked. In her mind, she thought Michael did not care much for her. After all, she had left him during time number three to marry another. The past ten years, for Sophia, included the wide range of the first year of blissful married life, to the last year ending in a painful divorce. Many other forms of dying to the old way of life and rebirth also occurred. It was a time of deep recovery. Sophia was reinventing herself.

Remaining sans man for a year following her divorce was one of the keys to her healing. Sophia truly did not want to inflict her wounded heart on another until the injuries had time to heal. She also needed to process her complicity in the failure of her marriage. Sophia believed she needed to wait until she gave herself sufficient time before attempting a relationship again.

However, that was about to change.

Sophia nervously called Michael's number from her cell phone, thinking about the message she would leave. She was not one to be easily annoyed. Most of the time she was quite patient, but that day she was not. She found herself thinking logically: *Most people do not answer the phone when*

*they can easily monitor their calls through voice messaging,
saving them needless time and energy. Isn't that one reason they
pay for such a service? However, on the other hand, waiting for
the usual absurd instructions on how to leave a phone message is
ridiculous. Anyone with the ability to use a phone does not need
to be instructed how to leave a message. The telephone has been
in operation since the late 19th century, long before the cell phone
and messaging systems were standard. It is the service provider's
way of adding two minutes on to the beginning of every call to
rack up minutes used...*

Oh no, she was not nervous. Her anxiety built by the
second, which is the amount of time the rambling intuitive
message took to purse through her lightning-quick mind,
but now that she thought about it, these particular seconds
of waiting for Michael's recorded greeting would give her
the chance to rehearse in her mind what to say. All of this
chatter was going through her mind, when of course, an
actual person answered on the other end. Michael's voice
had that familiar tone of warmth and humor. Sophia felt
immediately at ease. All that fuss was for nothing.

After the preliminary catch up of, "How have you been
all these years?" and "Tell me what are you up to," she
suggested, "Let's meet for coffee."

"How about dinner tonight instead?" Michael
responded.

Okay, then. That was easy.

Later that evening, following her directions, he drove
up in front a small two-story house. Michael thought he
must have misunderstood the address, or perhaps he had
driven down the wrong street, because in the driveway sat
an enormous recreational vehicle.

He doubted this was her mode of transportation. She would have to leap like a high jumper, running from twenty feet away to get enough momentum to hurdle herself between the seat and steering wheel. Michael always thought of Sophia as a 'cute little car' girl, or maybe a Corvette babe. Thinking the RV must have been her ex-husband's vehicle, he warily walked up to the gate and rang the doorbell.

On the other side of the gate, he saw the red-lacquered door open, and out she came, wrapped in an ankle length lace duster, slacks and high heels, all in her signature color of black. She wore a handcrafted silver cuff bracelet fashioned from graphic images of Zuni designs, long silver dangle earrings, and a necklace to match.

Sophia's bohemian style gave evidence of her mystical artistic nature. Michael thought it was characteristic of her *witchy way*. When he discovered that she had a black cat, he felt his thoughts were more than accurate. He was aware of some of her spiritual gifts that were beyond the norm. Unbeknownst to her at the time, Michael possessed some magic of his own.

She had a way that helped him feel good about himself, but there was so much more to her charismatic charm. Her long blonde hair that trailed well beyond her shoulders blew gently in the evening breeze of early autumn. It framed her slightly tanned face, which set off her teal blue eyes like labradorite catching rays of the sun. He did not remember her to be so strikingly beautiful.

Sophia watched him as he towered a couple of feet above the upper edge of the gate. She forgot how tall he was. Somewhere in his Irish heritage was the genetic component of the towering height of 6'5", blonde hair and green eyes, now tempered with a graying goatee. Sophia's romantic mind wondered if he came from Nordic Viking stock. What a striking combination. He was still so handsome, having matured nicely.

She noticed a slight smile as she approached. Michael possessed a quiet reserve much more deeply embedded than what Sophia had remembered. As she walked up to the gate to let him in, she was startled when she heard her wise inner voice calmly and quietly, but emphatically say, *I'm home!*

Chapter Eleven

*F*ollowing her divorce, and prior to Michael returning to her life, Sophia read several books on *how to find the perfect man,* and even more books on *how to keep from finding the same man disguised in a different suit.* But from all that reading - what she discovered was - it was *she* that needed to change. The feelings that came out of her thinking created her life experience, so if she wanted change for the better, she first had to alter her thought patterns.

When Sophia discovered that her thoughts created her conscious reality, life quickly changed. She began to understand that feeling was the key component in the creative process, and so she consciously became a co-creator, working *with* the universe instead of against it. Where she placed her interest with feeling created the fertile atmosphere for the universe to grant that very desire. She began to live by the goose bumps - the electricity that energetically charged her batteries.

She knew enough to not make a list of what she did *not* want, for if she focused on the feelings of what she did *not* want in her life, that was what she got. The universe did not discern between what she wanted or did not want. Its job was simply to say *Yes*, and to provide the experience upon which she placed most of her feeling and attention. To change her experience was to first change her thoughts.

This was science - the Observer Effect of Quantum Physics, collapsing the waves of possibility into the particular circumstance merely by her observation. Sophia began to discern instead of judge, taking care to act in the present moment to ask the right questions and to be truly mindful of where she placed her thoughts and energy. She learned to be acutely aware of where she placed her interest by taking responsibility for her choices. From there she incrementally created the life of her desires.

Being an artist, she decided to be creative and have fun by experimenting with this new way of thought. To draw the perfect man to enter into her life, Sophia composed *The List* in beautiful calligraphy, which detailed an inventory of everything she wanted in a man, extremely specific and worded very carefully. She left nothing out, right down to "tall and blonde." Following several false-start relationships, she decided to go about her search in a different way. She had to laugh, because she found that she chose the attributes of her dearly departed dog, Miles, to fashion the template to call in that perfect man.

Sophia and Miles were clearly soul family from the moment they saw each other. There was a palpable understanding between them - that unspoken soul connection - a knowing. He was strong, yet gentle, sweet, and very powerful. He had a gorgeous physique with rich, deep black fur, and a red undercoat. He had an air of self-confidence like no other animal she had ever known. His temperament was steady and secure, and rarely did he ever bark. Miles was quite intelligent and his loyalty unswerving. He was her fierce protector, yet he never hesitated to reveal his vulnerability and deep desire for her love. Sophia and Miles felt comfortable and entirely at home with each other. Best of all, Miles just loved being loved. If she could find a man with Miles' qualities, he would certainly be just about all that she could desire - without the red undercoat and doggy breath, of course.

Sophia took the experiment to greater levels. She designed a special box to create the life she would love to live. On the outside of the box, she painted swirls of color finished with a big bow, treating it as a special gift for herself. Inside, she placed photos of the little house she had envisioned, with each room painted in a different shade of red, her favorite color. White crown molding and deep baseboards framed the walls. The dream house had hardwood floors with cozy furnishings, mostly antiques. Distinctive pieces of artwork and memorabilia, prominently displayed among a virtual forest of plants. Built-in bookcases held volumes of wonderful reads.

She envisioned a cozy master suite that invited a well-rested night of dreaming, along with a guest room and art studio. The open kitchen and living room with a fireplace made a warm environment for entertaining. Photos of a beautiful fenced-in garden, with many green plants, trees, and flowers left her desiring the outdoors to invite serenity and beauty into her home environment. However, she did not have a picture of a garage.

Inside the box was also a Matchbox red Mini Cooper. She wanted one since 2002, when the new model came out on the market. Besides, she wanted something much smaller and more colorful than the white gargantuan 'Big-ass bus,' as Michael called it - the RV she used during her out-of-town art shows.

A crystal from her mother's original chandelier hung inside the box to remind Sophia to keep her consciousness clear. She kept a running list of her deepest dreams and desires - what she would most love to do - within the next couple of years, including a trip to Delphi, Greece. She had no idea the reason why White Buffalo recommended that she go, but the only way she could find out was to follow through. Her journey to Delphi would be a pilgrimage, a spiritual calling not yet defined.

She had no way of knowing how she would afford the trip, or when it would occur. The only thing she had to be clear about was what she most desired. It was the same as her intentions for the perfect man and the ideal home. She just needed to be certain of what she longed for, with visions of her desires activated by her determination to set each into motion. All she needed to do was clearly define *what* she wanted and the *how* would readily reveal itself in due time.

Up to that point, Sophia had written stories and articles for magazines. Since she was a child, she dreamed of writing books, particularly a children's novel, and to illustrate the story herself. A photo went into the vision box of the *New York Times* bestsellers display at the local bookstore. She decided on a title, and then designed a cover for the book she had not yet written. She wrapped another hardcover book with her newly designed cover and placed it on her desk to envision it as a reality each day. She also put a copy of the cover art into her vision box.

Sophia included photos and drawings that invoked feelings of joy, peace, and harmony - of beautiful, loving dreams and intentions for her life. Desiring to make an impact on the most people at one time, becoming a world-renowned speaker/author/artist would do the trick, so, she included a picture of a woman standing on a stage, giving a lecture to a receptive overflowing audience. She also had photos of locations throughout the world where she wanted to travel - beautiful places in nature, and places of historic significance.

Sophia envisioned meeting people within their own environment, rather than being a tourist, and so she had photos of many cultures from all over the world. She included images of money that represented the earnings from her books, lectures, and sales from her artwork. There were images of charitable causes she desired to help, with names of foundations for people, animals and worldly efforts to bring positive change to the world. Whatever her desire, she found photos, drew pictures, or made a list and placed them in her vision box. Sophia was calling forth, from the Field of Infinite Possibilities, to create a life for herself - one she would love to live - one that would have great meaning and purpose for others. And so, her life vision began.

Each night, before bed, she looked at every photo and drawing in her vision box. She imagined each item in her mind's eye, trying it on, envisioning what it would feel like when she accomplished her desires. These were the last thoughts etched into her subconscious before she crawled under the covers.

Sophia knew the revelation of her life's purpose would

come to her in the same way the ideal house and perfect man would appear. She would intuitively know when each heart's desire became manifest. The search for her home was easier, because she remembered her desires from the images she had set in her mind. It helped her pare down the choices, because if the desired feelings were not present when she toured a prospective home, she would quickly make the decision to leave and continue her search. She knew that when she arrived at that perfect house, a sense of deep peace would come over her, letting her know that her vision was completed.

After making several failed real estate offers, Sophia knew she needed to make a declaration to the Divine. She got up one Sunday morning and clearly spoke aloud, "Today is the day I will find my home. I don't know how it will happen, but I will not spend another day wondering where I will live. Today, I will find my perfect home. That's it! Thank you so very much, in advance!"

That afternoon, she drove past a townhome she found charming. As she drove around the neighborhood, she deeply tuned in to the feelings in her body, asking if this was the right home for her. Immediately, she sensed that it was not. Off the list of potential homes it came. As she drove a mile to the south, arriving at a stoplight, Sophia inquired, *which way do I turn, left or right?* She put her hands in front of her. In whichever hand she felt a tingling, she turned the car in that direction. Following her internal GPS of intuition at each stop, she eventually found a neighborhood of small two-story homes. She immediately felt a sense of excitement because she liked the architectural style. She thought if she found one for sale, it would most likely be less expensive than those she had recently toured. Within minutes, Sophia drove up to a little green house with a "For Sale" sign in the front yard. The asking price was twenty thousand less than the homes she had previously toured. There was a huge crabapple tree in the fenced yard, and a beautiful ash tree in front. Big trees! This was a good sign.

Sophia sensed this home was to be hers before she ever looked inside. At 9:00 a.m. the next day, her realtor arranged a tour through the house. Her intuition was right on. Sophia made an offer that morning, and the sellers accepted her proposal. The house had four bedrooms and two baths, all with hardwood floors hidden under a thirty-year-old green shag carpet. One of the bedrooms was an upstairs loft. The kitchen, living room, and family room had an open design, making entertaining much more inviting and enjoyable. There were two fireplaces, and two built-in bookcases. French doors opened to the deck outside, which wrapped around the fifty-year-old crabapple tree surrounded by flowers, shrubs, and groundcover of myrtle and violets. The deck was larger than any room inside the house.

She hired someone to remove the carpet, refinish the oak floors, and paint the interior walls in a neutral shade. She painted accent walls in a glorious mixture of red merlot faux finishes mixed with a gold that complimented the home's 1950s contemporary style. It was the perfect home for her and her animals. Remarkably, the house had no garage, something that did not appear in her original vision. Sophia's dream home manifested into a reality far better than she had imagined.

Not long after she moved in, on the night when Michael stood at the threshold of her house, the precursor to their fourth-first date was absolutely perfect. Sophia knew she had finally come home to where her heart was leading her. The two of them fit together like French vanilla ice cream and chocolate sauce - Michael, the ice cream, and Sophia the saucy one. They melted into each other.

Michael drove a beautiful car in her favorite color of Chinese red. The tall blonde knight in shining armor held the door open for her. *Yes! Chivalry is not dead!* she thought. Although Sophia was a very independent woman, she appreciated his genteel nature - that of treating her with respect. After all, synchronicity was at play.

They had not made previous plans for the date, but Sophia suggested going to the First Friday art event on the north end of town, where they previously lived together during time number three. Michael had the same thought. Two of his friends happened to be displaying their artwork at different galleries. During their dinner conversation, Sophia and Michael caught up on the past ten years. She revealed some of what had developed during that time. Michael knew her history from time number one, two, and three, and he patiently listened to her most recent account of the past ten years.

As a spiritual empath, Sophia could read people well, oftentimes beyond their own awareness of themselves. Many people immediately wanted to be her friend, but some tried to take more than she could give, and she found herself manipulated because of her sensitive nature. Sophia tended to attract energy vampires that attempted to suck the life from her. They wanted to possess and control her to obtain some of her power for themselves. This, of course, never worked, but it was Sophia's task to learn how to avoid these types of people.

Michael was the polar opposite of these people. He was an independent and solitary man - rock solid. From the day they met in high school, he demanded nothing from her, which may have been the reason they struggled to make their relationship work in the past. He always recognized and owned his faults and mistakes. He was never her project to fix. As Sophia matured, she let go of the need to save someone from himself. She learned to set strong boundaries and to take responsibility only for her own thoughts and action.

When she paused during their conversation that evening, which was unusual for her, especially when she was nervous, Michael asked, "Sophia, why were you with those other men? I would never cheat on you. I would never abuse you. I have been in love with you since we first met."

Sophia was stunned. She never knew his feelings for her. She was dumfounded and had nothing to say - not a common occurrence. All those years, through times number one, two and three, he had never told her how she felt. But in that moment, it was instantly clear to her that what they were individually seeking had just become a reality. He was seeking the relationship he dreamed they might have had, and Sophia finally came home to a man who was within her reach all along.

The List was finally competed. It was necessary that they both matured and endured life's experiences to bring them back together again. What instantly took place in that moment was the timeless, space-less silence that occurs when a quantum shift takes dominion. They were now ready to commit to what they had both desired for so very long.

Extreme loss made both Michael and Sophia grow up. They discovered that their task, whether they liked it or not, was to face their demons. One of these demons was grief, to feel the deep pain of the loss, and to wear it for a while. They grieved deeply because they had loved so well. Both had learned to release previous acquisitions, in relationships as well as in the material world. They both realized, after all, what truly matters in the long run is what lies within the soul's journey. One of the indications of the passage into the soul is re-discovering joy returning to life. Here it was, joyful bliss, wrapped in the packaging of the past, present, and the promise of a brand new bright future.

And so, it began - time number four, the fourth and final time they would date - for the first time.

CHAPTER
Twelve

*D*eath has a way of diminishing those left among the living. Michael was still healing after a year spent intimately entwined with death. He felt old. Aging, at that time for Michael, had a life of its own, oozing into every cell of his body. Most every experience included comments about getting old, "Oh my back...my knees hurt...my hips grind."

It was a challenge for his six-foot, five-inch frame, beaten by many years of rough play on the basketball court. Instead of service ribbons displayed on a military uniform jacket, Michael wore his badges of honor as mended bones and scars up and down his shins, with an accompanying tale about each injury. However, the past two years took the greatest toll on his life. The invisible injury of heartache turned Michael's blonde hair to gray. His eyes chronicled the tale of how the deep chasm of grief can diminish one's life force.

For Sophia, the age thing was nonsense, or so she liked to believe. Sophia thought of herself having only smile lines. She flaunted the fact that her hair was not yet gray, and her youthful genetic makeup prevented her from sporting the proverbial chicken neck. In Sophia's mind, she was not old - just experienced - taking that statement from White Buffalo, but there truly was something timeless about her that she was just beginning to understand.

In many ways, Michael and Sophia were the classic Yin Yang couple. She was a quick-thinker and fast-mover. He was well tempered and deliberate. She was the enthusiastic optimist, and he, the cautious skeptic, grounded like a rock and inherently suspicious of angles. However, Michael was the one who never gave up on Sophia. Something about her enchanted him. Her mystic demeanor kept calling him back like a whisper from the shadows lurking beyond the veils of his memory.

When in council with White Buffalo, he told Sophia she was a master healer/teacher. Evidently, she had been one for many lifetimes, as evidenced by animals and small children that naturally came to her, knowing they were safe in her company. The injured and sick were magnetized to her high vibration, which created a palpable, radiant energy that allowed them to heal naturally in her presence. Although many considered her a healer, she humbly considered herself more of a teacher who helped those willing to heal themselves. She merely became the open vessel, filled by the healing energy of the Infinite. The person or animal would attune their energy with hers, becoming a vibrational match and thus displacing the energy of illness.

Sophia knew it was not she herself, but *they* who were the true healers. Each person's body, mind, and spirit did the work when they were willing. She simply held the energy to a level where they could tap in and heal themselves. Small children and those of a pure nature easily recognized her light. She could walk into a chaotic situation and everything would immediately settle into a harmonious calm.

Considered a gifted mystic endowed with capacities the average person could not attain, she seemed to have it all. She had no idea of where she obtained her knowledge and abilities, hidden somewhere in the depths of her being, which set her aside from most of society. Some people were jealous of what she innately knew.

As a result, she turned inward and became an avid student. Her library at home was extensive. She typically had several books going at the same time, reading a chapter or two from one book, only to switch to another. Ever a student, she absorbed information, storing it away with the knowledge that it would later serve her. She was enchanted by history's layers of time, which included classical Greek philosophy and ancient Greek history. She could not identify the reason for her fascination, but found herself attracted to the specific cultures of Greece, Rome, Egypt, Britain, and the American South. She was naturally attracted to many indigenous peoples, and their histories - particularly Native American, Tibetan, and Peruvian cultures - and they to her.

Ceremonial ritual deeply moved her, which allowed her to delve into her mystical awareness. It would not be long before she made the connection between her interests and her own history. Unusual relationships were the result of her mystical nature, but she remained strong and confident within her solitary existence until Michael entered back into her life. Only three weeks from their fourth-first date, they spent every day, 24/7, together.

Michael worked at home. Sophia, a part-time student, was just beginning to write her first book while developing her art. Michael was a successful published author, and therefore understood Sophia's desire to write. He found her to be a promising talent, and he offered to edit her work. She was in good hands with Michael, for he was quite independent and desired the same for her. They were mutually supportive of each other's personal, professional, and in her case, spiritual development.

Michael helped around the house, fixing things that needed repair for some time. Since going through his own messy divorce many years before, he had lived alone. During his 'marriage remission' as he called it, he said the only thing he missed were home improvement projects. He said he liked to walk through a hardware store, "just so I can look at their stuff."

When he reunited with Sophia, he said he longed to get his hands dirty again in the manly art of home repair. Sophia couldn't help but laugh. It was on *The List - handy around the house*. Upon her return from a weekend retreat, she found Michael had cleaned up her yard, trimmed bushes and trees, and replaced a dilapidated old fence in the back yard. Sophia never had to ask him to do a thing. He just helped out, wherever needed. He even broke a few things just for the joy of fixing them – or so he said.

They discussed what to call each other. They were too old – or, too 'experienced' - to refer to each other as 'girlfriend and boyfriend.' 'Husband and wife?' Not yet. That would be a decision down the line. She once read a book by a renowned author and spiritual leader who wrote, "Marriage ruins a relationship." She had to agree, because she had a lot of experience in both marriage and ruined relationships. From being single to married, to divorced, then married and divorced again, Sophia decided that she would refer to herself as permanently, irrevocably, and forevermore single, in perpetuity. Michael was married "for about fifteen minutes," as he would say, and had no desire to marry any time soon. Yes, they both wanted a committed relationship, but marriage was negotiable.

So, what would they call each other? 'Partner' sounded like something out of the old West. Partner did not fit. 'Beloved' was too formal. 'Paramour' was right out of the silent film era, and 'Guy and Gal' would only work if he were a gangster and she, his moll. 'Fella,' 'Sweetie,' 'Honey-baby,' and 'Sugah,' came from the old *Thin Man* movies that were quaint but still not quite right. The list continued. Then there was the legal terminology for two people who live together in the State of Colorado, as *registered domestic partner.*

"If you please, I would like to introduce you to my registered domestic partner, Michael." They agreed that didn't fly either, unless they were going to open a law firm together. They never arrived at the right title for each other, deciding that it's all energy until you name it. Therefore, using that logic, they concluded that maybe, if they didn't name their relationship, it would continue to grow with a good chance for survival. Perhaps it would even have the opportunity to flourish.

By the time Michael and Sophia got back together, Rufus, Miles, Emmy, and Zaide were gone. Sophia still had the two older dogs, who were both about twelve years of age. Frankie, the alpha dog, was an Australian Shepherd/Wolf-dog. Saxon, Sophia's protector, was a

Rottweiler mix. Rounding out the family was a tiny black polydactyl cat, Digit, so named because of her extra toes that caused her feet to look like little black mittens. Sophia's animal family fell in love with Michael immediately. Animals just know. There's no fooling them. That was on *The List* regarding her perfect guy - *the animals must approve*.

Wherever Michael sat, the dogs would lie at his feet, and five-pound Digit would curl up on his lap, looking like a kitten against his large frame. He held her gently and treated her as the precious cargo she was. Digit came from the great state of Texas, where everything is bigger, except her. She was very small, most likely the runt of the litter. She had travelled to Colorado underneath the front driver's seat of a car. The kitten was rescued that particular day from the inevitability of the three-day wait on death row.

At the time when Sophia was married, her husband Joe had gone to Texas to spend time with his son from a previous marriage. Joe was staying at a motel, and Digit wandered into his room one morning, obviously hungry. Joe gave Digit some scraps, and she returned the next three mornings for some genuine cat food Joe bought for her. On the morning Joe was due to return to Colorado, Digit didn't show up. He inquired at the office, asking if the kitten belonged to someone there, but the clerk told him Animal Control had just left the property. Joe and his son drove to the shelter just as the truck arrived. He asked the driver, "Did you pick up a black kitten this morning?"

"Yep, she's in the back of the truck."

"What are the chances of her being adopted?"

"They have three days before they are put down. There are thirty cats in there right now."

It was obvious that the tiny black kitten had no chance for adoption within the three-day limit. Black cats were the least likely to be taken in because of archaic belief systems about them being bad luck. Joe said to the young guy, "Why don't you let me have the cat?"

"I can't do that. I'm not allowed."

"She doesn't have a chance. Do the right thing and give her to me..."

Her sentence commuted, Digit traveled for nine hours to Denver under the seat of Joe's car.

When Sophia arrived home from work, she sat in the living room with Joe, catching up on details about his trip. Suddenly, to Sophia's surprise and delight, Digit wandered in and sat like a regal queen in the middle of the living room floor. There she sat upright and oh so important as the new member of the family. Sophia came up with the name Digit, for being a magnanimously extra-toed polydactyl cat with twenty-seven toes.

Zaide, the beautiful alpha female cat liked her well enough. Emmy, however, did not care for Digit's presumption that she was now in charge. Frankie, Saxon, and Miles walked in through the front door and immediately noticed the new addition. However, none of them got very close, giving her a wide berth of at least eight feet. Each of the dogs weighed about 80 pounds, and Digit might have weighed three, but she carried herself like a black panther, and the dogs wisely chose to avoid her highness. She did respectfully concede to Zaide, the queen of the house, but Digit was, without a doubt, now the diva princess.

CHAPTER
Thirteen

Whenever Sophia experienced great changes, information came through from her past lives to catapult her into a greater expansive awareness. Answers regarding the question of her unusual fascination with Greek history began with the dream of her former life in Akrotiri. Michael's entrance into her life somehow spawned the next dream, bringing more clarity about Sophia's former life as it related to the pre-historic Ancient Minoan culture.

Her dreams came in vivid color and detail just before daylight's coral hues broke upon the eastern plains. The suspension of time and space in the dream world provided Sophia vast information that could fill a novel the size of *War and Peace*. In the realm of time and space, the story unfolding in one evening spanned many months, and sometimes years. Sophia's mind filled with images in the full spectrum of color and detail like an instantaneous downloaded file in her mind's eye.

She had studied Plato's work, written around 360 B.C.E., in which he wrote about the allegorical city of Atlantis, later theorized by some scholars to have been inspired by the island of Thera. Its Minoan culture was

Europe's oldest and most advanced civilization. Plato wrote that Atlantis was a city built in concentric circles, alternating water and land surrounding an acropolis with a temple in the center. Extensive bridge systems connected the outer rim of the island to the hub like the spokes of a wheel.

In reality, Plato was not far off, for Thera was a circular island with two waterways filling the central sea-filled caldera, one fed by the Aegean Sea, the other fed by geothermal sources coming from deep beneath the island. Three major volcanic eruptions over millions of years had caused the mountainous volcano to collapse in the island's center, allowing the Aegean Sea to fill the cavity. Growing out of the center of its water-filled depths, the mountainous volcano was rising again.

In Plato's writings, the people of the city had become so decadent and malevolent that Poseidon, the God of the Sea, released a great flood to destroy them. Plato's theory hinged on the belief system of the Greek pantheon of gods that began around the eighth century B.C.E. at the start of the Classical Age, but Sophia's memory of Akrotiri was 800 years before that belief system took hold. The gods of the prehistoric Ancient Minoan culture were not the gods to whom Plato referred.

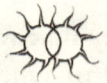

Thera's mountain peak was bulging - distorting its perfect conical shape into something foreboding and grotesque. Sulfurous gasses filled the air, leaving yet another warning for those who remained that nothing good could possibly come to their island home. They would soon need to leave before an enormous disaster would hit. Already, over six inches of heavy gray ash covered the entire village of Akrotiri from gaseous plumes spewing from the splitting crevices on the volcano's peak.

Most of the inhabitants had already sailed to nearby islands, leaving behind only the elders and the High Priestess. Only one boat remained in the harbor awaiting their departure, stocked only with their most precious belongings. Each elder pushed through the thick ash, trudging from home to home, calling out to ensure that everyone found safe passage to the shore. When their search was finished, they agreed to meet at the village entrance. From there, they would leave together, except Roxana, who held back.

One of the elders grabbed her arm, insisting she come with him to the ship. She resisted and pulled away from his grasp. Even under the circumstances, she, as the High Priestess, was obligated to the gods to be the last to leave the island. She needed to perform one last ritual for the island's future, and to give blessings for all who had sailed to destinations unknown. The elders reluctantly left her behind as they lumbered through the fallen ash toward the waiting ship in the harbor.

Her waist-length ebony hair was ashen gray. Normally, she was strikingly beautiful with olive skin and eyes of polished bronze. Her towering height of 5'9", much taller than the average height of her people, naturally demanded attention and respect. However, the ashen effect of the island's anger made her appear as if she had risen from the depths of the underworld where death made its claim. She wore layers of linen and woolen tunics covered with two cloaks - all that she could easily carry in such dire circumstances.

Roxana had been the High Priestess since the sun made its seventeenth complete cycle around Gaia. Now only in her early twenties, yet wise from her lifetimes of experience, she made sure that she was the last person to leave the island as instructed by her mother many years before. She had not forgotten the lesson imparted by Althaia, its importance etched into her memory. The fulfillment of her soul's journey would only happen once she left her island home. She must let go of the life she knew and loved to call in the one that was beckoning her forward.

Roxana's father, Nikolas, died at sea two years before, and her grandmother Elene had also recently transitioned into other lifetimes. Althaia had long since fled to a destination unknown, and Roxana feared she would never see her mother again. Only Roxana could invoke the power of the golden vessel, using the sacred waters of the spring to generate its energetic force. Only she could use the amulet to tell future timelines. She was the keeper of the eternal flame representing the all knowing, all powerful, and ever-present gods. From its flame, the knowledge of fire would spread throughout the world to invoke spiritual power. The eternal flame could create warmth, light, and means for cooking. It would be essential for centuries to come as it represented cleansing light, divine truth, and the almighty power of the gods.

Through her bloodline, she had inherited the authority

of being a healer and teacher. Such were the primary responsibilities of a high priestess. Her use of the bowl, amulet, and eternal flame enabled her to heal, transform, and interpret what she saw in the future. These golden objects were her most sacred possessions. Used separately, they evoked great power for individual purposes. Used together, they emitted information and authority that came through Roxana, making her a great instrument of the gods. The golden objects aided her in saving the island's inhabitants, having warned Roxana far in advance to urge the people to flee to other ports long before the foreseen destruction occurred. No one on Thera lost their life to the wrath of the gods.

When she reached the temple atop the southern hillside overlooking the volcano, Roxana quickly went inside. For the first time ever, she did not cleanse herself in the pool before entering the sanctuary, certain that the gods would pardon this single transgression. Despite the ashen dust that filled the air, her golden vessel remained luminous on the altar. Roxana filled it one last time from the sacred water flowing into the central basin of the almond-shaped pool. At once, she felt the familiar tingling in her hands, up her arms, and throughout her body, instantly shifting her to an altered state of awareness. As she took a deep breath, she raised the vessel above her head. She envisioned the heavens above, the stars shining brightly upon worlds without end. She spoke the final words ever uttered to the gods from the ancient temple. This was her final act as the last High Priestess of Akrotiri.

"I thank thee, all the gods, for you are wondrous and great. I praise each one of the gods, knowing that we, as beings of Gaia, are also a part of your magnificence, for how could it be otherwise that we exist? Here, on Thera, we have lived good and prosperous lives for many generations. Scores of children will grow, remembering their island home, telling their children's children the stories of our life here. Our grandmothers' and grandfathers' spirits thank you. I ask the gods to bless those who have sailed away, so they might find safety and well-being in establishing new and abundant lives. May they live in serenity, may they be joyful, and may they be prosperous, to live in a way that is good for all, using the knowledge they gained from their life here on our beautiful island home.

"May the gods of the mountain and earth wait to unleash their full anger until we travel a safe distance away from here. Lastly, I ask that the gods give us still seas so we arrive safely to live and thrive, so that we may continue to bless the gods for generations to come. I offer thanksgiving for all that we have received here on Thera. In gratitude, I present to the gods the lives of the animals left here on the island as an offering for what we may receive in our future. May their souls rise to live harmoniously in another time and place. Blessings upon this island, and when it is home again to those in the future, may their lives be as blessed as our lives were. In great gratitude, knowing that this prayer is already granted, I release it into the power of the gods. Praise be to the gods. So be it!"

Only a few small bowls of oil were left on the altar, burning the flame of blessing for those who were about to depart. She snuffed out the flames, for they soon would be gone. The day before, she took her golden oil lamp with the eternal flame to the ship. She would sail to the mainland and transport the flame to her eventual destiny below Mt. Parnassus.

From her neck, she removed the golden chain and amulet. Allowing the chain to drape over the back of her fingers, she held it steady with her forefinger and thumb. The amulet freely swung below the palm of her hand. She stilled the amethyst crystal to begin her inquiry, "My name is Roxana. I am the High Priestess of Akrotiri." The amulet circled to the right, indicating that it agreed with her statement. She then spoke an untruth, "I am standing in the middle of the river." The amulet switched, turning to the left. This helped her to know which direction was affirmative.

Roxana then asked the question that she truly needed to know. "How many days do we have on Thera before the volcano unleashes its ultimate power? Fifteen days?" The amulet circled to the left. Roxana knew this indicated that the crystal was not in agreement with her statement. "Ten days, or less..." The amulet changed and swung in agreement to the right. "Eight days, or less..." The circle continued, but became smaller. She was coming closer to the answer she sought. "Six days." The chain vibrated as the amulet immediately came to a complete halt. She inquired twice again to confirm the timeline, each with the same result. In six days, Thera would be no more.

She looked one last time into the golden vessel filled with the sacred waters of Akrotiri, seeing a vision of what was to come. She saw millions of varied races living in future generations all over the earth. Instead of a flashback in time, she envisioned a flash forward with thousands of years laid out before her. The earth would continue, changing from season to season, as far as she could see. However, in contrast, the fate of humankind was at stake at its own hand. She was destined to pass on her knowledge to help make a difference for humankind, and therefore on behalf of the earth and all its inhabitants. Life on the mainland beckoned her forward. It was time to say good-bye to Akrotiri. From her golden vessel, she poured the water onto the freestanding eternal flame. The fire remained, as the steaming water pooled down onto the ashen floor at her feet.

Other than the clothes on her back, the three golden objects were all that she carried off the island. She laid the golden vessel in a leather pouch and pulled the drawstring, then placing the loops around her neck and shoulders. She made sure to put her grandmother's golden necklace and amulet around her neck and tucked it inside her blouse, keeping it close to her heart. Taking one last glance at the extraordinarily beautiful sanctuary, she felt her heart breaking. Tears flowed down her ashen cheeks.

The temple had been a stunning place of worship for many thousands of years, passed down through her ancestral family of priests and priestesses for generations. Many miracles had occurred there, but she knew more were to come on the mainland. They had all lived a good and fruitful life in Akrotiri. The Minoan culture thrived for more than a millennium, but Roxana saw through the waters that the era was just days from its end.

It was time for her to leave. She left aflame all the crystal lights that hung from the ceiling and the torches along the walls. The sacred water continued to flow from the mouth of the sculpted dolphin. Roxana turned toward the doorway and left the temple behind.

Wrapped in many layers, Roxana covered her nose and mouth with a cloak to keep from breathing in the ash, which now filled the air with spitting embers from the mountain's crevices. The island was the antithesis of what it had been for thousands of years. It was now a dangerous and volatile environment. Roxana did her best to wade through the ash that filled the corridors of the village streets. The ash was much deeper than when she earlier entered the temple.

She made it safely down the mountain, but just as she was about to leave through the last corridor, she heard a child's cry. She thought the council had cleared the area, but it was evident that someone still lingered in the abandoned village. The mountain overhead spewed such great quantities of ash and cinders, making it difficult for her to see much farther than a few feet ahead of her. Instead, she let her hearing guide her toward the source of the cries. Roxana covered her face with her cloak, stepping gingerly through the heavy ash.

The cry came from the stables. Inside, hidden behind the back stall, she found a small boy about five years old, covered with ashen soot. He trembled as if he were standing in frigidly cold temperatures. She knelt in front of him and brushed off as much ash as possible from his clothes, wiping the tears from his face.

"There, there. Fear not. Everything is going to be all right. My name is Roxana, what is yours?"

"I am Theo."

"That is a good omen." She looked deep into his eyes.

"Do you know that your name means *gift of the gods*?"

He nodded.

"This must mean that you are a gift to me on this day." She smiled and wrapped her arms around him. "You are safe now. I will not let any harm come to you. Where is your mother or father?"

"My father is a fisherman on the sea. He has been gone a long time. My mother is dead," Theo said.

Roxana assumed that his father was dead, too. She looked around to see that Theo had been barely surviving alone in the stable. He was very scrawny, and it was evident that he had not eaten a decent meal in a very long time.

"How would you like to go on a boat trip to see other lands?"

His eyes grew very big, and a smile formed on his grimy face.

"I would like to take you with me. Would that be alright with you?"

He nodded enthusiastically.

"Do you have any extra clothes?"

He pointed to what looked like a pile of rags. She quickly went through them to find the best pieces and wrapped them in a small bundle for Theo to carry. "I am going to take you to the boat now. Ready?"

He shook his head, pointing to the back of the stables. "My goat - I don't want to leave her."

Knowing the goat was all he had, she said, "Do you have a rope?"

He shook his head again.

Roxana quickly took the remaining rags from his pile of clothing. She ripped them into strips and tied them together to make a long rope. She looped it around the goat's neck and tied the other end to Theo's wrist. Then she tied rags around the goat's body and head to protect it from the falling cinders. She looked at Theo and forced a smile. "Put your arms around my neck and hang on tight." She scooped Theo into her arms, and with his head on her shoulder, she wrapped her cloak around them both, sheltering them from the red-hot embers. Before she stepped out into the ashen air, she checked to be certain she still had the golden vessel.

The ground shook beneath her feet, challenging her to keep from falling as she carried Theo, who in turn pulled the goat behind them. She trudged through the ash until arriving at the shoreline, where it was not as deep. She ran toward the waiting ship, the earth violently shaking and making her stumble as she fell to her knees, dropping Theo. Ash covered Sophia, Theo, and his goat from head to toe as they struggled to their feet and together ran for the shore. An elder stood out in waist-deep water, clinging to a small fishing boat that would transport them to the last awaiting ship. Roxana told Theo to take his goat and wade out to the boat, and she would follow. She took one final look at her dying island, and then turned and waded out to the fishing boat, which transported them to the ship already with its sails raised. Roxana was the last human soul to step from the soil of Thera.

The mountainous volcano overhead bulged. Roxana took one last glance at the temple, knowing it would be her last reminiscence of the sacred site. She made sure to secure Theo and his goat on the lower deck where they would be safe. She gave him some bread, cheese, and two bunches of grapes, one for him and the other for the goat. All the passengers, including Roxana, took to the oars, sitting alongside the oarsmen to help speedily row away from their dying home. None of them had any idea of the magnitude of what would soon occur, but the many months of violent warnings were enough to convince them to leave before they found out firsthand.

Most who already left Thera sailed to Crete, the southernmost island in the Aegean Sea. The captain of the ship knew that, when the volcano exploded, the winds would carry the caustic ash to the east, affecting any land in its wake. The elders also knew that the sea would swell from the impact, taking with it the nearby islands. They decided to sail northwest toward the Mycenaean Greek city of Athens. If they arrived at the mainland before the eruption, they sensed they would all be safe there.

They stopped to stock up on food and water at one other island on their way to Athens. As best they could, some would rest, while others rowed when the winds were not strong enough to fill the sails. Only their arrival on the mainland would assure their safety. They reached a port on the coastline near Athens in three days. Upon setting foot on the soil, Roxana knelt on the ground and immediately gave thanks to the gods for their safe arrival. She knew they had much to do to find shelter and sustenance. Again, she thanked the gods for what they were about to venture toward, having faith that she and her people would be guided and supplied with all they needed. They hired carts to take them to Athens, still a day away.

The anticipated massive eruption took place two days after their arrival in Athens, which brought alarm to the entire city. The explosive blast was terrifying. From atop of a high plateau - one of the highest points in the city later called the Acropolis - Roxana could see the massive mushroom cloud of fiery ash to the southeast. She was certain that her island of Thera and the village of Akrotiri were no more. She dropped to her knees, wailing deep tears of grief for the demise of her ancestral home. Fine gray ash rained down upon the city of Athens, the remains of Roxana's island home falling down around her. Theo came up with his goat in tow and wiped the tears from Roxana's face.

"I will protect you, Roxana. I am mighty."

She cupped his face in her hands, smiling at her little hero. "Come, let us go to our shelter and get something to eat. We must rest well, for we have much to do once the volcano has finished its anger."

In the weeks and months that followed, news came to Athens about the thousands of people killed on the neighboring islands near Thera, specifically Crete. A sixty-foot tsunami caused by the Theran eruption destroyed lands as far as Egypt. The ash cloud blocked the sun for weeks. Many died of starvation from destroyed crops that left very little to feed the people and their livestock. For the following fourteen years, the volcano spewed ash and lava. It was the largest volcanic eruption in the history of the world.

Roxana was certain there was nothing left of her little island home, thinking she would never return, but that was not necessarily so, for time, when bent, opened up to a world of possibilities. In fact, she would return in another lifetime to find a thriving community built out of the volcano's ash and soot. It would be familiar to her, calling her home again...

When Sophia awoke from her dream, she immediately recorded it on her computer. This was one dream she would not forget. Somehow, she knew there would be a time when the memory of that dream would serve her. She was accumulating a chronology of her past lives, realizing what an influential and powerful life she had led. It left her feeling that the purpose of her past was melding with the calling of her soul.

CHAPTER
Fourteen

It was Sophia's birthday. She spent the early July morning having brunch with a friend at a lovely parkside restaurant. She enjoyed a delectable meal of Eggs Benedict, served with avocado, tomatoes, and hollandaise. Their server asked, "How are we doing here?"

"May we have two more mimosas, please?" Sophia's friend asked.

Sophia suddenly felt the familiar intuitive nudge, *Do not drink any more today. You need to keep your mind clear.* Sophia did not listen.

The mimosas arrived at the table, and Sophia's friend toasted her birthday, but the incessant directive continued, *Check your phone.* She was looking so forward to spending that evening with Michael and some friends who were throwing her a birthday dinner. It was so nice just to relax and allow others to slather her with attention.

After catching up with her friend, Sophia waved for the server. "Would you please bring us two coffees, with cream and sugar?" She, again, heard her intuitive voice. *You must check your phone, now!* The server brought the coffees to the table, and Sophia added cream to hers, making the coffee that perfect caramel color. Before she took a sip, she pulled out her phone and noticed three messages left by the same caller. She listened to the last message.

"Sophia, this is Maria from Mountain View Assisted Living. It is now 11:20 a.m. We have tried to reach you for a couple of hours. Your father has been having trouble breathing this morning, and we just now called for an ambulance to take him to Mercy Hospital. Please return my call as soon as possible."

This was not going to be a celebratory birthday after all. Sophia returned Maria's call and then left to meet her father at the hospital.

Congestive heart failure limited Patrick's oxygen levels to dangerously low levels. Doctors admitted him to the hospital to perform several tests and scans over the next two days, none of which returned good news. The final doctor to review his case was a pulmonologist on call that day.

Sophia was with her father when the doctor entered the room. The doctor was irritated and responded to Sophia's questions with short, curt answers. Clearly agitated by the interruption of his afternoon golf game, the doctor's options were dismal, one of which was that Patrick remain in the hospital and be pumped full of drugs to keep him alive.

The doctor's grim prognosis and rather abrupt conclusion left Sophia feeling disconcerted. Even more so, she thought his extremely unprofessional attitude and disrespect for his patient was unfounded. At that point, she did the only thing she could to bring her comfort. She went within with the expectant belief that her silent prayer would make a difference. *Please help us to know the best answers for my dad. I ask now that this doctor gets himself out of his own way, to speak to my father with the respect and compassion he deserves.*

Sophia slowly rose to her feet, looked directly at the doctor, and with assertive calm said, "I have looked into options for hospice care for him, knowing this day was coming."

A palpable shift happened in the room. The doctor paused for a moment, clearly his mood interrupted.

Patrick broke the silence and weakly asked the doctor, "Do you think hospice is my only option?"

The doctor shifted his stance and calmed down. There was a silent pause as his entire demeanor changed. "Mr. Delaney, I'm very sorry, but according to all the tests, there is very little I can do for you, other than to try to minimize your discomfort with medication. We could keep you here in the hospital a while longer, but we would only be delaying the inevitable outcome. You will be more comfortable under hospice care."

"Alright then, let's do that," Patrick said.

"The staff here can make all the arrangements to have you transferred tomorrow."

Sophia's eyes filled with tears, knowing that her father had made the right decision. She shook the doctor's hand. "Thank you for taking the time to explain his options. I appreciate your being here today."

The doctor was humbled. He first shook her hand and then her father's hand. "You're welcome. I am glad I was able to be here..."

The next day, Patrick was relocated to a nearby short-term hospice facility, a care center that accepted patients whose foreseeable death was expected in less than two weeks.

Indeed, Sophia had prepared for this moment, for her 96-year-old father's inevitable demise had been a slow and difficult transition. Months before, in December, Patrick was sick with bronchitis. He suffered from COPD for several years, and the congestion from the bronchitis made it even more difficult for him to catch his breath. He was on oxygen, but it no longer gave him much comfort.

Sophia typically visited Patrick two or three times per week and called him most every night around 8:00 p.m., no matter where she was. On a Sunday afternoon that December, she stopped by for a brief visit and was concerned when she noticed his diminished energy. Patrick sat upright in his recliner. She noticed his stilted breathing, making it difficult for him to engage easily in conversation. When Patrick made an effort to speak, he was clearly visible to Sophia. But when the words did not easily come, she witnessed his energy vanish, and his physical essence almost disappeared as if he melted into the chair.

This was the first time that Sophia witnessed a person's life force fade to the point of near disappearance. Because she was so close to her father, the situation was unfathomable. She sat with him for another fifteen minutes, observing him as he energetically came and went. She left the assisted living center that day, taking this as a warning that her father would soon permanently leave his body.

When she returned home that afternoon, she asked for

help from her divine guidance to determine future timelines so she could make some important decisions. Sophia found that using a crystal pendulum helped her bypass her emotions when she needed to make critical choices. The pendulum was an extension of her intuition, sensitive to her subtle energies - the vibrations with which her body resonated. Sophia used the pendulum as a tool and an enhancement when she needed additional support. She was not certain why it worked for her, but the pendulum helped her make many decisions in the past that turned out to be for her benefit.

When using the pendulum, rather than asking yes or no questions, Sophia found the device to be more accurate if she made an affirmative statement, as if it were a fact. If the statement was true for her, the pendulum circled clockwise, responding affirmatively to Sophia's vibrational frequency. When in disagreement, it circled counter-clockwise. When the statement had to do with a specific time, the pendulum would stop swinging, and the chain would slightly vibrate. Just to be certain, she inquired several times to acknowledge the veracity of the pendulum's direction.

To receive the best resonance with the crystal, Sophia allowed the chain to loop over her forefinger as the pendulum swung freely from the chain. Sophia first said a prayer, asking to receive what she needed to know to serve her in the best way, knowing that the answers she sought would help her take the right course of action.

She wanted to know when her father would be leaving this world, because she needed to make some life-changing decisions that would assist her in spending significant time with him. She stated aloud, "My father will be permanently leaving his body within a year's time." The pendulum swung to the right in agreement with the statement. "He will leave between now and October." It continued swinging to the right. "He will leave in September." The pendulum changed direction, to the left in disagreement. "August..." It changed and again swung to the right, indicating that August would be the month of her father's death. Then she asked specifically which day it would be. "He will live through the third week in August." The pendulum swung to the left. After some time, Sophia arrived at August 13th. When she stated the date, the pendulum ceased swinging and the chain vibrated. August was only nine months away.

Sophia wanted to spend more quality time with her father while he was still able, but the projected requirements of her business would most likely demand too much of her time. She received invitations to show her artwork in San Francisco and New Orleans. The time required to create, travel, and sell her paintings took a great deal of physical and emotional energy. The deadline for entry into the San Francisco show was due by the end of the month, so she opted out of that offer, but something told her she might want to leave the New Orleans date open for consideration, since it was later in the year. Sophia made a radical decision only to contract with art shows in the Denver metro area for the next several months. It would leave her with less financial security, but with fewer commitments. She would then be available to spend significant time with her father.

Patrick spent his last six weeks in hospice, four weeks

longer than anticipated, which seemed to Sophia an unwelcome ending to a well-lived life. She later realized that his prolonged time in hospice prepared her to release him. She and her father were very close. She was his spiritual connection to the next world, and she believed that it was particularly important to assist him as he transitioned, for he had great difficulty letting go.

For two years, Patrick told her of many dreams about standing at the river's edge, not yet able to cross over to the other side. Relaying his first dream to her, he said, "I had a very unusual dream last night."

Sophia responded, "Tell me about it. I know something about dream interpretation."

"I dreamt of a large river, and I couldn't see the opposite bank."

"Tell me what the water looked like. Was it smooth, or was it rushing?"

"There was white water - too vast and way too deep to cross - like an ocean," he said.

She knew he was trying to find a way to cross over – to leave his earthly life behind - but she did not discuss this with him on that level. "Could you see any bridges to cross?" She asked.

"No. I cannot find a way to the other side. I cannot see the other bank of the river. It is far too dangerous to cross."

With each consecutive dream about the river, the scenery changed. In one dream, on Patrick's side of the river was a steep slope with many boulders yet to climb to reach the water's edge. Others were with him, traversing the rough terrain. No bridges or still water was available for his safe crossing. He evidently still had much to do and many people yet to settle with before he could envision a new life for himself. He would remain a while longer.

In one of his last dreams, no longer were there other people climbing the boulders with him. Patrick was all alone. Eventually, he saw green fields bathed in wildflowers beyond the opposite river bank with the promise of a better life. Patrick had an affinity for all flowers, with the exception of those that were white.

As a young man, Patrick achieved the esteemed accomplishment of climbing all fifty-three of Colorado's 'fourteeners' - the peaks above 14,000 feet in elevation. A field of wildflowers along the trail was like a trophy to him, an acknowledgement for making such a concerted effort to the top of each peak. His vision of wildflowers let her know that he was clearly able to see the other side. He was getting close to finding a way to cross over - to reach his final destination. He had been in the hospice for five weeks when he told her about his most recent dream.

"Last night I saw Roy standing in the middle of the stream." Roy was Patrick's younger brother who died when he was only three years old. Patrick was six at the time, and he never quit grieving the loss of his little brother. Perhaps Roy was letting him know it was safe to join him.

"The water must have been shallow and still," she said. "Did Roy have hip waders on?"

He nodded. "Yes!"

"It sounds like the river is safe to cross. Was there a bridge?"

"I couldn't see one."

Patrick was a fly fisherman and had spent over ninety years of his life in a relationship with the river. He had one final journey to make. Perhaps it was nearly time for him to make a safe crossing to the other side.

For weeks, Sophia felt a tapping on her shoulder, on her arm, or her elbow, as if someone was trying to get her attention. She would turn toward the tapping, but no one was there, yet she felt her father's spirit next to her. She felt comforted, knowing he was coming to her throughout those challenging days as she slowly let him go. During one of her last visits to the hospice, he had a childlike look on his face. He began to tell Sophia a tale.

"I shot a rattlesnake!" he said.

"You did? Tell me about it." She could tell that her father was not his typical self. He was like a child telling a tale.

"I shot him right between the eyes," he continued.

"Did you eat him? I hear they taste like chicken," she said.

"No. He had feet."

"Feet... tell me about that. How many feet did he have?"

"He had ninety-eight feet."

"Ninety-eight...? I can't imagine a snake with ninety-eight feet."

"He was wearing shoes," Patrick said, making sure she heard him.

"What kind of shoes?" she asked.

"They are called Red Zongies."

"What are Red Zongies?"

He leaned in close and whispered slowly, as if he was telling a secret for no one else to hear. "They are very special shoes!"

She just smiled.

"I stole a car," he then said with a twinkle in his eye.

Surprised, Sophia prodded, "Tell me more about that."

"It's a Zephyr."

"I have never heard of a Zephyr."

"It's the top of the line," he said. The Lincoln Zephyr was one of the best American vehicles in the 1940s.

"Did you sell it?"

"Yeah, I made good money, so I stole another car."

"Are you going into a new line of work, like grand theft auto?" she asked.

With an impish look in his eyes, he smiled and said, "Yeah!"

It was like having a conversation with a child with a vivid imagination. It didn't seem like she was talking with an elderly man on the edge of death. There was a look in his eyes and an expression on his face not reflecting a man about to leave his earthly body. He was lit up, radiant from the inside out. She thought it was not only sweet, but it gave her a window into who he was, knowing that even in his last days he was still vibrant and alive on a different level.

Patrick's body was growing septic. His liver was failing.

That might have explained his convoluted stories, but Sophia herself had dreams that would have seemed to another like a fantasy, when in fact they were nothing of the sort. Perhaps he was telling the truth. Her logical mind told her what she intellectually knew was going on with him. It could have been a recall from another dimension within the Quantum Universe. The realm of time and space is where humans relate to circumstances within the Law of Cause and Effect. Sophia believed it was possible that her father was bypassing "time," and had entered a parallel universe.

No matter what her father's reality was, she stayed with it to honor his journey, allowing him to experience his own recall. Whoever he was, from her perspective, Patrick was still her father. From her viewpoint, she was hearing him tell a tale about himself as a young man, doing things that she never thought he could have done, but it did not matter.

The look in his eyes suddenly changed, and he shifted his gaze from her face to a far off place beyond the corner of the room. His radiance dimmed. He became her dying father again.

"Now is the time to write your book," he said

In response to the change in him, Sophia shifted her energy to join him right where he was. There seemed to be a prophetic tone to his words. Earlier in the summer, she wrote a story about the neighborhood wildlife. From the vantage point of her little green house she befriended two dozen squirrels, three raccoons, a skunk, a beautiful red fox, three coyotes, rabbits, a pair of mourning doves, two black-capped chickadees, two types of woodpeckers, a red-tailed hawk, and a huge yellow feral cat who lived under her bushes. On her property were two massive trees and many bushes filled with hundreds of singing finches, sparrows, and grackles. All the animals, including her cat and two dogs, sensed the safe and inviting environment in their little corner of the world. Every day, a mass of critters came to visit.

She began to draw and paint some of the animals she encountered, intending eventually to create an illustrated children's book. Every time she visited her father, or called him on the phone, she relayed the latest antics of the little beings that lived in her yard. He loved to hear the stories, adding his piece now and then and giving each animal a name of his own, such as "Girly," the tiny female squirrel, distinguished from the other squirrels by her unibrow. She often came down the crabapple tree to eat raw almonds from Sophia's hand. Who could resist such exotic fare?

The dozens of stories Sophia shared with her father did not leave him, and in that precious moment they shared in the hospice, he still encouraged her to pursue her writing and her art.

Patrick paused. It was clear how weary he was. He had little energy left in him for much more conversation. Sophia took his hand in hers and said, "You know, Daddy, I am going to miss you."

"I'm going to miss me, too," he responded. Even in his last moments, he didn't hesitate to express his humor.

She couldn't decide whether to laugh or cry, so she did both, knowing this may be one of the last conversations she would share with him.

She stroked his hand, trying to choke back the tears. "Do you have anything you need to say to me before you leave?"

He looked off into the distance as if in an altered state, and said, "Know Thyself. Know Thyself."

Patrick was a spiritual man, but never had Sophia heard him speak with such formality, never in "thees" or "thous". She was told her great-great grandfather prayed like that, but never had she heard her father speak in such a way. Sophia would soon search for the meaning of these powerful words he left with her, taking her on a journey to the other side of the world. A year later, the answer would begin to reveal itself.

These precious moments created a memory that would never leave her. Their relationship of cherished souls traveling through many dimensions would continue with such richness and grace beyond description. From her own near-death experience, she knew this was true.

Propped up in his chair with pillows and wrapped in blankets, Patrick said, "You are my precious darling little girl!"

His words instantly opened Sophia to the vast expanse of love between them. It was as if the universe poured its infinite grace over her, healing any and all barriers between them. Without knowing it, Sophia had waited her entire life to hear those unexpected words from him, healing everything that was ever unsettled and unspoken.

Patrick was solid and down to earth, logically grounded in all that he did. Sophia, on the other hand, was a right-brained, artistic bohemian, of sorts, who made her decisions based on intuition. For a man raised during the Great Depression, this was a combination that made a linear businessman like her father want to scream. Sophia always believed she was not what he wanted in a daughter, she being the opposite of his personality. He told her many times that he could not understand how she thought. It bothered him that she did not operate in a logical fashion as he did. His final words to her were like a blessing from God that wiped the slate clean.

With tears running down her cheeks, she hoped he could not see her grief. Her voice broke as she told him, "I love you so very much, Daddy!" She kissed him on the forehead and left for the evening. That was the last earthly conversation they shared.

The date was August 13th.

Over the next three days, Patrick quit eating and lay in bed seemingly unaware of who was in the room. On the fourth day, the hospice notified Sophia. Patrick had made a dramatic shift. The hospice caregivers knew to watch for the different stages of dying as their patients prepared to leave their bodies. Patrick had made such a change.

When Sophia arrived at the hospice late that morning, she found him propped up in bed, rocking back and forth, and gasping for breath. He grabbed at the sheets, the oxygen tubes, and catheter. Sophia's heart literally hurt. Her empathic nature allowed her to feel his anguish. It was torment to watch him struggle so.

Patrick's close friends came to say their goodbyes. Each had the opportunity to spend time with him. As the day made way for the night, everyone, except Sophia, went home. The hospice staff nurse estimated that he might have yet a couple more days before he would leave.

His room was completely dark, with the exception of light streaming in from a lone streetlight outside the window. Her father was blind in his left eye, and he had severe macular degeneration in his right. The artificial light that night bothered him, causing extreme sensory stimulation. In between gasps for air, he let Sophia know that any light bothered him. She sat in the chair on the left side of the bed, while he rocked back and forth, gasping for breath and grasping at the sheets. The death rattle began. It was a hellish experience for Sophia, yet she knew she needed to remain at his side.

She tried to remain calm, thinking, if she could go into a meditative state, it would help her deal with her torment of grief. When she achieved that state of calm, her father settled down. He sat back and rested a bit more easily. When she came out of the meditation, she looked at him through the shadows of the room. He began to struggle again, as if in his grasp he could find more oxygen to breathe. She went back into the quiet of her mind, which allowed him to settle down again. This happened several times.

She sat on his blind side, but the mere shift of her awareness toward him brought him back. He evidently felt her energetic attention directed toward him. Until then, she never realized how one could affect the field of energy of another just by altering their gaze or shifting their attention. When she was at peace, so was her father, but when she directed her attention toward him out of concern or worry, he responded with anxiety. Only love's presence was needed. Any sense of apprehension stripped the atmosphere of love's existing tranquility and harmony.

It was getting late. The nurses came into the room, turned on the lights, and announced that it was time to change the sheets and clean him up. Their intrusion shifted the sacredness of Sophia's time with her father. She went to the right side of the bed, where he could see her out of the corner of his eye, and asked him, "Would it be okay with you if I went home to get some rest? I will come back in the morning."

He said, "Okay."

Sophia kissed him on the forehead. "Goodnight, Daddy. I love you."

Just as she was leaving the building, she noticed the nurse who had admitted her father into the hospice six weeks before. Having just finished her shift, she was waiting for her ride home. Out of kindness and compassion, the nurse asked Sophia, "How are you doing?"

"I'm not sure right now, but maybe you can help me. I just spent most of the day with my dad. He is struggling just to hang on. I'm not quite sure what I just experienced." Sophia told her about how her father responded to her that evening.

The nurse said, "That's because you are deeply connected on a spiritual level. The love and compassion you have for your father shows up through your ability to sit with him while he is struggling to let go of his life. Our energy either uplifts or drains others. When we realize how we affect another, we become more conscientious of the energy we radiate. Your ability to meditate with your dad in such an emotional time raised your vibrational frequency to the highest level of love. Your father automatically resonated with your higher energy, bringing him to peace. In this poignant time, you have come together to remember who you have always been, joining together as one with the essence of the Divine."

Sophia was awestruck by what the nurse said to her. She turned away for a few seconds to find a tissue in her purse. When she turned back around, the woman was no longer there. She did not say good night, nor did Sophia hear her leave through the door. It seemed as if she disappeared into thin air. Sophia had so much on her mind that she didn't give it much thought until weeks later. Perhaps she was an angel who appeared to her as the trusted nurse when Sophia most needed the support. She was there at the right time to help Sophia come to a greater understanding of the subtle energies and their not so subtle effects.

That night, Sophia stayed with Michael. She had gotten little sleep for six weeks. She fell asleep around eleven. About midnight, she felt someone sit on the edge of the bed next to her. The energy remained. She awoke, thinking it was Michael, because he often sat next to her on the bed in the early morning hours before he went about his work, but Michael was asleep, lying next to her on the other side of the bed. Sophia soon realized that she was feeling the same energy of her dad, who had been tapping on her shoulder for many weeks.

Feeling the peace from his visitation, she quickly fell back to sleep, but this time she went into one of her dream-visions, the kind in which she was completely engaged. It was obvious to her that her father was afraid to let go. Perhaps he didn't know how to leave. In her dream, she suddenly thought, *I will build him a bridge to help him cross over to the Other Side*.

She grew up spending many weekends at their family cabin in the Rocky Mountains. On the property was a bridge over a river that flowed thirty feet from the cabin's front door. She didn't want to walk him across that bridge, because it would then be forever related to his death in her memory. Instead, she decided to build him a similar bridge in her mind specifically for this purpose alone. She created an arched footbridge, just wide enough for two people.

On the earthly end, they stood facing the bridge together. Sophia told her father, "Dad, come with me, I will help you across the bridge."

"No! I don't want to go." He withdrew his arms and turned his body away from her like a small child.

She held out her hand for him to hold. "Take my hand, and I will walk across the bridge with you."

He slowly took her hand, and she looked into his eyes and smiled with a deep love that would last for eternity.

Step by step, she slowly walked with him until they reached the apex of the bridge. From Sophia's vantage point, she could see the other side of green flowering fields. There, waiting for her father, she saw her mother and other family members. Sophia's childhood dog, Buffy, whom her dad had deeply loved, was anxiously waiting for him. Sophia knew this was no longer her journey to take. The remainder of the passage across the bridge was her father's sole journey. She led him ahead of her and released his hand as she watched him continue to the other side.

Then, the bridge and her father disappeared. The dream ended. Sophia woke up to a feeling of tremendous peace, not yet remembering what she had just dreamt. Then wide-awake, she got out of bed and went downstairs to make a cup of hot tea. The clock on the stove read 12:17 a.m. She sat on the sofa in the living room, sipping her tea, when Michael came down the stairs with her cell phone in his hand. The hospice chaplain was calling. Her father was gone. The nursing staff had checked him at midnight and found his vital signs to be strong. At 12:30 a.m., they checked him again and found that he died.

Sophia was so relieved and happy he was no longer suffering. She then realized what occurred and was grateful to have been with him in a way she would never have expected, and perhaps this was the better way for her to be with her dad in his last moments. The peace that she experienced when she created the bridge remained with her.

For several months following his death, Sophia continued to feel her dad's familiar tapping on her shoulder from time to time. She believed the bridge that she created was for her as well, providing a way to traverse the challenge. It created a knowing that she could generate whatever she needed for any circumstance, providing she acted out of authentic love.

Chapter
Fifteen

Time faded away when Sophia was deeply enraptured in her painting. Her nighttime ventures from the ethereal plane became ribbons of colored hues that transferred from palette to brush, and onto the canvas with blissful ease. Images arose as if by magic from some unfamiliar cache deeply hidden within her subconscious. Only when she tapped into that secreted reserve did she make known, through her creativity, such wonders that became inspired artistic revelations. It had been an exceptionally good day of painting, and she looked forward to another good night's sleep, feeling a satisfied sense of accomplishment.

Sophia enjoyed preparing herself to be fully receptive to what might come in her dreams. Before she laid her head on the pillow, she went into her library to take part in her nightly spiritual practice. She found that the more busy or tired she was, the greater the need for meditation. The best way for her to meditate was a practice she had followed since she was quite young. Water was her element. Meditating through a bowl of water was a way she could easily connect with Spirit at any time.

On her altar, the chalice glowed with the eternal flame.

On a table across the room was a silver tray of beeswax candles that emitted their sweet scent amidst her sanctuary's ambient light. Shelves filled with books, artwork, and mementos lined the golden walls of the room, filling the atmosphere with the eternal creative nature of every writer and artist who gave freely of themselves. Pulled back tapestry draperies revealed the crystalline cosmic wonders suspended in the skies outside her window.

Sophia gently crossed her legs as she sat on her meditation cushion in front of her altar, leaving her bare feet upon the Persian rug atop oaken floors. She wrapped herself in a warm woolen shawl that blanketed her in a cocoon of warmth and security as she closed her eyes and ventured into the eternal abyss - that of *apeiros* - the cause of all unity and the measure of all things.

Sophia left her earthly world behind and rose into the infinite realm. Her dream-life from several consecutive nights left her weary. Not much sleep had occurred, and yet she relished the next encounter with who she once was. The activity of her dreams left her exhausted, yet at the same time ready for the next challenge. Her body and mind ached for a good sound sleep, but meditation revived her from deep within, bypassing all time and space, while it united her with the Source of All - the Divine - the Universal Intelligence.

Her dream-filled nights left her with many questions. Sophia knew she must open up to new inspiration if she wanted to find answers, which meant she had to let go of old thoughts that kept her stagnant. Sophia had recorded her own guided meditation, entitled *The River*, to sell along with her artwork and books. She listened to the recording when she was weary. It played in the background as she relaxed into the journey:

Sit in a quiet place with no distractions. Close your eyes, breathe deeply, and exhale, clearing your mind of anything that has your attention. As you breathe in, know that you are breathing the breath of God, for God is breathing you. As you exhale, release any stress and burdens from your day. Breathe in... Breathe out... Breathe in... Breathe out.

Now bring your imagination to a beautifully wooded forest. You are walking along a path among gigantic redwood trees that tower high above your head, far into the zenith above. Sense their magnificence. Take in the exhilarating scents of the forest - conifers, mosses, flowers, ferns, and all plant and animal life. The loam beneath your feet, deep black and mineral-rich, cushions your every step. Honor these eternal earthly sentinels that rise into the heavens with their never-ending ancient wisdom. Give thanks to them, in advance, for what you are about to receive. Listen to the deep silence of the forest and feel its extraordinary wonder.

Follow the well-worn path as it takes you to a clearing at the edge of the woods. Continue along the trail as it leads you slightly downhill through a field of flowers and grasses, waving their welcome as you enter into the valley. The colors of flowering meadows are more vibrant than anything you have yet seen. Their fragrance refreshes your mind and body so you can fully take in the beauty and grace of the natural surroundings. You see the soft golden grasses swaying in the gentle breeze, hearing their soft symphony like harmonious waves upon the ocean. You notice, high in the distance, snowcapped mountains that surround the flowering meadow in which you stand. They are pristine and elegant in their vast expanse as they rise into the perpetual atmosphere of blue skies overhead. Know that you are an integral part in the order of the Universe. What you are now witnessing is a part of who you are, or you would not be able to recognize the splendor of your surroundings. Maintain your walk along the pathway as it winds down through the peaceful field until you come to an enormous grove of aspen trees. Black-speckled white bark repeats in vertical patterns. The leaves now turned gold, shimmer in the breeze like countless golden coins reflecting brilliant sunrays.

This aspen grove sits on the bank of a peaceful flowing stream, shading a thick mossy carpet that invites you to stop and rest. You are compelled to remove your shoes to feel the cool, plush textures beneath your feet. The gently flowing stream beckons you to enter. You step barefoot into the clear, cool water on the sandy edge of the riverbank. The water laps at your ankles, inviting you to enter more deeply into its currents.

You have not noticed until now that you are wearing a suit of armor that represents the burdens you bear. You are accustomed to the weight because you have carried it for so long, and you keep adding to it, thinking that this burden is yours and yours alone, but you now have a deep desire to swim in the cool clear water. It is calling you to join in its welcoming flow, inviting you to come deeper into the dancing stream, but the suit of armor is so heavy, you fear it will drag you down and you will not survive.

However, there is a way out of this dilemma. If you choose to remove the armor, piece by piece, you will eventually be able to enter into the river's depths. First, take off your leggings. One by one, let them loose into the flow of the stream. Attach something that you need to release to each section of the armor...it could be pieces of your wounded heart, regrets, a shameful experience, or something you have denied yourself. You could attach responsibilities that are no longer yours to carry. Could it be that you placed there the long denied unforgiveness for another, but more so for yourself?

As you take off your armor piece by piece, place it into the stream and watch it float away until it disappears beyond the horizon in the distance. The armor will float with the current, occasionally getting caught on an obstruction, but the clear cool water will eventually catch it with its persistent wave, dislodging it from its hold, *washing the armor away until you see it no more. Continue this process until every piece of armor is gone, specifically the breastplate that has shielded your heart all this time. Watch it float down the living waters until it is no longer visible.*

Now you are standing free of the armor, liberated from the weight of guilt, shame, and all that has blocked you from your heart's desires. You are naked and free of all encumbrances, and liberated to feel the immersion of your rightful place in the flowing waters.

At birth, your body consisted of seventy-five percent water. Water is your original home. Lie back and feel it wash over your body as you drift in the stream. Feel the baptism of its cleansing powers. Float facing up, viewing the blue skies overhead, allowing the current to take you gently downriver to where it becomes a serene lake. Play in the water as a little child. Splash and kick all you want. Laugh and rejoice in your newfound freedom. Now released of all burdens that have held you down, you are free. Liberation is your way of life from this point forward. Stay here in the lake as long as you desire. You are safe, and supplied with all you need. You are home.

When you are ready, swim to the shore and leave the lake. Return to the aspen grove to put on your clothes and shoes. Walk away from the shade of the aspen's golden leaves' applause in the gentle mountain breeze.

Remember how it feels to be free of what weighed so heavily upon you. This is now your task, so that you may be a crystalline reflection of water wherever your journey takes you. In this truth, you will remember others beyond the armor that they wear, for they too are free to choose, to live in the awareness of their birthright, that of being the life-giving water that ever cleanses, changes and transforms.

Return to the path, to ascend through the meadow's colorful flowers and grasses. Listen for their joyous laughter, celebrating your liberation. Walk past the protective ring of majestic mountains. Give thanks to them for their watchful nature. Continue to follow up the pathway toward the woods, taking in all the beauty surrounding you. With a grateful heart, walk through the majestic redwood forest, remembering yourself with renewed vitality, delivered from what once held you back. Send thoughts of appreciation to the forest, the meadow, the mountains, the stream, and all of its inhabitants for the honor of their service to you.

You may at any time return to this place where the aspen trees shade the moss by the river. The forest, meadow, mountains, and river want you to know they are ever available to serve you in the release of your burdens, as forgiveness and release cleanse you of your grievances, again renewing you to who you have ever been within your eternality.

Rest in the assurance of the love you have just permitted yourself to realize. Take a deep breath and now release it. Allow yourself to feel the seat beneath you and the floor underneath your feet. Listen to the sounds in the room, and take in the scents of your surroundings. When you are ready, open your eyes and bring yourself fully back into the room.

Sophia became aware of the floor beneath her. She opened her eyes and brought her gaze into clear focus, seeing the eternal flame dancing on the oil's surface inside the golden chalice. She came out of the meditation, knowing she had once again released all concerns. Feeling a sense of completion, she returned to her bedroom and crawled under the covers with a clear mind. Soon, she was traveling into her dream's adventures of Roxana settling into her new life in Athens.

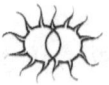

Chapter
Sixteen

A thens was a densely populated city comprised of small, one- or two-story houses. The architecture was not as advanced as that found in Akrotiri, and Athenians had no hot water piped into the homes, for there were no thermal underground sources. Although the city was massive, it seemed antiquated compared to Roxana's former island home of Thera. The best she could do was adapt, for the time being. She raised Theo as her own child, and they lived together in a village with the elders and others that sailed from Thera. Most were highly educated and had been successful trades people in Akrotiri, and all were starting over from new beginnings.

Roxana began to acquire herbs for medicinal remedies as she quickly developed a reputation in Athens as a healer. Available all hours of the day, she drew people from far distances who had many varied health challenges. The herbs were used mostly as a placebo, for true and lasting healing came from Roxana's ability to open herself as a vessel to the gods, allowing them to fill her with their infinite energy. Her healing power raised the patient's level of vibration to an elevated frequency in which illness could not thrive. Roxana merely held the higher frequency long enough for them to rise to that level. In actuality, the patients became the healers themselves, being receptive to Roxana's curative energies. Nevertheless, Athenians were beginning to consider her a miracle worker.

Roxana could recognize a person's highest qualities, or those shortcomings that blocked healing. She helped her patients rise above their challenges. Part of her work as High Priestess was to educate people about their inner nature. Everything they needed was already within. Word spread of the beautiful healer who taught people to heal themselves. Most every other high priest, shaman, or healer sought dominion over his or her subjects. If they could convince the people of their own powerlessness, they would have ultimate control, or so they believed.

Roxana thought differently. If the people were aware of their innate abilities, these empowered individuals would garner strong families and growing communities of health and well-being. Confidence and courage, instead of control and manipulation, would become a way of life. She quickly gained an enormous following that grew into an equanimous, bountiful community.

One particular day would change the course of events for Roxana and Theo. A horseman riding north of Athens came across an injured man who had fallen from his horse. He suffered a broken leg and hit his head, which knocked him unconscious. After helping the man come out of his dazed stupor, the horseman quickly rode to a nearby farm to borrow a hay cart to bring the injured man to Roxana, for he had heard the stories about her healing ways.

It was late afternoon when they arrived at her village. He called out for help, and one of the elders from Roxana's village helped him walk the injured man into her home.

Together, they laid him on a bed as Roxana placed down-filled pillows behind his head. She lit an oil lamp on the table nearby, while Theo brought both men water to drink.

The horseman expected to meet an aging crone, because the reputation she held for healing led him to believe only an aged woman could possibly possess such restorative abilities. However, he was pleasantly surprised to find standing before him a tall, elegant woman who seemed to radiate golden light.

She smiled, proudly holding her son's shoulders. "Welcome to our home. My name is Roxana, and this is my son, Theo. Please sit." She motioned for the horseman to be seated at the table. "First, I must attend to the wound on your head," she said, addressing the injured man on the bed. Roxana quickly cleaned the gash, applied a salve of healing herbs, and wrapped his head in clean strips of cloth. "And what are you called?" she asked.

"I am Yiorgos," the injured man replied.

"I am called Demosthenes," the horseman said. "We are grateful for your help."

"Yiorgos will be our guest until he is able to travel again. Would you like to join us for supper, Demosthenes?" Roxana asked.

He gratefully accepted. She left the room and soon returned with Theo at her side, carrying plates of flatbread, goat cheese, herbed hummus, grapes, and olives. She poured wine into three cups. For Theo, she poured a tiny bit of wine into his, and topped it off with water.

"Yiorgos, I would like you to drink as much of the wine as you can, for it contains an infusion of the healing herbs:

arnica, oregano, rosemary, and thyme. They will help the swelling and aid in alleviating the pain."

The two men were famished after their ordeal. Yiorgos was clearly in a great deal of pain, supporting his weight with his right arm, while he ate some of the food sitting on a plate next to him on the bed. The pain did not curtail him from eating, nor from expressing his gratitude. "Thank you for your help today, Demosthenes. I owe you more than I can offer in payment, but please accept this." Yiorgos offered him a pouch of gold coins.

It was a generous sum of money. Demosthenes accepted, but took out only a few coins. He shook Yiorgos' hand and returned the leather pouch. "It was my honor, Yiorgos, and I thank you for your generous offer. I will but take only a few coins for the farmer who was kind enough to loan me his cart. I am a fortunate man, for many have given me aid when I had nothing to offer in return. Being of service to you today is a way to give back their kindness. Perhaps someday you could help another in the same way. I now live comfortably with more than I need."

Yiorgos smiled. "I will not forget your benevolence today, Demosthenes." He winced at the tremendous pain. His left leg was swelling, with the bone not yet set.

"You will be here for a few days," Roxana said. "You must gather your strength. I will first set your leg, and then we will clean you up. Please drink your wine, for it will cloud your senses and ease the pain." She gathered her golden bowl filled with water, healing oils, clean strips of cloth, and two ten-inch tree branches stripped and fashioned into splints.

After Yiorgos drank the wine, Roxana asked Theo to

summon one of the elders named Gennadios. When he arrived, she instructed him to steady Yiorgos, as she planned to set his broken leg. Demosthenes helped, as well.

"I am going to place this leather strap between your teeth for you to bite," said Roxana.

Gennadios sat behind Yiorgos and wrapped one arm around his shoulders, and the other around his ribcage. Demosthenes firmly supported his leg at the knee. Before Yiorgos could resist, Roxana quickly pulled just above his ankle with a jolt, putting her full weight into setting his leg. Yiorgos moaned, leaving permanent teeth marks in the strap, but the worst was over. Roxana quickly cleaned his leg and then gently rubbed a healing salve of arnica over the area where the bone was broken. She wrapped his leg in clean cloths and placed the splints on the inside and outside of the lower leg, wrapping them with more strips of cloth and finishing with a knot tied just below the knee. She asked Gennadios if he would gently help Yiorgos place his injured leg on pillows to elevate it.

Yiorgos lay back on the bed and blew a heavy sigh. "Well, I certainly fixed myself this time," he said.

Roxana offered him more wine while she gently washed the dirt and sweat from his body. "How did you injure yourself?"

"Foolish, really, I was riding through the woods – a shortcut to the king's palace – when a sturdy tree had the gall to jump in front of me. It swept me off my horse like a whirlwind."

Demosthenes chuckled. "Trees can be ruthless if you don't keep an eye out for them."

"So I have learned," Yiorgos sighed. "Unfortunately, not for the first time, I might add."

Roxana smiled and finished bathing Yiorgos, who could not help but notice that the vessel she used for clean water was a gleaming golden bowl. With every stroke of the sponge, he felt his body release tension as it warmed and filled him with an unfamiliar heat and energy.

It was getting dark. Demosthenes said, "I now must take my leave. Thank you, Roxana and Theo, for your hospitality. And Yiorgos, may your health return to you soon, to bring you into great favor of the gods."

"It seems that their favor has already begun." Yiorgos looked at Roxana and smiled.

Beneath all the dirt and grime was a stunningly handsome man in his thirtieth year looking at Roxana with green eyes. She oiled and combed his shoulder-length curly ebony hair. He was well muscled and tan from working outdoors.

Averting her gaze and trying not to blush for fear that he would notice her attention, she shifted her interest to his injured leg, massaging both his knee and foot with oil of arnica and rosemary to help alleviate bruising and pain. With every touch of her hand, he felt an unfamiliar, but warm tingling sensation. He evidently had also cracked one of the bones in his lower left arm in the fall. It was not broken, but gave him tremendous pain when he put his weight on it. Roxana attended it in the same way, splinting it with smaller sticks and strips of cloth. She placed pillows under his left arm and head, making sure he was as comfortable as possible, and finally covered him with a blanket to keep him warm after the shock set in from his injuries.

She sat next to him on the bed and gently placed one hand on his injured arm, and the other on his broken leg. Yiorgos thought he could see a golden band of light around her as she sat with him in silence, but he thought he just might be woozy from the wine. A tingling sensation radiated from her hands throughout his body, leaving him vibrantly aware, even though he was inebriated. He also noticed her necklace, from which a lustrous amethyst hung from the chain.

"Yiorgos, within each of us is a power that comes from the gods," Roxana said. "It has always been present, and it is *within* you. This power is the authority that knows which decisions are correct and good. It is the same power within that naturally heals from deep inside. Here at your center is where this power lies." She placed her hand on the center of his chest and could not help but feel his well-developed muscles. She continued, albeit a bit distracted, "Place your attention here. Breathe into this part of your body. The gods are breathing you. Know that from the breath comes healing to every other aspect of your being. This is what you are to do in these next several days while you are here to heal. Concentrate your energy here, rest within your breath, and the part of you that knows how to heal will take immediate action."

He placed his right hand on her arm. "I am so grateful to you, Roxana." She looked into his green eyes, and for the first time since she was a youth, she felt a spark. As a young woman, she spent so much of her adolescence in training. Yes, there were flirtations with the young men in the village, but only one in particular captured her heart. Toward the others, she gave no effort to their attentions, for nothing was to deter her from her dedication to the great responsibilities of becoming the High Priestess of Akrotiri.

Since leaving Thera, she was committed to establishing a safe community for Theo and her people so they could all find their right livelihood and live comfortably. She devoted her efforts to establish herself as a healer. She gave little thought to romantic entanglements, until she tended to the wounded man who would remain in her care until he was well enough to return to his home.

The dark of night settled in by the time she finished attending to Yiorgos. She prepared fruit, nuts, and cheese for Theo and her dinner. While they were sitting at the table eating, she caught up with Theo about his day. Even though Yiorgos was quite intoxicated, to say the least, he could discern the atmosphere surrounding him. There was a welcome quality to the room beginning with the light yellow-toned walls made of limestone bricks. The house was small, but it contained a warm atmosphere with woven rugs in shades of gold, crimson, persimmon, and eggplant that covered the floors and provided window coverings to keep out the cold night air.

She had placed several oil lamps into the niches carved into the limestone walls, reflecting their firelight back into the room's atmosphere. Elaborate hand-carved wood made up the table, chairs, a long chest for clothing, and the bed-stand directly across the room. The designs were quite sophisticated and pleasing to the eye. Yiorgos had never seen anything like the woodwork in her small abode. What caught his attention most was the exquisitely painted wall of tall lilies in bloom that surrounded the corner hearth ablaze with a warm fire. The artistic qualities in the room were phenomenal.

Several days passed. Roxana re-dressed Yiorgos' shoulder and arm. Curiosity urged Yiorgos to ask, "Roxana, your home is appointed so beautifully. It is obvious to me that you are not from Athens or from anywhere nearby. May I ask of your origin?"

"Nine months ago, my people came from Thera. We were the last to leave the island before the eruption. We have been fortunate to find this village for us to settle into Greek life. One of my people is a master woodcarver. Another works with textiles, having made these beautiful rugs and window coverings. Each has come with their vast knowledge to make our community self-sufficient and strong. We are greatly blessed."

"You speak of them as 'your people,' and you also were the last to leave. That tells me that you were of a high standing and authority in Akrotiri."

She finished dressing his arm and shoulder. Rarely did she speak about herself, for the reputation of a high priestess must come from the people, not from her own boasting. She had but a few people she served in that capacity, so she kept that to herself. However, she did feel a growing sense of trust in Yiorgos – enough trust for her to say, "In Akrotiri, on our island home of Thera, I was the High Priestess."

Greatly surprised by her answer, his green eyes widened. "This explains why you have such healing powers, but it is so much more beyond herbs and treatments. It is the essence of you that knows your source, and that is what emanates through you from the gods. That is the difference of your power. I have never experienced such a thing until now. What is more magnificent about you is that you are extremely humble, not being in the illusion of power for your own sake. You have helped me to believe that I also have that same capability, thus enabling me to heal from what is the natural ability within me."

"Every one of us has this power within us," Roxana responded, "but most think it is something outside us that we cannot acquire. We feel we have to earn it or suffer for it, but that is not so. The gods created us to witness to the world of their powers through us, and as us. We are the origin of their immensity. We have just begun to tap into the abilities that we have at our fingertips, to do wondrous works for mankind and for all of nature."

Yiorgos witnessed her strength and compassion for all beings. While he recovered, he watched her caring ways with Theo, her community, and with all the animals that came to the window or door at feeding time. None would enter. They seemed to know the outdoors was where they belonged. She fed them specially prepared food. The dogs were her guards, but also were her animal family. Donkeys and horses all received her caring caress, giving her love and devotion in return, while Theo's goat continued to hold a special place in their family.

She asked, "May I inquire of your origins, Yiorgos?"

"Forgive me for not telling you about myself. I am a fortunate son from generations of merchants and landowners from the mountainous valley northwest of Athens. I tend hundreds of acres that produce the finest quality olive oil. Before I fell from my horse, I was on my way to the king's palace to negotiate trade on behalf of Greece with Macedon and Italia. I will resume my trade agreements when I am well enough to ride again." Roxana was impressed at his well-rounded nature. She recognized his educated intellect as a merchant, but he also had within him a sensibility and kindness.

During his stay, Yiorgos taught Theo games of strategy that would later serve him as he grew. They soon became good friends. When it came time that Yiorgos was well enough to leave, he admitted to himself that he would rather stay in the presence of Roxana's loving essence and with the growing young boy. Yiorgos placed his right hand on her shoulder as she bid him goodbye at the door, and asked, "Would it be of interest to you if I were to call on you? I must confess my deep feelings for you, Roxana."

She could hardly contain herself, but all those years of training came in handy, having learned how to control her emotions. "I have not heard you mention a wife or family," she said.

"No. I have not found the time nor interest, but I will make the time to visit you and Theo, if you so choose."

"Yes, I am sure I can speak for Theo. We will both welcome your return," she said with a smile that revealed her desires.

He looked deeply into her beautiful bronze eyes, and she into his. He took her hand in his and raised it to his lips. Still holding her hand, he pulled her to him and kissed her gently on the cheek, and then turned his head to kiss her on the lips. In response, she reached up to hold his face as she ardently returned his kiss. Both felt the energy course through their bodies that had been stirring for the four weeks he stayed during his time of healing, and they were now certain of their feelings for each other. Yiorgos left that day, knowing that he would spend the rest of his life with Roxana.

CHAPTER
Seventeen

R oxana would often ride a donkey to the top of the Acropolis to clear her mind of the densely populated city and all its chaos. There were a few buildings on top of the citadel, but nothing like the Parthenon and other temples that later were constructed eight hundred years into the future. She had now lived in Athens for nearly two years since fleeing the doomed island of Thera. Having gained the reputation of a powerfully strong healer, Roxana had developed a large following, but she was about to embark upon something for which she was not yet prepared. She needed solitude for her prayers to the gods so she would be ready and willing to serve when the time came.

Her relationship with Yiorgos had grown very strong. It was thirteen months since he came to her after falling off his horse. Because he was a man of such means and influence, Yiorgos persuaded many people of power to utilize Roxana's gifts. Her community of master craftsmen and artists had raised the aesthetic bar for Athens' societal arts. They included architects, engineers, builders, and stonemasons. Master artisans of textiles, frescoes, mosaics, woodworkers, metal smiths and potters also lived and traded in the community. Vintners cultivated vineyards nearby and produced wine reminiscent of the sweet vintages of Akrotiri. Roxana created an apothecary shop, offering healing poultices and tinctures for clients to purchase as needed.

The number of people who came to Roxana for healing steadily increased since her arrival in Athens. Her herbal remedies were extremely effective, but her healing gifts enhanced her meditations over the golden bowl. She had always been a seer and a prophetess, but she had not readily used her energetic powers. She felt they were of secondary importance while she established herself in Athens, but this was not so.

Her unique abilities set her aside from all other healers. Roxana became a seer for military leaders and local politicians, and would soon face her greatest test to date. The following day, she was to meet with King Krios at her home at midday, accompanied by his royal entourage.

When the ailing king heard of her powers many weeks before, he summoned her to the palace. She came, as directed, but informed him that she could better serve him within the walls of her home, where all of her healing herbs and concoctions were readily at hand. The truth of the matter was that she needed her golden bowl and chalice to see into his future, and she never removed either from their protected surroundings. For the sake and well-being of Athens and all of Greece, she could not take the chance of anyone gaining knowledge of her power. The healing arts were a guise, drawing attention from the golden vessels that she held most dear. Being a reasonable man, the king agreed to meet on her terms.

Roxana prepared for weeks, cleaning, organizing, and

beautifying the property for the king's visit. There was nothing more for her to do, and so she took the day to clear her mind to commune with the gods.

The next day, she arose before dawn to bathe and ready herself with perfumed oils. Her hair, pulled back from her face with strands of pearls holding up the mass of curling tendrils, gently draped down the nape of her neck. Donning her best *chiton*, she wrapped her waist with her red zonai, adorned with the Tyrian purple spiral designs. After tying her leather sandals, Roxana was ready to receive the king.

As planned, King Krios arrived when the sun shone directly overhead. He entered her home accompanied by his highest appointed general, Nikomedes, his younger brother. The king's physician, Timaeus, and the king's high priest, Capaneus, also accompanied him, as did Queen Melaina.

Roxana immediately took notice that the king's health had failed since she last saw him at the palace. She also could not help but notice the dark, cold countenance of the flaming red-haired Queen Melaina, and the harsh demeanor of the general.

"If you would please be seated, Your Highnesses." She invited the king and queen to sit in beautifully carved chairs crafted especially for their arrival. She motioned for the other three to be seated on the opposite side of the room, yet the general chose to remain standing near the door. Roxana served her best wine in beautiful polished bronze wine goblets. She then sat opposite the king.

"With your permission, my King, may I hold your hand?" Roxana asked. She gently took his hand between hers and looked deeply into his eyes. She felt a scarce amount of vital energy in her sovereign, indicating that, at this rate, it might be only days before he was dead. The king did not realize that Roxana was infusing into his body and mind life-giving energy through her hands.

While she continued to hold the king's hand, Roxana asked Timaeus, the king's physician, "If you please, it would be greatly beneficial for me to know the king's symptoms. And if you could also relay in what ways you have treated his illness?"

Timaeus listed a number of issues. "His Highness has felt tremendous fatigue from the beginning of his illness, which has persisted for many weeks now. Even at the beginning of his day his vitality wanes. The cooks prepare his favorite dishes, but he has no appetite. Pain in his stomach and abdomen leave him with little vigor. He purges whatever he eats. Because the king has not kept much food in his body, he experiences a great amount of dizziness and is extremely weak. I have administered various herbs, waters, and wine. Capaneus has performed many rituals to bring him back to health, but nothing has changed, except to say that he is more ill as each day passes."

As Roxana spoke to Timaeus, she felt an exchange across the room between Queen Melaina and General Nikomedes that belied a casual glance. The king was substantially older than his brother, who was next in line to the throne. Roxana could read the general's dark and foreboding energy under the layers of armor and leather. She could see right through him, for nothing could mask one's radiant energy, or in Nikomedes' case, the lack thereof. Queen Melaina was equally obvious in her discomfort, exhibiting agitation and impatience, while at the same time a cold indifference to her husband's distress.

It was apparent to Roxana that it was time to look into the sacred waters of her golden bowl. There, the revealing of truth would make itself known. "If you will please excuse me while I take a brief leave," Roxana said. "It is necessary that I prepare an herbal concoction to bring the king to health." As she rose from her chair, she bowed her head to the king and queen as she backed out of the room. The look in the queen's eye was deadly.

Roxana took notice that the High Priest Capaneus, without consent, arose from his seat and walked around the room, taking note of a variety of items she had displayed on a table. He picked up large crystal specimens, one of amethyst, and another of aquamarine. It was more than curiosity compelling him to look into containers and sniff the oils. A selenite ceremonial wand decorated with a large quartz crystal, beads, and eagle feathers caught his interest, as well as a stone bowl containing several papyrus scrolls. Word of Roxana's incredible powers had circulated like wildfire throughout the city, and Capaneus was clearly seeking the source of her abilities. He was rapidly losing the trust of the king and desired to obtain Roxana's powers for himself. Long before that day, Capaneus secretly planned to take drastic measures to rid Athens of Roxana and what he thought was her witchery.

He took one of the scrolls and began to walk into the next room where she had left the golden vessel. Calmly, Roxana walked up and blocked him from entering her apothecary. She took the scroll from his hand. "Good Sir, I invited you into my home as a guest and respectfully request that you take your seat. Please enjoy more wine, if you choose."

Startled by her bluntness, Capaneus threw his head back and looked down his nose at her in disdain. He sniffed and turned away to take his seat. Even in his weakened state, King Krios looked disapprovingly at Capaneus as Roxana stepped into the next room to retrieve her golden bowl. The chalice, lit with the eternal flame, sat on a bronze tripod above and behind the sacred vessel. The flame reflected onto the water's surface. Roxana sat on a stool and placed her hands on either side of the bowl. She peered into the flame's reflection in the water. She felt the eternal energy course through her body and immediately entered a higher state of mind, mentally asking the gods to reveal the truth of the king's health.

Her suspicions were confirmed as she saw through the waters the intimate involvement of the queen and the king's brother. They were systematically poisoning the king. Greek law stated once a woman was widowed she would immediately become the wife of her husband's brother. Upon the death of King Krios, Nikomedes would take the throne and, as a matter of course, Queen Melaina as his bride.

Raising her head from the vision that she saw in the bowl, Roxana asked, "How am I to prevent this terrible betrayal of my king?" She gave a silent prayer and quickly prepared a combination of herbs and powders that would help the king's body rid itself of the poison. "To all the gods," she prayed, "please guide me toward what is needed to save the king."

Suddenly, the answer entered her mind. She went into the next room and gave the king a cocktail of apple cider vinegar mixed with natron mineral water and sliced ginger. "Forgive me, my King, for this will not delight your tongue, but if you drink quickly, it will go down with ease. In very little time, you will begin to feel better. It is my recommendation that you remain here with me for several days, so that I may oversee your return to full health."

The king nodded. He sensed he could trust her. "I appreciate your diligent care, Roxana."

Then Roxana said with authority, glaring at Capaneus, Queen Melaina, and Nikomedes, "You are no longer needed here. You may return to the palace. I will send a messenger each day to inform you of the king's progress."

The queen angrily rose from her chair. "This is unacceptable! I see no reason for my husband to stay in your care. He will return to the palace immed-"

"You will take your leave," the king interrupted with a wave of his hand, dismissing them from his company.

"We will not leave you here unprotected," Nikomedes said.

"The palace guards and the king's physician may remain," Roxana said.

"This is preposterous!" Capaneus angrily said. "Your Highness, I must object to this charlatan and her magic potions!"

"Enough!" the king said. "Take your leave! I will not say it again!"

"You will be hearing from me, witch," Queen Melaina

angrily snarled. "You will not dismiss your queen without consequence. You will live to regret this day, I assure you. Come, Nikomedes!" She skulked out of the room, taking Nikomedes' arm as they left the king and his physician behind. More than annoyed, Capaneus could not have displayed greater displeasure by Roxana's earlier reprimand and dismissal by a woman he felt was beneath him. He followed the queen and general out the door, but not before he angrily threw his wine goblet onto the floor. After the door slammed shut, the physician, Timaeus, picked up the goblet and meekly handed it to Roxana as she cleaned up the mess.

The king, still too weak to concern himself with the outburst, simply put his head back and closed his eyes.

Roxana rinsed her hands in the water basin on the table and dried them on her apron.

"Roxana," Timaeus asked, "may I inquire into your findings? I have tried everything in my power to bring the king back to health, but I have failed in every effort."

She invited him to sit next to the king, who slowly turned his head to her. "Your Highness, there is no easy way for me to tell you this, but you are being poisoned in small increments each day, so as to draw little attention to your diminishing health."

The king weakly rose out of his chair. "Poison! How could I be poisoned? I have people to test my food before I dine. This is not possible."

Roxana rose to her feet to meet the king's gaze. "Yes, Your Highness, I understand you have tasters to sample your meals, but have you thought about the many times during your day that you drink water or wine?" She paused before she continued. "Who is it that casually brings you water or wine throughout the day? Who is it that prepares your bath? If your bathwater is tainted, it seeps through your skin, eventually affecting your health. Please give it some thought, Your Highness. With the greatest respect, it is my belief that you may already know the answer."

The king collapsed back in the chair. With his head in his hand, he said, "My wife is the last to test the water for my bath. My brother and the queen both serve me water and wine throughout the day." He looked at Timaeus. "How can this be true?"

Timaeus sadly nodded. "This is such despicable betrayal!"

"I considered their care to be of kindness, for once," the king said, "when all the while they were poisoning me? Their treachery is now clear."

Roxana nodded. Timaeus shook his head and sighed in disbelief. The king called out, "Guard!" A guard outside the door entered the room. "Guard, tell me your name and rank?"

"I am called Cleisthenes, Your Highness. I am second in command to General Nikomedes."

The king looked at Roxana. "Tell me Roxana, what do you see of this man?"

Roxana carefully considered the guard's curious eyes. She contemplated for a moment and then nodded. "I sense his innocence. You may trust him."

"Cleisthenes," said the king, "name your next in

command immediately." Just outside the door, the guard motioned for another to enter into the room. The king continued, "And what are you called?"

"Leontios, my King."

"Cleisthenes, I name you Supreme General. Leontios, you are now his second. General Nikomedes is no longer in command. You will bring the King's Guard here at once and provide me ultimate protection. You are to detain Nikomedes and Queen Melaina in separate cells in the dungeon beneath the palace. Do this tonight, before the moon sets in the west. In no way is either one to communicate with anyone, for neither one are any longer in authority. Arrange for your best guards at each of their cell doors. These guards will be those that remain true to your command, and ultimately to me. They must not waiver. Do you understand?"

Both men stood at attention, and Cleisthenes said, "Yes, Your Highness. I will immediately attend to your orders."

"Timaeus, you will go with General Cleisthenes and Major General Leontios as my witness of their new authority. Roxana, I will need a piece of papyrus, a quill and ink. If you please, write the following directions for General Cleisthenes to give to my council. General, tomorrow you will return here to report to me of the completion of my commands."

Roxana wrote out the directions of her king, immediately dissolving his marriage with Melaina and his relation to his brother, Nikomedes. He ordered both of them detained without privileges, until the council met to determine their fate. After he signed the directive, she rolled the papyrus, tied it with a ribbon, and sealed it with the king's stamp, which carried the unmistakable symbol of his reign.

She handed the directive to Timaeus. "You may all take your leave," said the king.

Before leaving, Timaeus said, "We are grateful to you, Roxana. I will take my leave tonight, and with your permission, return tomorrow to see how the king is faring." She smiled as he turned and departed.

King Krios looked at Roxana. "You saved my life and my kingdom. You shall be richly rewarded, so that you and your family will not want for generations to come."

Roxana bowed in reverence. She smiled and said, "I am in your service, Your Highness, but I must insist that you drink more of this tasty drink I have made for you." She smiled, handing him the cup. "I will bring you beef broth and flatbread to give you strength." The king gratefully drank her concoction and later ate the food.

"Allow me to assist you into my personal sleeping chambers, Your Highness. You may have my bed. I will sleep with my son tonight. Tomorrow, with your permission, I will introduce my son to you. He will be honored to meet his king."

"A fine and sturdy lad, I am sure," the king said. "I see no man of this house. Has he no father?"

"I fear not," Roxana said, helping him to his feet and walking him into the bedchamber. "He is lost at sea, and his mother perished before the great volcano destroyed our island of Thera. I have adopted Theo as my own."

King Krios weakly edged to the bed with Roxana's help. "You are an extraordinary woman, my dear Roxana.

I assure you – you and your son will want for nothing from this day forward."

Sitting him down on the edge of the bed, Roxana carefully asked, "My King, would you like me to help you undress?"

The king could not help but be embarrassed by his frailty. If he were healthy, he might have enjoyed such an offer, while surely the outcome of such a proposal would be one of great pleasure. Instead, he reluctantly surrendered to her help. After she undressed him, she gave him a linen chiton to sleep in. On a tray, she brought him a bowl of warm broth, a cup of wine infused with healing herbs, and the golden chalice lit with the eternal flame. The king thought he was imagining things, for the room lit up with a radiant light like nothing he had ever seen. He believed it to be a sign of hope for his recovery.

Before leaving the room, Roxana opened a small door. "In here is the water closet for your private use." He was unaware of her reference, for such technology was unheard of in Athens. She explained, "On Thera, there was such a system for every house. One of my engineers designed piping to come from the well, for use throughout the house. The water closet is our greatest convenience."

"I must meet this engineer of yours," the king said. "I shall engage him to construct the same in my palace."

Roxana covered the king with down blankets and placed her hands on his. "It is evident that you are feeling much better. The herbs are already gently detoxifying your body. My King, may I have permission to teach you something that will serve you not only in your health, but in all things?"

"Yes, by all means."

He felt a strong tingling sensation come from her hands as she laid her left hand on the top of his head, and her right hand gently over his heart. His body filled with unfamiliar, soothing warmth.

She lovingly looked into his eyes. "You, my King, are your own healer. I am here to assist you, but ultimately it is up to you whether you heal or not. You are at choice. You must tell the gods that you will live to the best of your ability, and not only believe that it is true, but feel it deep into your bones. Therefore, the gods respond to you by supporting you where your mind and heart join, evidenced by your feelings that tell you what you need to know.

"I can already sense the increase in your life force. Keep your concentration on this life force energy. It is right here in your heart. Just thinking of what fills you with peace, and that which brings you joy, will automatically fill your body with the same. These are just two of the life-giving states of being that regenerate our health and wellness. Remain in this state of mind, and you will make decisions inspired by the gods. It is a simple formula to live by, in which many people are unable to follow, because they believe they must suffer through life. With a life-giving belief, you will rise above earthly circumstances and avail yourself as the wisest, most powerful sovereign Greece shall ever know."

He looked at her with a tear in his eye. "I thought I was reaching the end of my days, but I can now feel my health returning. I am grateful."

She nodded and gently smiled. He noticed her zonai with the Tyrian purple threads. He knew this color indicated royalty, piquing his interest. Later, he would have questions for her, but for now, he rested in the assurance that peace finally filled him with all he needed to heal.

She stayed a few minutes more, channeling the gods' energy into the king's feeble body, and sensing the king filling his mind with pleasurable memories that would generate his recovery. When she left the room, she smiled back at the king as she shut the door. Never would she again feel so safe in her house, for there were forty guards posted about the premises.

Two weeks later, following the decision made by the King's Counsel, Nikomedes and Queen Melaina were put to death by poison. An eye-for-an-eye was typically the way of justice in the King's Court. Even though they were gone, their toxic residue still lingered. Roxana was clearly aware that she had greater work to do to free the king - and Athens - of their evil doings.

Once King Krios returned to full health, he regularly conferred with Roxana. It was not long before the king realized that Roxana's remedies were rich in the wisdom she shared that first night at the turning point of his recovery. It was her clear mind and bearing of the heart that empowered her to heal and assist others. Roxana gained her power from the gods - a secret the king wanted to master. Until he could embody these same truths of higher wisdom, he would consult with Roxana on all of his major decisions.

It was yet another turning point in Roxana's life.

CHAPTER
Eighteen

The citizens of Athens could not help but notice the King's Guard surrounding the complex where Roxana lived during the time of the king's recuperation. Word of his recovery traveled fast, as did Roxana's reputation as a seer and healer. Not only did she uncover Queen Melaina's diabolical plot to poison the king, but she also nursed the king back to health, both physically and spiritually, from the anguish of betrayal by his wife and brother. Patrons now came to Roxana from the far reaches of Greece, seeking cures to illness and consultations for their future, but consequences emerged.

In light of Roxana's newfound fame, some people out of jealousy or fear wanted to discredit her. Curiosity developed and inquiry spawned gossip and innuendo. *Roxana bewitched the king. She must have had her way with him. The king poisoned the queen to make room for this temptress.* Roxana had openly and honestly gained the king's favor and was now one of his most trusted advisors, but that did not keep the gossipmongers from spreading unfounded rumors.

Those threatened by her power plotted to have her removed from the king's court. They believed she usurped their influence. Some of the men on the king's council, Capaneus the High Priest among them, wanted her gone, and it mattered not how it happened. He, in particular, took measures to make it so.

She found it difficult to travel into the heart of the city, for she attracted unwanted attention, either glorified for her accomplishments, or treated with vile contempt. The wives of city officials and military leaders loyal to the former queen banded together and placed a hex upon Roxana. They cast spells upon her and chanted incantations to doom her current life and every future incarnation.

Roxana learned of this hex from one of Theo's young playmates, who innocently told Theo he overheard his mother talking amongst her friends about their intention to bring ruin and destruction upon Roxana. The child had difficulty understanding his mother's guile, because he found Roxana to be kind and caring. He could not fathom why anyone would want to hurt her.

Theo feared for Roxana's safety and he was understandably upset, but she reassured him they were safe. She told him oftentimes people lashed out due to ignorance and fear of that which they did not understand. Secretly, however, Roxana did feel a certain disquiet. No matter where she went, she no longer had any sense of anonymity, and she quickly grew weary of the attention.

Late one summer evening, she walked home alone after attending to a young mother who gave birth to twins. She quickly took notice of a man following her. Purposefully misleading her potential assailant down alleyways and odd streets, she took unusual routes toward her destination to test her assumption. Her aggressor appeared to be a young man with dark hair, dressed in neutral-colored clothing so he would not call attention to himself. He did not hesitate in his obvious pursuit, remaining far enough behind to intimidate her, but not too close so she could identify him. Fear rose within her, which was not a common response, but never before had she felt so threatened by another person. Having spent most of her life on Thera where she knew everyone, she felt vulnerable in the still unfamiliar atmosphere of Athens.

She sought refuge at a nearby inn, where she knew the proprietor whose son she had once treated for an illness. Her assailant did not enter the inn, but stood outside, waiting for her to emerge. Upon hearing Roxana's story, the proprietor hid her away from any outside portico. He then talked to his son, who was a large and now very healthy young man in no small measure due to Roxana's healing treatments. When his father told him about the intimidating stranger lingering outside, he bounded out and confronted her assailant. He grabbed the man by the throat and slammed him against a wall.

"You have no business here!" he growled. He threw the stalker to the ground and beat him just short of his life. "I promise you, if I hear that Roxana is harassed in any way, I will find you, and next time I won't be so gentle. Now be gone, and tell your lord, Capaneus, the same awaits him if he ever tries to bring harm to Roxana!"

The beaten man pulled himself to his feet and fled into the night without a word.

Two days later, after returning from the countryside where Roxana gathered mushrooms, herbs, and healing roots, she found that someone had rummaged through her home and apothecary shop. Whoever had broken in did not know what they were looking for, because they left nothing in place. Her furnishings were left upturned, and some of her fine pieces destroyed. Her apothecary was all but ruined. She sensed that it was the work of Capaneus.

Knowing she was ever at risk for theft, Roxana had a vault built to safely hide precious belongings, riches, and her golden bowl and eternal flame. She could not take the chance that someone would attempt to use, or worse, steal either one of her golden treasures. From out of the wall, next to the hearth, her stonemason notched out a section with a channel into the chimney that allowed vapors from the eternal flame to vent. He carved a stone that fit the hole with precision, creating a hidden compartment for the safekeeping of valuables. So masterful was the hiding place, even Roxana sometimes had difficulty finding the right stone to remove from the wall. In such a case, she used her amethyst crystal amulet, energetically linked to the other two items. All Roxana had to do was touch the amethyst with the intention of finding either piece, and the bowl would sing out a high-toned frequency, somewhat like a high-toned brass singing bowl.

Not long after the invasion of her home, Roxana received a package from an anonymous sender that contained a dagger and a note inside the wrapping, threatening the safety of her son, herself, and her community. This threat finally pushed Roxana to her limit. She determined at that very moment to make radical changes to protect herself and Theo. Fearing that someone might kidnap or kill him, she removed Theo from the academy and kept him with her at all times. She also ceased her healing and consulting work and went to King Krios to plead for his protection.

Greatly alarmed, the king sent a messenger to inform Yiorgos about the danger surrounding Roxana and Theo. He offered them refuge within the palace walls, but, suspicious of Capaneus and yet unable to provide proof of his murderous intentions, she requested instead that the king spare a palace guard to watch over her home. King Krios agreed and posted several guards outside her home and within her community.

Following the notification of their plight, Yiorgos put a plan into action. He came to Athens and tricked Roxana into believing one of his neighbors who was ill needed her. He picked up Roxana and Theo in his two-wheeled horse-drawn carriage, and they rode northwest out of Athens toward the mountains. Along the way, he told her of his deception to get her out of the city. They traveled for three days through fields and along steep hillsides, each night staying at a roadside inn before they reached their destiny.

Eventually, they arrived at his home, a complex of buildings not far to the north of the Gulf of Corinth. Roxana had no idea how much she needed the stillness until she left the hectic environment of Athens. Surrounding her was a peaceful serenity she had not experienced since she lived on Thera. Everywhere she looked were grey-green valleys of olive trees cast in the amber glow of sundown.

Yiorgos invited them into his home, which was a small palace with outbuildings built upon the hillside of Mt. Parnassus. Above them, the mountain peak rose into the ethers of the dusky evening sky. It did not take long for the servants to prepare the simple evening meal of bread, cheese, olives, and a few garden vegetables. They were all famished and exhausted after three days of travel in the chariot. Theo ate all his food, quickly finishing every bite. He then left the table, with his mother's permission, to play with the baby goats outside. Before long, Roxana tucked Theo into bed. His head barely hit the pillow before he fell fast asleep.

She was so relieved to be far from the terrorization in Athens. Now she could spend some needed time with Yiorgos, regenerating her soul and planning what to do next. Many questions arose regarding the best course of action. There was much to consider.

They returned to their meal and drank delectable sweet wine. The firelight from the chalices on the table illuminated Roxana's beauty. Yiorgos could hardly contain himself with the deep love that he felt for her. He took her outside onto the terrace to view the skies overhead, where there was no city glow of Athens to obscure their view of starlight. Not since she had been on Thera had she seen such a vision of stars that seemed to radiate their brightest illumination. Tears rose in her eyes at the magnificent vast wonderment of the universe. She felt both humbled and fulfilled by its splendid glory. She turned to face Yiorgos as he wrapped his muscular arms around her, lovingly enveloping her in his embrace.

They returned to the great room where the fire was ablaze. On the floor in front of the hearth were several sheepskins where they sat and leaned back onto large pillows while they enjoyed more wine. Warmth from the golden firelight was welcoming. The cool night of early autumn had already begun, bringing with it a chill of the clear mountain air.

They loved each other's company. It was too long since they last shared time together. The constant threat to Theo and her safety continuously built up over the several months since the king's health returned. She had no idea how troubled she had become, because the intensity incrementally increased. Being with Yiorgos seemed to remove all fear.

"Yiorgos, I am in great appreciation for your thoughtfulness in bringing us here, away from the city," she said. "It is such a wonderful and much needed surprise - too occupied have I been with the recent events. I am also entirely too engaged with my responsibilities. Rarely do I need another patron, but people come from far and near, seeking healing and advice. I feel burdened by guilt to take pause from my service, because there are so many in need. Please do not think of me as ungrateful for your gesture to bring us here, but I must say I am overwhelmed. And I could not be more appreciative to the king for his tremendous generosity, for I am left without concern for my financial future." Yiorgos remained silent, knowing that she needed someone to listen.

"I am challenged every time I travel into the city," she said with a sigh. "I have little patience left for people with small minds and dark hearts who wish to bring me to ruin. And this I do know: whenever we begin a new journey... that which is comfortable and ordinary holds us back if we remain in that reassurance of what is commonplace. I have moved far beyond what is comfortable, and I know I can never go back to my life before my work with the king. It is simply impossible, but for the safety of Theo, myself, and my community, I find myself at a loss of what to do."

"I dare say that I am heartened by your words," Yiorgos said.

Angered by his response, she said, "You'll forgive me if I find little comfort in that!"

"Wait! Before I stumble on my words further, please allow me to continue." He poured more wine. "My summer has been spent building this home and the surrounding complex. I have many plans for it."

"It is no wonder why you have not frequented my home in Athens. I must say, Yiorgos, what you have built is stunningly beautiful. I see details much like that of the palace in Akrotiri. The view of the rolling hills of olive groves and the sea far down the valley is heavenly, but I am still not yet clear why you are pleased at my discontent."

"Roxana, I built all this for you and Theo. I took to heart your description of where you lived in Akrotiri. Are you not in wonder why I hired the architect, Kephalos, from your village? We collaborated to design this home, to which he brought many details I could never have gathered from your descriptions alone.

"From the moment I first met you, my love, even though I was in great physical pain, I knew I did not want to live without you. Now, with your circumstances as they are, it is time for you to come to me."

She was awestruck. He drank in her essence and took her hand in his. "It would be my great honor, Roxana, if you consent to be my wife. I would be a good father for

Theo, and we can begin a new life and family here. Will you join me in marriage?"

She placed her goblet on the floor and broke into a smile that warmed his heart. Taking his face into her hands, she kissed his lips and said, "I can think of nothing that would bring me more joy than to be your wife. Theo already thinks of you as his father. He has endured tremendous loss for such a young boy, with the death of his mother and father, living alone in a stable with his pet goat, and then losing his homeland. The most recent events have caused him great strife. He feels it his responsibility to protect me. Here, he can just be a little boy, and we can begin again in safety with the gods surrounding us in all this beauty."

He arose to his knees, took her into his arms, and they embraced. They kissed long and deeply. Yiorgos slipped her chiton off her shoulders, allowing it to fall to the rug, baring her body in the firelight. He caressed her breasts and gently kissed her on the neck. She helped him remove his tunic, and they lay next to each other naked upon the sheepskins. The fire cast warm shadows upon their skin as their bodies intertwined in lovemaking. As the evening turned to the early morning hours, they laid entangled and slept soundly in each other's arms.

As dawn approached, she awoke to Yiorgos adding wood to the fire. Teasing, she asked, "Tell me, what was your alternate plan with this well-made replica of a Theran palace, had I said no?"

"Well, I am certain that I would have no problem quickly attaining another woman from Akrotiri to take your place." She hit him with a pillow, laughing. He continued, "I would be most proud if you will allow me to show you its fine features."

He placed a blanket over her shoulders and took one for himself. He offered his hand and helped her to her feet. "Put your sandals on. We will be going outside. You already know the Great Room and the Dining Hall. Theo is asleep in his own bed chamber." He then showed her the details of the kitchen with a large open hearth, tables for preparation of the meals, and many covered shelves for storing all the kitchen accoutrements. Best of all was the large inset washbasin with running water. "There is a large cistern outside filled by the Kassotis Spring that flows from the top of Mt. Parnassus. From it, water flows in here and to the water closet in the house through an ingenious pipe system engineered by Kephalos. There is also a washbasin outside the kitchen for washing clothes. It is like that of Akrotiri, yes?"

"It is even better. I am greatly impressed, but surely you do not have hot running water."

"Was that a question? Because if it was, you will be surprised to find the answer is yes. There are many hot springs on the mountain, from which we are able to tap in and provide the hot water you so greatly deserve."

"I am impressed!" Roxana said.

"Let me show you our bed chamber." He led her down a hallway, first showing her two rooms for guests - or eventually for children of their own. The best room of the house was at the end of the hall. "Here is what I call the Grand Playroom. As you can see, it has a sunken bath with hot and cold running water, and a water closet with two doors. One is accessed from this room, and the other through the hallway for others to use."

On all the walls were torches radiating light onto the twenty-foot-high polished copper ceiling. The bed sat on a platform large enough for several people.

"Are you expecting others to join us?" she said, teasingly.

"Only if you desire, my love. I built this house for you. It is yours. You may do with it as you please," he said. "There's more! Outside, there are stables, and the other buildings we can discuss later, for I have great plans, but I need your counsel before we implement them. One of the buildings is most important. Come. I cannot wait for you to see it."

Behind the house on the hillside was a rectangular building, aligned so the east entrance faced the rising sun at the Summer Solstice, and the west entrance aligned with the setting sun at the Winter Solstice. As they entered, he said, "I built this for you to give your spiritual readings, and to attend to your patrons."

"It is humid in here. It feels like a bath," Roxana said.

Mounted to the walls were torches between twenty-foot porphyry columns supporting the high ceiling. Yiorgos lit a reed from his chalice and proceeded to light each torch to illuminate the room. The light revealed a pool in the center of the room. A bronze dolphin was perched above the pool's marble edge with a waterfall flowing from its mouth, generated from the Kassotis Spring. Roxana was delighted to see this so resembled the fountain at the temple's bath on Thera. Hanging from the indigo painted ceiling were crystalline chalices overhead. He lit the lamps with his reed, making their fiery reflection on the water below.

Yiorgos had captured the essence of the temple of Akrotiri, only Roxana found it to be better than the original. The building, constructed of large granite blocks, contained one large room instead of two.

"The walls have been freshly plastered," Yiorgos said, "waiting for you to paint them with the images of your pleasing. As you can see, polished marble covers the overlapping circular floors. Surrounding the circles outside is granite flooring along the perimeter of the rectangular walls. The two circles represent heaven and earth. The left side is the feminine, and the right, masculine, linked at the center where they come together in oneness. There the pool fills the sunken bath."

Roxana was stunned. All she could do was smile.

"I had the stone mason carve a triangular altar for you, here in the corner. Next to it, the woodworker from Akrotiri designed three cushioned chairs for you and your patrons to sit in counsel. The chairs sit on a circular woven rug, beautifully crafted by the textile merchant from Akrotiri who lives in your village."

"You thought of everything," Roxana said, clearly enchanted. "It is as if you transported my past from Thera and placed it here on Mt. Parnassus. Your thoughtfulness overwhelms me, my love. There is one thing that is different, however. There is a sweet scent filling the air, unlike anything of my familiarity. Can you identify it?"

"The scent emanates from a fissure underground. The fissure revealed itself after the temple was completed.

Some say the scent is natural gas that helps one see the heavenly realm. Honeybees made their hive inside the fissure. We moved them outside to a manmade hive. I imagine you will befriend them as you do with all of your animals."

Roxana laughed. "But of course!"

"I instructed the stone mason to create a flat stone platform over the fissure so no one would be injured. On top of it, as you can see, is a beautiful table that will hold the eternal flame, once it is brought from Athens."

He led her to the sitting area. "Please be seated. I have greater issues of importance to reveal." She sat in wonder of all that he had done for she and Theo. Roxana felt humbled by his loving efforts.

Yiorgos began to fill in the many details of his plan. "Roxana, I had a dream shortly after we met, more-so a great revelation. I was informed that, here on the mountainside, you are to resume your position as High Priestess. Your spiritual lineage will be passed on to our daughter and onto our granddaughters, who will follow in the tradition you have been taught. You are to instruct them to use their gifts of healing and insight and, in turn, they will pass along what they have learned onto the many generations that follow. You, Roxana, are the beginning of a great spiritual tradition that will make Greece known until the end of days."

What she heard from him were nearly the same words her mother told her before her initiation as the High Priestess of Akrotiri.

"It is my desire that you are pleased, Roxana."

"I am greatly touched, Yiorgos. I can see that many lives will transform for the better here. Theo and I are the first. This new temple already has the blessing of the gods. I feel their presence. They are smiling down upon us now."

Yiorgos' smile filled his face. "I couldn't risk your saying no to me. I want you to feel at home again, for you have experienced a plethora of grievances in your short life. You deserve only your heart's desires, Roxana."

"You have gone to so much trouble. This is all so amazing, Yiorgos! But how shall I find a patronage this far into the mountain wilderness?"

"Word of your great power has now spread throughout the land. People will come from all over, seeking your wisdom."

"Seeking wisdom or revenge?" Roxana cautioned.

"I had a long discussion with the king before I snatched you up for our journey here. You will be relieved to know that Capaneus is no longer in service as high priest. He was exiled to Anatolia, never to set foot upon Greek soil again."

"I never said a word to the king about Capaneus, for fear that he would take his retribution upon me," she said.

"Roxana, the king is an intelligent man. The betrayal of the queen and his brother taught him to be more wary and cautious. He knew the plot against you was sourced from members of his council, and so they have been exiled as well."

"But who will now serve the king?"

"I advised him to seek out Demosthenes, the man who rescued me along the road and then brought me to you. His honesty and humility impressed me. I placed him in the back of my mind to return the favor. King Krios will soon summon him to serve as his supreme advisor. In addition, the King's physician, Timaeus, has risen to a higher rank. He is a loyal and trusted friend to the king through all of the recent troubles, and he will continue to advise him in matters of health."

"This is all very well," Roxana said, "but how may I continue to serve our king from this great distance?"

"He and I agree it is best for you to stay away from Athens. The king will come here on each moon, for you are his most trusted spiritual advisor. As High Priestess of Greece, you shall join Demosthenes, Timaeus, and I as Royal Council to benefit the King during his reign."

Roxana was astounded. "When the king was in my company, I never revealed that I was formally the High Priestess of Akrotiri."

"He and I have discussed many things, Roxana. When he was in your care, he noticed the Tyrian purple stitching on the zonai you wear around your waist. Only royalty or those of great wealth and high standing wear such a color. When I informed him who you are, he was greatly pleased and not surprised because of your gifts of insight and healing."

"Never had I imagined to be in service in such a way," Roxana said, slightly overwhelmed.

"This is your calling, my love. If you are in agreement, we shall move you and Theo here, straight away."

There was little to think about. She threw her arms around him. The problems of yesterday solved. Life would begin anew as her mother had told her when Roxana was young. If only Althaia could have known her insights were now coming to pass.

Roxana walked to the poolside and leaned over to feel the warm water flow from the dolphin's mouth. She let the blanket fall from her shoulders and entered the pool. Yiorgos joined her, and they made love again with the crystal firelight appearing like starlight against the indigo heavens of the new temple, dedicating themselves to their upcoming union.

Within the month, she and Theo moved to their new home with Yiorgos. They had a small wedding on the hillside with her community of people from Athens, most of them originally of Akrotiri. One surprise guest arrived just before the ceremony began. It was King Krios, who wanted to escort Roxana into the ceremony.

"If another man must have you, may I instead be the one to give your hand to him?" the king asked.

"My dear King, my wedding day wouldn't be complete without you."

Presiding over the ceremony was the king's new high priest, Makarios, who was enchanted with Roxana's powers. When the king and Demosthenes came to counsel with Roxana once per month, Makarios came along and stayed a few more days to study with her. They became good friends and colleagues.

The ceremony took place outside upon the terrace overlooking the valley and hills of olive trees with the Gulf of Corinth in the far distance. All the guests stood in a circle, each holding an unlit candle. Yiorgos stood with

Theo and Makarios at the center of the circle alongside a small table where the golden chalice contained the eternal flame. King Krios escorted Roxana to the center and gave her hand to Yiorgos. He then joined those standing in the circle.

She wore an elegant ivory silk gown, held at the shoulders with golden laurel leaves. She carried an unlit beeswax candle wrapped in wildflowers. She wore a wreath of laurel leaves on her head, intertwined with flowers, with her long dark hair cascading down her back in curls. She, Yiorgos, and Theo faced the high priest as he addressed them with the marriage rites. As they said their vows to each other, Makarios intertwined a garland of vines and flowers over and around their hands to indicate sacred union. Then Theo placed his hands on top of theirs, and Makarios finished wrapping the hands of all three with the garland. Officially, they were now a family.

At the end of the ceremony, Roxana and Yiorgos lit their individual candles from the eternal flame. Together they lit Theo's candle. He, in turn, walked over to light the candle of King Krios to begin the circle of light. The king spoke a blessing, which meant *to confer prosperity upon*. He then turned to Timaeus on his right to light his candle continuing the sanction over their union. Everyone within the circle followed suit, completing a most sacred ceremony while Roxana, Yiorgos, and Theo received loving thoughts and wishes from their friends.

Yiorgos placed on Roxana's finger a gold ring set with an aquamarine oval cabochon. She recognized the quality of the metalwork, noticing the luminous gold band etched with the same otherworldly runes as all of her golden possessions. The amulet hanging from her neck vibrated in unison with the ring as Yiorgos placed it on her finger. A numinous light filled the circle causing everyone to stir. Roxana just smiled.

Yiorgos later told her how he encountered an aging jewelry smith who had previously heard of the betrothal. The old man presented to Yiorgos an unusual box with a lid elaborately carved with two interlocking circles. Inside the box was a silken pouch that contained the ring. Yiorgos had no doubt that this was the perfect ring for his bride.

Afterwards, the large throng of guests entered the Great Room and celebrated with good food and an abundance of wine. Yiorgos had yet one more surprise for Roxana. He announced, "My lovely wife, today you have made me a most happy man. Never have I dreamed that I would be so fortunate. I have one last gift to present to you."

He walked out into the crowd and approached a middle-aged woman seated at the back of the room. He offered his hand to help her to her feet. The woman smiled at Yiorgos as he led her to Roxana. When the woman came close, Roxana immediately recognized her and put her hands over her mouth to keep from bursting into tears. The woman standing before her was her mother, Althaia. She had been living in a shoreline village off the Gulf of Corinth, not far from their home on Mt. Parnassus. She contacted Yiorgos when she heard about his impending marriage, remembering the insights she shared with her daughter many years before.

Roxana embraced Althaia, and they cried great tears of joy. Yiorgos then brought Theo over to meet her. Althaia knelt down, offering her hand to Theo. Instead, he threw his arms around her neck, so excited to have a grandmother again.

They all enjoyed a sumptuous feast, and before the celebration of music and dance, Yiorgos made an announcement. "My beloved Roxana and I would like all of you, our friends, to join us here permanently. We have plans to create a wonderful artisan village as a welcome to all who travel here. We already have the support of our king. It has been foreseen that many will travel from far and wide to take advantage of the offerings here on our mountainside." The room was abuzz with excitement at the idea of the community that evolved two hundred years later into Delphi, Greece.

A baby girl soon came into their family, whom they called Melissa - after the honeybees that gathered upon the mountainside. Theo grew up to follow his father's example as the owner of hundreds of acres of olive groves, becoming a respected, fair, and wealthy businessman. Roxana became the High Priestess of Greece, who generations later became the Oracle of Delphi. People came from hundreds of miles to hear her wisdom. As in the tradition of the High Priestess of Akrotiri, Roxana passed on her knowledge to her daughter, Melissa, with the help of Althaia, carrying on the family line of seers and prophetesses.

CHAPTER
Nineteen

It had been several tough years for Michael and Sophia. Michael lost both parents within a few months of each other, and Sophia's father died around the same time. The death of the final parent often leaves one feeling orphaned, no longer with a sense of foundation. It is an experience, like no other, that causes one to finally grow up. Decisions no longer echo the voice of a parent's wisdom as life reveals fresh territory for expansion beyond custom and history. Yet, what remains is a void, one so deep beyond experience or memory. It is a loss of the underpinning at the core of one's beliefs. Such emptiness calls one to question the mundane as an invitation to ascend beyond what is comfortable into expansive territories that reveal their reawakening.

Living through the death of a loved one can cause rebirth for those who remain, allowing emergence, regeneration, and a renaissance of the soul. Michael and Sophia found quiet respite in each other's arms. Their empathy for each other helped them unite in compassion and strength while they healed.

Nonetheless, challenging emotions remained.

A couple of months passed since their fourth-first date.

It was November and growing cold. Frankie, her sweet Australian Shepherd, was very sick, and Sophia could not bring herself to make that dreadful phone call to the vet. It was not that long since she put down Miles, Zaide, and Emmy, but it clearly was time to let Frankie go. She held onto her beautiful dog for too long, having experienced so much loss over the past couple years. The thought of losing yet another sweet being was almost unbearable, but Frankie let her know his time had arrived. He stopped eating, and he slept for hours on end - so unlike his usual pattern of high energy.

Sophia believed that Frankie lost his will to live after Miles passed, for they had been such good buddies. When they used to run in the park, their sides touched as if harnessed together. Frankie obviously grieved the loss of his friend, and he never regained the same zest for life. He once weighed eighty pounds, but now he was less than forty. Arthritis often made his hips give out when he stood. Unable to get up on his own, Sophia had to straddle his body and lift him to his feet.

Frankie originally came to Sophia on a mid-December night. She was married to Joe at that time, and they had just moved to their new home south of Denver. She had been working late, managing a flower shop in a major hotel downtown. It was one of the busiest times of the year, for people were celebrating the holidays in one form or another. Sophia and her staff were busy making table centerpieces and holiday gift baskets for parties, as well as creating flowers for holiday weddings and fresh bouquets for Christmas church services. She worked many hours of overtime helping others rejoice in their holiday parties, but having little energy for her own celebration.

Around 5:30 p.m. that evening, she received a phone call from her husband with the dreadful news that Rufus, her eight year-old Lhasa Apso, had gotten out of the yard. When Sophia got off the phone, she went into the flower cooler, which was the only private place in the bustling shop. She had a foreboding sense that it was too late for Rufus. Sophia prayed that, if it was Rufus' time to leave this earth, that his life would end quickly and he would not suffer. She also asked that she could find him, no matter what the situation, for she did not want to forever question his whereabouts. Right then, in her mind's eye, she envisioned the large sign of a business from a specific vantage point just up the street from her home. She wondered if she would find Rufus there.

On her way home, she drove past the business she envisioned earlier. No Rufus. She picked up Joe, and they drove through the neighborhood for thirty minutes before coming across two young men walking through the warehouse district. Sophia described Rufus and told them where they lived, in case the boys found him. They then drove across the street into a parking lot, hoping they might find Rufus hiding somewhere in a corner. Suddenly, a large Australian Shepherd puppy appeared seemingly from nowhere and came right up to Sophia's window. He was very friendly, wagging his tail and craving attention. Sophia couldn't help but smile and call out to the young dog, but Joe's attention was quickly drawn to the two young men they had spoken with earlier. They ran up to the car, clearly upset.

"I'm really sorry," one said, "but we found your dog.

He got hit by a car over there, across the street."

Devastated, Sophia and Joe left the puppy behind and drove to where the young men said they found Rufus. Someone had picked up his body from the street and left him on the sidewalk, covered with a plastic sheet. Sophia was very grateful to whoever had been thoughtful enough to remove him from the road. It was evident that Rufus never knew what hit him.

Sophia tearfully picked up her precious dog, and Joe knelt down in anguish, for he felt responsible for letting Rufus escape the yard. There was no life left in Rufus' sweet little cold body. Crying out in tremendous grief, Sophia looked up to see a sign on the building across the street - the very sign she had envisioned earlier - from the vantage point she had seen in her mind's eye. They found Rufus in the exact spot where her intuition directed her to search for him.

At home, Sophia took her favorite sweater and placed it around Rufus, with the arms wrapped around his small, broken body. They buried him underneath the crabapple tree in the backyard with his harness and a tiny dog jean jacket that she put on him before they took their walks in cold weather. Sophia's heart was broken. Rufus had been her loving and loyal companion for eight years. He traveled with her and adapted well each time she moved to a new home. Rufus loved her unconditionally. A great void remained in her heart that night.

Not long after they buried Rufus, they decided to go back to the parking lot, where they found the young Australian Shepherd puppy still wandering about. There was no indication that he had a home, for they often found abandoned dogs in that part of town. Sophia and Joe agreed that they had fortuitously come across this dog at the perfect time for them all. They agreed to take him in, at least for the night, but they had a difficult time getting him into the car. He was a big dog, and they had to lift him into the front seat with Sophia holding him on her lap.

The dog was part wolf, with webbed toes and sturdy, long legs. His eyes were almond-shaped, and his muzzle long and narrow, clearly like that of a wolf. On his tail was the telltale pre-caudal gland indicating his wolf heritage. For some reason, the dog never learned how to navigate stairs easily, and he had a peculiar phobia for different floor surfaces, putting on the brakes when he walked from hardwood flooring onto the tiled kitchen. No matter his quirks, Sophia and Joe had found a wonderfully sweet dog. They named him "Frankie," after Saint Francis of Assisi, the patron saint of animals, because he saved them during their time of grief.

It seemed that Rufus' spirit passed on to Frankie. Sophia used to find Rufus asleep, upside-down, beneath the dining table, between the legs of the chair. The morning after they brought Frankie home, Sophia was shocked to find Frankie sleeping upside-down under the dining room table in the exact spot Rufus slept - between the legs of the same dining chair. She never again found Frankie under the table again, nor sleeping upside down. It was as if, on that first night of terrible sadness, Rufus sent her a sign through Frankie, telling her that he was all right, and that Frankie would carry on where he left off.

Frankie was a brilliant dog, always plotting out new strategies for mischief. He would stand at the corner of the front yard fence with each foot in the chain link, first looking both ways to make sure no one was watching before he climbed over and escaped to explore the neighborhood.

Unable to scold him out of the habit, Joe finally rigged a hose from the back yard, through the family room window, and along the fence, positioning the nozzle to aim at the exact spot where Frankie would climb the fence. As if on a mission from God, the determined Joe sat watching from the family room for hours, waiting for Frankie to make his move.

Joe's vigil paid off when Frankie finally skulked up to the corner of the fence and stealthily looked around to see that no one was watching. When the coast seemed clear, Frankie put his foot into the chain link, and Joe turned on the faucet. The power stream of water hit Frankie in the ribs, and he sprang away from the fence and ran for cover. Sophia laughed at this epic battle of manly wits, but she had to admit that Frankie never attempted to jump the fence again.

Twelve years had passed since Frankie came into Sophia's life. It was a frigid day with an icy mist in the air. Sophia worked from nine to five, so she left Frankie, Saxon, and Digit inside to shelter them from the cold. Michael was home with them for a portion of the day, until he left to meet Sophia for dinner. Upon their return, Sophia appeared at the door, and seeing her through the glass panel, Frankie tried to rise to his feet. He had always greeted her with a wagging tail, but that night he struggled, yelping as he tried to stand. Sophia couldn't unlock the door fast enough. She ran into the room, dropped immediately to her knees, and wrapped her arms around her beautiful dog. She helped him to his feet and noticed his heart racing wildly. Frankie's body froze, and his eyes went blank as Sophia held him. She gently eased him down onto his dog pillow, and then curled up next to him and wrapped her body around his.

Her beautiful dog, Frankie, had a stroke in her arms.

She caressed his beautiful coat. "I love you so much, Frankie, but it is okay for you to go," Sophia said, tears choking her words. Frankie knew what she was saying, for it is not about the words, but the feeling conveyed. "I have kept you here too long, and now it is time for you to move on. You have done such a good job being my wonderful dog and my dear friend. I promise we will know each other again." Frankie's gray mottled body was still, the shell of a beautiful, stately, and elegant dog. He died there in her arms.

Frankie was the fourth of her six animals that she had to let go within two years' time. The grief was almost too much to bear. She thought, *somehow it seems to be more difficult to let my animals go than when my father died*. Was it because they were completely dependent upon her care? Was it because her care for them filled a need within her? There was no baggage between Sophia and her animals, allowing only the sweet and tender exchange of love. That extraordinary love was what remained from their short time together long after they were gone. That selfless love was one of the many gifts she gained from her animals through the privilege of being their human. From them she learned how to love wholeheartedly.

Michael knelt next to Sophia, gently holding her when

Frankie died. They grieved together, for he also struggled in the depths of loss that seemed to never end. Michael was everything Sophia could have wanted in a man, and more. All that he was becoming to her was now much greater than the relationship she had ever desired.

CHAPTER
Twenty

*S*ophia had been in such deep grief over the many losses she recently endured, she was feeling quite humbled by it all. The grief had reduced her to a state of unconditional surrender. Within the realm of vulnerability, where emotions are raw and the soul lay bare, sometimes the most miraculous things occur.

Journaling was a tool she used to work through her challenges. After all, she *was* a writer. No other process helped her work through her pain more than putting pen to paper.

She wrote:

> *Who am I without these wonderful beings? I was a daughter, but now I am that no longer. I now feel the aloneness of being orphaned without the anchors of defined relationship. I was a wife, but not anymore. Divorce is also the release of home, family and friends, but more so the loss of the dream of a life once imagined. I was a human to five beautiful four-legged beings, but they have moved on. I miss them so.*
>
> *I had a great and successful livelihood, but I put it on hold to be with my father in his last*

months. I loved my business, the creativity, the community with my clients, with the sense that I was bringing beauty into the world.

I am without a foundation, feeling undefined, with less importance without these beings - without these things - to help me to identify who I am.

Who am I now? What is my importance - my purpose - my calling? I am stripped clean. I am cleared of any and all relationships I once knew, including my relationship with myself, for I am not who I once was. I am empty.

Memories are all that I have connecting me to what I used to know as myself. The void runs deep, like a chasm into the dark abyss. I am falling, falling, rapidly falling.

I once defined myself through my relationships. I thought I was who I was, because of who I knew, and what I had. Not so. I find that is the great gift of The Dark Night of the Soul, which bared me to the bone. And if anything was left, I was picked clean by the residual anguish of grief, and at times regret.

I redefine myself from what I once knew, leaving me to flail and thrash around to find new meaning. In this moment, this present moment, I step out, in trust, again to spread my wings - to jump off the cliff - allowing the breeze to catch me, to save me, to bring me to a soft landing.

And so it is, I begin again. I know that I am

complete without anyone or anything to fill in the spaces, emptied of idle attachments. I am whole in my solitude, fulfilled from within. Aligned and true. Blissful. What I have now are endless opportunities to live within the possibility of everything I have ever imagined myself to be.

Having lived many lifetimes before, I am of the gnosis that I will again live on. I am endless, omnipotent, and eternal. I Am!

It was the last day of the weekend at the New Orleans Autumn Art Show. Sophia was tiring and looking forward to packing up and making the long drive back to Colorado and to Michael's loving arms. She contentedly watched the crowd wander by, when an older gentleman came into her booth and became keenly absorbed in her largest painting. A few minutes passed before Sophia approached him. "You like that piece," she said with a smile.

He did not take his eyes off the painting. "Exquisite," he said.

"May I introduce myself? I am the artist, Sophia Delaney."

"Good day to you," he tipped his hat. "Darius MacPhaidin. It is my pleasure to make your acquaintance, Ms. Delaney." His southern accent exuded sophisticated charm.

"What an interesting name, Mr. MacPhaidin. It appears that I am in the company of a fellow Scots-Irishman."

"Right you are. But please, call me Darius." He was

clearly a traditional southern gentlemen - charming, suave, debonair and tremendously elegant. Sophia had an eye for men of graceful refinement, and Darius was the epitome of polish and finesse.

He was dressed in light grey woolen slacks, a white linen shirt with a ruby paisley cravat tucked inside the collar, and a navy light wool blazer. When he removed his black classic fedora, he revealed a head of curly white hair that framed his handsome face. He sported a well-groomed white goatee and moustache, and he smelled of fine pipe tobacco. He carried a silver handled, hand-carved wooden walking stick, but it did not appear that he used it as a cane, but rather a finishing touch to his wardrobe. Enchanted, Sophia felt drawn to him by something more than the ambiance of her potential client. *Who is this man? I want to know more about him - his history - his story - even his ancestry. I am truly intrigued!*

Sophia could almost feel herself blush. "May I offer you something to drink, perhaps some mineral water or a glass of my favorite blend of red wine?" She motioned to the two director's chairs at the edge of the booth.

"I would be delighted. Yes, a bit of wine would be most appreciated."

As he sat, she poured two glasses. "May I answer any questions you might have about the painting?"

"I typically like landscapes, but I cannot take my eyes from this abstract of yours. Please tell me what inspired you to paint something with no apparent subject matter?"

"Well, in this case, I was deeply motivated. The colors and textures came to me from my most inspirational dreams."

"My, you must have quite vivid dreams if all of these paintings are inspired works."

"You could say that. My dreams inform my reality, my writing, and my art, as you can see."

"Fascinating," Darius said with a wry smile. Sophia detected a mischievous twinkle in his eye that implied he just might know more about dreams than he was letting on. "I am intrigued by your work, Ms. Delaney."

"Ah-ah!" Sophia scolded. "You must call me Sophia."

"Sophia, yes," he said. "Your work is so clean, clear, and quite sophisticated. The intricate use of color and texture leaves one to question your process and also what inspired your technique."

"Thank you, Darius. I appreciate your keen eye."

Darius gave a wry, almost embarrassed smile. "Sophia, I must confess that I did not come here today by chance. I have a friend who referred me to you - White Buffalo."

"Why yes!" Sophia said. "He is a dear friend and my spiritual guru, you might say. How do you know him?"

"He and I come from a similar school of thought, you might say, considered by some to be seers, intuitive healers, or shamans. I believe you also fit into the same category. I would not be claiming to be such if I did not think I was also in company with one who understood."

"Yes, well, this conversation is taking a different direction."

"I must apologize," Darius said. "I don't want to deceive you. I knew that you were coming here to New Orleans this weekend. I am one of the people White Buffalo mentioned who has been waiting to meet with you."

Sophia shifted in her chair, not expecting such an encounter that day, but when would she ever be prepared to meet one of these sages? She took a sip of wine. "I must say, I am honored that you have taken time to meet with me, Darius."

"Oh, dear Sophia," he laughed, "time is not of my world, nor is it of yours. I think you understand what that means. I knew at some point you would come to New Orleans and we would meet."

"You did?" Sophia said, still rather bewildered.

"Oh, where are my manners," Darius said. "This is far too important to discuss here. You must come to my home for dinner." He fished in his pocket and pulled out a card. "Here is the address and phone. I live just ten miles west of the city. Shall we say seven o'clock tomorrow evening?"

"How lovely, I'd be happy to join you for dinner."

"By the way, bring this painting with you tomorrow, and I will pay you in cash."

"Wonderful! Tomorrow at seven o'clock, it is. Thank you, Darius." She shook his hand as he left her booth. She happily put a "SOLD" sign on her most expensive piece of art, priced at $28,000. She brought the painting as a showpiece, truly never thinking it would sell. What excited her even more was the opportunity to engage further with this most interesting man.

The art show concluded at 5:00 p.m. Even without the sale of the painting to Darius MacPhaidin, the show was a tremendous success. She packed up her remaining paintings and stored them in her motor home. She then took down the tent and all the tables, along with the lighting and display pieces. When everything was neatly packed away in the RV, she drove to the RV park to settle down for the evening. She had to call Michael to share her exciting news. She did not expect to sleep well, wondering about the next evening's meeting with Darius, but, oddly enough, she awoke the next morning completely refreshed, having enjoyed a restful night's sleep.

Sophia began her day early at Cafe du Monde, open 24 hours a day, located on the edge of the Mississippi River in Jackson Square. She looked forward to a cup of Café au lait with chicory and fresh beignets - the famous fried dough dusted with powdered sugar. She took her seat among many others on the outdoor covered patio. Just as she took a bite, a gust of wind came along and blew the powdered sugar all over her. Several patrons around her politely tried without success to hide their laughter at the woman dressed completely in black...and now white.

She joined in, laughing at herself, "I'm so glad I could be of great entertainment for you all!"

Her charming waiter approached. "May I bring you anything else – more coffee? A broom?"

"Smart aleck," she giggled as she cleaned herself off.

He winked as he left the check accompanied by a single beignet with the powdered sugar intact. "Sweets for the sweet..."

Sophia then walked along the Mississippi River and over to the French Quarter along Bourbon Street. She found Royal and Chartres Street in the upper French Quarter much more to her liking with shops loaded with many exquisite antiques, some of which dated back to the French Baroque, Rococo, Neoclassic, and Romantic periods, leaving Sophia in wonderment of the extravagance and attention to detail by the artistes of the day.

Enchanted by the lavish furnishings, she found the area to have the finest selection of antiques than anywhere else in the world she had travelled. She loved to find mementos to remind her of her journeys. Walking through several of the shops, she searched for that one special item that called to her. She would intuitively know it right away.

Suddenly, she found herself drawn to a charming little place across the street. A sign over the ornate front door read, in an old Middle English script: *Nothing But Tyme*. Sophia smiled. *This is right up my alley!* she thought. When she entered, she heard the delightful ring of bells attached to the door. Immediately she took note of the shop's atmosphere, saturated in the scents of centuries-old tapestries, upholstery, leather and aged wood. An elderly man who sat at the counter looked up from his newspaper.

"Good day, and welcome," he said.

"Hello," Sophia said. "Mind if I browse?"

"My time is yours," he said with a lovely smile. "In fact, in here, you'll find nothing but time."

Cute, she thought. She wandered into the shop, which was much larger than it appeared from outside. Aisles of dining room sets, divans, armoires, and hand-painted end tables lined up row after row. She couldn't help but notice dozens of crystal chandeliers, large enough for an opera house, hanging from every inch of the ceiling. Displayed all over the shop were shining sterling silver candlesticks, porcelain lamps, fine linens, and hand-painted vases. *That's it...I just found heaven!* she thought.

Of course, as a jewelry designer herself, Sophia had to peruse the antique jewelry counters. Rubies, emeralds, sapphires, pearls, and diamonds glistened among the ornate gold and platinum settings. However, as if targeted by a spotlight, one piece stood out above the rest.

Sophia caught her breath when she saw a stunning amethyst crystal amulet hanging from a golden chain necklace, so highly polished it appeared to be completely free of flaws. She wondered how it was possible that any antique jewelry could look so perfect. There was no tarnish, nor scratches on the piece. The design was very simple, explaining why it stood out in the glass case among so many other elaborate pieces. The necklace called to Sophia, and she could not take her eyes from it.

"Is there something I could show you?"

Startled, Sophia turned to the elderly gentleman, who seemed to come from nowhere. "Yes, if you wouldn't mind, may I see that exquisite amethyst on the gold chain?"

"Why, of course." The proprietor opened the case and took out the amulet. He reminded her of Darius, quite refined with his southern charm. Sophia guessed him to be in his late sixties, clean-shaven, with salt and pepper hair. He dressed with casual sophistication, and his dialect was a deep southern drawl that made every word seem important. He spoke slowly and deliberately, but Sophia couldn't quite place his accent.

He held the necklace with care. "If I may point out to

you the remarkable properties of this necklace, this piece has quite distinctive assets, if you will. Notice the markings etched into the sides of the crystal? I'm told they are ancient runes, yet no one I know is able to identify their origin. I have not been able to categorize the metal itself, but it clearly is not gold."

Sophia looked at the necklace, hoping he would allow her to hold it. "You know, I've worked with many precious stones and metals..."

"It cannot be scratched, bent, chipped, burnt, or destroyed," the man said. He looked around and lowered his voice, even though no one else was in the shop that day. "It is my strong and honest opinion that the piece not of this world." He finally handed her the chain with an almost playful smile. She suddenly sensed a strange familiarity about this man.

As she took the amulet in her hands, it gave her a palpable energy so strong that it lit up the room. The chandeliers overhead reflected the necklace's brilliance, and the individual crystals vibrated a tone, matching that of the amulet, as if they sang in unison. They were attuning themselves - something she knew as entrainment - when a higher frequency held long enough causes lower frequencies to rise to its level.

Sophia was speechless. She looked around the room in awe. The proprietor, however, did not seem fazed. She turned the crystal in her hands, carefully examining the etched designs.

"Care to try it on?" the man said.

"Oh, may I?"

"By all means, mademoiselle. In here, we have nothing but time." He winked.

She curiously smiled. *Contrarily so, something tells me, time does not exist here.* She placed the chain around her neck and instantly transported in her consciousness to Ireland, hundreds of years in the past. She was a young girl with red hair, dancing barefoot with wide-open arms in a field of green grass as the sun shined brightly on her upturned face. Beyond a nearby cliff, she could hear ocean waves crashing on the rocky beach below. In that vision, she experienced pure ecstatic joy.

As Sophia rubbed the different markings along the amulet's edge, she saw flashes of herself wearing the necklace in one time or another. She saw herself as a young maiden picking crocus on a small island. Then later, having grown into adulthood, she was a grand woman empowered to lead her people. Sophia was all too familiar with the memory, having dreamt of her life as Roxana. However, this was the first time she accessed her past life without being in her dreams.

She rubbed another etching on the amulet and saw herself sitting on a tripod in a torch-lit room while peering into a golden bowl. She was advising a young man about his future. Then she shifted again into another lifetime, seeing herself dressed for high society on an ocean liner, again in possession of yet another talisman. Flashes of memory showed her with other visionaries and healers like herself, all working for the well-being of humankind.

She clearly knew this crystal amulet. It was familiar to her. In fact, somehow she knew it rightfully belonged to her. It must have been the very amulet that she saw herself, as Roxana, wear in her past life. *Maybe,* she thought, *that is why I have an affinity for pendulums.* There was something innate transferring knowledge to her, through them. This amulet had obviously traveled with her through parts of her history, and it had come home to her again. But why?

Suddenly, Sophia found herself back in the shop as if she just awoke from a dream. Embarrassed, she looked at the gentleman, who all the while stood back, watching her with a knowing smile. A bit bewildered, she said, "I must have this. Please sir, if you would be so kind as to wrap it up for me?"

"I must tell you that I have held onto this piece for over fifty years. My elderly aunt entrusted my father to keep the necklace safe. I was a youth at the time. I remember when she told him that a woman would someday enter this establishment and claim the piece to be her own. She said he would know the woman was true by the reaction of the crystal necklace when she held it in her hands. He could not say no to her. To be perfectly frank, we both found ourselves enchanted by her abilities. You see, my aunt had, you might say, magical powers, which is common among the Irish, Cajun, and Creole here in New Orleans. Many of us in this part of the South live between the veils of time and space. It is my sense that you catch my reference?"

"Yes, I completely understand."

"We can always recognize the mystic in another, can we not?" he said with a sparkle in his eye.

Sophia smiled and nodded as she looked away, knowing her face was turning red. She oftentimes felt tremendous solitude with the spiritual gifts she possessed. Such was the plight of a strong intuitive. She could read others well, able to connect and communicate quickly on a very personal level, but rarely did she feel supported in the same way. It took another intuitive to empathize with her. Sophia felt relieved to be in the company of one who also shared similar spiritual or psychic abilities. She felt a certain trust for this apparent stranger, as if she had known him before.

She opened her handbag. "The necklace, please tell me how much are you asking for it?"

He smiled and continued, "Well, you see, it is my duty to honor my dear departed aunt's dying wish. She implicitly stated that I was not to sell it, but only keep it for the right person to claim it. That appears to be you, mademoiselle."

Sophia stopped. "Excuse me?"

"The necklace is clearly yours," he calmly said.

"I – uh –"

"Shall I wrap it, or would you care to wear it home?"

"You're saying this is a gift?"

"Yes, in a manner of speaking."

"But I can't just take this. We don't even know each other."

"Permit me to introduce myself. Gaston Menard, at your service."

Sophia extended her hand, and he warmly took it, for a proper southern gentleman never reached out to shake a lady's hand unless she first initiated the invitation. "I'm Sophia Delaney."

"Delaney?" he said with a chuckle. "Of course! Well,

now we know each other. I think you should wear it. It matches your lovely ensemble."

Sophia nervously laughed. "Oh, Gaston, I don't know what to say. I'm stunned by your generosity. I so appreciate this. Thank you!"

"It is my pleasure, dear Sophia Delaney."

"Your name is French?"

"Yes, I am a mixture of many origins, as most of us are here in the United States. I originally have the blood of the Spanish, French, African, and Native American in me. I am Creole."

Sophia enjoyed beautiful people, but more important, she found herself drawn to them in resonance with how well, or not so well, she attuned to their energetic vibration. In the case of Gaston Menard, she felt right at home in his company. It was as if she had found a long lost friend.

She intentionally turned her attention back to the glass case in front of her. She pointed to another enchanting piece. "Gaston, I also have my eye on this hourglass. But first you must know I shall insist on paying for anything else I might find here."

"I wouldn't have it any other way," Gaston said.

Sophia laughed. "Would you mind showing it to me?"

"You have exquisite taste, Sophia. This piece is from the mid 15th century. The hourglass is Italian, from Genoa to be precise. The story, as passed down through my ancestry, is that the sand inside the glass comes from a marble quarry in Greece. It is quite interesting that you chose this particular one. The tripod frame is made of Mycenaean bronze. There was a wooden box in which the hourglass originally came, but it is not in my possession."

"Perhaps it would shed some light upon the source of the hourglass," she said as she turned it so the sand easily sifted down into the empty glass below.

"I am sure it does," he said with that same knowing grin.

"Well, I seem to be drawn to this, as well, or perhaps it is calling out to me. In any case, I would like to purchase the hourglass."

"Well, now that presents another problem. This is another piece my aunt gave me, which was evidently also waiting for you. I cannot take money for it, either."

"Now, stop, Gaston! I insisted on paying for anything else, and you agreed."

"I know," Gaston said. "But I fibbed. I should have said you may pay for anything, except the hourglass."

Sophia paused for a time, wondering what to do. "You aren't going to let me pay for anything here, are you?"

Gaston shrugged. "I still owe a few thousand on my Cadillac, if that would make you feel any better."

Sophia laughed. "Please, Gaston, I'm serious! I don't feel right about not paying for either piece."

"You will have to take that up with my departed aunt - if you see her sometime…"

Sophia curiously looked at his playful eyes. She decided not to go there for now. "Alright, I tell you what, I happen to be a landscape artist. Would you be willing accept one of my paintings as my gift to you? It is obviously not antique, but my landscapes of this area tend to bring in a good dollar or two down here." She pulled out a tablet from her handbag to show him some photos of her paintings. You may pick out whichever one you want. What do you say?"

"Oh my, this is exquisite work. Very well – twist my arm. I will accept your gift in exchange. My aunt probably would approve of such a barter." He chose a sunset scene of the bayou. "I must say that we have done some remarkable business today, have we not?"

She agreed and left her business card, thanking him for his kindness. They arranged a time the next morning when she would deliver the painting. It was 5:00 p.m., time to get ready for dinner with Darius MacPhaidin.

They shook hands. "Gaston, I can't say when I have enjoyed a more delightful afternoon."

Gaston kissed her hand, and she was surprised to see a tear well in his eye. "I have so longed for this day, my dear Sophia."

She smiled, questioningly. "I'll see you tomorrow then?"

"I'll be here. As you know, in here-"

"You have nothing but time?" Sophia said with a wry smile. He laughed, and she walked out the door as the ringing bells bid her good-bye.

CHAPTER
Twenty~one

Although Sophia had no choice but to drive her oversized RV to Darius MacPhaidin's home, she thoroughly enjoyed the scenery along the country roads west of New Orleans. She would have rented a car, but she needed something large enough to transport the painting he purchased. She arrived with plenty of time to spare, turning the RV into the long drive leading to the house.

She was astonished to see that Darius lived in a large restored plantation house from the antebellum days of the old South. Ancient oaks draped in Spanish moss welcomed her along the drive as the two-story Greek Revival mansion emerged in the distance. Dormer windows dotted the roofline supported by Corinthian columns along the wraparound porch. White wrought iron railings ran the length of the second floor veranda, and each window sported full-length black shutters.

Sophia laughed to herself. Feeling entirely underdressed, she imagined herself more appropriately attired in an off the shoulder floor-length satin gown, with a hoopskirt adorned with ruffles, ribbons, and lace. Underneath the skirt would be layers of petticoats, pantaloons, and of course a laced up corset and silk hosiery tied with satin ribbons just above the knees. Nevertheless, she would have to present herself as she was. The only thing she wore that was anything close to the dress of that period was her floor-length black jersey skirt and coral satin slippers.

After parking the RV on the side of the house, she walked up to the black French doors and knocked the bronze doorknocker crafted in the image of a Greek Goddess. A butler opened the door and showed Sophia into the parlor. He invited her to take a seat. "Mr. MacPhaidin will join you shortly."

She sat, absorbing the 19th century opulence. Persian carpets accented the oaken floors. Crown molding and deep baseboards framed the room with an elegance long gone by. A fire blazed in the baroque French marble fireplace, filling the house with an inviting scent that only came from burning hardwoods. Antiques filled the room, some from Louis XVI France. Most of the pieces were from the pre-Civil War era. A few were contemporary additions that made the room delightfully eclectic. Surrounding her were the features and details of a life lived in luxurious fashion long ago, with very few details carried on into the present day. Draperies, fabrics, tassels and trim, polished silver, Chinese porcelain - all displayed with the greatest attention to detail. Enchanted by it all, Sophia felt honored to witness this extraordinary piece of Louisiana history. Most of the antebellum homes of the Deep South did not survive the Civil War, but this one was an exception.

Darius entered the room, looking a bit like Mark Twain with thick, curly white hair and a goatee. He wore a dark grey double-breasted tweed suit with a white polished cotton shirt and bow tie. He held a pipe in his left hand. Time seemed to revert to the days of the Antebellum South, leaving Sophia feeling a bit disoriented.

She stood and offered her hand in greeting. When he took her hand, the same golden-white light lit up the room as when she first met White Buffalo. The light was not unlike when she held the amulet in her hand earlier that day at Gaston's shop. Sophia smiled, *I am beginning to get used to this numinous light.* Darius didn't make much of it himself, but he had a glimmer in his eye. She offered him a rare gift of Glenmorangie Cellar 13 Single Malt Scotch Whiskey.

"How delightful," Darius said. "I haven't enjoyed a bottle of this since I last visited Scotland. You know, they don't even make this anymore – it's quite rare!"

"I thought it an appropriate gift for a discerning Scots-Irishman," Sophia said.

"Ah, indeed!" Darius said with a laugh. "It will just be the two of us for dinner this evening. We have so much to discuss. Did you bring the painting, my dear?"

"Yes. It is in my RV."

"I was watching as you drove up alongside the house. You are such a tiny little thing to navigate that monstrous beast of a vehicle."

"I need something large enough to transport all my art and equipment. It also makes it easier for me to have the convenience of living in familiar surroundings while I travel to these shows. Allow me to run outside and get the painting for you right now."

She brought the painting in, along with her newly

purchased hourglass to show Darius. "I thought you might find this of interest. I bought it at a lovely antique store on Royal Street this afternoon."

Darius carefully examined the hourglass, but did not say a word about it. Instead, a grin appeared as he thoughtfully placed his pipe in his mouth. "If you will allow me, I will place this exquisite piece in the library, where we might discuss it after our evening meal?"

"Of course!"

A space for her painting had already been prepared over the fireplace in the dining room. Charles, the butler, hung it while they observed. It complemented the decor beautifully, and Darius was quite pleased. He handed her an envelope, already prepared for her prior to her arrival. She placed it in her purse and thanked him.

"Aren't you going to count it?" he said, smiling.

"I am sure that you are more than good with your word. Besides, I am an excellent judge of character. I feel I can trust you."

"I appreciate that, for this is the beginning of not only a wonderful evening, but a long and lasting relationship."

She wondered what he meant. Perhaps he was planning to be her wealthy patron, which she thought would be something she would certainly enjoy.

The table was set with 19th century china and sterling silver flatware on a linen tablecloth with matching napkins. A pair of sterling silver candelabra lit with three candles each flanked a floral centerpiece of garden flowers, creating an elegant atmosphere by which to dine. Sophia and Darius enjoyed a delectable meal that began with a bowl of corn and crab bisque, followed by a fresh salad made with homegrown garden vegetables. Charles placed on the table a platter of Shrimp Étouffée, paired with a nice German Riesling served in antique crystal stemware. He also served them fresh asparagus, topped with Hollandaise sauce, accompanied by hot Creole cornbread.

They engaged in small talk for a time, exchanging simple pleasantries. Sophia briefly told Darius about her life in Denver. She shared how she and Michael reunited for a fourth time after many years of trying to make it work. He enjoyed sitting back and just listening. Too long had it been since he had such delightful company to share his table.

To finish off the meal, they enjoyed their Café au lait, with chicory of course, and Crème brûlée with fresh blueberries for dessert. Sophia told Darius about her dream's images that inspired the painting he just purchased. Of course, she did not reveal that she had been frequenting her past life, but only about fiery images of volcanic activity. He asked, "Sophia, have you ever seen a volcano erupt?"

"I have to admit, I have only seen such images in television documentaries. It must seem odd to you that I dream such things."

"Not at all," Darius said. "Our dreams are portals into other worlds far beyond the physical dimension. I know there are times when I travel to other places I could only imagine. I am certain that I have frequented worlds outside our own, where I feel perfectly supported, completely loved, and accepted."

"Yes, I have done such things myself. It is amazing to

know that we are able to exist simultaneously in another time and space where we are just as much an integral part of life as we are here. I am ever in awe of what my dreams teach me," she easily responded.

"Let us retire to the library for an after dinner cocktail - perhaps a glass of that fine Cellar 13." Darius, ever a gentleman, held her chair as she rose from the table. He then motioned toward the door, allowing her to precede him into the next room. "Let us open the Glenmorangie, some of the finest single malt scotch one can acquire. Tell me, how is it that you were able to find Cellar 13 here, on this side of the Atlantic?"

"Actually, I didn't. When I last traveled to Britain, I bought a few bottles to give as gifts. It happens to be my favorite. A pity you can't get it anymore."

"Rocks, or neat?"

"Rocks, please. I'm probably not a proper Scot, mixing my scotch with ice."

"A proper Scot drinks scotch with water," Darius said as he poured. He winked, "But ice is water, now, isn't it?" He handed Sophia her drink. He poured himself a glass straight-up. "In the tradition of my French ancestors, I drink my scotch neat." He raised his glass to her, as did she in return.

She noticed a portrait over the mantle of a young blonde woman dressed in a stunning floor-length evening gown. Sophia assumed the woman was most likely one of his ancestors. She thought the woman seemed oddly familiar, but there were so many details to take in that evening. She put the thought aside for the time being while she curiously perused the room's rare books, art, paintings, and memorabilia - not unlike that which filled her own library at home. Because of her wide interest in history and art, her inquisitive mind basked in fascination with the room's atmosphere.

Darius motioned for her to sit in the 18th century settee placed in front of the roaring fire. He took his seat in the Louis XVI Bergere chair next to hers, separated only by a hand-painted end table. Sophia was feeling a bit anxious, for Darius had not yet made mention why he had invited her to his home.

The warmth of the fire was a welcome comfort, as the autumn night brought with it a chill. Darius sipped the fine scotch, placed his crystal glass on the table, and paused for a moment before picking up the hourglass. "What an exquisite piece. Tell me about it."

"I found it this afternoon at the most charming antique shop down on Royal Street. I was drawn to it and also to this unusual amethyst amulet necklace." She removed the necklace and handed it to Darius.

He compared the etchings on the crystal to those on the hourglass. "Aren't these interesting markings? Did the shop owner shed any light on their translation?"

"He had no idea, but they must be of the same origin. Don't you agree?"

"Indeed, I have no doubt that is true." He stood up and walked behind her, holding out the chain and offering to clasp the necklace for her.

"Anyway, I'm leaving out the best part. When I first held the necklace in my hand, I had the most extraordinary experience. Darius, I have seen this necklace in my dreams of a life I once lived long ago, and right there in the shop I had visions of myself in other past lives, wearing the necklace."

"Indeed," Darius said.

"The proprietor, a lovely man named Gaston, told me he had been holding onto both the necklace and the hourglass for over fifty years at the request of his deceased aunt. She said a woman would someday enter his shop and experience something unusual when she held the crystal. He said that I was the rightful owner of both pieces, and he insisted I take them. I offered to purchase them, but he wouldn't accept my money."

"My word," Darius said. "That is remarkable."

Sophia looked curiously into his eyes. "Remarkable - but you don't sound too surprised."

Darius sat back down and took a sip of scotch. "I am sure you are wondering why I invited you here, Sophia."

"Yes, I must admit, I am a bit on edge."

"You took note of the portrait, I see."

"She is beautiful. Is she one of your ancestors?"

"She is my great-great-great-grandmother, Maeve. This portrait was painted in 1839, when she was twenty-two years old. She originally came from a family of innkeepers from Dublin, Ireland. Her husband, Liam, began working for Maeve's father as a youth, in exchange for room and board. Liam was a distant cousin of Maeve, many times. He learned the trade, and before long, Liam was well known for his excellence as an innkeeper.

"He and Maeve grew up together, working side by side. From the very beginning, it was Liam's intention to marry Maeve, drawn to both her beauty and brilliance. She was unlike the majority of girls of that time - most of them groomed solely to be a wife and mother. Maeve, on the other hand, was highly educated, and she learned every aspect of her father's business, hoping somehow to inherit it all, but the laws of that time did not allow a daughter to succeed her father. Only the son or the closest male relative could inherit the holdings of the estate. Liam was, by law, deemed the legal successor. By marrying him, Maeve would remain linked to the family innkeeper trade and to her father's legacy. Fortunately, for her, Liam was a good and honorable man, and they grew to love and respect each other. They joined in marriage in 1835, and they left Ireland the same year during the Great Potato Famine."

"What an interesting history!"

"Ah, the story gets better. They crossed the Atlantic in a cotton ship that previously unloaded its cargo in Liverpool. The tragedy of the Great Potato Famine became the answer to the dilemma for a ship's captain during that time in history. He simply used people as ballast, but let me say, the conditions of their transport were far less than desirable. Over one million Irish fled their homeland from 1820 to 1840 because of the famine. Those on the cotton ships were mislead to believe that they were destined to disembark in New York City, or somewhere on the east coast of the new Promised Land, when in fact the ship set sail for New Orleans the entire time.

"New Orleans, however, was the greatest city in this part of the South, so Liam and Maeve decided to settle here. Liam became one of the first successful hoteliers in New Orleans. He named the hotel *Hibernia*, from the early Greek reference to Ireland."

Sophia's eyes widened. *Hibernia,* she thought. The name *Laurinda* instantly entered her mind... *Perhaps it is another past life to come from out of my dreams,* she thought.

Darius continued, "Maeve was not only his wife, but she fully partnered with him in business. She was in charge of the staff and the hotel's highly successful restaurant. Liam handled the finances and made all the business decisions. Together, they made a fine team.

"Maeve eventually gave birth to Alannah in 1842, having had two miscarriages prior to her birth. Alannah then bore a daughter in 1863, named Fiona. Fiona subsequently had Bridget in 1887. Bridget, my grandmother, gave birth to my mother, Siobhan, in 1910. I was born in 1937, the first male child in seven generations. We were each the only surviving child born in our individual generation."

"I, too, am an only child," Sophia said.

"Yes, that is interesting, isn't it?"

She thought the tone of his last statement was peculiar. He skimmed past her comment almost as if he did not hear her.

"The family business has been passed down for five generations, now a chain called *Delaney Hotels*."

"I have heard of Delaney Hotels – no relation, unfortunately!"

Darius again did not seem to take note of what she said.

He continued without missing a beat. He walked over to the fireplace, and from atop the mantle, he took a hand-carved wooden box and handed it to Sophia. "This finely crafted dark walnut box is for you."

"For me?" She curiously took the box and examined the fine engraving of a hand-carved design of two interconnecting circles that created the vesica piscis where the circles joined. Triangles and squares formed from the points of intersection, creating what Sophia recognized as sacred geometry. "My goodness, I've seen this design before."

In her mind's eye, she flashed to her memory of the almond shaped pool formed by the union of the two rounded sides of the temple in Akrotiri. Elaborate textures filled the shapes on all sides, making the box a sensual pleasure to touch, but there was something even more intriguing about the familiarity of the design.

Many questions were beginning quickly to arise, but she stayed focused. The lid attached to the box with bronze hinges and a latch designed of Celtic knots, all anchored to the front by a bronze pin. The interior of the box was empty, except for a velvet form shaped like a hollow eight. There was a silver plaque on the inside of the lid, engraved in French.

"May I translate for you?" Darius asked.

"Yes, please."

"It reads, 'I leave this hourglass of infinite time to Luciana Nervetti, a descendant of the Delphic Oracle, for her gift of vision, healing, and great heart. Its golden tripod is the symbol of prophetic powers. The glass, in the shape of infinity, holds the Greek marble sands of time, ever flowing, and never ending. I leave you with my blessing of apeiros, knowing you will continue to receive great gifts through the eternal, boundless, expansive love of God. I also leave you with my endless love and devotion, for we are forever one from this point forward. Devotedly, Michele du Nostredame'."

Sophia's mind was spinning. "Hourglass!" she said. "Gaston mentioned a box for the hourglass! Is this it?"

"It appears so," Darius said.

Sophia paused for a moment. There was so much to take in. "Wait! Michel du Nostredame? Nostradamus?"

Darius picked up the hourglass and handed it to Sophia. "Yes, Nostradamus was a patron, and it appears also Luciana's lover. She was one of my ancestors. Her surname, Nervetti, meant 'innkeeper.' It was from her that our family business evolved. If you do not mind, we will temporarily postpone the conversation about Nostradamus, for I have so much more information to share with you before the night's end."

Sophia acquiesced, yet her interest was piqued with wonder about the details of the legendary seer. *What was that about Luciana being a descendant of the Oracle of Delphi?* There it was again - the Oracle. It seemed that quite a few odd puzzle pieces were falling into place. The picture was becoming clearer. Evidently, she would have to wait, with great anticipation, until the time presented itself for her to know more.

In the back of her mind, she recalled her life as Roxana.

Yes! That's it, Yiorgos gave Roxana an aquamarine ring

set in gold. Etchings on the golden band matched those of her other golden possessions...and the wooden box for the ring was carved with the same designs as on this box now holding the hourglass!

She returned from her epiphany to give her full attention to Darius.

"The markings on these two items, now in your possession, are a type of rune, not yet identified of their origin. I imagine you are wondering how I know this."

"Yes, of course!"

"I invite you to, again, take a good look at the portrait of my Grandmother Maeve," Darius said.

Sophia got out of her chair to stand at the back of the library. "Oh, my, there is an hourglass on the table next to her!"

"Yes. Look further."

It took her another moment to notice the necklace on Maeve. "She is wearing the crystal amulet! How is it that I received these from Gaston today if they belonged to her?"

"Maeve's daughter, Alannah, died in childbirth when her daughter, Fiona, was born. To pay for Alannah's medical services, my grandfather, Connor, bartered with the physician and gave him a golden bowl, this hourglass, and your amulet necklace. He kept the box for the hourglass, hoping that someday it would return to the family. He may have had no idea of their great value, or of their mystical power, otherwise I am sure he would have found some other way to pay the physician.

"It was the time of the Civil War, and my grandfather

had difficulty making ends meet. Lucky for him, although Union Troops occupied the house during the war, they did not burn it down like so many others. The Hibernia became the hospital for the Confederate soldiers in this part of the South. Although Grandfather Connor owned the building, Fiona was not born there. If so, the physicians might have saved Alannah's life. After the war, Connor first restored the hotel. As time allowed, he refurbished this house and raised Fiona on his own, for he never remarried."

"So, why do I have a feeling you already knew that Gaston gave me the hourglass and amulet today?"

Darius smiled. "I apologize for not telling you right away, my dear, but I have a bit of a flair for the dramatic. Gaston and I grew up together. He is my brother-in-law. His sister - my wife - passed away many years ago."

"Oh, Darius, I'm sorry for your loss."

Darius nodded at her sympathetic gesture.

"So if you will, allow me to sort this out then," Sophia said. "Gaston's aunt – the woman who insisted the amulet necklace and hourglass be saved for me - must have been related to the physician who took the items in trade from your ancestor?"

"Precisely," Darius said. "Yes, the physician was Gaston's aunt's great-great-grandfather. It seems our families were destined to intertwine through the ages. Gaston's aunt, who was a rather mystical being herself, apparently recognized that these items had powers that only the rightful possessor could utilize. She believed someday that woman – you, my dear - would come to find them, and so Gaston agreed to display them at his antique store. He was very excited to discover that you were the rightful owner. He called me after you left the shop. There is more for you to know, Sophia."

He knew this was a lot of information for her to process. She was scheduled to drive back to Denver the next day, and he didn't want to leave her guessing.

"The amulet necklace, when in your possession, is powerful, yes?" Darius asked.

"I cannot deny it, yet I don't understand why."

"It is said that the story of the amulet, a chalice with an eternal flame, and a golden bowl came from pre-Ancient Greece, as passed down from one generation to the next, through the females in the family, but this was not necessarily a case of material inheritance, but rather of divine legacy.

"The Delphic Oracle's ancestry traces back to the High Priestess of Akrotiri, who was the last to survive the volcanic destruction of the ancient island of Thera around 1630 B.C.E., now called Santorini, Greece. The High Priestess possessed a golden vessel, marked with an unidentifiable script etched along the edge of the bowl by which she could foretell the future. She also had an amulet with the same etchings on the face of the crystal. In sacred ceremony, she used a golden chalice filled with oil, lit with a luminous eternal flame.

"All three items, in the possession of the rightful owner, enabled him or her to acquire powers beyond this world, but only for those who were initiated with the temple rites. No one else could utilize the powers of these amulets. They were passed down through the generations, mostly through their daughters with the sacred knowledge of being a seer, intuitive healer, and prophetess."

Darius had no way of knowing that Sophia intimately knew the details of which he was speaking, or so she thought.

"My grandmothers Maeve and Alannah possessed the amulet necklace and the golden bowl, but there is no evidence that the eternal flame passed through my family – it apparently has journeyed elsewhere through time. Gaston's aunt said she found a letter with the items, written by Maeve, telling of their mystical powers. That is how Gaston's aunt knew they were not for anyone else but a woman descended from the original Oracle.

"Maeve and Alannah were healers and seers, initiated by their grandmothers' heritage. However, their female descendants, Fiona, Bridget, and my mother, Siobhan, had powers that set them aside from ordinary women, but they did not know how to use their abilities. No one remained to train them, for Alannah's death interrupted the Oracle tradition, including the inheritance of the necklace and golden bowl. If her heirs could have had in their possession the golden bowl, eternal flame, or the necklace, they may have been able to access the powers, but evidently, this was not to be. Instead, a writer and artist from Colorado happened to be the one drawn to them."

She sat back in her seat and sighed, trying her best to keep all the history he spoke of clear in her mind. "You keep mentioning a golden bowl," Sophia said. "What happened to it?"

"It was given to a couple that came into Gaston's shop here in New Orleans on their honeymoon back in the

1970s. The woman was enchanted by the bowl, and Gaston discovered that she had the power within her, most likely through her heritage as you apparently do, Sophia. I remember him telling the story about when she held the bowl, and how the room became luminous as if the sun shined directly from the bowl itself. The young woman also said that she transported into a different time for a few moments when she held the bowl. Gaston knew this woman was the rightful owner. He took no money for it, and instead gave it to them as a wedding gift."

"But why didn't he give her the necklace, too?"

"The woman never noticed it, although it was right there in plain sight. Apparently, she was not attracted to its power like you, and therefore the necklace was not hers. It is my belief that many Oracles have existed, holding either one or two of the sacred items. A woman for whom all three were meant would be as powerful as the Delphic Oracle's ancestor – the High Priestess of Akrotiri."

"The woman who accepted the golden bowl from Gaston," Sophia said, longingly, "I wonder who she was."

"Perhaps you'll know someday…when you are ready," Darius said.

Sophia looked at him quizzically. "What do you mean?"

"Anyway," Darius continued with a wry smile, "before the couple left the shop, Gaston gave them the letter written by Maeve. Now, let me tell you something that will give you a perfect chill." Darius smiled like a child about to tell a secret. He lowered his voice and took Sophia's arm. "Gaston said, when he handed the letter to this woman…it vanished the moment it touched her hand." He snapped his fingers. "Vanished, like that, into thin air!"

Sophia laughed. "Oh, Darius, now stop."

"Oh, but I cannot! Gaston, while an accomplished drinker, tells me he was perfectly sober at the time!" They laughed like children. "He swore to me, on his mother's grave, that the letter vanished – but there's more. The woman looked at her empty hand as if she was still holding it. She thanked Gaston as if nothing happened, and she appeared to put it into her handbag."

"Darius, you're telling tales now!"

"It's all quite extraordinary, don't you think? No more than what you experienced today in Gaston's shop, no?"

Sophia had to agree. He had told her much of what she had already recalled from her many dreams.

"Would you care for another scotch?" Darius asked.

"No!" Sophia laughed. "I've had quite enough, thank you!"

"As you wish," he said with a shrug. He poured himself another.

"Now, the hourglass. Do I understand it correctly – that it was a gift from Nostradamus to another of your great-grandmothers?"

"Luciana Nervetti, yes," Darius said. "Nostradamus, one of the most gifted seers the world has ever known. And you resonate with the hourglass, don't you..." He playfully raised his eyebrows up and down as he sipped his scotch.

"Ok," Sophia said, "let's get back to something else here. You are telling me that I am also a descendant of

Luciana, the Delphic Oracle, and the High Priestess of Akrotiri? That would make me a distant relative of yours, wouldn't it?"

Of course, she was aware of her life as Roxana, the High Priestess of Akrotiri, but someone else mirroring the same information back to her, and not just a reoccurring dream, brought the importance of her lineage to the forefront.

He took her hands in his and looked deeply into her eyes. "Yes, my dear. We might need a calculator, but I estimate that we are cousins, about seventeen times removed!"

They burst out laughing, enjoying a lighter moment on this evening of deep revelation.

"Well, Darius, here's some information for you. When I last met with White Buffalo, he gave me a gift of a golden chalice containing the eternal flame, with the same etchings of the amulet and the hourglass. White Buffalo, as we speak, is watching over the chalice during my travels."

"So, there is no doubt that you are the rightful holder of these sacred pieces," Darius said. "I know, Sophia, that you were thinking that I might become a patron of your work. In a way I am already."

Sophia cocked her head to the side and waited for Darius to explain himself.

"You see, I have been waiting for you for many years. I knew you would eventually reveal yourself. Others are waiting for you, as well. They have much to share with you. You will know them over time. This, you already know from White Buffalo.

"I am a very wealthy man, Sophia." Darius paused and

took a deep breath. "There is no easy way to tell you what I am about to say, so if you will settle back and get comfortable in your seat, my dear. There will be a day when I leave this world, and when I do, *you* will inherit all of my possessions. This mansion will be yours, along with its contents and the several hundred acres surrounding it. You will also inherit my hotels and all the related businesses. My estate will be yours in its entirety."

Sophia stared at him in disbelief. She sat back, crossed her legs and arms in front of her, and shook her head. "Darius, I am astounded! Do you not have someone you have worked with for years who is close to you? Surely, someone on your staff, here in your home, is more qualified than I am. You must have a relative more closely related to you than me." She was adamant."I do not deserve this. I just met you yesterday."

"My dear, Sophia, all of my people will be well cared for when I am gone. There is more than enough to spread around. Have you truly looked at the painting of my grandmother Maeve? Do you not see the resemblance?"

Sophia uncrossed her legs and placed her hands on the edge of the seat as she leaned forward to look at the portrait again. Maeve's blonde hair, pulled back away from her face... and her eyes were blue. *No, they are teal!* Then, Sophia recalled when she first entered the mansion, imagining herself dressed in a satin evening gown, off the shoulders, with a hoop skirt. She pulled up the hem of her long black skirt to look down at her coral satin slippers. In the portrait, Maeve was wearing the same feminine shoes. Sophia was not imagining it after all. Instead, she was recalling being Maeve, herself. What astounded her more was that Darius knew it too.

"Maeve's father's name was Luciano Delaney, a descendant of Luciana's, and of Nostradamus fame," Darius said. "Not only was the golden bowl, hourglass, and amulet necklace passed down through the family line, but so was the knowledge of being an innkeeper. On many levels, Sophia, you and I are related. You will inherit all this from me when the time comes, but that will not be for many years. We have a lot of catching up to do. There is, however, one catch."

Sophia sat still, just taking it all in, incredible as it all seemed to be. The moment could not have been more tense than if a large organ was playing a funeral dirge in the background. She shifted in her seat and looked directly into Darius' eyes.

He had to admit that he already greatly admired her direct nature. She was not one to play games of manipulation. He felt that he was in company of a genuine and authentic woman - one he could trust with not only his fortune, but also his life.

"Sophia, my wealth has increased exponentially only because what I do with my businesses and their holdings are for the greater good of those I serve. When you inherit all this, only if you continue in business - doing what is best for all - doing philanthropic and life-giving good for others - will you thrive financially. If not, I guarantee that your financial status will quickly fail. This is true to the laws of prosperity. Do you understand what I am saying?"

"Darius, I am astounded that you want to make me your heir, but let me assure you of how I do my work in the world. I make all my decisions, business and otherwise, through my intuition. I never made a decision based on money. Never! I discern what will best benefit all involved, including myself, of course. I truly try to do the right thing. Then the money follows and quite often in a much more prosperous way than if I had engineered the course of action.

"Oftentimes my intuition guides me in ways that I have to step out in full faith and trust in the unseen, because what I am guided to do does not make logical sense. As I am certain you know, the thinking mind does not generate intuition. It never leads us to doing something that will bring harm, but it can guide us away from harm. I also find that my intuition leads me to miraculous findings, bypassing time and space with results that would never occur if I had acted on my own egoic, earthly mindset.

"If I don't follow my intuitive guidance, I always regret it. More often than not, I immediately know that I have made an enormous mistake when I have not been wise enough to listen to my intuition and follow through with it. Therefore, even though I would like to think that I am smart enough to make decisions on my own volition, I do far better trusting that which is greater than I am - that which speaks to me as my intuitive voice.

"That is the only way I work, Darius. Politics or power cannot sway me. Worldly power is an illusion. It is fleeting, and most often deceptive."

"Well Sophia, I must tell you I already knew all this about you, for I have kept an eye on you since your birth."

"My birth..." Sophia said. "But how-"

"I can't reveal everything just yet," Darius said. "You

will know more when you are ready. For now, I must say I am most pleased to hear that you know yourself. I have no doubt that we are going to do great things together. You will carry on well with my legacy, and now that you are aware of your southern roots, it is now *your* legacy." He reached out to place his hand over hers in a gesture of assurance that all was well.

She paused with a sigh and gently placed the hourglass into the box. It fit perfectly. Over 150 years had passed since it sat inside the lush velvet interior. Sophia closed the lid and clasped the Celtic bronze latch. In the same way as when she and Michael reunited, Sophia sensed a feeling of *home*.

CHAPTER
Twenty~two

*D*arius invited Sophia to remain as his guest for a few days before her return to Colorado. He told her she was welcome to stay as long as she desired. Sophia had to admit she felt an affinity for Darius. Already, there was an invisible bond between them, causing her to feel at ease in his company. However, she felt a childlike vulnerability, not only in his home, but also throughout New Orleans. Such was the paradox that left her wondering.

She attempted to logically put the pieces together. Darius lived in traditional formality, while Sophia was true to her bohemian nature as an artist. He was from the South. She was not. He was older, and she was, well... a couple decades away from qualifying as such. He was a successful, wealthy businessman of old money, and she was just beginning to gain her own credibility in the art world, and far from yet finding her voice as a writer. *So, what could possibly be the problem, when I am, after all, his heir apparent?* she thought.

There was another very important piece of the puzzle left for Sophia to put into place. It was something she did not expect, never having travelled to New Orleans before.

She could not help but notice the palpable heaviness that permeated the area's atmosphere. She could feel the countless spirits left behind, just waiting for someone to set them free. Sophia could sense the immensity of the area's dramatic history that included the exploitation and abuse of not only African slaves, but also indentured servants from Ireland, France, England, and the Caribbean. The sorrow she felt was an aged magnification of anguish, not yet forgotten, nor forgiven. Any place of destruction and death carried its grief and sorrow until something of greater purpose breathed life back into the atmosphere.

From another perspective, Sophia felt herself drawn to the mystic flair of one of the truly unique cities of the United States, built along the Mississippi River on the edge of the Gulf of Mexico, and surrounded by lakes and levees. The city's enchantment and well-known hospitality of the Old South kept people coming back for more. She could certainly understand why the historic French Quarter, with its food, music, and freedoms drew millions of tourists to the city each year, well beyond the famed week of Mardi Gras. It was there, in New Orleans, where cultures melded together to create Jazz, one of the original art forms of the United States.

However, there was a great deal more that called Sophia to wonder into the mystery to which she became more accustomed as each day passed.

Sophia needed to take in all that happened that day, *and* felt it necessary to delve more deeply into the questions of her life's purpose. She was certain the two were an intricate, intertwined web. A quiet respite away from her responsibilities certainly was welcome, and so she accepted

Darius' generous offer of hospitality.

Until she arrived back home in Colorado, Sophia did not share any of the news with Michael. She wanted to wait to tell him in person. Besides, something told her that Michael was already familiar with the day's events anyway. She laughed to herself, thinking, *I would not be surprised if Michael knows Darius. They probably belong to a highly esteemed Secret Sage Society, or something...*

Late that night, Sophia settled into the second floor guest room that faced the lane leading up to the house. An antique oil lamp burned on the dressing table, reminding Sophia of her golden chalice, which she left in the care of White Buffalo. The antique four-poster bed invited her to sink onto the silk down-filled duvet, but first, she spent a few moments outside on the veranda.

Before she washed her face, she brushed out her long blonde hair and bundled it into a twisted, messy knot behind her neck. Just as she patted her face dry with a thick white terry cloth towel, she found herself looking into her eyes in the mirror. She saw a different woman looking back than the one who arrived in New Orleans only a few days before. As tired as she was, her mind raced with questions about her life that seemed to offer nothing but greater adventures to come. She felt overwhelmed.

She prepared for bed and wrapped herself in a rich plum-colored floor-length silk robe that she found on a hanger in the antique walnut armoire. The color, alone, made her feel as if tranquility swathed her in the sweet assurance she sought that night.

In her bare feet, she stepped onto the veranda that overlooked the long lane of oak trees heavily laden with silver streamers of Spanish moss. A padded wicker loveseat sat, perfectly placed in the moonlight, draped with a beautifully handcrafted quilted afghan. She sat with her feet up on the seat, and her back resting against the armrest as she wrapped the afghan around her legs. She leaned back, taking in the peaceful ambience of the plantation, softened by the glow of the moonlight. Then, she finally took in a few deep breaths of the cool air of the surrounding autumn countryside, allowing herself to relax.

As she often did when she needed support and guidance, she turned within, through meditation and prayer, to gain access to wisdom not available through her thinking mind. The result was exponential, resulting in increased calm and confidence. Her spiritual awareness and intuitive gifts increased, causing her to shift into higher domains closer to the consciousness she experienced when she was in the next dimension. It was there that answers awaited her.

That night, she felt a serious need for all the help she could get. If she was to accomplish whatever it was that she was about to embark upon, it was past time to get her small self out of the way. She wanted to access that infinite, all-knowing soul she witnessed during her near-death experience. It was time for her emergence - time for the Phoenix within her to rise, but she could not do it alone.

Sophia closed her eyes while she held the amethyst crystal firmly in her hand. She felt the vibration permeate her being as she went into a meditative state. The sound of crickets chirped in unison in a gentle mantra that helped her rise above her concerns. She spoke a prayer as a whisper into the winds of change:

> *"Tonight I humbly come to join my mind and heart with my guides, my angels, and with the infinite intelligence, which I call God, the Divine. I come to release my thinking mind's barriers so I may open up to be the teacher and the taught, the speaker and one who is spoken to, the writer who scribes words of wisdom from that which has already been written. May I see, hear, and know that I am the healer, and therefore healed from that which keeps me separated from my greatness, my god-ness, my good. May I be the artist painting with colors not yet seen, and with unfamiliar textures, so that I, too, may become both created and the creator. May I allow myself to be guided to easily live in grace, celebrating joyful bliss, in my return to the way of the heart. And from that place may I serve, returning to others all I have been given. I am so thankful for all I have, and all that I am. I truly am blessed!"*

Sophia found herself falling away from the memory of her current life as she travelled into another past life, one she had not yet recalled, but would ever remember from that point forward.

A burning oil-filled chalice, passed through her ancestry, was the only light in the small room. She sat on the goatskin-covered platform built high above the floor, accessed by a wooden ladder next to the outside wall. Beneath the platform was a storage space for jars, baskets, and earthenware pots filled with olive oil, honey, and water. From the platform, another ladder led up to the roof where she would lay out her clothing to dry in the sun. It was there, on hot, windless summer nights, where she slept. Her two-level, three-room house was small, built with large uneven stones, the cracks packed with smaller stones and mortared with clay and straw. The floor, covered by a mixture of ash and clay, created a hard surface easier to keep clean than an earthen floor.

She was a young woman in her twenties with vibrant hazel eyes and olive skin. Her long, wavy, chestnut hair trailed down her back, held away from her face with a blue sash tied around her head and anchored at the base of her neck. She wore a floor-length ivory gown made of Egyptian cotton bordered in lapis blue, with sandals on her feet. She wore a few adornments of dangling gold earrings and an amethyst amulet hanging from her neck on a golden chain. They were the only indications of any wealth whatsoever. She lived simply, never calling attention to herself. Her name was Rachel.

There was great upheaval in her part of the world. People in surrounding cities and other nations competed for power. Tension rose among the many communities of Judea as the Roman occupation increased. The Hebrews awaited the Messiah - the anointed one - the one true messenger of God, whose arrival, prophesied for hundreds of years, had not yet occurred. They believed the divinely appointed one would bring to fruition God's plan for all humankind, but specifically for the Hebrews. He would bring peace, material prosperity, and spiritual harmony. They believed the Messiah would also be a warrior - one who would force the Romans to rectify the wrongdoings they had for too long perpetrated upon the Jews.

However, Rachel knew the Messiah would have to be a humble servant unencumbered by ego. He would not be someone who sought such power, but one who naturally obtained it from many previous lifetimes that led to his calling. Clearly, this unique individual, having achieved oneness with the Source of All, would arrive to bring great change to the world, but most likely not in the way people had hoped for hundreds of years.

Rachel was a seer, a prophetess who carried on the Oracle tradition from a different land and time. Those who sought power felt threatened by her mystic nature, but she gave no attention to them, for her only desire was to help others help themselves, so they could live a healthy, more grace-filled life.

Many people stood for hours outside Rachel's door, waiting to meet with her. She attained a reputation as a mystic healer and teacher. Some sought healing, and others desired love, or greater prosperity. They brought their deepest desires to her, hoping she might bring them greater fortune. But Rachel could only help people to the level that they themselves allowed for change and growth.

There were some that wanted change but were unwilling to alter their ways. Others, however, were willing to do the inner work necessary to transform their lives. Only they would be the ones to grow and see the fruits of their labor, because they sacrificed the lesser for something better. They knew their good would come as they let go of what they no longer needed, but these types of people were rare. Most wanted something more for a very small price, if they had to pay anything at all.

Four days of the week, Rachel was available for readings and healings. One day per week, she reserved to visit the sick that were unable to come to her. For them, she administered herbal remedies, energetic healings, and prayers for anyone who asked. The last two days she saved for herself, for personal reflection and rejuvenation so she would be fully empowered to be of greater service the following week.

Her patrons paid her well, both in coinage and precious olive oil for her prophetic services. The use of olive oil, a most important commodity, was for food and cooking, hygiene and healing, lighting oil lamps, and for anointing in religious ceremonies. Olive trees were prolific among the rocky terrain of Galilee, where she lived. She could have lived in lavish opulence, but instead she chose to live simply, giving much of her wealth for services to aid those not as fortunate as she. Without the desire to live in excess, she felt well cared for and supplied with all she needed to live comfortably.

Always, there were many more people waiting for her than she was able to see on any particular day. For those left waiting when nighttime approached, she gave them an assigned priority number to be the first in line the following day.

One such individual who returned after waiting an

entire day stood out among the rest. In fact, Rachel had never met anyone like him. Immediately, as he crossed the threshold, Rachel felt the surrounding atmosphere shift to a higher level. She looked around the room and noticed the air filled with a palpable sparkling radiance, so apparent she could practically wave her hand through the light as if it was water.

He was noticeably handsome, tall, and slender, wearing a long plain linen tunic cinched at the waist with a wine colored sash that accentuated his lean, muscular body. Laced over his ankles were simple leather sandals. Taller than the average man, he stood about six feet in height with dark skin and black hair falling to his shoulders that was curly and well-oiled. A cropped, well-groomed beard and mustache made him appear older, but he was most likely in his late twenties. His soft brown eyes had a depth and intensity of wisdom beyond the ages.

Rachel had difficulty looking away from him as he maintained her gaze. She finally lowered her eyes and bowed her head in reverence. "Forgive me for hesitating. My name is Rachel. Welcome to my home."

"Thank you for seeing me today. I am called Yeshua ben Yosef."

She had heard of this man. If he was who she thought he was, word of his healings and compassion spread widely throughout the land. But why had he come to see her? When she looked into his eyes, she could see the universe in its entirety - everything in existence. Through him she knew all there was to know, recognizing his omnipotence, omniscience, and omnipresence. Being in his company transferred his knowledge to her, raising her vibrational frequency well beyond her current awareness of all that she knew within her capacity.

She was instantaneously changed and sustained for lifetimes to come. Such was the power of people who obtained elevated frequencies. They shifted the energies around them just by being in the room. But Rachel still wondered why had he come to her? Clearly, he was not in need of her services, for he was far more accomplished than she.

Sensing his visit was a special occasion and one not likely repeated again, she invited him to dine with her, offering freshly made flatbread, with a mixture of olives and vegetables in herbs and olive oil. A separate plate of figs, pomegranate and goat cheese was served with her best wine. They sat on the floor of the platform with the food at their feet.

"I have been waiting to meet with you for some time," he said. "You have brought aid to many people." He smiled, and to honor her, he raised his cup before sipping the wine.

She nodded, smiling in return. "Yes, I remember. You are one to whom I gave a number yesterday, in case you desired to return. While waiting in line, you could have asked anyone to step ahead of them, and they would have gladly granted you their place, but instead, you waited until today like everyone else. I am even more impressed and find myself greatly intrigued by your presence."

"Rachel, I have an important reason for being here. I want you to know that the angels continually surround you. Nothing can bring you harm, except that which you bring into your own experience when you cannot remove yourself from your own limited thinking. You are ever safe, protected, guided, and sourced. As you go about your days knowing this, you will be greatly empowered, for you will then not be seeking anything outside yourself. Whatever you need is within you. All you must do is inquire of the Divine in humble sincerity, feeling that very desire is already manifest, for your deepest, most sincere longings will come to pass.

"God sources every need. I invite you to keep in mind, take care of that for which you yearn, notice where you place your attention, for that which lies within, when acted upon with feeling, becomes the answer to your prayer. Rachel, you are ever at choice. If you are not pleased with life, change your thoughts to that which is life giving - to that which serves you well. Shift your attention from the thoughts that govern the world, to where your heart leads you. In this, your life will flow, and you will find ease and grace all around you."

Rachel responded, "I am visited in my dreams from my past lives, where I have done similar work. So, what you are saying is an acknowledgement of what my dreams reveal to me."

"As you continue to advance through each lifetime doing this work," Yeshua said, "you will become even more powerful as each life progresses. Over time, your tasks will change in various ways and reveal themselves to you. You are to treat each person who comes to you as if they are your kin. Love them wholly with a compassionate heart. See each of them at their best, and support them to make better changes for their advancement. You are to hold them in your heart, so they can be the best they can possibly be.

"Know this, Rachel, when we are in agreement to change, everything that is not of that new realm will remind us of our smallness and insignificance. Old ways keep us trapped, for they fool us to think we cannot rise above our habitual thoughts and behaviors. This is one of the discomforts of change. Therefore, the key is to remain in the uneasiness of change just long enough so that what we are seeking to become will develop into our new normal.

"Rachel, from your compassionate care, the people you serve will pass along the higher wisdom and vibration they gain from you. They will recognize that they, too, have within them everything they need to live well in the fullness of life. I have come here to do the same work. I came to this life, utilizing all the power of God that is mine. I am here to teach all people that they are able to do the same. Anyone can do this, but very few are aware of their innate abilities. Of those that *are* aware, very few will make the commitment to join in union with God. I seek out a handful of people to do this work with me. Those of this highest vibration can shift thousands - even millions of people from the lower frequencies, saving humanity from self-destruction and thus saving the world and the earth - Gaia herself.

"This kind of existence can be a solitary life, for one must stay within the quiet recesses of the heart. You must continuously seek guidance, staying open to receive. In this you will remain humble and of greater service to others, uninfluenced by your surroundings, and able to avoid the minds of the masses. You will find this way of life one of great reward beyond anything I can convey. I have chosen you, Rachel. I ask that you accept this calling. Will you join me?"

She felt outside herself, almost as if she was an observer from above the rafters. His presence was so powerful and yet peace-filled. She desired to do the same work he was doing in the world. "Yes, of course, I accept," she said. "I am unsure how, but I will do my best. I am honored that you chose me."

Rachel truly had no idea what she was saying yes to, but she knew she had already been about this work in her own way. Her past life as High Priestess and the Oracle were similar callings. She knew, even before he came to her, that she must carry on as she had for thousands of years, doing the work of her soul's passion.

"Rachel, I'm going to reveal to you a power that we all possess. It is so simple that most bypass its importance. We do not have to know how to do anything. We only need to be clear about what we desire. We see it in our mind's eye in detail, color and texture. We feel it as if it is already in our experience - as if it is a manifest reality - living as if it has already come into fruition. From that level of certainty, how to fulfill the desire will reveal itself. Sometimes the answers will come to us as an epiphany. Other times they will come through another's expertise, but be assured it will happen. Oftentimes, what will manifest will be even greater than the original desire. The key is to be clear of what it is you desire, not what you do not want to occur. God says yes to that upon which we place our greatest attention. This is the truth in our healing work."

Yeshua then held Rachel's hands so her palms faced upward. "I want you to feel the energy in your hands,

Rachel." She sensed the vibration in her palms and nodded. "Now breathe in deeply, then exhale, concentrating your breath into your hands. Do this several times. Can you feel the energy increasing?"

"Yes. It is quite enhanced."

"This energy is always there," Yeshua said. "The difference is now you are aware of its presence. As you breathe this way, envision the Light of God coming through the crown of your head. You are not doing the work - you are the instrument through which God heals. Your task is to be aware of your receptivity to God's eternal power within you, operating through you and as you. Think of yourself like a human funnel as the light pours into and through you. In turn, you fill another with this healing light. This is my task, as well.

"As you work with those who are infirmed, breathe the light of God into them through the power of your hands. See them whole and healed - living a life of joy - liberated from their challenges. The lesser nature of their illness will not be able to survive, because you will have displaced it with God's higher energy. This is how you energetically heal others with physical ailments and with issues of the mind.

"For every meal you prepare, charge the food with this energy. Purify your drinking water simply through your intention. Bring God into everything you do, and into all you physically touch and mentally engage. The power is yours by knowing that God surrounds you, comes through you, and is within your every breath.

"When you give prophecies, breathe the light of God into your hands as you hold the golden vessel. What will come through the water for you to see will be magnified. Blessed are all when you breathe the same light of God into that which you believe. Whether you are in company or not with those for whom you pray, enhance your prayers with your sensitivity as you envision and feel in your mind and body their absolute complete health and wellness. See in your mind's eye that their illness has ended. Sense from your heart that all is well. Envision them living a happy and prosperous life with those they love.

"The feeling of God within you truly is what makes you the channel. That level of feeling is what brings healing through the words you choose both in prayer and in your everyday existence. Within the sensitivity of feeling the effervescent joy within you - that which *is* the love of God - you create what we call miracles. When, in truth, the simplicity of what you are doing is calling to the surface that which has ever been present."

Yeshua then smiled and gazed gently into her eyes. "Would you like to try an experiment?"

"Yes!" Rachel excitedly said.

"Bring in your next patron. Whatever their concern, before you help them, take several breaths and feel the energy fill you completely until it comes through, radiating from your hands. Without any doubt, know for those you serve that the Almighty God knows all, is everywhere, and is all-powerful. We are all of this same godly essence, and this power of God is also your power to use for the good of all. And because of this truth, you have within you the same almighty power to the degree of your belief. This is what it means to Know Thyself. Breathe this knowing into your hands and then give your reading. Lay your hands upon your patron to bring healing and well-being to the situation. The infinite, eternal God knows all. The only thing you need to do is believe that it is so. Allow the Divine to work through you and as you. Now let us see what transpires."

Rachel went to the door. The people at the front of the line insisted that she help a man who sat on the ground waiting to see her. Yeshua helped the middle-aged man to his feet and into the house. He eased the man to the cushions on the floor in front of the fire pit, and then sat next to Rachel.

"My name is Rachel, and this is Yeshua ben Yosef."

The man winced in pain as he straightened his leg. He looked at Yeshua and said, "I am Ananias ben Simeon."

"How did you injure your leg?" Rachel asked.

"I am a stone mason. This morning, while working at the quarry, a large block of stone fell on me. Some of my fellow workers brought me to you for healing." His knee and foot were badly bloodied and bruised.

Rachel arose and retrieved a bowl of water, clean cloths, herbal tinctures, and honey. "May I tend to your wounds?" she asked.

"I gratefully accept anything you can do to help me. Until I am better, I cannot return to my work."

She knelt in front of him and cleaned his wounds. He winced in pain, withdrawing his leg from her touch. Rachel paused, took another deep breath, and smiled at him. She placed her hand upon his shoulder while she looked into his eyes, compassionately bringing him to calm. She then proceeded to mix the herbal healing tinctures with the honey. With a wooden knife, she gently applied the mixture to the wounds while she asked him to tell her about his family. With his mind on those he loved, she wrapped his leg and foot in clean cloths, tying them at the ankle.

"Now, let us thank God in advance for this experience of learning, and for healing you." She took several deep breaths, feeling the vibration in her hands increase to a radiating energy. Then she placed her left hand on the top of his head and her right hand on the clean bandage.

"Yeshua, Ananias, and I have gathered here in this moment, clearly knowing that God is present in the fullest, as the All Knowing, All Powerful, and ever-present Divinity. We can feel God's magnificence and power here and now. We know that we, too, are a part of the All There Is, which is God, the Divine, in and as us. It is who we are, and we claim it now to be so. I know, in this moment, that the health and wholeness of God is also that of Ananias. This is who he is. Right now, all that appear as bruises and wounds return to full health in this instant. The pain is gone, his energy restored. We see Ananias already returned to work. We see him able to give of his good to his family and community. Already, fully restored health is his. We thank you, dear God! We bless your name and praise you, for we are grateful, knowing that you have granted this good to already happen. We simply release this prayer to the mind of God, which takes this declaration and makes it so. We know that it is complete. And so it is. Amen."

Ananias opened his eyes, astonished. "Your hands - I feel the vibration - so powerful and warm. I feel no more pain." He sat on the floor rubbing the bandage. "I believe I can go to the quarry tomorrow. Oh, bless you. I give thanks to you!"

"I am so pleased you are feeling better. Not I, but you allowed yourself to come to your healing - to that place that already resides within you. Keep the bandages on until tomorrow. Come back to see me after your workday is completed. I will remove them and redress your leg and foot, if need be," Rachel said.

He stood and walked around the room without a limp. "I will gladly see you then. I am amazed!" Ananias bowed and handed her a bag of coins and left the room.

"He is healed," Yeshua said.

"I could feel the pain move from him. I could see the darkness turn to light. That was a remarkable experience!"

"If you do not allow yourself to get in your way and let God do the work, you will perform what seem like miracles, when in fact what you are doing is bypassing the concern to reveal the reality of the good of God, which is ever present and eternal. We are empowered to do wondrous things beyond our imagining, Rachel. That is why we are here."

Rachel placed her hands on her heart and bowed her head in awe of Yeshua. He stood and took her hands in his, helping her to her feet. He wrapped his strong arms around her and gently held her. She looked up into his eyes and then kissed him on the cheek. Immediately, Rachel saw before her a golden entity about the size of Yeshua's chest. The crystal clear Christ energy emitted from his body like a ball of light. The light briefly hovered in the air between them and then immediately entered deep into her heart.

She took a step back. Tears filled her eyes, for she knew she was instantly changed. He smiled as he took her face in his hands. Yeshua wiped the tears from her cheeks and gently kissed her on the lips. Filling her was the inner knowing that she was in the loving embrace of the one true Messiah.

Clearly, Yeshua's presence and wisdom separated him from others' teachings of religion and spirituality. The source of his knowledge came not from the history of the world down through the ages, but was fresh, inspiring, and radical.

He taught that his Heavenly Father's kingdom was within each person, regardless of his or her origin, age, gender, education, lifestyle, or level of understanding. This higher order was available to all who believed, as a power that bypassed religion and government, or anything of the earthly realm. This supremacy came from the expansive nature beyond the human imagination. This was how Yeshua empowered not only Hebrews, but also anyone willing to go within to find that their existence had no end within the eternal cause of all unity and measure of all things – the power of God. All they had to do was make a declaration, and believe wholeheartedly that it was so.

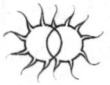

CHAPTER
Twenty~three

In her sleep, Sophia traveled back to Delphi, where Roxana and Yiorgos lived out the rest of their days together, but the time changed to 1300 years later than her last visitation into her past. The year was 340 B.C.E. In this lifetime, her name was Hypatia, a fair-skinned beauty of auburn hair and hazel eyes. Delphi had grown along the mountainside of olive groves from a small village of mostly one-story, one-room dwellings, into a sophisticated hillside city constructed of clay bricks, limestone, granite, and marble.

Ancient Greeks believed that Zeus released two eagles into the sky, which flew in opposite directions, encircling the earth. Zeus declared that the completion of their individual flights, resulting in their intersection, would mark the center of the world. This was the location of Delphi, as marked by the Omphalos Stone, meaning center or navel. The stone, carved into a 30 inch-tall shape of a beehive, stood inside the Temple of Apollo.

The temple site was located at the intersection of two fault lines - the Delphic Fault that ran from east to west, and the Kerna Fault, from north to south. At this intersection flowed the sacred Kassotis spring, creating fissures that emitted trance-inducing gases, primarily the sweet-smelling ethylene gas. The temple, intentionally constructed directly over these important geological points, was for the use of the Oracle tradition. Hundreds of years before, bees thrived inside the fissure, drawn to the increased electromagnetic energy that was common to such geological formations. Ancient Greeks considered bees sacred.

Before Delphi became the most sacred of religious sites in Greece, the people believed the Python protected the mountainside as the guardian of Gaia - Mother Earth. Apollo, son of Zeus, known for his marksmanship with a bow and arrow, reputedly shot several arrows into the powerful Python, killing it to claim the mountain as his own. There, the Greeks built the Temple to Apollo to honor Python. The High Priestess was also known as the Delphic Oracle. She was the ultimate authority over both religious and civil issues, quite unusual in male-dominated ancient Greece. In most traditions, the gender of the priest or priestess was the same as the divinity they served. However, in honor of Apollo, the Delphic Oracle, also known as the Pythia, was female, for she originally served Gaia.

She gave prophecies to both citizens of Greece and foreigners alike. Those who most sought her council were kings deciding on matters of state and law, philosophers pondering deeper knowledge and wisdom, and military leaders seeking prophecies of upcoming battles. Anyone could utilize her services once selected by lottery. However, those given precedence over those picked by the draw were patrons who paid large sums to the treasury.

Apollo, believed to be the most powerful and complex of all the Greek gods, was the god of light, god of the sun, and god of truth. He was also the god of healing and medicine, capable of bringing someone to good, or ill health. He was the leader of the Muses as the god of music, dance, and poetry. He had dominion over colonists and was the patron defender of herds and flocks. Most honored for being an oracular god, Apollo was the prophetic deity for the Delphic Oracle.

Apollo inhabited Delphi during the nine warm months of the year, beginning in the spring. These were the months when the Oracle gave her prophecies. Dionysus, the god of wine, ecstasy, and the Greek stage, inhabited Delphi during the three remaining colder months.

The Temple of Apollo was the largest and most noticeable edifice among dozens of buildings high on the hill beneath the summit of Mt. Parnassus. The temple, built in the center of the temple complex, was similar in architectural style to the Parthenon in Athens, yet not as large. Surrounding it were many treasury buildings that housed the massive assets offered to Apollo by people of neighboring cities and countries. Many tithed ten percent of their spoils of war in gratitude to Apollo for the prophecy of conquering their foe, making Delphi the most prosperous storehouse of wealth in Greece.

Theatre had its roots in Athens and soon spread to other cities in the Mediterranean, including Delphi. The Delphic theatre was located on a hill above the Temple of Apollo, with the stage located on the lowest level surrounded by the half-round theatre in rows of ascended seating. Musicians, poets, and philosophers such as Plato and Aristotle performed and orated at the theatre.

The summer Pythian Games, held in Delphi, were part of the Pan-Hellenic Games that occurred every four years. A three month period called the Holy Delphic Peace occurred prior to, and after the games, thus guaranteeing both competitors and the thousands of audience members safe passage. The accomplishment of attaining spiritual perfection through the events of cultural exchange could only occur in times of peace.

On this particular year, Hypatia attended the games in honor of Apollo. The Pythian Games included competition in music, literature and sport, each participant competing as an individual. Those allowed to compete were only Greek men and those from Greek colonies from as far as Asia Minor to Spain. The games began with an animal sacrifice offered at the temple's altar to appease the gods. Even though this was the tradition for centuries, Hypatia did not agree with animal sacrifice. She had an affinity for animals and believed it a barbaric practice. She believed the gods were most powerful and did not need to be placated in any way. Instead, she believed the best way to honor the gods was to praise and give thanks, in advance, for whatever was about to commence. To live life everyday in celebration of one's gifts and talents was how one would truly honor the gods.

The games commenced in the theatre with a performance reenacting the mythical struggle between Apollo and the Python. A procession of the competitors followed in the final event of opening day. On the second day in the gymnasium, a banquet was held in honor of each competitor and all visitors. At the theatre were the music, literature, and dance contests, which took place on the third day. These were Hypatia's favorite part of the games. The fourth day, sporting events of discus and running took place at the stadium located at the highest point of the temple compound. Some competitors dressed in full armor, while others competed in the nude. Boxing and wrestling competitions were in the gymnasium. The four-horse chariot races were the last of the competitions held off the grounds on the plain of Krisa.

Either a laurel wreath to wear on his head, or a palm frond to carry was the award for the winner of each competition. There was no monetary prize granted. It was enough for the winner to achieve eternal glory and fame. Delphi often erected bronze statues of the champions, displayed as a tribute to the Greek ideal of excellence.

Hypatia enjoyed spending time in the Agora, or marketplace - the grand emporium for the arts, with wares and artworks sold to the thousands who came to observe and participate in the games. She found dresses and cloaks in beautiful fabrics. She also purchased a new pair of leather sandals and shoes for the winter months. Even in ancient Greece, a woman could never have too many shoes. Food, jewelry, and items for her home were aplenty, not to mention an art piece or two.

Although Hypatia attended most every event, she covered her head and shoulders with a shawl to avoid drawing attention. Hypatia was in her twenty-ninth year, easily noticed because of her striking beauty. She hid her identity as the Delphic Oracle to avoid recognition for her prophetic powers. Only a few knew who she was, for her patrons never saw her in person when she was in service at the temple.

Prior to when Hypatia was the Oracle, the women before her were selected for their more advanced age and less attractive nature - albeit they were powerful prophetesses. Hundreds of years earlier, one of the Oracle's patrons abducted her, who not only wanted to take advantage of her powers, but also wanted her to be his. She left her sacred calling as the Oracle and fled with him to another country. From that time forward, the only women chosen to be the Oracle were plain, undesirable middle-aged women, who were also well educated and most likely wealthy.

However, when Hypatia became the Oracle, a widespread illness had taken the lives of many of the aged. There were no middle-aged women well enough, or endowed with the needed prophetic abilities to be the Pythia. Hypatia, known for her powerful healing abilities since childhood, was by far the best choice to be the High Priestess of Delphi. Her mother, who was the Oracle before her, told Hypatia the stories of her ancestry, passed down for over a thousand years. Her name, Hypatia, meant *most high – supreme* - and was evidently even more powerful than her predecessors. Because she was so young, she would serve the prophetic deity many more years than most. Apollo selected her by divine appointment, and she was reputedly the most extraordinary healer and seer ever known to Delphi.

It would not be long before the time for the olive harvest to commence throughout the countryside. The fruit of the olive trees were turning purple, ready for harvest and pressed for their precious oils. Olive fruit and oil were the area's greatest commodities, with honey the next most profitable product for trade. In that particular valley, hundreds of square miles of well-tended olive groves grew for a thousand years, which yielded premium olive oil traded far beyond the Mediterranean.

Just before dawn, Hypatia walked along the familiar road under indigo skies filled with crystalline starlight. She entered the sanctuary complex dedicated to Athena, the Greek goddess of wisdom and military victory, and the patron of the city of Athens. Athena's father was Zeus, god of the sky, and ruler of the Olympian Gods. Her mother was a nymph named Metis, which meant *wisdom* or *thought.*

Zeus heard a prophecy that the boy child born to Metis, following the birth of Athena, would become lord of the heavens. If that prophecy came true, the boy child would overthrow Zeus in the same way he overthrew his father and grandfather before him. To take preventative measures, he swallowed Metis while she was still pregnant with Athena. When the time came for Athena to be born, the god of smiths, Hephaestus - son of Zeus and half-brother of Athena - took an axe to Zeus' head. Athena stepped out as a beautiful young woman, fully grown and dressed in full armor. Metis, her mother, did not survive. Because of the mode of her birth, Athena obtained dominion over all things of the intellect. She was the defender of heroes and male causes, because she was born out of the male mind and not from the female womb. Zeus remained as god of the sky, and ruler of the Olympian Gods.

The Tholos was located next to the Temple of Athena Pronaia, meaning *Athena before the temple.* One arrived at the Temple of Athena before the higher climb up the mountainside to the Temple of Apollo. In Hypatia's opinion, the Tholos was the most beautiful of all the buildings among the dozens that made up the temple complex. Instead of a massive rectangular masculine building, common to Greek architecture, the Tholos was round and feminine in its style, measuring thirteen feet in diameter with two circles of marble columns, one inside the other. The exterior Doric Columns held up the double tiered, red-tiled roof. The interior ring of Corinthian columns stood inside the small circular room, which was just big enough for one or two people to sit comfortably.

Use of the Tholos was quite secretive, not known to many. As the Oracle and high priestess, Hypatia was one of the few allowed entrance to the Tholos, for it was the sanctum sanctorum - *inner sanctum* - and sacred chamber used for prayer and meditation by the priests and high priestesses.

Each morning in the early hours, while it was still dark, Hypatia would enter the Tholos and sit upon a small stool. Particularly during that time of day there would be no interruptions, no noise, except the singing of the birds in anticipation of dawn. Their song enhanced her communion with the gods as a melodious offering to the source of her being. An eternal flame burned in a copper oil pot on the small altar. She burned incense to fill the room with sweet perfume. Once a week she placed on the altar a vase of handpicked flowers filled with water from the sacred spring. Occasionally, she would leave a gift of food.

Hypatia would remain in the inner sanctum until the light of day became evident. She sat in communion with the gods, in particular Apollo. It was there where she became aware of a higher truth that all the Greek gods were aspects of an all-inclusive highest god. Yet it was to Apollo she prayed, and with whom she joined during her meditation.

While in the meditative state of mind, she entered a higher state of consciousness that raised her mindset above all earthly conditions. She melded her soul with that part of her that knew all there was to know - aware of that which she could not conceive in her human mind. This ability enabled her to better prepare for her prophetic visions during the one day per month she served as the Oracle. It was important that she remained pure and uncluttered by the world's events so she could offer the best of her abilities to those seeking her prophecies.

The Tholos stood next to the Temple to Athena below the gymnasium, which was the most frequently used building in all of Delphi. The immense gymnasium housed an indoor track in addition to the open-air track outside. Men used it for athletic training and exercise. In times of war, military training took place in the gymnasium. A bathhouse contained hot and cold baths popular to both men and women. The gymnasium, additionally used as a place for informal education, hosted visiting lecturers on topics such as literature, philosophy, music, and medicine. Those who travelled hundreds of miles to see the Oracle on the seventh day of the month had access to the gymnasium to take advantage of its numerous amenities.

The calendar year differed in each Greek state, developed during the classical period - the same time when scholars and philosophers wrote the most significant

ancient Greek literature - between 500 and 400 B.C.E. The
Attic Calendar of Athens used June as the first month of the
year. The Delphic Calendar began the year with September.
All were lunisolar calendars linked to the cycles of both the
sun and the moon. The New Moon, or *Noumenia*, indicated
the beginning of the month. Since the lunar calendar
contained 354 days in the year - 12 less days than the solar
calendar - an additional month was repeated every three
years to make up for the lost days.

In Delphi, it was the seventh day of *Bucatios* -
September - and the beginning of a new year. The weather
was warm, but not swelteringly hot as it was during the
previous three months. Hypatia walked up the road from
the Tholos, where she spent her morning hour in
communion with the gods. She carried a satchel containing
her golden bowl and the ritual gown and sash she would
wear in the temple. Before she could enter the temple, she
cleansed and purified herself in the Castalian Spring
located between the lower sanctuary of Athena and the
higher Temple of Apollo.

Hypatia bathed in the waters cascading down the
mountainside from the top of Mt. Parnassus, allowing the
sacred waters to purify and infuse her with inspiration.
Once dried off, she dressed in a pure white gown,
anchored at the shoulders with golden laurel leaves in
honor of Apollo. She tied a ruby sash at her waist and wore
a deep purple cloak around her shoulders, for it was cold
in the small room where she gave her prophecies. She tied
her hair high upon her head, held with a long strand of
pearls. After she tied her leather strapped sandals around
her ankles, she was ready to walk the slanted marble-

paved Sacred Way, past the treasuries and statues, and up the steep hillside to the base of the Temple of Apollo. Inscribed on the temple walls at the entrance were the words *Know Thyself*.

Instead of entering through the main entrance on the ground level, she walked to the southern side of the temple. A private stairway led to the lower level, where she entered a small room approximately 9'x12', known as the *adyton*, meaning inaccessible, or do not enter. On the stone floor of the adyton was a twelve-inch-deep stone platform, specific for the use of the Delphic Oracle. It was a 4'x4' section of stone with three indentations chiseled into the platform's surface for the legs of the iron tripod upon which she sat. The platform held the seat in place and gave her greater stability while sitting on the high, throne-type chair. The tripod signified divine revelation, as a symbol of the high status of worldly and prophetic power.

On the platform in front of the tripod at her feet was the Omphalos Stone, flanked by two golden eagles. Someone had painstakingly drilled a four-inch-diameter vertical hole thirty inches through the center of the Omphalos Stone, and down through the four-inch stone platform beneath it. The opening allowed ethylene gases to rise into the Oracle's chamber from the ground beneath the temple's foundation. The gases, called *pneuma* - meaning breath of life, spirit, and soul - directly correlated to the breath, spirit, and soul of Apollo.

Under the temple, the Kassotis Spring joined at the intersection of the two faults - the Delphic Fault and the Kerna Fault. Engineers re-routed the sacred Kassotis Spring to flow through a channel carved along the surface of the stone platform between the tripod and the Omphalos Stone at the Oracle's feet.

Ethylene, methane, and ethane gasses emitted through the waters of the spring. Breathing the gasses induced the Oracle to enter a trancelike state. She occasionally chewed on laurel leaves, which induced a psychotropic effect. Prior to giving the prophetic rites, she was required to drink water from the sacred Kassotis Spring. She filled her golden vessel with the spring water, and gave her prophecies by peering through the water in the bowl.

A rock wedged into the top of the Omphalos Stone acted like a stopper, allowing the Oracle to control the level of sweet-smelling gasses flowing into the adyton. She did not remove the stone until the seventh day of the month, when she entered the adyton. As she left her day's work, she plugged the opening again to allow the gasses to build up until she returned on the 7th day of the following month.

Those who sought her prophecy brought offerings of many kinds, mostly tremendous golden treasure, to gain the favor of Apollo. The Oracles before her demanded a sacrificial offering of an animal before the patron could enter the adyton. However, being a woman of great power as the High Priestess of the Temple of Apollo - the Delphic Oracle - Hypatia declared all life sacred. She would no longer allow such barbarism and brought animal sacrifice to a halt. Because she honored their lives, animals naturally gravitated toward her and surrounded her in protection.

Some people traveled hundreds of miles, hoping to meet with the Oracle. Anyone, rich or poor, Greek or foreigner, could confer with the Oracle as long as he or she gave an appropriate offer to the god Apollo, according to his or her means. It was a form of tithing, but as it had ever been in all of history, those who offered greater riches were the first to speak with the Oracle, while those of lesser means stood in long lines, awaiting lottery selection.

Available only on the seventh day of each month, from *Bysios* through *Apellaios* - March through November - Hypatia would give readings to those fortunate enough to be chosen. The remainder of patrons always had the option to return the following month.

Hypatia sat on the tripod with a stem of laurel leaves in her hair to honor Apollo. She held the golden bowl, filled with the sacred water from the Kassotis Spring that flowed beneath her feet. She had already uncorked the Omphalos Stone, allowing the pneuma of gasses to fill the room with its sweet scent. Draped over her shoulders was her cloak, for it was cold and clammy in her small 9' x 12' sanctuary. There were no windows - only torchlight illuminated the walls of gray stone that surrounded her. A fabric drapery separated Hypatia from the priest and the patron who stood on the other side of the makeshift wall.

For the generations of Oracles before her, the priest would translate the Pythia's ecstatic ravings for the patron. Often what was said, or sometimes screamed, made no sense, so the priest served as a translator. However, Hypatia was much more pragmatic, preferring a more down-to-earth approach. Rarely did the priest need to act as an intercessor in her behalf, but she appreciated his presence, for he also acted as a guard, protecting her from some who wanted to take advantage or bring her harm.

The first patron of that day entered the adyton. Hypatia

listened for the question. "I am called Tyrion. I travel the sea as a tradesman from port to port, trading many wares. I have everything I could ever want, for great wealth is mine. However, great Oracle, I am coming into a time in my life when I no longer need material gain. No satisfaction does it bring me. There must be something more. I speak many languages and am well educated. During my travels, I obtain papyrus scrolls of written teachings, some from ancient days far into the past. In the dark hours of night's stillness, I find myself entranced in my reading, sometimes until the break of day. It leaves me in wonder. Sacred Oracle, please advise me about a direction that will lead me to happiness. I desire so much more than earthly pursuits."

She sat in stillness while looking into her golden bowl, receiving from Apollo the needed guidance to serve her patron. Then she spoke: "For as long as you depend solely on your human mind, you will receive only human results in return, which often is comprised of doubt and limitation. However, you are to journey to a different port, to that of the heart, which is endless in adventure. The heart is where you join with the gods, finding the extraordinary wonder of magic that only occurs when in such union. This journey, should you decide to completely accept and commit to the changes you must make, will lead you to become a great philosopher. The knowledge you have obtained of the world's varied ways, along with your education and wealth, will enable you to bypass time, arriving at gnosis in short order, which is necessary for your enlightenment. This is your new path and purpose. In turn, you will be of substantial influence to many people, wherever you adventure. I now give you the name Iaeiros, meaning *whom*

God enlightens. Go now, Tyrion Iaeiros, sail the seas of the Greater Mind and meld with higher wisdom, and be a grand influence in the world for the betterment of all."

"I am ever grateful, great Oracle. In my travels, I will spread the word of your generous nature. From my heart I give thanks to you and to the god, Apollo."

Over time, many heard the word of Tyrion Iaeiros, which made its way back to Hypatia, who was greatly pleased to know of his successes and influence.

The next patron who came forth was a woman. "I am called Zoe, great Oracle. It is love that I seek. I have had two husbands, both of them now dead. The first was a sailor who succumbed to the sea. The second, a stonemason, killed while building a temple not unlike this one. A column fell on top of him while he was working at its base. He never suffered, for death came instantly. I am still young and desire a family. Can the god Apollo help me?"

Hypatia saw for Zoe a life of tremendous possibility. The Oracle spoke to her with clarity. "First, you must cleanse yourself of these other men. Go to the white sands at the edge of the Gulf of Corinth. You are to spend three days in the blue waters on the seashore. There the sun shall cleanse you. The god Apollo is the god of the sun. He will purify you by day. At night, you are to spend your time sitting still in silence.

"During these three days, you must fast, taking in nothing but honey water. This is yours to do alone. No others are to be with you. You must take heed, for this may sound easy, but it is not. In the dark night and the silence, your demons will emerge. Fear will arise, causing you a great desire to flee. If you do, you will not meet another of significance. Until you clear yourself of these other men, no others will come to you, other than fleeting moments of meaningless encounters.

"The man of your dreams is dreaming of you in return. You must make him welcome, first by purifying yourself, for you will then become a maiden vessel filled to overflowing. Then you will live in astonishment of what occurs. If you follow my direction, you will both live out the rest of your days surrounded by your children and your children's children. Joy will be yours."

"Oh thank you, great Oracle. To you and the god Apollo, we will dedicate our marriage."

"Live and love well, Zoe."

She served nine more patrons before the sun was at its zenith. Apollo was pleased. Hypatia took time to replenish with food and drink. Eleven more patrons followed. It had been a wondrous day of prophecy. Hypatia was pleased with the variety of people who came to her. She believed what came through her, as an offering to them, was indeed sent from the God Most High, and from the god Apollo. However, the last reading she gave was one that she would never forget.

Much gold was paid in advance for the prophecy she was about to give. The wealthy patron was a powerful youth, tutored by Aristotle from thirteen until sixteen years of age. Aristotle educated him in geometry, astrology, and medicine, of which he was quite astute. He learned all things Greek and developed the attitude that everyone was a barbarian, other than those of Greece. However, it was his idea to merge foreigners with those of his country of

Macedon, northern Greece, to create new generations of warriors and citizens loyal only to him.

Aristotle also taught him ethics, self-control, and self-denial. The result of these disciplines taught the youth to give generously, keeping only a modest amount for his immediate needs. He regimented himself in diet and fitness, and was cautious of his relations where sex was concerned. What interested him most, of all his studies, was Greek poetry, especially the works of Homer. He fashioned his life after Homer's Achilles. His soldiers knew him as Alexander the Great.

At the age of 16, recently named Regent by his father, King Phillip II of Macedon, Alexander had no choice but to do battle with the rebels of the Thracian tribe of Maedi. He assembled an army, conquering the Maedi and renaming the city Alexandropolis, after himself. His responsibility of Regent ended his education with his most notable tutor, but not before Aristotle insisted that he meet with the Delphic Oracle.

Hypatia sat on her tripod awaiting the next patron to enter the adyton. The sun would soon fall below the mountain's crest, and she had spent the day breathing the sweet vapors of the pneuma rising from beneath the Omphalos Stone. She was deeply entranced and perhaps not as alert as she had been earlier in the day.

She immediately felt the young man's powerful presence, even though she could not see him. Her shoulders tensed, and she felt her heart constrict, while the hair on her neck raised a strong warning to be cautious. Without seeing him, she already knew who he was. The vision of what he would become directly entered her mind.

His words, not spoken in reverence of her position as the most powerful of all Oracles, were a display of arrogance beyond self-assurance.

"Pythia, I am called Alexander III of Macedon. My father is King Phillip II of Macedon. The one you know as Aristotle advised me to come to you. Until recently, he was my tutor. I have come here for you to confirm that I will soon conquer all lands to the edge of the world."

Hypatia was stunned. No one yet had the audacity to dictate what she was to tell him. What would truly be the reason for coming to her in the first place? However, this young man endeavored to display his superiority in every way. She took a deep breath and gathered herself as she peered through the sacred waters of her golden bowl. Through her mind, she asked Apollo to reveal what she was to know on behalf of this young warrior. The power of the golden bowl struck her body like lightning. The life vision of Alexander spilled out into the waters with a future prophecy, difficult for Hypatia to fathom.

He stood before her at the age of sixteen, but soon he would prevail in his first conquest, and several would follow in the next four years. His father, Phillip, soon to be assassinated, would elevate Alexander to the throne of Macedon by the age of twenty. Over the following thirteen years, he would prevail over her homeland of Greece, conquering Thebes and burning it to the ground. Six thousand Thebian citizens would perish, and thirty thousand more sold as slaves, clearly sending a message to the remainder of Greece to submit to his rule. Not once would he lose a battle, conquering Asia Minor, Levant, Egypt, the Persian Empire, Mesopotamia, Assyria, Central

Asia, and parts of India. In addition to inheriting the kingdom of Macedon, Alexander would be named Lord of Asia, Shahanshah of Persia, King of Babylon, Hegemon of the Hellenic League, and Pharaoh of Egypt, where he was deemed the son of Zeus Ammon, the providential ruler of the world. At this point, he himself would truly believe that he was a god.

From the Gulf of Corinth to the Himalayas, and from the Adriatic Sea to the Indus River, Alexander would overtake all. He would name over twenty cities after himself, the most notable being Alexandria, Egypt, which he would never see. He would inject Greek customs into every land he conquered. Greek would become the international language, because it was one of the few languages written. So many other spoken languages had not yet developed into record.

His excessiveness eventually would lead to his ruin. Several people plotted against his life, some his own military leaders. Although Alexander prided himself on his varied means of self-control, his desire for wine was his undoing, with speculation that it was the primary cause of his death. His life would end at the young age of 32, the result of a long night of drinking. Several factors were involved, making it difficult for Hypatia to know, but she believed poison would be the cause of his death.

It was rare that Hypatia saw such detail in a prophecy. Not only did it tell the life of Alexander the Great, but also it revealed his influence on the future of civilization. She saw the hundreds of thousands, from many different countries, forced into slavery and servitude against their will. It was bloody and horrible, difficult to fathom.

Hypatia did not want to give the young man any satisfaction of knowing all this in advance.

"I cannot clearly see your destiny and have no comment for you at this point in time," she said. "Return to me in the future, and perhaps I will be better able to have answers for you."

In a fit of rage, Alexander forcibly tore the curtain from the ceiling, which was the only barrier that separated them. He was furious that she would not succumb to his demand to tell him he would conquer the world. The priest frantically followed and tried to wedge himself between Hypatia and the angry young prince. Alexander shoved the priest aside, knocking him to the floor. He seized Hypatia by the arm and pulled her off the tripod that tumbled off the granite platform, its bronze legs entangled in her gown. She screamed in terror.

"You will tell me what I desire!" he demanded, grabbing her by the hair and dragging her up the stairs.

"Unhand me now!" she cried. "You are unconquerable!"

They stumbled outside the temple, and he threw her to the ground. Alexander looked at her with rage with his one blue eye and the other black. "I now have the response I came to hear!" The short, blonde-haired, and oddly fair-skinned future warrior-king stomped away like a little boy in a bad temper tantrum.

Many who stood in line awaiting the Oracle's prophecies watched in horror. The priests came out of the temple to comfort her. She lay on the ground in a heap, crying, certainly from the abuse, but more from the shock of the vision she saw. The world as she knew it was about to transform beyond her imagining, and she could do nothing to change it.

Sophia suddenly awoke with a start, still feeling the pain of the assault. She ran her fingers through her hair, expecting her scalp to be sore. Then, she realized that she just returned from a dream of her past life as the Delphic Oracle. She took a deep breath, relieved that she was back in the present day.

As Sophia stretched her arms and legs, she sat up on the edge of the bed, exhausted and quite sure that the wild journey into her past had allowed her very little rest. At the same time, she felt rejuvenated, because she gained perspective. Her world was tame compared to what she had seen in her vision. Nothing that occurred in the last several years matched what she had seen in her past lives. Sophia breathed a great sigh of relief, knowing she would simply start another day, grateful for the life she was living.

The greatest gift she received was the answer to the question that had plagued her for months. Know Thyself was etched into the wall of the Temple of Apollo, and evidently the words were imprinted in the depth of Hypatia's memory. Sophia recalled her dying father saying those very words during her final conversation with him. She now knew why it became such an obsession for her to seek understanding of its meaning.

Hypatia, the Delphic Oracle, had read that simple, yet

profound statement engraved upon the wall of the temple for the many years she served, and she lived its philosophy her entire life. It remained in the depths of her soul's consciousness for over two thousand years. Sophia's father must have called forth those two words from somewhere deep in his past as well.

Some say, in past life experiences, one travels with some of the same souls through many lifetimes. She wondered if perhaps she and her father had some type of relationship in Ancient Greece. She felt a sense of release, having now made the connection of that poignant statement of those two words, *Know Thyself,* which formulated her life's journey and would remain her spiritual mantra.

CHAPTER
Twenty~four

When they resumed their relationship for the fourth time, Sophia told Michael about her desire to travel to Delphi and Santorini, Greece. She didn't know exactly how he might respond, but his answer was unexpected. He gave her an odd smile, as if he already knew she wanted to go there. "I'm in," he simply said. "When do you want to go?"

October was only a month away, so they decided to wait until spring, as advised by White Buffalo. Michael took charge of making the reservations, but he could not decide which time was best, so Sophia used her etched amethyst pendulum to ask the deeper questions beyond her capability of thought. She found that the pendulum, intended as a divination tool, was a good device for deeper inquiry, specifically when asking about future events. It never failed her.

Sophia made the affirmative statement, "April is the optimal time for us to travel to Greece." The pendulum swung to the left, indicating *no*. "March is the best month for our trip to Greece." The pendulum swung to the right. They planned to travel for two weeks. According to her pendulum, mid-March was the best time. Just to be certain, she made the same inquiry several times, receiving the same answer each instance. Michael made the reservations for their departure on the 18th of March, with the return date on the 30th. Decision made.

The week before they planned to leave, labor strikes broke out in Greece, shutting down the airports and interrupting commerce. Michael considered postponing the trip, but Sophia suggested they be patient and wait. Two days before their scheduled departure, the strike ended and the Athens airport re-opened.

They flew from Denver to Washington D.C. for a two-hour layover before boarding a flight to Frankfort. From there they would fly to Athens. Just as their plane began to board at Dulles, Michael and Sophia parted ways for a restroom stop before the long flight to Germany. What followed was a classic Sophia & Michael moment straight out of a script from *I Love Lucy*.

Michael never took longer in a restroom than Sophia did, so when she came out and didn't find him waiting, she thought he probably walked on down to their gate. She went to find him. In this case, however, Michael *did* take longer in the restroom, and when he came out, he waited outside the women's restroom, believing he *never* took longer.

In the meantime, Sophia arrived at their gate, still looking for Michael. The plane was fully boarded by then, and the United gate official announced both Michael and Sophia's names, warning that the flight was about to depart. Sophia asked the gate official to hold the plane, and she ran back down the terminal. From a distance, she saw Michael standing outside the women's restroom, blankly staring at the door despite the fact he had been waiting more than twenty minutes.

Sophia put her fingers to her lips and blew her shrill, not-so-lady-like whistle. That got his attention - and everyone else's, as well. She motioned for him to follow, and they ran to the gate, laughing all the way. They breathlessly boarded the plane, receiving several annoyed stares from a few of their fellow passengers as they took their seats. They may not have been a married couple, but they certainly acted like one...

Unusual circumstances filled the entire trip, beginning the day they visited the Parthenon in Athens. Sophia drove their tiny foreign rental car, and Michael navigated, using his trusty GPS. The Parthenon was about twenty miles from their hotel, with the majority of the drive along a busy highway. She drove about 80 mph, yet cars passed by as if she was driving in reverse gear. Motorcyclists weaved between the cars at speeds exceeding 100 mph. The mortality rate for drivers in Greece was the highest of any European country, and Michael reminded Sophia of that fact every two to three miles.

The ride to the top of the Acropolis, where the Parthenon was located, was at first highlighted by a drive through the streets of Plaka, an historic neighborhood of Athens where many ruins remained from the Roman occupation of 146 B.C.E. to 330 A.D. The one-way road was narrow and congested with cars parked halfway onto the sidewalk, tipping inward from both sides of the street. At one point, Sophia squeezed her eyes shut in anticipation of scraping the next car they passed. Fortunately, she missed, but Michael did not pass up the opportunity to mention the

Greek highway mortality statistic again.

Sophia believed the Greek gods were protecting them, but Michael invoked a few Irish leprechauns from his neck of the ancestral woods – just for good measure. They followed the narrow labyrinth of cobblestone roads, which led to the top of the citadel.

Parking at the base of the monument was practically impossible, with cars and tour buses wedged into any available empty space on the pavement. Logic and reason obtained its beginnings in ancient Greece, but something was lost in translation for public parking in Athens. Because mathematics also originated in Greece, the hypotenuse of the tour busses triangulated with smaller cars would have made Pythagoras proud. There was no symmetry, no order, and no way out for many cars stuck in the center of the lot.

However, nothing would stop nor intimidate Sophia. Marking the only available parking space was a sign, "Police Only," as stated in both English and Greek. She took it as an invitation. When they returned to the car after their tour of the Parthenon, several other drivers also deemed themselves police for the day. Athens police, they decided, had no better luck finding a spot to park than tourists.

They found the Parthenon an astonishing sight. Among the greatest cultural monuments in the world, and one of the few buildings of Classical Greece still in existence, the Parthenon has remained the definitive example of ancient Greek architecture. The skill and ability to design such a massive architectural achievement in the 5th century B.C.E. seemed unfathomable by modern standards.

In 438 B.C.E., the Parthenon was completed and dedicated to Athena, the patron of Athens. The building, 228' x 101', was constructed of limestone, with the fluted columns carved out of Pentelic marble transported nearly ten miles from Mount Pentelicus. The cost of construction was an exorbitant expenditure of 489 silver talons. A talon weighed approximately 75 pounds - the amount of silver needed to pay a month's wages for a 200-man crew upon a *Trireme*, the warship of Ancient Greece. Michael calculated the current market value for a silver talent would be worth $300,000 U.S. dollars, translating the cost to be nearly 147 million dollars to build the Parthenon in the present time.

Eight Doric columns were constructed on each end of the building, and seventeen on the sides, equaling forty-six outer columns with twenty-three in the interior. Each line of the Parthenon's architecture intentionally curved inward, designed to create an optical illusion of straight lines from one's point of view at ground level.

Originally, the Parthenon, used as a treasury, held a massive forty-foot statue of Athena made of ivory and 44 talents (2400 pounds) of gold, most of the treasury used on the statue itself. The statue of Athena was removed by Romans in the 5th century. In the late 6th century, the Parthenon housed a Christian Church to the Virgin Mary. Ottoman Turks took over the building in the 15th century and changed it to an Islamic mosque. In 1687, a Venetian mortar round fired into the interior of the Parthenon, where a Turkish gunpowder magazine was stored, which destroyed the roof and interior of the building, including six columns on one side, and eight on the other.

Also on the Acropolis was the Erechtheion, constructed entirely of white marble with friezes in black limestone. The Caryatids were supporting columns carved in the likeness of beautiful Greek maidens, each carved individually with a different face, hairstyle, and stance in classical feminine Greek drapery. The Erechtheion was originally dedicated to Athena and Poseidon. Throughout its history, it was a burial place, an altar, church, palace, and a harem.

Sophia was in her element, taking photos for her paintings and drawings. She had an affinity for animals, and she felt right at home at the Acropolis, where dozens of dogs laid in the sun and freely wandered the grounds. Atop the Acropolis, Sophia and Michael enjoyed a 360-degree view of the sprawling city of Athens. Most of the architecture of the city was comprised of four- to five-story white buildings tightly packed together like sardines. There were narrow streets, and very few trees or parks in between. Athens was a massive city of shallow white buildings, with a beauty of its own, flowing over the hills and down toward the sea.

The following day, they left Athens. Michael continued to navigate while Sophia drove over 100 miles northwest to Delphi. The roadside billboards, all in Greek, reminded them of their vulnerability. Some of the words on the signs were over 25 letters long. *It's all Greek to me* made perfect sense, because neither could read the Greek alphabet. Michael used his trusty GPS to guide them to their destination of Aracova, a mountain town near Delphi, but even without his GPS, Michael seemed to know his way to their mountain destination.

Aracova resembled a traditional Italian hillside village. Terraced cobblestone streets on the steep hillside of Mt. Parnassus added to the charm of 14th century buildings nestled between the more contemporary three- and four-story white stucco structures. Wooden shutters flanked windows with a view of the valley below, while French doors opened onto tiny verandas bordered by wrought iron railings. The red tiled roofs in contrast to the gray-green of the surrounding olive trees made a beautiful complement of color.

As they drove through the smaller villages, they noticed mostly men socializing in public while smoking and drinking at the small cafes and bistros along the main road. As they approached Aracova's village center, a bit of Colorado welcomed them as they observed skiers from Mt. Parnassus gathered together for après ski cocktails at an outdoor plaza. On the narrow road in front of the plaza, several buses engaged in a standoff with the tourist traffic coming from Delphi to the west. Dozens of vehicles lined up along the road, and no one was able to back their cars to allow the other to pass. Both sides inched along, nearly scraping doors and mirrors while a few brave volunteers stepped into the road and directed traffic. It was quite the event for the elderly Greek men in their flannel caps, who lined up on the edges of the sidewalk to watch the spectacle. After forty-five minutes, Michael and Sophia finally navigated through the traffic jam and began an epic search for their hotel.

Michael made a reservation at a hotel in Aracova, but his trusty GPS was failing him. So steep were the inclines and switchbacks on Mt. Parnassus, the GPS could not differentiate the roads. At one point, Michael directed Sophia the wrong way up a one-way road, much to the chagrin of an oncoming motorcyclist coming swiftly toward them. He waved his arms wildly and yelled something in Greek that they guessed was not, "Welcome, lovely Americans!"

Sophia angrily turned the car around, and in one of the few times she ever became frustrated with Michael, she said, "So, what's your GPS say now!"

After several more wrong turns, narrow escapes, and snide comments, they finally found their hotel, a lovely traditional Greek inn not far from Delphi. They were surprised to discover they were the only guests in the 400-room hotel because the tourist season started on Easter weekend, still three weeks away. Not only was the hotel owner happy to have paying guests, he gave them the best room on the top floor overlooking the valley to the west.

That afternoon, they took the winding drive to Delphi along hairpin turns, at times waiting for flocks of sheep to cross the road. The mountainside was peaceful, with endless acres of olive trees for many miles. The only sounds were distant bells clanging from the goatherds up along the hillside.

As they drove around the bend, Sophia caught her breath when she first spotted the Temple of Apollo on the rise above them. It seemed so familiar to both of them, for Sophia did not yet know of Michael's affinity for Delphi. So caught up in her own reverie, Sophia paid little attention to Michael's experience. She loved history and antiquity, but even the magnificence of the Acropolis did not move her in the same way as the Delphic ruins.

They spent the late afternoon exploring the lower level of the ruins at the Temple of Athena Pronaia. Before walking through the site, they stopped at a little souvenir shop at the entry to the grounds. The shop proprietor was an elderly man who had owned the shop for decades. Many of the trinkets had been there nearly as long. Sophia found herself charmed and tremendously intrigued by the man.

She could not speak Greek, except to say please – *parrakallo*, and thank you - *efkaristo*. He spoke very little English, but they had no difficulty communicating. Sophia and Michael were thirsty after their drive, so they decided to have a Coca Cola, which to Sophia was the American nectar of the gods. The man sold Coke in 8-ounce glass bottles no longer found in the U.S. He invited them to sit outside on the veranda, where they could see the Temple of Apollo on the hillside.

They sat at a small wrought iron table in matching cafe chairs. The proprietor served them in the tradition of formal European hospitality, with a white towel laid over his left forearm and carrying a small round tray with two glasses and two bottles of Coca Cola. He poured the soda into the glasses and left Sophia and Michael to enjoy the view. There, at the shop, they also bought their entry tickets to the Sanctuary of Athena and some Greek worry beads often used in prayer and contemplation. They also purchased several bottles of ouzo to take back to friends in the States - at least that was their initial intention.

The Tholos, at the Sanctuary of Athena Pronaia, which meant *before the temple of Apollo*, displayed its distinctive round architecture with a partial reconstruction of a few columns showing the detail and scale of the original building. Sophia felt a sense of awe as she stood before the Tholos remains, seeing in her mind's eye its beauty and grandeur when it once stood in full splendor. She humbly remembered herself as Hypatia, sitting inside the tiny round room as the Oracle, praying to the god Apollo.

As with most temple sites of the last several thousand years, the feminine, round temple was located below the masculine, rectangular temple. The atmosphere of the entire site was much gentler than the grounds of the Temple of Apollo, located a half mile up the hill.

Later that day, they wandered through the shops in the small village of Delphi. Sophia would fondly remember a tiny grocery store owned by a very old widow who wore the traditional mourning garb of a floor-length black dress and a black kerchief over her head. When Sophia met the woman, she looked deeply into her eyes and saw years of pain, loss, and a lifetime of stories. They shared a kind exchange of heart that remained with Sophia.

Later, they bought a plaque with a copy of the only artwork ever found depicting the Oracle, seated on her tripod, draped in a long gown with a stem of laurel in her right hand, while looking into a bowl of water. King Aegeus stands before her, awaiting prophecy.

That evening, Michael and Sophia enjoyed great food and wonderful hospitality at a restaurant in the center of the town of Delphi. Later, while sitting under the stars on their hotel balcony, they decided to open one of the half-pint bottles of ouzo intended for their friends in the States. Upon further examination, they opened a second bottle. Their tolerance of alcohol was much greater at the low sea level of Greece than when they were home in the Mile High City of Denver. The licorice flavored drink went down very easily, one half-pint at a time, as they decided their friends might not care for ouzo anyway. At least, Michael concluded, what they didn't know wouldn't hurt them.

The hotel provided a breakfast fit for royalty, serving varieties of bread, scrambled eggs, Greek olives, cheese, ham, sausage, and beverages. A big cup of coffee was the only thing missing. In Greece, coffee was either instant Nescafé or the Greek version thick with sugar and spices, and served in a demitasse cup that Michael couldn't get his big finger in. They both lamented over how could they possibly get their caffeine fix a quarter cup at a time.

They spent their first morning at the Delphi Archeological Museum. Few of the antiquities remained for display in Delphi after centuries of plundering the sacred site's many treasuries and artworks. The majority of the statues, frescoes, and art are displayed in museums throughout Europe, mostly Germany, Paris, Rome and London. What little remained in Delphi were remarkable works of art and craftsmanship from well over 2500 years before.

After touring the museum, Michael and Sophia found a table on the outdoor plaza to enjoy a flavored ice. Cats roamed everywhere, under the tables, on the seats, and all over the mountainside at the temple site. One tiny calico kitten came up to Sophia. Unable to ignore this precious being, Sophia picked her up and placed her on her lap, only to find that the kitten was pregnant. She could not have been much older than six months and still quite tiny, but her little belly was swollen, not far from the time for her to give birth. The kitten relished the attention as Sophia scratched her behind the ears while she tenderly held her. She wanted to bring her back to the States, but that was not possible. Sophia left the kitten with a silent prayer, blessing her to have an easy birth and healthy kittens.

Michael suggested they wait to tour the ruins of the Temple of Apollo until later, after the tour buses were gone. Before they toured the temple, they stopped by the Castalian Spring, where the Oracle bathed in the sacred waters prior to her walk to the temple. Water still flowed from the top of Mt. Parnassus as it had 2800 years earlier. Sophia felt an affinity for the spring, recalling from her dreams that she bathed there numerous times in the past. An enormous olive tree stood at the edge of the spring. Perhaps it was a mere sapling at the time when she was Hypatia.

Upon entering the plaza at the base of the temple site, Sophia was surprised to find the same tiny calico kitten she earlier held on her lap five hours before. Cats were all over the mountainside, but only the little kitten greeted them at the plaza entrance. The kitten had walked all the way from the museum, half a mile away. Sophia thought of her as the cat ambassador, waiting to greet them before they made their trek up to the temple site. The tiny kitten stretched her neck sky-high to receive a scratch on the head from Sophia. One of the Greek women volunteers sat nearby and laughed, watching the kitten's response. The people who worked there left plates of food and many bowls of water for the dozens of cats packed together like a cat conference. Cats made their home on the steps, upon the ruins, and along the pathways. They were all healthy and tame. None appeared to be feral. It was evident that they were greatly loved and well cared for.

Michael and Sophia made their way up the steep steps toward the temple. Sophia did little research on the Oracle before they left the States. She wanted to naturally experience why White Buffalo advised her to visit the famous site. They walked past the ruins of the many treasuries, originally meant as storehouses of a fortune in golden treasure and art left by neighboring cities and countries in exchange for the prophecy of the Oracle. Pillaging of the treasuries, many times over, occurred for centuries. Very little wealth remained, and yet Delphi continued to be the most sacred of all the temple sites of the Gods throughout Ancient Greece. For Sophia, visiting Delphi had very little to do with ancient statues and antiquities, but rather, it was about being in the sacred atmosphere that permeated the site for nearly three thousand years.

Sophia and Michael walked past the Treasury of Athenians. The city of Athens completely restored the treasury building on the site, displaying the original beauty and architecture of Delphi from 7th Century B.C.E. The remains of other buildings on the temple site were scattered about, over the centuries either destroyed by fire and earthquakes, or plundered by the Romans following the advent of Christianity.

The treasuries stood along the Sacred Way, an uphill pathway paved in marble that zigzagged up the hill, ending at the temple terrace. Sophia enjoyed the view along the upward climb that overlooked the valley below. As she stepped upon the temple mount, she noticed to her left a wall positioned at the east end of the temple. She immediately sensed a dark foreboding feeling, later to discover that area was the altar where animal sacrifices took place. Before a patron would enter the temple to confer with the Oracle, one would give an animal, typically a goat, as a sacrificial offering to the god, Apollo, hoping to receive favorable prophesies in return.

At the center of the ruins was the rectangular foundation of the Temple of Apollo. It was there that the Oracle gave her prophecies for nearly 1200 years in the lower level of the temple. Sophia felt a sense of wonder as she walked around the temple's foundation. She knew it well. She recalled having been there centuries before. It was all too familiar.

Originally, on the wall of the temple, *Know Thyself* was inscribed. She recalled her father Patrick's last words spoken to her, not knowing at the time what he meant. Having visited the site, it now made perfect sense. It was as if her father left her a calling to discover on her own. Sophia finally came full circle, having returned to a memory of long ago, and yet the adventure leading her to understand the knowledge of her gifts became clearer. She was awakening to a newness of being as these greater dimensions revealed themselves. Yet, there was still a mystery about her life not yet answered.

Sophia felt in a daze as they walked around the temple, suddenly coming across a hidden stairway she found quite intriguing. She recalled herself as Hypatia, walking down those very stairs to enter the darkness of the adyton, the small room where she, as the Oracle, waited for her patron's request. Many people travelled hundreds of miles on foot or by sea to take a chance to consult with her. If chosen by lottery, even then they could not see her in person. The patron entered the adyton, accompanied by a priest, both separated from the Oracle by a drapery. After the patron asked their question, the Oracle answered with enigmatic impassioned ravings, followed by the priest's translation.

Sophia was too enthralled in her surroundings to notice that Michael seemed to be curiously familiar with the temple site. He climbed over the ropes surrounding the Temple of Apollo, meant to keep tourists out. Acting as if he owned the place, he wandered up onto the temple's foundation. He certainly did not consider himself a tourist. He was, after all, the first resident to have lived there over 3600 years earlier...

He built a replica of the Temple of Akrotiri for Roxana on that very site. Michael wanted to see if there was anything left of his original foundation. The stone platform on the floor of the adyton, used to engineer water flowing from the Kassotis spring, was the very same stone he placed over the intersection of the Kerna and Delphic faults. It was right where he left it.

Sophia finally noticed Michael as he studied the temple foundation. Then she suddenly saw him as Yiorgos. She was stunned as she realized that Michael's green eyes were exactly the same shape and color as Yiorgos'. Even though Michael was a foot taller and of fair complexion, his manner was identical. For a moment, she shifted and became Roxana standing in the temple he built for her. At the center, she envisioned the almond-shaped pool filling with sacred spring water that flowed from the mouth of the bronze dolphin resting on the pool's edge. Overhead, the crystal oil lamps illuminated the ceiling painted in indigo, supported by enormous columns carved from porphyry.

Questions began to arise in her mind as she shifted back to being Sophia. Why had she not noticed until now that Michael was Yiorgos? He knew how to fix most any problem. His temperament and even his humor matched that of Yiorgos'. He was the same protector, and she deeply loved this man, who was evidently her soul mate for over three millennia.

Later, they sat on the edge of the temple mount, looking out over the valley below. Sophia sat in silence and then turned to look at Michael in astonishment.

"You finally figured out who I am," he said, smiling. He put his arm around her shoulders and pulled her close.

"Why did you not tell me?" Sophia asked.

"I kept my history to myself, so you could remember yours in due time. If I told you, it may have distorted the recall of your memory."

"So, you've known all along about our past?"

"I began to recall my life as Yiorgos about the time of our third first date."

"That was over ten years ago." She shook her head. The revelation was unfathomable for her to put all the pieces in place. "All this time..."

"Why do you think I've been trying to find you since then?" he said.

"Not only have we come together four times in this lifetime, but through other lifetimes as well? So who are you in the other lives that I am just beginning to recall? Are you aware of those, too?"

"Some of them, but you will have to find out for yourself. It would be wrong to tell you who I was from the past, until you remember on your own."

"How is it that you have known about your history, and I am just now finding out who I have been?"

"That will become clear over time. I suppose my memories came back to me because I have spent years searching for my ancestry. There's another thing I have been keeping from you."

"Really! What's that?" she asked, undoubtedly exasperated.

"Now is as good a time as any to tell you – I'm one of the sages that White Buffalo told you about."

"What?" She pulled away and punched him on the arm, clearly frustrated. "I feel like such a fool! You have known all this time?"

Michael smiled and rubbed his arm. Understanding her frustration, he put his arm around her again and said, "That has been the main reason for my search for you. I have much to tell you - to teach you - to learn from you. And the greatest thing about all of this is that I am madly in love with you. Sophia, you are my beloved. What Yiorgos and Roxana had was nothing compared to the life we are just beginning."

She melted into his arms and said nothing, for she had no comeback - for once.

That night, Sophia's dreams came to life. First, she

recalled Roxana living along the hillside, sharing her life with Yiorgos, Theo, and Melissa. They created a well-rounded, family-driven, thriving community of artisans and craftsmen, philosophers and teachers, herders and olive farmers, engineers, and healers, of course.

Yiorgos' brilliance facilitated the organization of the village terraced along the hillside. Roxana's gifts drew people from far distances, many of whom decided to remain and settle in among the flourishing community. Theo grew up to be a very successful businessman and tradesman like his father. He, too, became a wise sage with powerful intuitive abilities. Melissa grew to be a beautiful woman who assumed the responsibilities of her mother, as the Temple High Priestess, and passed along her knowledge to her daughter. They all lived out their days not realizing their legacy would influence not only Greek history, but also the entire world.

Recollections from Sophia's past life as the Oracle also returned in full vision and color, like images coming into full view through the dense fog of time. She dreamt of bathing in the Castilian Spring, cleansing herself prior to walking past the grand monuments and treasuries a half mile up the hill along the Sacred Way to the temple. Flashes of memory came to her like fast forward photography with images of the thousands of people she served. Astounded at the impact of what she recalled, it was incredible to her that only one day of the month, for nine months of the year, did she serve as the Oracle. Yet, it was as if she recalled her past life to remember who she had become. The Oracle affected world decisions for 1200 years. Kingdom and country made assessments on war and policy because of her prophecies.

The lineage of the Oracle passed down to Sophia. It was humbling, yet clearly important for her to think how she could use her powers for good, now that she was beginning to understand her origins. Roxana and Hypatia's lives left a tremendous impact on the future, and so would Sophia's choices.

Sophia and Michael visited the temple site for three consecutive days late in the afternoon following the tourists' exodus. They were the only tourists present as they sat on the ancient granite blocks inscribed in either Greek or Latin. Hundreds of square miles of olive trees stretched out before them like a gray-green sea bordered by granite mountain peaks. The palpable history of nearly 3000 years of sacred Greek religious belief was still in the atmosphere, drawing thousands of tourists per year, some who came to Delphi in pilgrimage.

The theatre above the temple was still intact. Michael stood on the platform, gazing at the half circle of seats rising above. He stood where Plato and Aristotle spoke. Perhaps Michael was one of their descendants - anything was possible.

Taking photographic records later helped Sophia recall even more details of her life as the Oracle. Her name, Sophia, was of Greek origin, meaning *wisdom*. Following their visit, she felt appropriately named, finally linking her ancient history to who she was in this life. Each night, following their time spent in Delphi, her dreams filled with the imagery of two of her past lives spent there on the hillside of Mt. Parnassus. The revelation of Michael's past-life history helped her understand both of their abilities beyond her imagining. They stepped together into the greater dimensional field of eternity's vast expanse.

CHAPTER
Twenty~five

M ichael and Sophia drove back to Athens along the edge of the beautiful Gulf of Corinth. They spent the night at a hotel across from the Athens airport so they could easily catch their flight to Santorini early the following morning. When they arrived on the island, they rented a car from a friendly Greek named Markos, who would later prove to be quite an extraordinary man.

Santorini is the southernmost volcanic island among the Cyclades in the south Aegean Sea. Once called Thera, Santorini consists of layers of white, red, and black volcanic rock, including olivine and hornblende left by numerous cataclysmic eruptions over the last two million years. What remains of modern Santorini is a crescent shaped ring of five islands surrounding a 12x7-mile caldera filled by the Aegean Sea to a depth of 1300 feet. The last major eruption of the super volcano occurred 3600 years before, around 1630 B.C.E., while the most recent eruption on Nea Kameni, the larger of the two islands in the center of the caldera, occurred in 1950.

Scientists believe the eruption that caused the destruction of Thera was among the largest volcanic eruptions on earth. Hundreds of years after, Greeks inhabited the island and carved traditional cave houses into the deep hillsides of volcanic rock, as did the people of Thera before them.

In modern Santorini, the cave openings exhibit the distinctive round white exterior cement facades. Most of the traditional houses have the doors and windows trimmed in varied shades of blue, replicating the changing colors of the caldera. The charm of the traditional housing built out of the remains of the volcano's destruction is evidence that life continues. Out of death and destruction comes a cleansing in preparation for something new and life giving.

Over the centuries, Byzantines, Venetians, Ottomans, and various private families occupied ancient Thera until the island united with Greece during the Greek War of Independence in 1830. The name Santorini evolved from the Latin empire's homage to Saint Irene, constructed in the village of Perissa in the 13th century.

Michael and Sophia stayed at a boutique hotel in Oia, a northern village of picturesque traditional houses over 1000 years old, carved into the volcanic hillside facing the caldera. The interior of their hotel suite was a cave with curved cement walls painted white. Beautifully furnished with antiques, the suite had a full kitchen, bedroom suite, and a bath finished in green marble.

During their four-night stay, they dined in the village every evening and later sipped wine while soaking in the hot tub on a private terrace under the stars. A full breakfast was set out for them each morning on the terrace. From there they observed the caldera's changing colors and the effects of the volcano's swelling magma slowly rising above the water's surface. Santorini's crescent-shaped island circled around the smaller islands of Nea Kameni, Palaia Kameni, Aspronisi, and Christiana. Nea Kameni is the evidence of continuing volcanic forces that will inevitably erupt again someday.

Enchanted by the magnetic quality of the caldera, Sophia spent hours writing and painting her watercolors, watching the changing colors of the water as the sun crossed overhead. The charm of the island presented unlimited subjects to capture in her paintings. A magical appeal to the caldera left Sophia and Michael acutely aware of their own mortality. The earth was growing and expanding beneath the calm veneer of the water's surface. The caldera's mysterious nature left Sophia filled with anxious emotion, not only from the sense that the volcano could again erupt at any time, but more from her recall of the frightening time so long ago when it did.

She experienced the same affinity for Santorini that she felt for Delphi, both calling from her ancient past. She awoke before dawn in anticipation of their planned visit to the archeological site of Akrotiri, located on the southern horn of the Santorini crest.

The drive took forty-five minutes to reach the other side of the island. They cautiously drove along the winding, nearly single-lane roadways around the perimeter of the hillsides as locals speedily swerved around them, reminiscent of their drive through Athens. Contrarily, they inched their way through bumper-to-bumper congestion in Fira, the island's main town, until they reached the countryside site where the excavations were taking place. Michael was especially interested in the archeological site, because he earned his master's degree in archaeology from the Australian National University.

Still feeling the anxiety of the drive, Sophia tentatively walked along the unearthed community of ashen framework buildings. Before long, the awe of witnessing the effects of the volcano's destructive power took over as she recalled the memory of her life as Roxana, the last person to leave the island prior to the ancient eruption. As Sophia walked through the ruins, she suddenly began to sense the hard edges of her physical reality fading as she stepped from the 21st Century into the 17th Century B.C.E. and morphed into Roxana. Familiar corridors materialized from her memory as recognizable features came to life in the bustling village that emerged before her.

Children played along the narrow streets, and fishermen returned with the morning catch slung over their shoulders. A woman beat the dust from her woven rug of brilliant colors outside her home. Houses painted in shades of gold and terracotta lined the village corridors. Bold purple-red porphyry columns supported many of the balconies. The temple of Akrotiri stood on the top of the mountain, far above the village, and all was well.

Roxana was in the final weeks of her instruction to become High Priestess, yet not entirely immersed in her training. A young artist named Dimitrios caught her eye. Many weeks had passed since she last saw him, but that morning she watched him far down the passageway. Dimitrios' father was a merchant who took his three sons on trading ventures to other lands. They had just returned from a journey to Egypt, and Dimitrios brought back drawings of animals and plant life from Africa to paint in his frescoes. He worked as an artist, assuming the trade from his paternal grandfather, who was the muralist for Akrotiri before him. His work was wonderfully fresh, colorful, and inventive.

For one home, he painted an entire room of blue monkeys playing. Other walls illustrated graceful gazelles, flying swallows, flowers, or elegant papyrus plants swaying in the breeze, while beautiful young Theran maidens picked crocus on the hillside. On many larger pieces, his artwork decorated pottery with images of spirals, swallows, dolphins, and flowers. Enchanted by his beautiful depictions of animal and plant life, Roxana promised herself that one day she would also see such wonders beyond the waters of Thera.

Not expecting to see Dimitrios that morning, Roxana was delighted when she noticed him in the distance. He was just a few years older than her, and they frequently shared flirtations, occasionally stealing a glance or a smile. Roxana was infatuated with the dream that perhaps someday she and Dimitrios would marry.

But that would never happen.

Roxana continued her walk through the village to visit her grandmother, Elene, who lived in the next row of houses beyond a set of stairs wedged between the walls of two homes. Roxana took her first step up when a massive earthquake suddenly jolted the island with such devastating force that the entire stairway compressed and crushed between the supporting walls, splitting the stairway vertically and making the passage half-again as narrow. The force of the quake knocked Roxana to the ground, but she luckily escaped injury. Some were not as fortunate.

The earthquake subsided to light tremors, for the time being, as Roxana swiftly scrambled up the twisted stairway, the stone slabs at her feet in small pieces and at odd angles. She reached the village corridors, jostled around by frenzied people who screamed and chaotically ran in all directions. When she finally reached her grandmother's home, she found that no damage had occurred, nor was Elene injured. However, in several surrounding homes, walls and ceilings had collapsed and scattered into the streets, blocking many passageways. Roxana left her grandmother to see if she could be of help to anyone affected by the earthquake. She was sure that her mother was at the temple, most likely safe from harm. Her father, Nikolas, was out to sea.

She came across several men outside one of the destroyed homes. They lined up in a human chain, passing off rocks and wooden framework from fallen walls. The men were attempting to clear the area to gain access to someone trapped inside. Roxana noticed that some of the stones were painted. One of the frescoed walls of the house must have collapsed.

Not until the sun shined directly overhead did they pull a young man from the rubble. They placed him on a blanket, and four men carried him down the path just as Althaia arrived from the temple to meet them. She told the men to bring the injured man to her home and place him on a bed in the living area. Roxana ran into the house to assist her mother, only to discover in horror that the injured man was Dimitrios. He was severely wounded and unconscious, his breathing wet and shallow.

"Roxana," Althaia said, "quickly bring me a basin of

hot water, two sponges, and several clean cloths. I will also need the healing herbs and oils. You know which ones to get."

Roxana rushed to bring her mother what she requested. Althaia cut the clothes from Dimitrios' body, revealing a crushed upper torso and severely broken ribs. Both of his arms and one leg were broken in several places. The bruising over his body was so immense that he was almost entirely purple. His injuries were grave.

Althaia stepped out of the room to keep Roxana from hearing her direct one of the men. "Quickly, find Dimitrios' father and mother. Notify his brothers to come as well. I fear he will not be with us much longer." She came back into the room and found Roxana slumped onto the floor next to Dimitrios. Tears ran down through the accumulated dust from the day's events caked on her face.

Aftershocks from the earthquake continued, causing greater alarm outside, but Althaia was calm. "Roxana, I am sure this is difficult for you, but I need you to help me clean him before his family arrives." Althaia took a clean cloth, poured water into the fabric, and gently wiped her daughter's tear-stained face. She put her arms around her and held her close for a moment before Roxana proceeded to follow through with her mother's directions.

Roxana took a damp sponge and washed away the dust from Dimitrios' face, arms, and chest, and then dried him with a clean towel. She gently rubbed oil of Arnica over the bruises covering most of his body. Althaia had already cleaned his lower torso, legs, and feet. She draped a blanket over him, knowing there was nothing more she could do. Only the gods could save him.

Rinsing the dust from his hair, Roxana combed the black curls that framed his face, knowing that her dream to marry the handsome young man was no longer a possibility. Dimitrios stirred and slightly opened his eyes.

She placed her left hand on his head and her right on his uninjured hand, knowing that this would help to energize his life force through her touch.

"The house where you were working collapsed," she whispered. "The gods displayed their anger this morning, shaking our island and bringing much destruction to Akrotiri. I am sorry to say you have been badly injured."

"Your family will be here soon," Althaia said. "Roxana, bring him some wine. It will help ease his pain."

"I feel no pain," Dimitrios said. He weakly smiled and looked into Roxana's eyes.

Roxana tenderly spooned water into his mouth. Silently, she prayed to the gods to bring him healing, but she knew that sometimes healing meant that someone would be relieved from what they could no longer call life. Dimitrios' family soon arrived, and Althaia spoke with them before they came in. Roxana stepped away and stood at the back of the room with her mother as Dimitrios' family lovingly surrounded their son and brother, supporting him and each other in the best way possible. Their demonstration of grace touched Roxana.

Althaia put her arm around Roxana, so very proud of her daughter. Roxana showed much compassion for Dimitrios that day, caring for him so gently and lovingly. She demonstrated great dignity in the midst of her feelings for the young man, which made Althaia realize her daughter was ready to assume the duties of the High Priestess of Akrotiri.

Sundown approached. Roxana requested that the family allow her to speak with Dimitrios. She could see the life slipping away from him, but she had no more tears to cry. A quiet calm washed over her as she looked lovingly into his eyes with a sweet smile. Then, she leaned over, tenderly kissed him on the lips, and softly whispered, "You are my love, Dimitrios. I promise you our paths will cross again." The look in his eyes told her that he returned her love. "Go now, the time has come for you to go."

They all gathered around him. Several oil lamps lit up the room with a golden glow. She watched the life force, like golden fire, slip from his body and rise above him. She looked up into the corner of the ceiling and saw the light of his spirit briefly hover overhead and then disappear. He was gone. It was done...

As Sophia returned to the present day, the colorful buildings turned back into ashen gray ruins. Residual feelings penetrated her mind and heart of the grief left from Dimitrios' death. Tender love remained within her memory.

That afternoon, Sophia and Michael toured through the Museum of Prehistoric Thera, where they found pottery, artifacts, and frescoes of Akrotiri. One of the frescoes was one she had seen earlier that morning when she returned to her life as Roxana. The mural of lilies and flying swallows was in her grandmother's home. The relics reminded her of the simplicity of life in that earlier time. It seemed that her essence, as Roxana, was in some of the artifacts, while the soul of Dimitrios' artistry remained.

Throughout the museum, déjà vu flashed memories of mundane events through her mind - a family meal with her parents; picking crocus on the hillside; a wedding ceremony she presided over as the High Priestess; entering the temple, first to bathe in the temple pool before her daily lessons. Recollections began to unfold both in her waking moments and even more in her dreams as the days progressed.

On the third day of their stay, Sophia sat on the terrace, painting a small watercolor of Oia's traditional houses trimmed in varied blues and lavender. Michael was on a walk down the path with his camera. The small white domed facades rose in layers above the edge of the caldera, separated by painted white zigzag walkways and stairs decorated with mosaics of volcanic rock. The sun reflected off the water's surface like a million tiny diamonds. Amidst the sea of traditional cave homes was a splash of the bright blue domes of several Greek Orthodox churches.

Christofer, the owner of the hotel, approached Sophia and asked, "Do you mind if I sit and chat while you paint? I have refreshments!" He held a bottle of Santorini wine and two wine glasses.

"Oh, please do," Sophia said.

Santorini's wine was one of the great surprises of the island. Outside of tourism, this was their main industry. Wines produced from the island were exceptional because of the acidic soil. The growing season was very short - from late April to early September. Vines grew in a circular basket-type wreath, clustered on the soil's surface to protect them from the strong winds. Santorini vineyards were reputedly among the oldest in the world.

Christofer happened to be an owner of one of the vineyards. In the closet floor of Sophia and Michael's hotel suite was a round pit three feet deep and two feet in diameter, originally used to store crushed grapes for winemaking by people who lived in the caves as far back as 1000 A.D.

"I am so busy working on restoring these traditional homes," Christofer said. "It would be nice to take a break and visit."

"I would enjoy the company," she said. The wine was an exceptional sweet white wine. A pleasant westerly breeze blew in from the caldera.

Christofer was a handsome man with dark hair, brown eyes, and a medium build - about forty years old. Even though he was working, he was well dressed in expensive jeans and a crisp white shirt with the cuffs rolled back onto his forearms. Sophia could not help herself. *There is something about a man in well-fitting jeans and a white shirt. The only thing he's missing is cowboy boots and hat, with a finely tooled leather belt.* She laughed to herself. *Just because I'm on a diet doesn't mean I can't look at the menu!*

She collected herself. "Did you grow up here on Santorini?" She assumed he did not, because he possessed a polished continental demeanor.

"My mother was born here, but I was raised in the south of France, where I still keep a home. I was formally educated in London, but in the summer months I came here when I was a boy to help my grandparents, who rented these cave homes to the tourists. I inherited them and have been restoring them while acquiring more to increase my business."

"It seems like a lucrative venture."

"During the tourist season, from mid-April through November, the hotel is always full. Temperatures can get into the mid 80s during the summer months, and it is pleasant here all year around. Business slows down from December through March, so that is when I do renovations. I keep it open year-round for people who like to stay for an extended time during the winter. The rates are much lower than what I charge during the high season."

"I guess we will have to return in the off-season. I can see myself writing another book here."

"I'll offer you a great deal...one you cannot refuse."

"We'll do that!"

"You do beautiful work. Do you sell your paintings, or is this a hobby?"

"Thank you. I appreciate the compliment. Painting is a passion of mine, and some of what I do for a living. I paint, in addition to my writing and photography. I then sell my work, mostly in shows throughout the States, and now I am about to begin showing my art in Europe. I write during the months when I burn out of artistic creativity for my paintings. When I publish a book, I take a break and return to do my painting, drawing, and photography. It's a nice life. I am very fortunate."

"Where do you get your inspiration?" he asked.

"I get the most incredible subject matter for both my painting and writing wherever I go, as I meet very interesting people who are more than willing to share stories about their lives. We strike up conversations that lead to amazing revelations for them, and for me."

Sensing it was a good time to stop, she put some final touches on her painting. She rinsed out her brush and placed it on the table. Taking a sip of wine, Sophia sat back in her chair next to Christofer and placed her full attention on him. "Tell me, Christofer, what do you do when you are not running the hotel?"

"Oh, I am so occupied with my business – it fills up most of my time. I am very fortunate. I make an excellent income eight months out of the year. The remainder of the year I travel, mostly in Europe. I acquire more properties in Oia to upgrade during the winter months."

"This island seems so small. It must be hard to get help."

"Yes, good contractors are difficult to find, so I do most of the work myself. I have to ship in most everything to do the renovations. I employ a professional staff to run the property, including housekeepers, maintenance, and office assistants who are multilingual. It is more than a full-time business to maintain, but just for fun I have again taken up painting frescoes."

Sophia felt sudden warmth fill her. "Frescoes... isn't that when paint is applied to wet plaster?"

"Yes it is. When I was young, I painted frescoes – a hobby for the most part – but I made a few Euros painting walls of friends and neighbors. I have found renewed interest in painting again, so I did some in my home. It's not far from here - would you be interested in seeing them?"

"I would love to."

They took the short walk to his home, located on the top of a hill on the western edge of the village. It was a sea captain's house, originally built in the mid 1800s to view the comings and goings of sea vessels, with views overlooking both the caldera at the center of the island, and the sea to the west.

Hardwood plank flooring and white stucco walls were throughout the large home. His furnishings were antiques, similar to those found in his boutique hotel. Charmed by the exquisite surroundings, Sophia was enamored with the allure of his home, particularly when Christofer brought her into the dining room. The natural light from an overhead skylight brought every wall alive with images of plant-life, making Sophia feel as if she were in the middle of a jungle. Christofer's paintings were not unlike the frescoes of Akrotiri. The images were quite similar, except more greatly detailed in a wide array of sophisticated colors.

"Christofer, these are magnificent. You must have studied the murals at the museum for months to capture the likeness of the images. Your technique is quite similar."

"You might say that. My grandfather was a muralist - quite well known for his work. He taught me everything he knew. I got to travel quite a bit when I was a boy, and I suppose he instilled my love for the varied colors of beautiful landscapes."

"If you have any more frescoes, I would like to see them."

"Upstairs, in the master suite are some that you will most likely appreciate."

Just off the master bedroom, they entered the bathroom suite. Sophia was astounded to find the walls covered with images of lily plants with swallows flying above them. Clouds painted on the high inset ceiling appeared as if it was a summer day in Greece.

"Christofer, I don't know what to say. The papyrus is identical to that of the frescoes at Akrotiri." She paused. "Wait a minute - did you say that your grandfather was a well-known muralist, and he taught you everything you know?" She found a seat, feeling a bit lightheaded.

"Yes, I did say that."

"But we are not talking about your maternal grandfather, are we?"

"No, we are not. You catch on quite quickly... Roxana!"

She slowly rose to her feet, directly in front of him. Wide-eyed, she scanned his face, finally seeing the similarities in his features to that of Dimitrios. Then, she smiled. "I told you we would know each other again."

"Yes, and I believed you. That promise has carried me for many millennia. This is not the first time we have come together, Roxana."

"I suppose, like Michael, you cannot tell me when that was."

"Only when you recall that memory on your own will we then talk about those times."

"So, there are more lifetimes we've shared than these two?"

"There are several, in fact."

"It's nice to know that I can count on familiar souls to join me from one lifetime to the next. Is there anything else you would like to tell me?" she asked.

"You will come to know more before too long. Keep your mind and heart clear. I would suggest that you increase your meditation time. The deep silence will prepare you for what is next to come. That is all I can say for now."

"But..."

"It's time to get you back to the hotel. Michael will be looking for you."

"Thank you, but I will walk back by myself. I have a few things to put into perspective." She looked up into the eyes of the one she once knew as Dimitrios. He gently placed his hands on her shoulders and kissed her on the cheek. Sophia stood on her tiptoes to embrace him. She blushed and sweetly smiled, then slowly turned to leave the room.

As she walked back to the hotel, she remembered Roxana's thoughts of young love for the man she would never marry, and yet here he was. Perhaps in another lifetime they were able to share their life together. She just smiled at how life kept her in the wonderment of it all.

CHAPTER
Twenty~six

Other than breakfast, Michael and Sophia ate their meals at Oia's local restaurants. Santorini's tourist season did not officially begin until Easter, still two weeks away. So many restaurants were not yet open. Those that were had only a few items on the menu from which to choose. Sophia tried to order something Mediterranean. You know, she thought, when in Greece - which meant she typically ate chicken or fish with feta cheese, olives, basil, and tomatoes. She loved the simple and fresh Mediterranean fare. However, Michael was pleased to find on every Greek menu his favorite dish. For six out of the nine evening meals during their vacation, he ordered spaghetti.

Their last meal in Oia came at sundown in a small restaurant of eight tables for two, owned by a local couple. The wife worked hard, sweeping the floor and cleaning off the counters, while her husband sat in a drunken stupor at the bar. He had apparently broken into the ouzo supply ahead of the tourist rush. He did manage to rise to his feet and greet Michael and Sophia, welcoming them to a choice table at a window overlooking the caldera. He gave them menus, and with surprising coherence pointed out the five entrees the restaurant was serving that evening. He then stumbled back to the bar and almost fell before regaining his stool.

His wife stomped out of the kitchen and angrily yelled something in Greek at her husband while Michael and Sophia perused the menu, pretending they didn't hear. The woman ceased her diatribe and approached, breaking into a reasonable tone of hospitality. She spoke in English and was perfectly charming, suggesting a nice filet of sole for Sophia and a hardy Bolognese for Michael. They agreed and ordered appropriate wines at her suggestion.

The woman smiled and walked into the kitchen and relayed their dinner order to the cook, yelling again in Greek. She came back out to her husband and lowered a second boom, picking up where she left off without missing a Greek beat.

"I didn't know this place had a floor show," Michael whispered. Sophia giggled.

The rant continued for another minute, and the women then emerged with the wine, all smiles. Michael and Sophia almost broke their silence when their feisty server returned to the bar and exploded again, but they instead composed themselves as Michael proposed a toast.

"To our last night on the island of peace and serenity..."

Sophia broke into laughter as they touched glasses.

It was quite evident to them, while attempting to eat their meal in peace, the husband could not hear his wife, nor did he care.

By the time Sophia and Michael paid their check, the husband was slumped at the bar, his head hidden in his folded arms. He may have been dead - or wished he were.

The wife was on the phone, apparently expressing her continued displeasure to the unfortunate person on the other line, for she was madly shaking her free hand toward the mass of a man passed out on the counter.

She suddenly stopped her tirade to process Michael's credit card, and in a calm and pleasant voice thanked him, in English, for their business. They smiled in return as she resumed her phone call, determined to be heard by someone...somewhere.

They left the restaurant with a story to tell of unexpected Greek hospitality, and most importantly, Michael enjoyed yet another meal of spaghetti.

That final night, they soaked in the hot tub in the cool night air while drinking more of Santorini's fine wine. They sat under the stars, admiring the lights of the hillside town of Fira trickling down the steep incline to the caldera's watery abyss.

Sophia told Michael about her afternoon spent with Christofer. Of course, Michael already knew who Christofer was. It was no wonder why they stayed at his hotel out of the dozens of others on the island. Michael quickly wrapped his arms around her, "Sophia, my love, Dimitrios may have been your first love, but you and I have so much more history than the two of you ever had."

"Well, I don't know about that!" she teased. "Who knows what he and I had in other lifetimes."

"Well, I am staking my claim for you here and now. In this lifetime, you are mine. Christofer is just going to have to wait for another lifetime to have a chance to be with you, but not if I have anything to do with it."

She snuggled up inside his arms and ardently kissed him. They took advantage of their privacy under the stars to have a bit of fun before going into the room to sleep. The next few days of travel would be long ones.

At 3:00 a.m., a severe windstorm wreaked havoc on the island. If the strong winds continued, it was most likely their flight to Athens the next morning would be cancelled, hindering their plans to return to the States the following day. Her fears were confirmed when they arrived at the airport at 9:00 a.m. A rare tropical cyclone, or Mediterranean hurricane known as a *medicane*, was passing through the southern Cyclades, causing extreme storm conditions of wind and rain outside, while emotional temperatures were running high inside the airport. No flights left Santorini that day.

In spite of the obvious storm conditions making it too dangerous for small commuter planes to take off, lines formed with over 80 people in a panic, arguing with the staff at the airline ticket counter. A Greek Orthodox Priest, officially dressed in his exorasson and kalmafhion, was due in Athens for a special religious conclave that commenced that evening. He elbowed his way past others in line and was disappointed when told the same thing communicated to everyone else. Nature plays no favorites, and neither did Athens Airways. Michael and Sophia's scheduled flight from Athens to the States was to leave early the next morning. Without transportation off the island, they were going to miss their flight.

Sophia calmly stood in the middle of dozens of people all in a chaotic frenzy. She felt as if she was in the middle of a tornado, in the eye of the storm, surrounded by pandemonium. She had learned to ask herself, when facing a challenge, *What is the worst thing that could happen?* Imagining the worst helped her to realize creative options instead. From there she could take inspired action toward something better, creating momentum toward a solution.

Michael suddenly took her arm and said, "I just heard something in my heart just say that all is well and we will safely leave the island." Michael did not share such insights often, but when he did, she knew to take him at his word. There was truly nothing of concern, outside of a delay. If they missed their flight out of Athens the next morning, they would simply have to reschedule. "If nothing else," Sophia said, "we can return to Oia and stay at the hotel another night."

Just then, she noticed Markos, their rental car agent, standing at the edge of the flurry. He motioned for them to follow him. As they approached, Markos offered his hand to help pull Sophia out of the fray. When their hands touched, she suddenly shifted into the life of Roxana and saw the hand of Theo holding hers on the day they left Thera, only this time he was helping her. The pandemonium of angry passengers shifted to the chaos of the island's explosive rumbling and fumes. Roxana knew his soul well, their lives remaining forever linked. She looked into Theo's soulful eyes, and they became those of Markos again.

Sophia and Michael explained their predicament, and Markos gave them a reassuring smile. "Don't worry," he said with a wink. "This happens all the time. Come with me. I'll get you to Athens."

They followed Markos outside into the storm and

walked to his car in the airport parking lot. He and Michael loaded their luggage into the trunk. Sophia stopped to look into Markos' eyes as he opened the car door for her. Even though the storm was raging, she thought she saw a knowing glint in his gaze.

Michael sat in the passenger's seat. "So, Markos, is it a long swim to Athens?"

"Swim? No…if you're a dolphin!" Markos laughed. He smiled at Sophia in the back seat. "But if you need to escape this island in a hurry, I'd advise a boat." He winked.

Sophia got that feeling again. "And you have a boat?"

"Yes, if you want to go fishing, but I have something a bit more practical in mind. You see, there are 33 inhabited islands down here. We have as many ferries crossing these waters every day as you have taxicabs in New York. One is leaving right about now, but there will be another departing for Athens this afternoon around three."

"A ferry! Of course!" Sophia looked at Michael and jokingly said, "Why didn't you think of that?"

"I did, just now," Michael said. "With these cancelled flights, we should probably hurry to the port and get tickets."

"There's no rush," Markos said. "I'll take care of you." He threw that great smile back at Sophia again.

He took them to his home, a traditional cave house not unlike their boutique hotel suite, except much larger. Sophia was surprised to find his home appointed in elegant contemporary furnishings, all in white. On the terrace, an aquamarine infinity pool appeared to flow over the edge into the caldera. It did not make sense to her that someone operating a rental car business at the airport could live in such elegance.

Sophia looked out on the terrace and was suddenly delighted to see three goats appear near the pool. They played in the wind for a moment, and then scampered down the hill. "Oh, how cute!"

Markos offered his guests a seat in the spacious living room. "We will be safe here until the storm passes. That is one of the many advantages of living in a cave - weather poses no problems. Only our very own super volcano seems to be the challenge for us on this island. Here, we just keep floating along between the last eruption and the next."

Sophia couldn't help but shudder, remembering years of increasing terror felt by her people at the inevitability of the volcanic eruption. Markos offered some fruit, cheese, and breakfast rolls, breaking her away from the scenes in her mind's eye of earthquakes and falling ash. "Please enjoy, and if you'll excuse me for a moment, I'll be right back." He projected that infectious smile again and walked into his small office off the foyer.

Markos was a conundrum, a mystery, and a puzzle, and Sophia knew she was just the woman to solve each, but first, she and Michael dug into the pastries. Markos returned shortly with some documents and a metal box in hand. "I took the liberty to arrange for you to leave on the ferry this afternoon. It leaves the port at 3:30, and will arrive in Athens around 1:00 a.m. It's quite a long day ahead, but you will be able to make your flight from Athens in the morning."

"Wait a minute," Sophia said. "You made these

reservations for us, *before* you knew our flight to Athens would be cancelled?"

"As I said," Markos said, "these storms ground the flights all the time. Let's just say I had a hunch that you two might need my help. Now, you have a few hours on your hands, so you might as well be comfortable. I happen to know how Americans like their coffee. May I brew a fresh pot to go with your breakfast?"

Both Sophia and Michael said simultaneously, "Yes, please!"

"Oh, *god*, yes!" Sophia said again. "We haven't had a good cup of coffee since we left Colorado."

She sat on the sofa and looked through a coffee table book about the ruins of Akrotiri. She thumbed through the pages and stopped at a photo that showed the entire flight of a stone stairway, vertically cracked in two and compacted between two heavy walls made up of massive stone slabs. She suddenly recalled the earthquake while witnessing the force of nature snap the stairway right in front of her, albeit difficult to believe that she was standing there when that happened 3600 years before.

Michael sat on her right side, and Markos sat on her left, placing a tray on the coffee table with a carafe of fresh coffee, three mugs, and plenty of cream and sugar.

"I must admit I love an American mug of coffee myself," Markos said. "I have this specially imported from a great mystical supplier in the northwest region of your continent, imported here through the darkest regions of South America."

"Mystical supplier? What?" Sophia said.

"Starbucks – I get it on Amazon," Markos said with a shrug.

They had a good laugh as she thumbed through the book, looking at pictures of the ruins. Markos spoke of Plato's belief that Akrotiri was the original Atlantis, destroyed by the volcano. The story of Atlantis came from *Timaeus*, a Socratic dialogue written around 360 B.C.E.

Just prior to their trip, Sophia finished two college courses - Classical Philosophy, which included her study of *Timeaus*. The other course was The Wisdom of Islam - a study of the fundamentals of the Islamic religion. She discussed with Markos Plato's theory of Atlantis, based on a sophisticated culture of advanced engineering.

"Those theories passed down through the ages may very well have influenced Plato to believe that Akrotiri was the lost city of Atlantis," Markos said.

Of course, Sophia could see herself living in the reality from which the stories of Akrotiri became the basis for Plato's theory. Akrotiri was truly the envy of other societies as a nearly utopian civilization, which tragically ended at nature's behest, never again duplicated. Akrotiri was a stand-alone, once in a planet's lifetime anomaly, now only a legend, and Sophia, as the life of Roxana, was once a part of that legend.

Markos went on as if nothing between him and Sophia was rising to the surface. He revealed that his father had been the Greek Consulate to Egypt, where he lived for twenty-three years. He could speak eight languages, having been educated at the London School of Theology, where he received a master's degree in philosophy.

He had read the Koran nine times, nearly converting to Islam from Greek Orthodoxy, and he spoke with great authority about both the old and new testaments of the Bible. Sophia was able to keep up on most of Markos' points, for she was no novice on the topic of religion herself. Their conversation created a deep connection, for Sophia could not get the image of Theo out of her mind. There was more to Markos than she could have ever predicted, and more to him beyond the world of appearances. He seemed to know everything about Santorini, and he just happened to be at the airport right when Sophia and Michael needed him. Sophia was intrigued, to say the least.

"Markos," she said, "forgive me, but you are so extremely accomplished – I can't help but ask, why are you in the rental car business?"

Markos laughed. "We are many things in our lifetime, are we not? Or, should I say, lifetimes?"

Michael, who had barely uttered a word during their conversation, sat back with a knowing look in his eyes.

"Sophia, I must confess. I am not really a rental car guy."

"Well, that doesn't surprise me. Why would a man who is as highly educated as you rent out cars for a living?" Sophia said.

"Michael and I happen to know each other. We also have a mutual acquaintance in White Buffalo."

Sophia turned to Michael, thinking, *Maybe the Secret Sage Society was not so far from the truth.* "He isn't kidding, is he?" she said.

Michael laughed. "Just take a deep breath, honey, it'll be alright."

"So I suppose you also know Darius MacPhaidin?" she asked.

"Oh yes," Markos said. "He's one of us."

"Us?" she asked.

Michael took Sophia's hand in his, looking directly into her eyes. "My love, Markos, White Buffalo, Darius, and I are a part of a diminutive, but influential order that work collectively to help sustain and raise the consciousness of humankind."

Sophia stared at Michael. "Would you like to say that again, please?"

Markos interjected, "Those who have the insatiable need for power and greed have affected the well-being of the planet and its inhabitants for thousands of years. Small factions of people like us, knowingly and unknowingly energetically maintain, and at times, raise the frequency of lower vibrational fields to one that is higher. In that, people are better able to live in harmony and balance, as a peaceful, joy-filled community. Our presence on earth affects the field of energy, resulting in a positive outcome for many, even though they have no idea who we are or what we do. In fact, it is imperative that we are not known."

"You, Sophia," Michael continued, "are included in those who do this work naturally just by going about your day and raising the field of energy around you. You do this as God works through you, and as you. That is the most dynamic way to live, knowing that you are able to open up to your empowerment within the greater dimensional field we sometimes call God, Spirit, Great Spirit, the Universe, and the Infinite Intelligence. Because you have come to Know Thyself, as directed by your father, you allow the Divine to use you for the betterment of all. And now you are teaching others to do that as well. That is also who 'we' are."

She sat very still, taking in what they both said. "When Michael made plans to visit Santorini, he contacted me," Markos continued. "I have a friend who gave me a temporary job at her rental car company so I could meet you. I have been waiting for you to arrive. I am here to help you along your way, because you are finally arriving at who you were meant to be. Don't you see, Sophia, there are no accidents. All things work together in agreement with each other, if we let go of our resistance and allow our intuition to guide us in everything we do."

She laughed. "So, are you telling me you knew to take advantage of our inability to leave Santorini this morning?"

"I didn't know that it would happen as it did, but I knew that the opportunity to meet with you would avail itself easily. I think you know that we knew each other before, in another lifetime. We are soul-family and will ever be a part of each other's lives, just as you and Michael are so deeply connected."

"When you took my hand at the airport, I saw you as Theo, my son in another life," she said.

"Yes, I also saw us here, in Akrotiri on that fateful day, when you, as Roxana, the High Priestess of Akrotiri, assumed the role of my mother. I am also aware that

Michael was Yiorgos, my stepfather."

Sophia nodded at Markos and then laughed. "I always wanted to have a child. I just didn't think he would have a master's degree in philosophy, be able to speak eight languages, and be thirty-six hundred years old." Their laughter echoed through the cave.

"You don't look a day over three thousand," Michael said.

"The secret to longevity - vitamins, red wine, Starbucks, and a nice Cuban cigar now and then," Markos said with a wink. He took Sophia's hand and said, "I have something for you, Sophia. It is yours." From his metal box, he pulled out a leather pouch about six inches in diameter. The pouch was hand-stitched and quite old and worn. "This has been in my family for over three thousand years. My lineage comes from this island, and later from Delphi." In his mind's eye, he became Theo. "Long ago, my stepfather, Yiorgos, gave this to my adopted mother, Roxana, on their wedding day." He smiled at Sophia and Michael. "Its origin is believed to come from extraterrestrial beings that visited from outside our solar system. What you will find inside, legend reveals, is connected to other items of a similar type."

Sophia opened the drawstring and removed a small wooden box with the same carvings on its surface as the larger box that held the hourglass, given to her by Darius MacPhaidin. She smiled as she turned the box in her hands, feeling the textures and looking at the familiar elaborate pattern of interlocking circles of sacred geometry. She opened the lid to reveal inside something small, wrapped in a piece of very old sapphire blue silk.

She placed the box on the table and carefully laid open the fabric. Inside, she found a golden ring with an aquamarine oval cabochon set inside a golden bezel. Ancient etching on the band was the same as that on her golden chalice and amethyst amulet. The amulet hanging from her neck vibrated and sang out as if it were celebrating another lost piece of the ancient puzzle had returned to its rightful owner. The dome of the cave resonated with the amulet's song as golden white light filled the room. They all sat there in awe, as Sophia thought, *I never tire of the mystery!*

Michael lovingly took Sophia's left hand in his. "Allow me." He took the ring from the silk and placed it on her third finger. It fit perfectly. They suddenly became Yiorgos and Roxana on their wedding day, surrounded by loved ones on the mountainside of Mt. Parnassus, and next to them stood their son, Theo. They had come together again, united as a family of souls.

The storm had passed. The infinity pool was clear, flowing over its edges as if nothing had happened that day to disturb the even flow of water. It was nearly time to leave for the ferry, but Markos wanted to make just one more stop. He took them to the largest Greek Orthodox Church in the village of Fira. Next to the building's pristine white exterior, topped by the distinctive bright blue dome, the multi-arched bell tower rang twelve times, indicating that it was noon. They entered the round sanctuary. Patterns of polished inlaid marble covered the floors. Overhead, an elaborate crystal and gold chandelier hung from the center of the dome.

The face of Jesus, painted on the ceiling, looked over

them as if he watched everyone who entered the inner sanctum. Around the dome were the iconic stories of Jesus' life from birth to death, painted in a storyline, for most people of the era were uneducated and unable to read or write. They illustrated key moments in his history as told through colorful, detailed paintings. Sophia had toured through many Catholic cathedrals with stained glass windows that depicted the tale of Christ and the Saints, but the Greek iconography was even more meticulous.

"I wanted to share with you how painted frescoes have advanced here in Santorini," Markos said.

Again, Sophia slipped back into her memory, recalling the painted frescoes on the walls in Akrotiri that told of the lifestyle of Thera's people. She reflected upon Dimitrios' gifts of artistry - and as her first memory of sweet, young love.

"Thank you for bringing us here," she said, "I wonder, is Christofer the frescoe artist who did this work?"

"Ah, you spoke with him," Markos said.

"Yes - he and I, let's just say, re-discovered our common history, just as you and I have today."

"The discoveries of your past are just beginning, Sophia. White Buffalo started something for you when he encouraged you to travel to Delphi, didn't he?"

"And to think that you all know each other," Sophia said.

"You are our center," Markos said. "You will learn more about us soon."

"Markos," Michael said, "I think it's time we get to the ferry."

Markos drove them down the switchback road, 980 feet below Fira, to the water's edge of the caldera, where the ferry was just arriving. Markos and Michael shook hands, and then Markos turned to Sophia. "When you return, we will resume where we left off. I have much to share with you! Until then..." He kissed her on the cheek and then embraced her. Again, he was Theo and she, Roxana.

The ferry departed Santorini promptly at 3:30 p.m. It was more than an eventful ride for Michael and Sophia. They thought it curious that there was no security check prior to boarding the ferry. Trucks and cars simply drove onto the boat among hundreds of passengers carrying luggage and backpacks randomly stuffed onto shelves located on the lowest cargo level. This was similar to arriving at the Athens Airport, where Sophia and Michael were not required to clear customs or have their passports stamped. In all their worldly travels, they had never encountered such a lack of security as they had seen since arriving in Greece.

The ferry was four levels high. Upper levels had two passenger sections similar to an airplane cabin, with long rows of seats on either side of the aisle. The passengers appeared to sit in random seating, and since neither Sophia nor Michael could read the Greek printed on their tickets, they just chose two comfortable looking seats in the front row of one of the sections and relaxed in anticipation of the long journey to Athens.

Thirty minutes later, the ferry stopped at another island and took on new passengers. Two Greek women angrily approached and told Michael and Sophia that they were sitting in their seats. Although there were twenty or thirty vacant seats around them, Michael and Sophia apologized and wandered to a different section of the ferry and took two new seats. Again, they relaxed and resumed their journey for an hour this time, until they arrived at another island, approached again by two more angry Greek women.

Sophia took the diplomatic approach, while Michael bit his lip. "I'm sorry," she said. "Do you speak English?"

"I do," one woman curtly said.

"We can't read Greek, and we don't know where our seats are. Could you help us?"

The women tapped on her ticket with her long, fuchsia acrylic fingernail. "This is our seat number. You don't have a seat number, so you sit in the commons area."

"Oh, darn," Michael snapped. "I so hoped we could ride up here next to you."

Sophia elbowed him in the ribs. "Thank you," she said and then smiled, "*Efkharisto!*"

Her attempt to charm the women with one of the two Greek words she knew didn't work. The women sat and grumbled something in Greek that Sophia was certain was not, "What lovely Americans they are."

Sophia and Michael found the commons area, a food court occupied by a large crowd and very few chairs. They did not want to be there for another eight hours, so they got something to eat and went to the ship's purser to upgrade their seats. Even though Sophia and Michael were unable to speak Greek, and the purser could speak very little English, they managed to communicate well enough to get two seats that did not have any angry Greek women nearby. In fact, the friendly purser upgraded them to the fourth level premium seating for just a few extra Euros. They found only ten people seated there with a capacity of over 80. Michael suggested they go back and show the angry Greek women where they were sitting now, but Sophia talked him out of it.

They finally settled into their seats behind another couple. By then, they were very weary, and they still had a long ferry ride ahead of them. Michael settled back and tried to read his Kindle, occasionally executing what he called the 'Kindle Flop' - dozing between paragraphs and startling himself when he dropped the Kindle on his chest.

Sophia burrowed into her own reading. She couldn't help but notice that the woman in front of them was in her stocking feet. In her white ankle socks, fringed with lace, she played footsy with the man next to her, but he just sat with his feet planted firmly on the floor. *Funny, the things you notice,* Sophia thought. Michael didn't notice. He was alternating snoring and scaring himself doing the Kindle Flop.

Just then, a tall, slender man in his early thirties stuck his head through the doorway and nodded at someone in the back of the cabin. He looked oddly familiar to Sophia, and yet she had never met him before. Sophia, stunned by his striking good looks, mostly took notice of his dark energy.

Minutes later, Sophia looked up from her book and saw the very same man sitting across the aisle from the people in front of her. He calmly watched the man in the seat ahead of Michael. Sophia noticed the young man's clothes, in particular, his expensive leather coat and shoes. He kept his black curly hair and goatee neatly oiled and trimmed. The shade of his skin was quite dark, almost with a blue cast to it, accentuating his black eyes. Even his nails were well-manicured. He possessed a cultured air, that of great wealth, high education, and prestige, resulting in an intense confidence.

Sophia knew she should not meet his gaze, for he would detect her apprehension. She tried to return to her book, watching him out of the corner of her eye, when she heard her inner guidance tell her, *Go sit behind him and surround him in Light*. Again, this direction from her guidance did not make sense. Her intuition had never directed her to do such a thing. She proceeded silently to argue with her guidance. *Why should I do this?* Again, she heard the still small voice within say, *Go sit behind him and surround him in Light*. She argued back, in her mind, *I am afraid. There is such dark energy about him*. This time she heard, *You are ever protected, supplied and guided with all you need. Go sit behind him, now, and surround him in Light - before it is too late!* As she typically did when hearing the guidance three times, and specifically with a *now* attached, she followed through.

Sophia got up from her seat and told Michael she was going to sit across the aisle to meditate. This was more for the man's benefit, in case he wondered why she got up to sit behind him. Her intuition guided not to put her feet on the floor behind him, but instead upon the seat next to her. Then, unlike any other time in meditation, within seconds she fell deep into the field of stillness.

She envisioned both she and the man facing each other, looking into each other's eyes. From above, a brilliant light penetrated through the crown of her head and out of her heart, surrounding him in light. The light wrapped them in a never-ending energy spiral of swirling luminosity, connecting their souls forevermore. Then she heard *I Am! I am the light of Gaia - water, fire, earth, and air. I am the stars above and the earth below. I am one with all that has ever been and ever will be.* The light of the Divine came through her, spiritually linking them, never again to be strangers.

It seemed that she was there for hours, but it had been only a few minutes. When she came out of her meditative state, both men were gone. The woman with stocking feet stood while folding a sweater and organizing her bag. Sophia returned to her seat next to Michael, who was now enraptured in his reading.

She sat and gathered her senses, and then asked the still small voice from her mind, *Why did I have to sit behind the man? Why could I not have as easily blessed him from where I was sitting?* The answer quickly came back to her - *You know of heart math. It is its strongest within an eight-foot radius. You are a spiritual human, but most of what you do must be within the realm of humanity for it to take effect. This will be true for you until you realize that you are able to transcend your human limitations.*

She had been too far from the man to make that kind of heart connection. She knew not why her intuition guided her to surround him in light, but found that every time she thought of the man since that evening, she sent him, his family, and community great blessings.

The man who sat in front of them soon returned. It seemed that death had washed over him. The woman was happy to see him at first, but then she noticed the severe look in his eyes as he sternly held her attention. Her response then altered immediately to one of alarm. Without saying anything, they quickly gathered their belongings and left. The well-dressed young man did not return. Sophia had a foreboding feeling that something evil had just occurred. The memory of the young man stayed etched upon her mind. There was something oddly familiar about him. It would not make sense to her for another twenty-four hours.

They arrived in Athens at 1:00 a.m. quite exhausted, but they made their 8:00 a.m. flight out the next morning. Unfortunately, their flight delayed for several hours in Munich, where they sat on the tarmac with very little explanation from the cabin crew. Finally, the plane departed, and Sophia and Michael spent the nine-hour flight over the Atlantic trying to catch up on some sleep. When they finally returned to the States, they learned the reason for their delay in Germany. Terrorists had set off a bomb on a train outside of Moscow, disrupting travel throughout Europe.

Sophia and Michael finally arrived in Denver, suffering from severe jet lag after twenty-four grueling hours of airplanes and airports. Sophia could not sleep, for she could not escape the image in her mind of the man on the ferry. She suddenly remembered a dream-vision she had more than two years before. Sometimes her dreams were more like direction from Spirit - something she later knew as astral travel.

In this particular dream, she stood on a green hillside overlooking a three-story community of white stucco buildings. She was to pray for the villagers. She then found herself in a military hangar, surrounded by spirit animals protecting her. Many futuristic military vehicles parked inside the building, well advanced beyond the technology of present time. Some of the vehicle's drivers were making their way toward Sophia, but none of them seemed to notice her or the animals. They all had a look in their eyes like that of a shark - dead and lifeless.

Next, she stood in a room full of boxes of firearms. Sophia was not that familiar with the design of machine guns, but she observed a technology of computerized weapons that were a projection, far into the future. A man in the room walked toward Sophia, looking not at her, but beyond her. She was horrified as he walked *through* her, then realizing that she was there in spirit-form to bless what was occurring.

Many of Sophia's dreams were of a similar nature. She was there to bless the people and the situations in which they were involved, able to shift the energy and create a different outcome for the better. After such a dream, she was exhausted because she had not truly slept, but instead had been working in another dimension all night long.

The final part of the vision was the last and most important. She stood against a wall in a large formal room, surrounded by her animal protectors. In the middle of the room was a long oval-shaped board table surrounded by dignitaries from many nations discussing the fate of the same country Sophia already blessed. At the head of the table was a handsome man in his mid-forties, with oiled curly black hair and a goatee. He was dressed in a beautifully tailored dark blue wool suit, with a crisp white shirt and dark blue silk tie. The discussion of this enclave of dignitaries was to decide about the possible genocide of the community for which she had prayed. The leader at the head of the table was an older version of the young man Sophia had surrounded in light on the ferry.

Evidently, her task was to surround this man in light - to shift the negative circumstances in which the man was involved - energetically. Perhaps her spiritual presence in both instances modified the effect of what he was doing. When she recalled her dream from two years before, and the connection with the man from the ferry, she told Michael what had happened.

Sophia was learning not to be surprised at what Michael had to say. He was not outwardly a spiritual man, but he was just as connected as she was in his own way. Sophia cried as she told Michael what happened. He laid next to her with his big arms cradling her in safety.

"Maybe you were guided for a couple of years to go to Greece for this reason alone. That may have been the reason we needed to stay in Delphi for three days - so you could be spiritually prepared, as the Oracle. Our encounter with Markos was no accident. He had our ferry tickets already purchased for us before we saw him at the airport. I wouldn't be surprised if he knew the purser, telling him just where to seat us on the ferry. I am sure, however, Markos would not have known about the man you saw in relation to your dream, but we both know of these soul connections and their power.

"During the entire trip you were hyper-aware of everything happening around us, and that caused you to be conscious of what happened on the ferry. The windstorm on Santorini may have been part of the plan, keeping us from flying to Athens that day. Only the ferry could get us to Athens, and then no matter where we sat, we had to move until we sat on the top level. It seems to me that everything fell into place for us to be there so you could surround the man in light. You might have saved a nation and their future. You probably will never know the effect you had by saying yes to taking this trip to Greece."

Only a day after they returned, the Eyjafjallajokull volcano in southern Iceland erupted, causing all air travel in Europe to come to a halt for the following two weeks. Sophia, again, was grateful for having trusted her pendulum to help guide them to travel on the right dates for their trip. Looking back on those two weeks, there was nothing out of place. Everything seemed directed as if by divine intervention. Each step they took, every detour, every choice brought them to where Sophia and the man from the ferry joined souls.

CHAPTER
Twenty~seven

Saxon became Sophia's protector from the first day they found each other. When the other dogs were alive, they were more dominant and demanded more attention than Saxon, but it was finally his turn to get what he so long deserved.

Michael and Sophia relished the time outdoors walking him each day. It was not on her original list, but should have been at the top of every dog-lover's requirement - a principle attribute of Sophia's perfect man was the quality of being compassionate to animals. Michael not only volunteered to walk Saxon, but he cleaned up after him. Sophia deemed it the absolute test of whether or not the ideal guy stays or goes is the proof of true love, as evidenced by him carrying the little bag of poo to the trash.

They were able to spend two more months of blissful love and attention with Saxon before it soon became clear that it was time to let him go. He was old and very sick, clearly ready to move on. For months, Sophia talked with Saxon, telling him, when it was time, she would make it easy for him. She promised not to make him stay too long as she had with Miles and Frankie. This time, she was more prepared, or so she thought. Such a decision was never easy. Sophia continued to ask Spirit to guide her to know when the time was right to help Saxon on his way.

One night, Sophia dreamt that she was walking Saxon when a yellow coyote suddenly came and snatched him away. The coyote and Saxon simply disappeared into nothingness, leaving Sophia holding the leash as it limply fell to the ground. Sophia believed this was a message: If she did not take care of her dog, nature would.

The dream was significant for Sophia, because when she was small, she remembered a strong and wise spirit of a Native American man she called Yellow Coyote, who often entered Sophia's dreams, informing her that she was safe, surrounded, and deeply loved by many. White Buffalo later confirmed that the man in her dreams was also named Grandpa Napayshni, a former Lakota chief whom White Buffalo said had been with Sophia all her life. All she had to do was ask him for help, and he would be there. She did ask, and in her dream, he was the one who came to take Saxon.

During her walk in the park with Saxon the next evening, a coyote crossed their path. The animal was much larger than Saxon. Sophia sensed danger when she heard other coyotes communicating from different directions, their chat sounding almost like squeaking wheels. The following Sunday morning at 5:00 a.m., Michael and Sophia awoke to the same noise just outside the bedroom window. The predatory coyotes apparently sensed that Saxon was nearing death.

Later that morning, Sophia counseled with a woman whose concern was for her friends who were going put their dog down that afternoon. She was ever surprised to find those who approached her came with an issue she had already healed, but more often than not, she too was working on a similar concern. Life reflected back to her exactly what she needed to know. If she listened and paid attention to all that was happening around her, she would intuitively know the next step to take. Life could be just that simple if she would only allow it.

Sophia knew right then that the woman's concern for her friends, her own troubling dream of the yellow coyote, and the natural call of the coyotes signaling to each other, were Spirit's way of telling her it was time to let Saxon go.

That afternoon, she called the veterinarian to come to the cabin the next day to euthanize Saxon. She then drove to a hill overlooking the city to take her old friend for a walk. It rained that afternoon, and the eastern sky was dark gray with the brightest rainbow she had ever seen. Saxon and Sophia sat in the field overlooking the eastern plains. From Sophia's vantage point, the rainbow appeared to glow out of the top of Saxon's head, which reminded her of those who referred to the rainbow bridge for animals to cross over when they died. This seemed to be a gracious nudge in that direction.

That evening, both Michael and Sophia walked Saxon. The coyotes kept their distance from the two humans that clearly intended to protect their precious dog. Upon their return, Sophia walked around the corner of the cabin to unlock the gate. Michael stayed with Saxon, who was clearly tired from the walk, and yet he pulled Michael along, following Sophia to watch over her one last time. It was Saxon's job to be Sophia's protector. As she turned around, she suddenly stopped, catching her breath. There in the moonlight, Saxon looked like the same young, sweet, slender dog that she first saw standing outside her fence years before...

Thirteen years earlier, Sophia recalled Frankie barking at 3:00 a.m. It was not like him to bark that early in the morning. Sophia was alone that weekend. Her husband, Joe, and his son from a previous marriage had gone camping. She got out of bed and looked out the window to find a young dog on the other side of the chain-link fence. He was not much older than six months with a slender black body and gold markings through his chest and down his legs. Obviously, he was a Rottweiler mix, as evidenced by the distinctive batman-shaped insignia beneath his cropped tail. He just stood there, solid, regal, and still.

She brought Frankie inside, not thinking about the other dog until sundown the next day when he showed up outside the fence again. Sophia left food and water for him across the street in the park. That night, he slept at the edge of the property near the street. She did not see him during the day, but at sundown, he came around again. Each night he slept a bit closer to the house.

The evening of day three, she watered the flowers outside the gate and found the dog there again, looking at Sophia with his big, sorrowful copper-penny eyes. His deep, ferocious bark normally would have alarmed her, but she sensed he was afraid, for he backed away from her while he barked. As she walked toward the flower garden, he followed about five steps behind. If she turned to look at him, he barked, but as she walked away, he silently followed. As long as she did not look at him, he quietly followed her, five steps behind. She experimented by walking in a looping pattern on the driveway. He shadowed her as she changed directions several times.

On the fifth night, he slept right by the gate next to her home.

The next day, she expected Joe to return from camping. She left a message on his cell phone, warning him about the dog - not to allow him into the yard - in case he was sick. When Sophia returned from work that evening, she found the dog inside the yard, sitting on her stepson's lap. So much for caution, Saxon had found a home.

Someone abandoned him, like so many other dogs in their neighborhood. His coat was dull and grey, with the fur singed off his head and back. He was terribly thin, apparently suffering from abuse, for he was particularly skittish around men. Sophia and Joe brought him back to health. After a few months of loving care, he filled out, and his coat became black and shiny again.

They named him Saxon because of his German Rottweiler breeding. Originally, they thought of naming him Gromit, after the dog character of *Wallace and Gromit*. His great big copper-penny eyes seemed rather sad, but quite expressive, with gold markings above his eyes that looked like eyebrows.

When Joe and Sophia sat at the breakfast bar, Saxon stood motionless, facing them from the floor on the other side of the counter. His eyes were all that moved, from Joe to Sophia and back again. Only his eyebrows moved up and down with each shift of his gaze.

Saxon was silent and stealthy. Sophia often found him lying on the floor behind her when she had no idea he was there. She had to be careful not to trip over him. He was her protector, the best watchdog of the family. Miles was large, muscular, and pure black - appearing quite threatening to those who did not know him, but he never considered it his duty to stand guard like his pal, Saxon. Frankie barked at other animals, but he loved people. As a herding dog, his job was to please, and his only care was that people loved him in return. If it were up to Frankie, burglars were welcome if they had a treat and a kind word.

Saxon, on the other hand, was wary of anyone who came close to the house. He not only looked intimidating, but his deep bark warned of any stranger's approach. Whenever they all went for a walk in the country, Saxon was the last to follow. Frankie and Miles blazed the trail ahead, Sophia followed them, and Saxon remained five feet behind her, watching over everyone.

One summer, Saxon developed an autoimmune disease, common to his breed. At one point, he became so sick that the veterinarian suggested Sophia have him put down, but she arrived at a different decision. Instead, she prayed over Saxon. She laid her hands on his head and prayed for his full health to return. Within two weeks, the disease was gone. Children and animals respond best to prayer because they have not yet developed the emotional blocks that keep them from healing. Saxon trusted Sophia. He knew she loved him. He remained her protector for the rest of his life.

All the animals went through the divorce with her. They struggled with the changes, too. She moved the dogs to her new home, one by one. She brought the three cats first, along with Miles, who was not well and needed special care. She then brought Frankie and Saxon to join the rest of the family. They were seven - the six animals and Sophia.

When Frankie was sick, Saxon suffered great anxiety. He knew Frankie was about to die. It was stressful and heart-wrenching to watch each of them go through their individual process of letting go - Saxon releasing his good friend and companion, while Frankie readied himself to leave his body behind. Saxon took several weeks to recover from Frankie's death, but when he adjusted, he showed new signs of life.

Finally, it was his turn to get all the attention he so deserved - many walks each day, lots of hugs, and Sophia brushing his coat until it shined. When Michael came into their world, Saxon, Frankie, and little Digit immediately adopted him as if they had known him forever. Michael came into their family just before Sophia decided to put Frankie down. Since Frankie was the alpha male, Saxon was subservient to him. When Frankie passed, he immediately adopted Michael and deemed him the new alpha male. Saxon loved to lie at Michael's feet in front of the fireplace, like in a Norman Rockwell painting.

There was rarely a moment when Michael was without Saxon. When Michael used the bathroom or took a shower, Saxon waited outside the door. He slept on Michael's side of the bed, sat at his feet while he was working, and followed him into the kitchen at lunchtime. Sophia began to wonder if Saxon loved her anymore. When Michael was around, Saxon ignored her. However, when Sophia was away from the house, Saxon paid no attention to Michael, either. Part of his attachment to Michael was his way of protecting Sophia, keeping an eye on him all hours of the day.

Digit usually sat on the dining room chairs, or snuggled in a corner or on a bed somewhere. Her relationship with Saxon was no different from with the other dogs. They were tolerable but beneath her. They, after all, were dogs, inferior to a cat in every way. Occasionally, when Saxon came near, she swatted him with her tiny paw, just to remind him of his station in life. She had no claws, but she still frightened him every time. Only once did he snap back at her. For the most part, he was very tolerant of her catty ways.

During the summer, they all drove to the Lake of the Ozarks in Missouri for a vacation. It was swelteringly hot - the average temperature during the day was 104 degrees with high humidity. It was clear to them that Saxon did not feel well.

On their way back to Denver, they decided to stay at a hotel in Topeka for the night. Their room was on the third floor, and Saxon had never ridden in an elevator before. He stepped into the small metal room and cautiously watched the doors close. When the elevator began to rise, Saxon tensed up and stood up on the tips of his claws. With nothing to grip the floor, his legs began to spread apart. Michael and Sophia laughed at Saxon's unexpected reaction. Sophia quickly straddled over her frightened dog and cradled his belly in her hands to support his weight for the rest of the ride. The doors opened, and Saxon exited, wide-eyed and mystified by the experience. From then on, they used the stairs. Saxon distanced himself, walking as close to the wall as possible and keeping an eye on the evil elevator doors.

The cool nights of autumn returned, and Sophia and Michael were concerned how Saxon would handle the winter, but they did not have to find out. All the signs quickly pointed to the opportune time to let him go.

The day before they had Saxon put down, Michael had a private conversation with him, assuring he would take good care of Sophia. Sophia also had a talk with Digit. She sat on the couch, holding her little black cat face-up in her hands. Digit's body was perfectly still and relaxed. She looked up at Sophia with her golden eyes as Sophia gently told her that it was Saxon's last day with them. She asked Digit to be nice and not swat at him or scare him. When another animal is dying, the healthy animals chase it away. In the wild, the healthy pack drives away the sick animal, forcing it to go off and die on its own. Following their "conversation," Digit obliged. She did not hiss or hit him again.

Saxon slept outside their bedroom door that night, but Sophia could not sleep, knowing this was the last night she would spend with him. She got out of bed and lay next to Saxon on the floor. He snuggled next to her and slept while she held him. Sophia would forever remember Saxon with his copper-penny eyes. Long before, he established himself as her protector and defender. That was the last evening he would watch over her.

The next day was beautiful. The sun was warm and the air was cool. Unexpectedly, Saxon was feeling energetic. Sophia suddenly had her doubts about putting him down, but she knew from all too recent experience that animals sometimes rally when they sense they are moving on. "Animals are much more attuned to nature than we humans," Sophia would later say, for they have this life figured out.

Michael and Sophia took Saxon for his last walk, and when they returned, they fed him fresh hamburger and tuna. The vet arrived at four o'clock. As Sophia did with Miles, Zaide and Emmy, she moved the furniture around and layered blankets on the floor. Sophia lit a candle and placed some mementos on the hearth by the fireplace, among them a nearly perfect round rock that she had found once during a walk with Saxon, a pinecone from one of the trees in the yard, and also a piece of a meteor. Sophia floated a rose from the garden in a shallow glass bowl. Every earthly element was there, as well as a token from the heavens. The sound of the ocean played in the background from their sound system.

Saxon took a drink from the bowl as a friend, who came to say goodbye, read a poem and then said a prayer. Sophia lay next to Saxon on the blanket and scratched his head. Saxon licked her hand for the first time in thirteen years, and he then nudged her hand back on top of his head with his nose so she would continue scratching his head. He had never done that before, either.

The vet gave him a rawhide to chew, which he enjoyed until the first injection made him relax. He then laid his head down. It took four injections, layer by layer going deeper, to let him go. Sophia lay down in front of him so her face was the last thing he would see. She told him she would see him again. It was the same conversation as with the other four animals. It was true love between an animal and their human - a love that has no description, no destination, no time and no end. She told Saxon how deeply she loved him until she felt his last breath upon her face.

Sophia held him in her arms, her protector of thirteen years. He was gone. Her precious, quiet, strong, stealthy puppy was no longer. She was grateful that she and Michael had those last several months to give Saxon so much love and attention. She wrapped herself around her beloved dog and sobbed deep sorrow of ancient grief into his fur.

It was the fifth animal Sophia had put down in less than three years, and the second since she was with her beloved Michael. Again, she and Michael held each other during the release of another precious being into the eternal ethers of no time or space.

CHAPTER
Twenty~eight

Sophia and Michael later returned to Santorini and stayed at Christofer's hotel in Oia for several weeks. During that time, Sophia kept quite busy, taking hundreds of photographs with her digital camera, and walking through the village, chatting with many of the locals at their businesses. Sophia enjoyed getting to know people. Her easy demeanor made it comfortable for others to relax and open up to her.

She was beginning to learn Greek, which was always appreciated when she tried to converse with the locals. However, her attempts were quite humorous, for she couldn't help but discombobulate the language. She spoke Italian fluently, but her Greek was – well, Greek to her. Nevertheless, she tended to get a laugh or two.

She spent quite a bit of time painting watercolors from several scenic areas throughout the island, never without great subject matter from which to choose. The remainder of the time, she wrote most of the original draft for her next book.

Christofer introduced Sophia and Michael to Shoshana, the lead anthropologist at the Akrotiri Archaeological Site. Shoshana was from Israel, having earned her doctorate from Columbia University. Shortly after, she was awarded a two-year grant to continue the work in Akrotiri, which originally began in 1967.

Because of Michael's education and experience, he was able to lend a hand at the dig, enthralled at the opportunity to uncover pieces of the 3600-year-old ruins. Forty buildings had been unearthed, estimated to be one-third of the entire site, leaving the area, believed to be as large as twenty hectares - about the size of ten American football fields combined. At that time in history, a village that size was quite a large city.

Both Sophia and Michael gained entrance into the private areas kept from public view among Akrotiri's ruins. Along with her study of the artifacts and frescos at both the Museum of Prehistoric Thera and the National Archeological Museum of Athens, Sophia was able to fill in the details of her ancient memories, adding to the picture of her life on Thera. She realized that she, as Roxana, the High Priestess of Akrotiri, was of integral significance in the history of Minoan and Mycenaean Greek civilization and its influence on world history, politics, and religion.

The advancement of Akrotiri's civilization was well beyond surrounding cultures. Archeologists were amazed at their findings of the highly developed society, which first inhabited the island in the Late Neolithic period of the fourth millennium B.C.E. A dual ceramic pipe system throughout the village delivered both cold and hot running water, generated from the geothermic sources beneath the island. Each home had a water closet and drainage system that supported their advanced technology. This alone would take another two thousand years before Europe would have such conveniences. In Akrotiri, the invention of airflow management within the structures allowed natural venting by the strong trade winds. Akrotiri's advanced achievements reached far beyond other cultures of that time.

Their refined design in hand-carved wooden furnishings could have been the model for the similarity in Baroque pieces that developed 3200 years later. Sophisticated pottery design appealed to specific use, instead of one style fits all, as displayed by many surrounding cultures in subsequent centuries.

The Minoans' advanced use of design and color decorated the frescoes of their homes' interior walls that mirrored their flourishing and prosperous lifestyle. On one wall were images of children boxing with long black braids in their hair. Another was an illustration of young women gathering saffron from crocus upon the hillsides. Entire walls painted with beautiful maidens with their black hair pulled back away from their faces in long tendrils falling to their waist. They were shown wearing open fitted vests baring their breasts, and woven ankle length multi-colored skirts. Elaborate embroidery bordered the edge of their clothing with beads and tassels dangling from their sleeves. Their adornments of large gold hoop earrings and golden bracelets and armbands indicated wealth and affluence.

Illustrations on the walls of entire rooms were images of papyrus and swallows flying overhead. There were frescoes of svelte fishermen with their catch. One entire room illustrated blue monkeys playing, and another with leaping antelope.

The most elaborate fresco was a mural in a home, later called the West House, with an intricate painting of eight pleasure boats sailing from one island to another, each manned with at least twenty men rowing the ship with a dozen passengers aboard. On the left side of the mural was a small island with a three-story dwelling, showing people facing to the right. A river flowed in a circle around the dwellings on the mountain, not unlike Plato's version of Atlantis.

Above the hillside were trees, bushes, and two antelope chased by a female lion. The island to the right side of the fresco showed a multi-story complex or palace much more advanced than the island on the left. People in the rooms and on the rooftops faced toward the other island to the left.

At the base of the complex were twenty men standing like servants at the ready. It also displayed layers of caves carved into the island's volcanic surface, occupied as dwellings for many thousands of years during Thera's history. Tremendous detail and spectrum of colors used throughout the painting left the impression of the island's success, prosperity, and wealth, with much commerce and cooperation between flourishing and refined societies.

No evidence of bodies left from the eruption remained at the site of Akrotiri, unlike those found at Pompeii. Evidently, the island's inhabitants had enough warning for many months, and perhaps years of earthquake activity to make the necessary plans to evacuate.

Sophia and Michael's return to Santorini also gave them an opportunity to reunite with Markos. Their hasty departure the last time they were on the island, combined with Markos' revelation of his history as Theo, left Sophia with many questions. She departed the island feeling incomplete, and she wanted to spend more time with Markos. It was not so much about Roxana and Theo's history, but instead the conscious coming together of souls that traveled in different directions for over three millennia, only to join again for a greater purpose.

Sophia and Michael were on the island for a week when Markos invited them to a party held in their honor the following Saturday. He wanted to introduce them to some of his friends. For some reason, Sophia sensed this was to be a very special event, so she decided to go in elegant fashion by wearing an off the shoulder, floor length white chiffon gown with a sweetheart neckline, complimenting her slender curves. She never wore white, but when she went into Fira to shop, the dresses were either too formal or too casual. She pulled her hair back, away from her face in soft curls trailing down her neck. She wore her own beautifully handcrafted pearl drop earrings, and a delicate necklace of pearls and gold, along with the aquamarine ring that Markos gave her. Michael wore cream slacks and a white linen shirt. They looked like a couple from a society magazine, vacationing in the Mediterranean.

The deep, rich colors at sunset over the Aegean Sea reflected in Markos' infinity pool. The famed white stucco buildings along the caldera held the coral hues as the sun disappeared over the horizon. Amber lights all over the hillside lent a romantic atmosphere to accentuate the aqua tone of the infinity pool.

Markos had the affair beautifully catered, beginning with an outstanding variety of delectable hors d'oeuvres and cocktails. A five-course candlelight dinner, decorated with flowers, on fine linens would be served on the terrace next to the pool, accompanied by Santorini's finest wines, and finalized with a choice of desserts, coffee, and cognac.

Sophia and Michael arrived fashionably late at 6:15. The party had already begun. When Sophia and Michael walked into the room, everyone stopped talking. Markos greeted Sophia and Michael with wide-open arms, warmly embracing Sophia. Markos and Michael shook hands, looking at each other with a knowing glance.

"Welcome! We are all so happy that you have joined us this evening. May I offer you something to drink while the introductions commence?"

"Thank you for the invitation," Sophia said. "We have so looked forward to seeing you again. A glass of your Santorini wine would be lovely. I trust your choice, Markos."

Sophia looked around the room, taking notice of everyone who gathered around to greet them in warm welcome. She began to sense, again, that this would be more than a special occasion. She was already familiar with some who attended. Among those were White Buffalo, Darius, Shoshana, and Gaston. Including Markos and Michael, there were six, of what she called *spiritual sages,* she now knew.

Introductions began with those she would soon add to her list of acquaintances among her erudite and wise spiritual teachers. They were twelve in all, from every continent across the globe. Sophia would not remember all their names right away, but she did recall details of conversations, and she never forgot a face. Much to her surprise, the last to arrive at the party was Christofer. Now they were thirteen, leaving Sophia to think of the numerological meaning of thirteen, which meant transformation and change, instead of unlucky.

When all the introductions were finished, Sophia noticed that everyone wore white. How did she know to wear a color, or lack thereof, she rarely ever wore? She smiled, acknowledging to herself again that her intuition never failed her.

Markos raised his glass in a toast. "I welcome all of you who have come from far away to gather here this evening. We are all sages, intuitives, teachers, and healers, and tonight we welcome Sophia into the fold, if she so chooses."

Sophia was somewhat surprised. They all raised their glasses to her and took a sip of wine. "Sophia," Markos said, "we gather together, once per year, for an eight-day assemblage, each time hosted by one of us. Sometimes it is in our homeland, but always our gathering takes place in a most remarkable setting. We are a small order of thirteen, and we are extremely discerning about who becomes one of our organization.

"There is nothing that we do, or are involved in, that would cause anyone to question what happens 'behind the scenes,' but because we are so transparent it causes others to be oddly suspicious. The importance of this assembly is the level of awareness that each person possesses, so that the collective whole is tremendously powerful and more effective for our good work in the world. This year, we join together to receive you into what you humorously call 'the Secret Sage Society.'"

"Oh, I hope I have not offended anyone," Sophia said with chagrin.

Everyone laughed. "Actually Sophia, you're not far off," Markos said. "Individually, each one of us is tremendously powerful, gifted with specific spiritual and psychic abilities to empower universal energies using the individual and collective attributes of the Divine. These qualities are elemental, and always considered ordinary to most of humankind, but we know differently.

"These fundamental qualities are best experienced in feeling tones, which cannot be felt in the past, or in the future, but only in the present - here and now. They are pure and absolute, and when we completely immerse our self in one, we experience the rest of them in their entirety. You might say they are a package deal. We activate our task as individuals and then work together as a collective whole. Let me explain further by demonstration."

They formed a circle, facing each other, as Markos continued, "Every year, each one of us places our time and attention on one quality until we meet again the next year. Then we gather again and exchange qualities. Every thirteen years, we will return to the quality we had the first year. Through various forms of deepening - meditation, prayer, study, and practice - we each utilize our primary quality in everything we think and do - in all exchanges with our world - with people, animals, nature, mother earth, and even with our electronics." The group laughed. "The power works with all aspects of the earth and the universe, for that matter.

"There are twelve basic qualities of spiritual consciousness, otherwise known as Absolute Awareness, demonstrated through unconditional Love. This is what we in the western world refer to as the Christ Consciousness. In other parts of the world, it is Bodhi, Gnosis, the Buddha-nature, Samadhi, Taqwa, Illumination, and Enlightenment, to name a few. There are other aspects of these worldly spiritual qualities also included in what we hold as our task and mission each year. For instance, Health includes well-being for physical, mental, emotional, and spiritual strength and growth. Peace includes silence, tranquility, and serenity.

"These are the primary attributes of Spirit, or God. This last year the highest attribute, the one that is all-inclusive of the rest, the quality of Love and Absolute Awareness was held by Irina; Abundance, by Darius; Compassion, by Anja; Order, by Markos; Truth, by Michael; Beauty, by Christofer; Joy, by Yesinia; Oneness, by Gaston; Harmony, by Shoshana; Balance, by Ananta; Grace, by Lestari; and Health, by White Buffalo.

"There were thirteen of us, but one passed on this year," Lestari continued. "He is certainly with us, even more than before, now that he is liberated from his body. He held the attribute of Peace, as he has in the past for many centuries, and in many lifetimes. He was Patrick, your father."

Sophia gasped and put her hands over her mouth to hide her surprise. She had no idea her father was involved in anything of a mystical nature, but now it made sense. Ever since she could remember, Patrick would leave for two weeks each year, during which she remained behind to stay with a trusted neighbor. Once she recalled going on vacation for ten days with one of her childhood friends and her family. Her father did not join them. Perhaps that was when he hosted the group in Colorado.

"That is one of the reasons you are here, Sophia," Markos said. "It is our desire that you take his place. Many of us that you have met this year have been assessing how you show up in the world - to see if you are ready to join us."

"We collectively feel that you are more than qualified, but only by your choice will it be so," Ananta said.

All Sophia could do was smile at those she already knew. It all made perfect sense to her. She silently asked herself, *what if I do not choose to join them.*

"There is no pressure if you would rather not be a part of the order," Christofer said. "We will just have you bound and gagged and I'll hide you in one of my caves." He got several laughs. "Seriously, it is entirely up to you to decide."

"I have to say, it's an ingenious system!" Sophia said. "Since my near-death experience, when every one of these attributes occurred simultaneously, I have been searching for a way to reenact that ethereal reality, and here it is, as all of you. I am greatly humbled to be considered for such an honor." Tears began to well up in Sophia's eyes - tears of joy.

"We each have phenomenal abilities to do profoundly good work for the world," Darius said. "Together we can more easily bypass time and space, creating quantum shifts while affecting the earth in a beneficial way from the wider expanse of the dimensional field. I know you are already able to utilize these very gifts, Sophia, but working with us in community will affect even greater change. In addition, being a part of this small enclave, you can call on us at anytime and one, or all of us, will support you. If you need us to be present, at least two of us will join you within 24 hours. For each one of us this is more than our work, it is our sacred task. We pose in our everyday life, going about our livelihood, with our family and such, but we are ever about our work. It is our way of life.

"When we gather, we wear white the first evening in humble reverence to the clarity and grace of the Divine Intelligence, the Infinite Field, Allah, or Great Spirit - whatever each of us refers to as our God and Source. The almighty power is in everything that we are, and in all we think, say, and in our actions. If you are now in agreement, Sophia, would you join us tonight?"

The statement, *Home is where the heart is,* never had more truth to it. Sophia felt at ease with those she already knew, and sensed that she would soon be comfortable with the others. She felt both humbled and privileged to be included, and she nodded in agreement.

Michael pulled from his pocket her amethyst amulet. "Here, my love, I think you need to put this on." He clasped it around her neck. The amulet rang out the high frequency when in company with the other golden items, but she only had her aquamarine ring with her, with the two items already attuned. There was no reason for the amulet to respond in such a way. She then took notice of the others, with the exception of Markos, who wore a golden ring set with a cabochon aquamarine, much like her own. Even Michael was wearing a golden ring. She never saw him wear it before that evening. Each ring lit up with the radiant light that Sophia was now accustomed to witnessing. They all held out their hand towards the center of the circle, except Markos. She realized that he had given her his ring months before, which was hers, as Roxana, 3600 years earlier.

White Buffalo handed her a ring that she sensed belonged to her father, Patrick. Markos was standing to her right in the circle. She turned to him, took his right hand in hers, and placed her father's ring on his forefinger. The two joined with the group, placing their right hand into the circle. Each of their individual lights joined, creating one brilliant golden white light - a luminescent column at the center of the circle. They could barely look into the intensity of the light. For Sophia, it was an indication that these people could be trusted, and to join with them would be the wisest decision she could make.

"I would be most honored to be included in this gathering," she said.

Each one removed their hand from the union of light, and yet the light seemed to float about the room in perpetual floating golden flecks, not unlike the wonder of glowing fireflies on a balmy summer eve. She reflected upon her near-death experience, when she realized each of the tiny lights were individual angels.

Markos then passed out a white taper candle to each person. He brought a small round table to the center of the circle, revealing the golden chalice, lit with the eternal flame. They all gathered around the table. Sophia smiled at White Buffalo, knowing that he transported the precious item from Colorado. White Buffalo simply nodded.

"Sophia," Markos said, "if you will take your candle and ignite it from the eternal flame, then go to each person and light their candle."

As she did, she looked into each person's eyes.

"Now, each of you place your candle in the individual candle holders on the table and return to where you were standing." Each followed along. "Sophia, stand with me inside this sacred circle of trusted friends, whom you will now call family."

She stood with Markos, and for a brief moment saw him again as Theo. Markos, of course, knew what she was thinking and smiled at her as he took her hand. He held a small bowl of rose oil with its sweet aroma filling the air.

"Sophia, each person will anoint you with a blessing." He dipped his middle finger into the oil and touched the back of her hand that he held so gently, "I, Theo Markos, honor you as one who was once my mother, who is now of this family for lifetimes to come." Tears came to her eyes.

White Buffalo touched her shoulder with the oil. "I welcome you and bring you prayers from your Lakota family. Grandmother earth wants you to know that she is happy that you walk upon her back. Great Spirit and the Grandfathers surround you and support you, circling you in safety and wisdom. They want you to ask more often for their help. When you do, it will come to you in a good way. Aho, Mitakuye Oyasin."

"Aho." She responded, and looked down, not peering directly into his eyes, as a sign of respect.

Darius touched her cheek with oil. "I will leave you all my earthly goods, but I also reveal to you your Southern American heritage, rich in tradition, immersed in magic, and wealthy in God."

She smiled, took his hand in hers, and gently grasped it.

Christofer came to her and touched her throat with the oil. "Your words in all forms will ring out to the heavens and back with songs of the angels. You will always have a home here on Santorini. Your ancient Greek heritage and the world are very grateful to you as the gods smile upon you."

Gaston spoke in his deep French Creole accent as he touched her forehead with the oil. "Your radiance is like your mother's light. You do not yet know how, but soon you will recall who she was. I am here to help you remember your mother. She comes to me in my dreams to inform me of how I can better be one of your earthly protectors and guides. She wants you to know that she is here tonight, as is the spirit of your father. They send you their love."

Tears flowed down Sophia's cheeks as she lovingly remembered her father. The memory of her mother was so undefined, and yet her essence was so sweet and tender. That Gaston would know anything about her was beyond Sophia's comprehension, but for now, she would have to trust her mentor.

All the others, except one, gave their blessings and committed their support to her for what the future would bring. Michael waited to be the last. He placed a drop of oil on her décolletage, close to her heart. "As you know, I have loved you as Yiorgos, and now as Michael. As both, I continue to protect you in counsel, as your champion, and beloved. Until the end of time I will seek you out to love you wholly without reservation." He tenderly kissed her on the lips, and she put her arms around his neck in a tender embrace.

Darius concluded the ritual, "Welcome Sophia, to the Order of *Apeiros*. You might wonder where the name originated. Yes?"

"It is a beautiful name, and yes, I am intrigued," she said.

"It is derived from the brilliant works of Anaximander, from the 7th century B.C.E. Considered as 'the first' in many schools of thought; he is the first philosopher, first geographer, and first metaphysician. Having written the first surviving lines of Western philosophy, he speculated on the boundless and infinite, in his philosophical and theological arguments of the all that is, as an open universe. His work influenced many Greek philosophers, especially Plato's work on cosmology and that of Aristotle.

"Apeiros comes from the Greek, *Apeiron*," Gaston added, "meaning: *eternal, boundless, infinite, endless expansion. It is the cause of all unity and measure of all things.* This is who we are, as the Order of Apeiros, holding the infinite eternality for the earth, and for the universe itself."

The room filled with golden white light for the entire initiation. The caterers, outside on the terrace, thought there was some type of laser light show inside. The people gathered around Sophia had blocked the outsiders from seeing what occurred.

"Now, to conclude this evening's ceremony," Irina said, "we will proceed with our new assignments for the coming year." She turned her attention to Sophia, "Each person cycles on to the next attribute in consecutive order, returning to the same one every thirteen years. Shoshana will record each name and their mission for the coming year on the parchment pages in this ancient leather-bound book passed down for centuries through the Order."

When it came to Sophia, Ananta said, "Patrick was next in line for Love - Absolute Awareness. It is now yours, Sophia."

They all applauded, knowing that she was perfectly prepared to hold the high honor she was about to embrace. The only one who had any doubt concerning her ability to follow through was Sophia herself. The others reminded her that she would not be alone in her task.

The ceremony concluded. When Sophia took off her necklace, the light dimmed to the natural diffusion of twilight. Glowing candles and the eternal flame were now the brightest lights in the room.

All thirteen dined under the moonlight at the edge of the caldera, enjoying the food, good wine, and excellent company of souls. Sophia was certain she had known each one of them before in some other dimension or lifetime, and if it were for her to know of their association, she would discover their connection without effort.

The next day they would gather again to discuss the facts of world affairs, but they knew there was a difference between fact and truth, for what is in one's experience is merely the effect of past circumstance. Their task was to operate from the truth, from the highest potential, beyond what was obvious to the majority of the world. This, being their starting point, helped them etch out their greater vision for the upcoming year.

It was clear to Sophia that Patrick continued to hold the task of Peace, even beyond his earthly life, and in that, he would also be of support the following year as she held the honor of Love and Absolute Awareness. Knowing that, she felt more confident and courageous as she stepped into the adventure before her. Sophia took note of her father's calm presence. In fact, she realized for the past several weeks that she felt her father's familiar tapping on her shoulder. For the time being, he would remain with her, continuing to support her, and as she knew so well, love never dies.

Her visitation to Santorini was more than she could have imagined. There was a peaceful calm within her, a knowing. The purpose for her traveling back to those particular times in her history aided her to feel fulfilled, for she found clarity of purpose to be a gift. As her father had directed her to *Know Thyself*, it appeared that she had done so. She had just begun a new adventure with no idea of her direction, except that she sensed the blissful thrill at the journey set before her.

CHAPTER
Twenty~nine

Sophia again witnessed herself as Rachel, this time in early springtime, seated on a green grassy hillside along the upper east coastline of the Sea of Galilee. She sat in the midst of a multitude of people, observing Yeshua and his disciples as a young boy gave them his humble offering of a few barley loaves and fish to feed the masses. Rachel witnessed the people, who had gathered together in community from faraway places, as Yeshua spoke to them from love - bringing them back to themselves - back to their healing - to their wholeness. They joined in peaceful awareness as all shared much more than bits of food.

Sophia processed throughout her dream's recall the esoteric meaning of the elements of the miracle story. *Barley*, one of the oldest grains of humankind, was first cultivated in Jordan around 10,000 B.C.E. Considered a sacred grain, barley was given as an offering to the gods throughout the Middle East, Egypt, Greece and India. The mystical meaning of barley represented a gentle, nurturing force that stimulated the heart chakra, as it eased one's burdens by turning harsh feelings into love. The ancient grain embodied the good of truth recognized in life's pleasures. The *loaves* signified spiritual substance - food for the soul as fresh ideas and wisdom that lasted a lifetime. *Fish* represented increase and a wealth of new ideas. It was also a symbol of fertility. *Multitude* stood for hungry thoughts - longed-for words of wisdom, and the seeking of expansive ideas that would sustain.

So in essence, out of the faith of a young boy's selfless gift, Yeshua fed the people's hungry thoughts with longed-for words of wisdom, offering the good of truth, easing harsh feelings into love as food for the soul. He presented a wealth of new fertile ideas, with increasing wisdom that lasted a lifetime. The people's minds and hearts were filled to overflowing with the Spirit of Truth so they would be better able to recognize life's simple pleasures, as delivered by the one whom the Jewish people believed to be the deliverer, the prophet, the Messiah. Yeshua's message taught all people that anyone who believed could use the power of God to create the miraculous life they desired.

Yeshua's example of giving thanks in advance was the key element in receiving. He taught that being grateful was to appreciate, which multiplied and enhanced everything in existence through the greater awareness of one's multitude of blessings. As a result, love naturally revealed itself when a thankful heart allowed it.

Yeshua's teachings and example enlightened anyone in his company, shifting one's awareness from the lower frequencies of fear, shame, and scarcity, to the higher energy of love through peace, abundance, harmony, and joy. The enhancement of life thus included a sense of absolute fulfillment where healing automatically occurred in that higher realm of grace.

Days later, Yeshua came to Rachel's home to share food,

wine, and good company. That evening, at his request, Rachel peered into her golden bowl to perform a prophetic reading on his behalf. He asked her to do this for her sake, not his.

Rachel many times witnessed the very phenomenon of Yeshua's presence, and yet her eyes filled with tears for what she foresaw in his future. Through the waters, she envisioned his earthly end, as he would suffer significantly at the hands of Rome.

The Pharisees and chief priests would call together the Sanhedrin, the council of sages that made up the Jewish court. They would deliver a judgment against Yeshua, finding him guilty of blasphemy, thus condemning him for claiming to be the son of God. The Roman authorities, wishing to rid themselves of Yeshua's unconventionality, would brand him a heretic and act out their judgment of death. His death would greatly affect the world as far into the future as Rachel was able to foresee.

What she envisioned beyond his earthly life was phenomenal. Those who followed his example - in the love he had for life in its fullest expression - would teach the world in the role of master healer/teacher as many had done before him. Those who believed in him would write of his miraculous nature, outlining his acts of grace, compassion, and healing to illustrate that all believers who acted wholeheartedly and through higher spiritual perception could forego illness, death, fear, and the egoic mind's gripping tentacles.

Yeshua taught that all beings could live in the knowledge that anything was achievable within the field of infinite possibility - the God nature. This was his message:

to live life in simplicity infused with the all-knowing, all-powerful, and ever-present nature of the source of all things - to follow the sacred way of the heart. She could see that people would follow Yeshua and his teachings for thousands of years. He would leave the world expansive, yet simple lessons on how to live in love, compassion, and joy beyond human limitation. His teachings were timeless and infinite, so much that other master healer/teachers would take his example and adopt the same truths to teach in their part of the world, in their traditions, in their way. And so, he lived on.

Belief in the example of Yeshua would enable humanity to embrace the balance and order of the invisible nature of the Divine, manifested in all forms of life and the earth itself. Yeshua would teach humankind how to live in harmony with their souls' journey as empowered, miraculous humans, embracing the power of God within by ascending time and space.

All this and more, Rachel saw in the waters. Millennia of revelation flashed before her, and her understanding of what she envisioned through the passing of time was instantly clear to her. At the conclusion of her vision, she looked up at him wide-eyed, witnessing the radiant Christ before her. In that moment, she came into the full recognition that he was human, *and* divine. Because he was that, she realized she was, as well... as was everyone.

He lovingly smiled, speaking to her from the peace and assurance that he knew so well. "It is my belief that I am of God, and so are you, as is all humankind - all beings. This, I know, you now understand. There will be a day when the quintessence of unity will be a knowing throughout the universe. I want you to remember, I will continue to teach these truths beyond this worldly existence. Only my body will be gone from the earth, but my essence will remain.

"Rachel, you and others will continue with the work that I came here to do. Teach the people that never has there been, or will there ever be another one like them. If God is all there is, then everyone is of that expansive, loving presence as well. As you know this for yourself, you will know it for them, and that is when the miracles happen. Know this, when you bring people to their healing, it is simple. You are helping them to remember who they are - as the thought of love is evidenced in human form.

"This is the truth for all beings. It is just that we humans need a bit more help to keep in mind who we are. Remember, a person's perception is what colors the images they see. If they see through a restricted viewpoint, their decisions will reflect their limited vision. Likewise, within the temporary illusion of power over others, they can only see from a very small viewpoint. Your task is to facilitate the broadening of their spectrum - help the people to see with the eyes of God - to recognize all colors, hues, textures, shapes, and forms - to realize that they too have come to this life to celebrate their extraordinary excellence, using their individual gifts and talents well, in service to the world. In this, they will fully realize their purpose as they again become whole and healed. By assisting them, you will continue to come back home to yourself.

"In their illusion of control, those who don't understand wish to destroy me, believing my demise will rid them of their fears, but my death will instead open the floodgates. No one can destroy the sacred way of the heart. It is the way of life for every living being. After I am gone from this earth, I will continue on, for the sacred way of the heart is the way of the eternal soul. This has always been the truth, long before I came into the body in which I now reside. Rachel, there will come a time when all people will awaken to this magnificent truth. You will teach the sacred way, melding it with your soul's journey as you live your life being the woman you are."

She cried, looking into his eyes, unable to speak of her sorrow.

"My sweet one, please know I am at peace. In very little time, I will no longer dwell upon this earth. I have done what I came here to do. Many have accomplished similar works before me in their way, and others will do so far into the future. What they will achieve will be even better things, I might add. And so, the time has come for me to move on.

He paused and placed his hands upon her shoulders and looked intently into her eyes. "And so, Rachel, you must now leave this place. There is nothing to keep you here. I want you to go to my brother, Ya'aqov. As you know, he is a fisherman. I have arranged for him to take you to Italia, under the guise of being his wife.

"Once you are established there, seek out those who wear the ring, for they are awaiting your arrival." He raised her right hand and touched the aquamarine golden ring on her third finger. "There are many people like you with the same calling. From them, establish a counsel of twelve - the number twelve signifies perfection. To aid you in your work, in teaching the way of the heart, appoint each person with one of the twelve truths to hold - that of peace, joy, harmony, order, balance, abundance, health, compassion, oneness, truth, beauty, and grace, all in the over-arching love and absolute awareness, which you will embrace yourself. Teach each one of these truths until each person embodies the others, as all are forms of love and absolute awareness. All these qualities are the life-giving aspects of God, the Divine. None of them, by nature, is diminishing, but only of expansion and evolvement. Living fully in one of these truths expresses the others for all to witness. The fullness of compassion is also joy-filled. Appreciating beauty fills one with peace, and so on. It is a wondrous way of life. I charge you and your counsel of twelve to live these principles as the Sacred Way of the Heart. In this, you and your people will be empowered beyond your imagining, as individuals and as a collective group of teachers.

"By day, you are to live a simple life, calling little attention to yourself. However, at night, you will be the seer and prophetess that you now are, carrying on the ancient tradition of teaching the way, for it has been in your family line for millennia. In that high standing as a leader, you will share with others the power of God, teaching them that each person has within them what they need to live a full life.

"You already know that each and every person is equipped with gifts and talents that enable them to easily traverse their individual path, all done by their choosing. As they evolve, becoming more aware through the stages of advancement, they will tap into additional aspects of those talents that support them on their way.

"Your purpose is to help others remember who they

are. Forget not to take with you the golden bowl, eternal flame, ring, and pendulum, as given to the world from the Star People long before the existence of humankind. They are tools for evolvement, passed down through your ancestry for a reason. That reason is to continually bring the eternal truths of which I speak to the land where you and your lineage will reside, supporting you in the work that you will continue to do.

"Eventually, you will live in every corner of this earth - blessing the land, its people, and all sentient beings with the sacred waters that flow from the golden bowl, with the cleansing fire of the chalice, and of the winds of change that pass through the pendulum. Over time, you will acquire other tools and talismans that, when used together, will further empower you and all those you serve. Remember this: these are only tools that enhance your abilities. Your true power, as is the truth for every living being, lies within - the God essence within you that knows all. Eventually, you will need no tools, for you will fully realize you are of God, and all you need is the desire within you to propel you forward to the awakening of who you have been all along.

"You might wonder how I know of the history of these golden items in your possession. I have seen the Star People through the sacred waters. I am aware of the golden amulets they left, and those that will come to you in the future. You and I are family, Rachel, generated from the same ancestry. We come directly from the Star People, and of course, all of humanity - all beings are of the Divine. This is the most important part of our human journey - to remember just this one key truth - we are all of the goodness of God. Someday your descendants will return to the stars from whence we came, but not before you touch the entire world with the knowing you came here to share. Go now. Make haste to speak with Ya'aqov. Tell him he will remain in my heart."

He took Rachel's tearstained face in his hands and kissed her forehead, and then he looked deeply into her eyes. She drank in his essence, never to forget him or his words. Rachel wrapped her arms around his waist and buried her head in his chest. He lovingly held her before he left her with his last words.

"Goodbye, my beloved. I promise we will know each other again, in another lifetime, in another dimension. I am ever with you and you with me. Always remember, '*I Am. I am the light of Gaia - water, fire, earth, and air. I am the stars above and the earth below. And I am one with all that has ever been and ever will be.*'"

He released her and turned away, knowing she would carry on his work. The last words he spoke came as if in a dream. Rachel remembered them from somewhere in a distant mist from long before.

Never did Rachel speak with Yeshua again, at least not as a human in the physical world. The last time she saw him, only his body remained on the cross. Ya'aqov, Yeshua's brother, awaited Rachel on the ship, but she had one more thing to do before she left Jerusalem.

The Roman authorities could not abide by Yeshua's innate power that drew thousands to him. Yet, before he died, he emitted a radiant glow. The look in his eyes was of peaceful kindness and compassion. There was no blame or emotional charge within him. Only love remained. *How could this be?* Rachel thought. *How could he not hold any judgment toward his persecutors?*

She remembered, in all the miracles over which Yeshua presided, he had two questions for the person who came to him for healing. The first question was, "Do you believe in me and therefore the Source of all Creation?" The power of Yeshua came from the full knowledge that he was one with God, who had many names - Elohim, El Shaddai, and God Almighty, to name only a few.

Yeshua did not ask anyone to follow him or put him on a pedestal, but rather he led by example, for he had found the sacred way of the heart. If the people in need were truly in compliance, believing that Yeshua and God were one, they would know that they too were in union with the Divine. With that embodiment of wholehearted knowledge, all things of the earth were of no consequence because of their temporal nature. The belief that they were one with God, the Almighty - the invisible field of grace would create a personal recognition in which all things needed became known. By believing in Yeshua, the example of God on earth, they in turn believed in their own transcendent nature. Once fully realized, the concerns of the earthly world disappeared into the ethereal realm from whence they came.

The second question he had for them was, "Have you learned anything from your illness or challenge?" If the answer was no, healing did not take place, and the querent was released to learn what he or she needed to glean from their circumstances. Nothing left the body of experience until realization emerged from the teaching. There was no judgment from Yeshua. He extended compassion to them as they went on their way. If the answer was yes to both questions, then healing took place first in the mind, then within the needs of the physical body, and most importantly, healing reached into the depths of the soul.

Yeshua had the power that others sought, but it was available to any who accepted that they were of the same power of the Divine. It was not for him alone. He taught this wherever he went. Some listened, but very few believed that they were worthy of such grace. Nevertheless, they changed within the natural process of expansion, whether they knew it or not.

At the base of the cross, where Yeshua was nailed, Rachel laid a bouquet of wildflowers and poured sacred water over them from her golden bowl. She witnessed the flowers miraculously multiply into every color of the spectrum. She smiled as she remembered the many moments she shared with him, witnessing the miraculous healings, grateful in the knowing that he passed his wisdom on to her, and to so many others. Rachel then spoke a blessing for Yeshua, so he would easily return to the ethers from whence he came. She prayed he would know only the peace and love he spent his short life teaching others.

Yeshua left the world of effects without pain. Only his body experienced what appeared to be suffering, for his soul had already moved on before his body finished breathing the last breath. From the eternal realm - that which was everywhere, at all times - Yeshua would emit throughout the universe his essence of the sacred way of the heart. He continued to live through Rachel, and through all who knew and remembered him, into eternity.

Yeshua ben Yosef finished what he came to do. He accomplished his purpose, to live on earth as a human being within the realm of God's almighty power and infinite knowledge. He healed the sick, raised the dead, and transformed the physical into the eternal dominion of infinity. He performed miracles by which he tapped in to other dimensions, where he found that all things were possible, making them so in this world. His power came through his example of compassion, forgiveness, and non-judgment - that of pure love and absolute awareness.

He did all this and much more in a state of gratitude, giving thanks in advance for the manifest occurrence, knowing it was already complete in the mind of God. Therefore, the power was within his ability to accomplish the extraordinary, because he was of the same mind. Most importantly, he did it all with humility, knowing it was not him doing the work. Instead, he was a powerful conduit through which the authority of God flowed. As a humble servant of God, he taught everyone that they too could do the same as he, and even greater things still. He did it all from love - the most powerful force on earth - through the Sacred Way of the Heart, the greatest gift that can be both given and received.

He was done. Finished. He left the earth by teaching forgiveness with his final words, "Father, forgive them, for they know not what they do."

Rachel bid him farewell. His body completed its earthly journey. Yeshua left for all of humanity the example of how to live life fully and wholly in service to God - in service to others and in service to the self - all in oneness.

She placed the golden vessel in her leather pouch and

tied the tethers around her neck, along with her golden chalice and pendulum, keeping them safe for travel. She was unable to leave until the early hours of the following day. A massive storm developed just as Yeshua breathed his last breath. From mid afternoon into late evening, thunderstorms, lightning, and earthquakes left their mark.

Ya'aqov safely transported Rachel to Italia, leaving her in the hands of a Jewish community along the coastline of the Tyrrhenian Sea, not far from Rome.

Sophia barely awoke, as she realized that the sages mentioned by White Buffalo were not only of this world in the present time, but from other dimensions. Yeshua came to her through the life of Rachel, as did other great teachers that came to her through her dreams.

CHAPTER
Thirty

After Sophia and Michael returned from Greece, Sophia decided it was time to sell her little California style house. From her dreams, she created exactly what she desired for her home. She loved her little green house, having put her heart into it, but it was time to move on. Michael was a big man, and her house simply was too small for him. When someone shares their life with another, they sacrifice some of their personal wants for the betterment of both concerned.

Again, her intuition guided her to sell at that particular time, and her guidance was correct. The economy was in a downturn, making it difficult for buyers to qualify for a loan, but Sophia knew that appearances were not necessarily accurate or true. She proceeded as if opinions of the masses did not apply to her, ignoring the negativity and thus avoiding unnecessary tension. She simply did not accept what most everyone thought. Instead, she decided to create a ritual in order to easily and gracefully release her home to the next owner.

Sophia cleared her calendar and turned off her phone. The night before, she prepared for the ritual, taking a few hours to write three lists. The first was her forgiveness list naming everyone she needed to forgive, which included that which she needed to forgive in herself. All her issues with others began with her own perspective of hurt feelings and self-imposed wounds. By releasing the invisible tethers that tied her to the pain, she was liberated, set free, and ready to move on. She released wounds from her divorce, and she let go of indifferences she had from misunderstandings in the past. This included painful memories from past lifetimes she remembered through her dreams.

The second list contained guests, friends, family, her animal family, and even workers who helped her with home renovations. The third was a gratitude list of all for which she was thankful. It ended with her intention for what she was calling into her life, and being grateful in advance for what was to come.

In a stone bowl filled with fresh cold water, she added flowers and leaves from every variety of plant on her property, a pinecone, and a pretty little rock from her garden. A glass of red wine in an antique crystal goblet sat on the floor next to the stone bowl while soothing music played in the background. She sat on a sheepskin rug in front of the fireplace and built a fire. She began with crumpled newspaper, stacked kindling, and small sticks, followed by larger split logs on top. Something about building a fire brought Sophia pure joy.

She struck a match to the newspaper and watched the fire catch the kindling and quickly burst into flames. Sophia closed her eyes in communion with the Divine, allowing its presence to come through her - to bless her home and everyone who had entered. She meditated for twenty minutes to move into the ethereal realm where all things were possible. When Sophia felt herself arrive at that eternal realm of spaciousness, she knew she was ready to proceed. She opened her eyes and took a sip of wine, toasting what was about to commence.

She first read the forgiveness list aloud, seeing each person in her mind's eye as she read each name. When she finished, she tore up the list and threw the pieces into the fire, feeling liberated from what she had held onto from the past. Next was the list of all who had entered through the doors of her home. She gave thanks as she read each name, for what they shared, for their contribution made to her home and her life. She blessed them in their travels, whether they were still walking on the earth, or had left for greater adventures. After reading their names, she placed that list into the flames. She paid final tribute to her lengthy gratitude list, which took several minutes to complete. After she burned that list, she again toasted what she had released and blessed.

The last part of the ritual was a conversation with God. "I sit before you today, having released those I have held hostage in my mind, some from years of condemnation. Blessings I have given to the many that touched my life in this house, and I now bless the many that will enter beyond my time here. Most of all I sit here in awe of all my many blessings, for they are so magnificent. I am so thankful for all I have and all that I am. I am so fortunate to experience the lifetimes I have recalled, and for those that will come to me in the future. May I be ready and receptive to what my soul is calling me to become, and in my journey may I have a positive influence on everyone I encounter from this point forward as I continue to evolve within the expansive realm beyond time and space. I am so grateful.

"And so, I release this home to the next owner, knowing that they will be supported in their life's journey, and will soon find it to be a home of heart. I bless this little house, knowing that the word blessing means 'to confer prosperity upon'. Therefore, may this home continue to accommodate love in its joy, beauty, peace, harmony, health and well-being - all celebrated abundantly. And so it is! Amen."

She lifted her goblet one more time, toasting the house that had been her home, and took her last sip in gratitude.

The house sold just ten days after Sophia put it on the market.

She and Michael moved to Sophia's cabin in a small valley in the Rocky Mountains, alongside a river that flowed just thirty feet from the door. Surrounding the cabin were seven, eighty-foot blue spruce trees and numerous ponderosa pines standing like protective guardians of the mountain retreat. Shimmering aspens brought texture and a splash of autumn gold to the varied shades of green on the property.

Sophia grew up at the cabin, spending weekends there during the summer months with her father. The cabin had been theirs since she was seven years old. It was her favorite place to spend time, and it became her sanctuary as she matured. Nowhere else was there a place where she felt more at home. It was a summer retreat, so for Michael and Sophia to live there year-round, the entire cabin needed an upgrade.

They spent several months adding insulation and a furnace, and many custom touches - a wrought iron spiral staircase, granite countertops, and an entirely refurbished kitchen and bath. They installed large picture windows to frame the natural beauty of the mountain sunset, the river, and the trees. They converted the upstairs loft into a creative space with skylights to let in the natural light for Sophia's painting and writing.

They redesigned the back bedroom into a man cave for Michael, with an entire wall reserved for all his books. She positioned a leather recliner just right for him to watch his flat screen TV on the wall. Two long tables met in the corner that held his numerous laptops, monitors and keyboards, which appeared like the control panel for NASA. Every room was changed and upgraded from the hardwood floors to the skylights overhead. Although their mountain home was virtually new, to Sophia it would always be *The Cabin*.

Before they replaced the kitchen cabinets, Sophia had put most everything from the cupboards into boxes for the Salvation Army. She saved one old dusty cardboard box tucked away on a top shelf, for she had not yet had time to go through it. She did not remember ever seeing it before, and she nearly threw it away, thinking nothing could possibly be of value inside. She decided to open it up, just in case she was mistaken.

Inside, she discovered a finely handcrafted wooden box with dovetailed corners, bronze hinges, and an ornate clasp resembling Celtic knots with a bronze pin that anchored the lid through the clasp. Her eyes widened, for this was the same design carved into the box containing the hourglass that Darius gave her, as well as the box for her aquamarine ring.

Sophia's heart raced as she slipped the bronze pin from the loop on the clasp. The box sprung open, revealing a radiantly beautiful golden bowl cradled in dark blue velvet. *This looks like the bowl both Gaston and Darius described, but it can't be,* Sophia thought. *Talk about a strange coincidence...*

The inscription on the bowl's upper rim was the same as the markings on all the other golden treasures she had in her possession. It truly was luminous, albeit a bit dusty. Sophia shook her head. She squinted in the dim light of the kitchen and tried to clean the dust off the bowl to get a better look. The kitchen sink was full of paintbrushes and buckets, so she went outside to wash it off in the cove.

Since childhood, she had spent hours pondering life's questions while sitting in the small private inlet on the riverbank, watching the river swiftly flow downstream. In that moment, Sophia smiled as she realized that, since she was quite young, she had instinctively peered into nature's vessel of water that flowed into the cove. Without knowing it, she had naturally carried on the Oracle tradition in her own way, communing with God from the time she was seven years old.

Sophia sat on the root of a tall sentinel blue spruce tree at the river's edge. She dipped the bowl into the river and filled it with the purified water of the stream. Immediately, energy surged from the golden bowl, radiating a palpable force into Sophia's hands. She looked into the bowl through the water and instantly entered a trance. Her eyes naturally relaxed, and the single round image of the bowl split into two joined circles.

Staring through this shape into the foreign etching at the bottom of the bowl, she began to see images emerge. She flashed back to her lives as Roxana, Hypatia, and Rachel. This was the very same bowl - the golden vessel - from thousands of years before. The bowl appeared as if it were brand-new, with no scratches, dents, or tarnish. It was an astounding, flawless piece of craftsmanship. Beyond its appearance, the power that came from it while in Sophia's hands was unfathomable. Holding the bowl with the pure river water inside it made her feel as if she was the life force itself - the most powerful element on the earth.

It would be over an hour before Sophia would return to the cabin...

CHAPTER
Thirty~one

Sophia wandered into the cabin, her mind still swirling from the images evoked by the golden bowl. She picked up the box in which she found the bowl and sat at her large antique desk in the library. She still felt as if she was in a daze. *Where did this come from? How did it end up here?*

She looked outside and saw Michael pass by as he walked out to the shed. He was puttering. That could go on for hours.

Sophia looked at the bowl again, and then at the box. Something caught her eye, and she ran her finger along the dark blue velvet lining inside the box. She curiously pulled up a corner of the fabric, and underneath she noticed what looked like yellowed paper tucked in the bottom. She suddenly felt a warm tingling sensation throughout her body, for there seemed to be a palpable energy in the room. She carefully removed the paper and discovered it was a very old parchment letter, folded into the shape of an envelope and sealed with red wax.

Sophia felt her heart race, for indented in the red wax was the familiar sacred geometry. She gazed upon the ancient envelope, knowing the contents must yet be another piece of the puzzle.

She looked outside and saw Michael chopping wood for the upcoming winter months. The privacy in that moment gave her the opportunity to create a ritual that made opening the letter sacred and revered. She took a hand-cut crystal wine glass from the china cabinet and poured herself some Santorini wine from Christofer's vineyard. She sat on the Persian rug in front of the burning fire in the hearth.

The envelope was scribed with a fountain pen in beautiful calligraphy, written in Italian: *Per il portatore del Sacro Forza di Vita.* Sophia recalled her Italian lessons in college: *For the Bearer of the Sacred Life Force.* The Life Force was precious water - the most powerful earthly element - giving bountiful life to all beings upon the earth. The Bearer, or carrier, was a woman - a vessel - represented by the bowl. The word 'sacred' was defined as holy, blessed, revered, and sacrosanct.

In the days of the Delphic Oracle, Hypatia spoke on behalf of the god, Apollo, using the bowl through which she received his wisdom. In the present time, Sophia used a bowl containing sacred water for her prophetic readings on behalf of one's greater good - of one's divinity - of God. Therefore, the envelope was intended solely for Sophia, as she was the modern day Oracle, the sacred vessel that held the life force for those she served.

Sophia broke the red wax seal on the envelope and was startled when the fire in the hearth suddenly flared up as if she threw fuel into the flames. Opening the ancient parchment, she discovered a remarkably well preserved handwritten letter. Sophia had studied languages in college as part of her Art History curriculum. Although she never quite mastered Greek, she was proficient in the Romance languages. She recognized the script as a form of ancient Italian, a challenge for even the most learned scholar, but she, in some form of a miracle, was able to read the letter with amazing ease:

> *My dearest Sophia,*
>
> *I am your ancestral grandmother, Luciana Nervetti da Genova. I write to you from the coastal port of Genova, Italy, in the year of our Lord, 1541. I see your many lives through the veils of time with the aid of the golden vessel, and now it finally has come into your possession, for you are ready for its power.*
>
> *It has been necessary for you gradually to come to yourself through your dreams, because no one gave you the appropriate training to receive the rites when you were young. Sages, shamans, and wisdom keepers are gathering to align with you and your purpose. As you know, not all of them come to you from the physical realm.*
>
> *One of them, your beloved Michael, is the most notable of them all. He is your protector. He is tremendously wise and is with you, in part, for your success and well-being. Especially when you doubt yourself, listen to his wisdom. He will never fail you, for you know each other's soul. In the many lives you shared, in one way or another, you were the other's beloved.*

Your quest is to *Know Thyself*, and you are just in the beginnings of this pursuit to understand who you are. I am communicating with you over centuries of time to help you understand that you are the most powerful Oracle that has ever lived. This power possessed by our ancestors multiplies as we evolve through our lifetimes. You are to use it well, knowing the truth by following *The Sacred Way of the Heart* in love, peace, grace, and harmony.

By now, you have recalled some of your past lives. Roxana of Akrotiri was the first High Priestess of the land that later became Delphi, and her teachings and power progressed into the tradition of the Delphic Oracle. The greatest Oracle of Delphi, Hypatia, served the most patrons of any oracle for over fifty years, among them Alexander the Great. Rachel was the most blessed among them all, as taught by Yeshua, while they held each other in mutual companionship.

I, Luciana, had the privilege to know and commune with Michel de Nostredame. If you peer into the golden vessel, you will learn of my relationship with him, which occurred long before his fame. I know of his future through the waters. His gift of the hourglass completed the earthly elemental tools. You must know that he could see you through the wisdom of the bowl, and he gave me the hourglass to pass on to you. You will know how to use it when the time comes.

You will soon recall many more of your past lives, such as that of Laurinda, the youngest of Druid High Priestesses, who lived during one of the most volatile times in Ireland's history. Maeve brought her Irish magic to her days spent in Antebellum New Orleans. Jocelyn, who from the darkest depths of despair shall soon bring light to one of the greatest mysteries of your time.

As you recall your past lives, you will open to the wider perspective of your life on this earth. You will become aware of all knowledge needed to navigate through life's adventures. In turn, you are to write your insights to enlighten future generations of the wisdom you obtain. This is a crucial directive for you to follow. It is vital that you act in accordance with this instruction.

Some of the lives you witness are from your ancestral bloodline, while others are fragments from the journey of your soul. You and I are both. It matters not how you have gained your heritage. We are all linked - all one with the Source. My life is yours. My memory joins with your mind - we are one being. We think with the Mind of God, availing us to the powers of the Infinite. You are to open up to the highest possibilities - to obtain the knowledge and power of God - that which is yours to achieve. This is what it means to Know Thyself.

As you have learned through your dreams, they inform you how to apply your knowledge in service to those whose lives you touch. You are in possession of the four elemental tools, the most influential being the golden vessel, for everything about you is of water, the most powerful force on earth. You must learn to use these talismans simultaneously for the betterment of earth's enfoldment, for their power is not just for humankind, but for all beings, for the earth itself, as a living, breathing life form, and for the universe as a whole.

The golden bowl used with sacred water serves you in your prophecies as a seer, revealing both the wisdom of the world as it is, but more of what lies in other dimensions. Water is a symbol of transition as it moves from its liquid state, to ice, to vapor. It represents reflection, clarity, intuition, and life itself.

The chalice of the eternal flame cleanses, renews, and enables you to become instantly cleared of all that you wish to release. Fire represents energy, power, passion, and creativity - ever lighting the way to new adventure.

The hourglass holds sands of quartz crystals, representing the power of the earth. When used with the other golden objects, it shall take you far beyond time and space, into worlds without end.

The amulet pendulum represents air and motion, used to aid you in determining the best course of action for any given occurrence. It resonates with all elements, bringing them into synchronicity.

The aquamarine ring protects you from harm. You may venture into the world, knowing that wherever you are, you are ever safe. You will be naturally guided to those that possess the other rings similar to yours. These people are your council, those with whom you will share your journey. When gathered together, your rings emanate a powerful radiance that shifts the energy of the place where you join in unity. Each year, in a different location, that shift shall support the forward change of the earth and her inhabitants.

When used together, these golden talismans shall empower you so you are able to better increasingly perceive the unseen. Your awareness of other dimensional fields will become manifest, allowing you to Know Thyself by distinguishing the larger perspective - the dominion of the Divine.

I am the only one who had all five in my possession, yet I knew not how to best utilize their powers to their fullest potential, but I must tell you my accomplishments were astounding. I know already, these amulets attune to you, and your use of them will enable you to achieve wondrous events beyond your imagining. With these elemental tools, you will be the master practitioner of the elements. They will assist you in serving the earth, as was their purpose when given to us by the Star People. There will be a time when you will join with these beings, for your soul will evolve to dimensions beyond the realm of this earth. From there, your soul will journey onward, never to cease in its becoming.

Know that I am here in the spirit world, as are all who have gone before you. Call on us to assist you. Be still, know, and listen - the answers will come in a myriad of ways - remain open to the possibilities and you will never falter. Ease and grace in all things will come to you, if you inquire with a humble heart. Love surrounds you as you are greatly blessed to know thyself to be the Sacred Carrier of the Sacred Life Force. You, Sophia, are the sacred holy vessel of water - the most powerful force upon the earth.

Your true journey now begins. I send you great blessings,

With love,

Your grandmother, Luciana Nervetti da Genova, on this day of our Lord,

17 April 1541

Sophia sat back and took a deep breath. In her hands were the words of her grandmother from five centuries past, communicating through the mystic realm. The sacred bowl held the elemental key to the past and future. Sophia knew that she could now look into the sacred waters and join with the memory of Luciana and any of her past lives... and with her future. The other golden items were powerful, but the bowl was the final piece that would enable Sophia to accomplish great wonders. She no longer needed to wait until her dreams revealed her past - she could access them any time she desired through the golden bowl.

There were still questions hanging out there: How did Luciana's sacred bowl end up at the cabin? Sophia did not imagine that her mother, Elizabeth, left it there, for she died when Sophia was three years old, long before Patrick bought the cabin. The only logical conclusion remaining was that Patrick left it behind. Elizabeth remained a mysterious apparition about whom Patrick rarely spoke – a woman that Sophia only remembered as a loving but faint shadow.

"She died of cancer, far too young," was all Patrick ever offered, claiming his grief was unbearable and too difficult to discuss. He never remarried - a testament to his sorrow. Sophia had always longed for information, but Patrick was adamant – always the enigmatic loner of few words, who rarely, if ever, bared his soul.

She questioned even more so about why her father never revealed such a significant piece of her pre-history. Why did he keep information about her mother a secret? Sophia's dreams of Roxana clearly implied the significance of the maternal ancestry of the Oracle, and yet Sophia knew nothing of her mother's life, or of Elizabeth's mother before her. The revelation of the ancient sacred bowl hidden at the cabin presented more questions than answers. Sophia realized those answers would most probably reveal themselves in the sacred water once she learned how to harness its power.

She looked at the elegant simplicity of the bowl. She felt the energy vibrate from it, even without the water.

Thoughts of her mother entered her mind – a gentle, dark shadow that never quite left her. Suddenly, as if touched by fire, Sophia caught her breath and looked at the bowl, with the surge of realization that comes from an "Ah-ha!" moment.

The voice of Darius caught her ears as if he sat next to her:

"It was given to a couple that came into Gaston's shop here in New Orleans on their honeymoon back in the 1970s. The woman was enchanted by the bowl, and Gaston discovered that she had the power within her, most likely through her heritage as you apparently do, Sophia…"

Everything suddenly became crystal clear to her. The newlyweds to whom Gaston gave the bowl were her parents! The bowl belonged to Elizabeth – her mother. Sophia wondered for a brief moment, *Why is it that the most obvious answers seem to lie in obscurity?* She burst into tears.

The unsettled mysteries were just beginning to unravel. One thing she truly knew, when something from the past revealed itself from out of the shadows, more arose to the surface for examination. From there it could be released and therefore healed. She would never understand it all, but that was what the journey was about - the search for meaning…

Upon the revelation that her mother was the woman who discovered the golden bowl at Gaston's shop so long ago, Sophia called him at *"Nothing But Tyme,"* to tell him of her discovery. Perhaps he had some insight to share that would help Sophia connect with her mother. Gaston, in his usual enigmatic way, revealed little emotion at Sophia's epiphany, but he assured her that eventually he would help her learn more.

She knew little of her mother's ancestry, and nothing of her childhood. Sophia's father always told stories of his upbringing, but he did not speak about the early years of their marriage. To her knowledge, her mother had no psychic or intuitive powers, but the presence of the golden bowl changed that assumption. *How,* she wondered, *is it I never knew about Dad's involvement in the Order of Apeiros?* Apparently, the only way Sophia would be able to find out the details of their past would be to ask the golden bowl for answers.

Another question arose: *How was it that the letter inside the box remained unknown?* From Luciana to the present time, 500 years had gone by. It was not hidden that well – just placed under the lining. Surely, someone else should have found the envelope...

Michael returned from chopping wood outside. He grabbed a cold beer from the refrigerator and sat down with Sophia in the great room. Sophia left the letter from Luciana on the end table next to the sofa for him to read. Michael noticed the fine crystal goblet in her hand as she sat on the couch next to him.

"You don't break out the crystal unless we have company, or when you are doing a ritual. What's the occasion?"

"While you've been out there all day, I've had quite an afternoon in here," she said. "I'm not having a ritual right now. I just needed a drink."

"Uh-oh," Michael said.

She pulled out the bowl. "Have a look."

Michael took the bowl and turned it in his hands. He

looked at her, and then back at the bowl. He gave a soft, almost silent whistle. "Is this…what I think-"

"It is."

He gently ran his hand over the etchings. "Where-"

"Here," Sophia said. "In the cabin. It has been here, stashed away in a box all these years. Or, am I telling you something you already knew?"

"Oh no," Michael said, raising his hands in surrender. "See this quizzical look on my face? It's real. Where do you suppose it came from?"

"You remember I told you that Gaston gave it to a couple on their honeymoon down in New Orleans in the '70s? Guess who."

"Whoa," Michael said, shifting back in his seat and placing his arms wide on the back of the sofa. "I think you just learned more about your mom in one afternoon than you've known your entire life."

"Ya think?" Sophia said. "Get this: when I took the bowl from the box, I accidently pulled out the blue velvet lining inside. Underneath was an old letter. It's written in Italian from probably my 15-times-great-grandmother named Luciana during the mid 1500s. Luciana, remember her? The hourglass? The great-grandmother - many times removed - of Darius' lineage, who was involved with Nostradamus? She wrote this, addressed to me, Sophia – she called me by my name!"

"You're kidding! I have to see this. Where is it?"

"It's next to you on the end table." She pointed at the pages of aging parchment.

Michael appeared to look right at the letter. "Where? Did it fall on the floor?" He stood up and looked under the table.

Sophia curiously watched. "On the table, Sherlock. It's right in front of you!"

Michael looked at the table, and then turned to Sophia with a sarcastic shrug.

Sophia could not believe what she was witnessing. She got up from the couch, placed her wine glass on the end table, and picked up the pages of the letter. "Right here!" She waved them in front of him. "Well - no more beer for *you!*"

Michael blankly stared at her.

Sophia felt a sudden chill. "You see this, right?"

Michael's eyes shifted back and forth. "See what?"

"Right here - this letter. Michael?"

"Sweetheart, I don't see anything."

Sophia looked down and rustled the paper. "You're telling me you don't hear that?"

"No! Your hands are moving, but there is nothing there. Obviously, *one of us* needs to stop drinking."

Sophia heard the voice of Darius again: *"Gaston said, when he handed the letter to the woman...it vanished the moment it touched her hand - vanished! - into thin air!"*

Sophia sat down next to Michael with a sigh. "Well, that explains why nobody has seen this letter for 500 years. It was meant only for me – just like the other letter from Maeve must have been meant only for my mom."

Michael's eyes darted. "What? Your mom? Sweetheart, I'm a little lost here."

Sophia tried to speak, but words did not come out.

"What other letter?" Michael asked. "I feel like I just walked into the middle of a movie."

"Ok, just listen."

"Like, *The Twilight Zone* or something."

"Michael, just listen, ok? This is me. That is all you need to know. I *am* holding a letter in my hand. I know you cannot see it, but trust me, I found it in the same box where I found the bowl. I would like to read it to you, if you don't mind."

Always astounded by Sophia's mysterious ways, Michael just sat back knowing the mystery just kept getting better. "You're going to read me the letter that's not in your hands? And you think *I've* had too much beer?"

Sophia grew angry, but she calmly spoke. "There is a letter in my hand, although you can't see it. And I want to read it to you, if you don't mind."

"If I can't see it, do you think when you read it, I won't be able to hear you?"

Sophia's glare knocked the smirk off his face. "Do you want to hear it or not?"

"Okay, okay!" he said. He sat back, placed his arms on the back of the sofa again, and smiled. "Just when you think you've settled into your powers, something else shows up. Evidently, you are now able to see things that others can't. What's next in the life of Sophia Delaney?"

"For now, I'll read what Luciana wrote over 500 years

ago. It's in Italian, so even if you could see the letter, you wouldn't know what it says, anyway. You're just going to have to believe me when I tell you I see things that you cannot."

Sophia slowly read the letter. Michael listened intently, growing more astonished with every word. When she finished, he teasingly said, "It's about time that someone recognized how important I am."

"Please, Michael, enough with the jokes. I need to know what you think about this."

"I think it makes sense, now that you have all the elemental items together. Their collective power enables you to see into greater dimensions, melding them with the physical earthly dimension that we live in. If I were you, I would strap on my seatbelt, because you're about to take a wild ride."

"Well, I've got news for you. You are my traveling companion. So, buckle up, yourself!"

All Sophia could do was shake her head, taking in her new realization of what happened that day. Her work had just begun. Accompanied by her dreams and the talismans, she would bypass time and enter other dimensions – just as Luciana did. The question was whom would she recall next?

She was ever recalling her past lives and her ancestry, but what about her future lives? This brought up the question of who would be her heir. Sophia was in her forties, past the age of safe childbearing, and she clearly had not considered having children. She still had at least another fifty years to make her contribution to the world, but she still needed to consider who would be her successor to the Delaney fortune. To whom would she pass on her knowledge and use of the golden items? Hers was a task of great significance. It was something she would have to consider for the future of the Oracle tradition.

CHAPTER
Thirty~two

*T*hat night, Sophia dreamt of Luciana, which began the recall of her life during the Renaissance, in Genova, Liguria, Italy, otherwise known as Genoa in Sophia's timeline. Sophia smiled in her sleep, able to see Luciana, who had written to her from centuries before. She was a woman in her early thirties, with long dark hair accentuated by a few natural streaks of silver along her face, tied in a stylish chignon at the back of her neck. Her golden brown eyes showed great wisdom that only came from life's journeys and years of challenge.

Luciana's husband died several years before she wrote the letter to Sophia. He left her as the sole proprietor of a small but very successful inn along a busy seaside road on the outskirts of Genova. Not only was it a place for travelers to eat and sleep, it was also a center for people to gather for health, well-being, and spiritual guidance. In a way, it was a renaissance spa.

Extraordinarily skilled in the healing arts, Luciana created custom concoctions of herbal remedies and tonics to bring one to perfect health. She also had a gift for forecasting, using her golden bowl to read a person's life events. For many seers who used Tarot as a new technology of the occult, Luciana was a rival, but she felt no such challenge, knowing her work was through the guidance of the Divine.

However, it was the time of the Inquisition. Empirics, apothecaries, and those like her, with the gifts of prophecy and healing, were in danger. Only men could train in the university, particularly in the new field of medicine. People like Luciana had to do healing work behind closed doors and beyond the eyes of the church, lest they be condemned for witchcraft and sentenced to death.

The church sought out offenders, particularly women, to blame for issues of concern like bad weather, poor crops, and disease. Religious systems rooted in the belief that Eve was responsible for the fall of Adam took action against women as both inferior and the source of most evil. The plague had consumed the lives of millions, reducing the population in Europe by a third, and the church was hard pressed for answers. A scapegoat of blame placed on an earthly source was a way of control, otherwise, the church would lose faithful followers and wealthy patrons. Those connected to the powers of the earth - with knowledge of herbs and the shifting of energies - were at risk. Women, in general, including midwives, were in jeopardy.

Some healers were envious of Luciana's abilities, calling her a sorcerer or witch. By trade, Luciana was an innkeeper, while privately she was a seer and healer in the shadows. She consulted her angels when working with an ill patient, peering into the golden vessel of sacred waters and foretelling his or her needs to bring them to their wholeness. Beyond time and space, she communed with the spirits on high, knowing just what to do, which herbs to administer, the correct tonic to create, and knowing just how to pray for her client's well-being. She knew her power did not lie within her own abilities, but instead, authority came to her through her level of faith. If her patients' faith in God was equally strong, they would join in her belief and healing would take place in what appeared to be a miracle.

Energetically, her vibration was so high that it shifted most anyone from their level of malady and disease - that which was out of balance and out of the natural order - to that of a higher frequency, enabling them to receive what they needed to come back to full health. She healed livestock, thus increasing the farmer's prosperity, for animals were extremely receptive to her healing vibrations.

She brought her healing energy to farmers' crops, ridding them of insects and disease simply by aiding the farmer and his family to live in an environment of peace and harmony with the land and their surroundings. When the farmer experienced no dissension, he did not attract discord. His crops produced a larger, healthier yield, thus creating greater prosperity for the future. In a loving atmosphere, he and his wife raised healthy, happy children, and their lives operated in accord with the natural flow of nature's balance. Luciana's reputation for healing spread throughout Italy. Like her ancestor, the Oracle of Delphi, she performed miracles beyond any other healing modality of the time.

In the autumn of 1539, a stately and elegant man stayed at the inn, having traveled from the south of France. There was something intriguing about him, drawing Luciana's interest. Quiet and reserved, he appeared tremendously sad. One evening, she offered him a flagon of mead - honey wine made from her beehives. He gratefully accepted the offering, and when he reached for the pewter vessel, she noticed a long gash on his forearm.

"Come with me. I must dress your wound," she said.

"I would gratefully accept your aid," he responded.

Luciana washed the injury with fresh water and applied a poultice made of honey, calendula, myrrh, lavender, and comfrey. She wrapped a clean white rag around his arm and tied it at his wrist.

"I am called Luciana. I am the proprietor here. I will wash and change your dressing each day until you are healed."

He noticed the amethyst crystal pendulum hanging from her necklace. Enchanted by its elegance, never had he seen a piece of jewelry so simple and exquisite, and yet it emitted great power. He shifted his attention away to Luciana.

"This place will be a welcome resort for my healing. May I introduce myself, my name is Michel de Nostredame. I left my home in Saint Remy de Provence, where my wife and two children recently died of the plague. I was forced to flee, fearing persecution by the inquisitors." He could not help but notice all the bottles of concoctions on tables and shelves. From the rafters she hung clusters of varied herbs to dry. What called his greatest interest was the golden bowl sitting on the table next to a flaming chalice, both made of the same lustrous metal.

She responded, "I am humbly at your service, good sir.

My name is Luciana Nervetti da Genova - my condolences for your tremendous loss. You are most welcome to stay as long as you like so you are able to rejuvenate for your upcoming travels. I too must resist the questioning eyes of the church. I keep my deeper healing arts in the shadows, only offering them in the night's darkest hours. It is clear that I may be of some assistance as you move toward your future. May I offer you a reading?"

"That would be most welcome."

"Come and sit with me as I prepare my golden vessel..."

Sophia suddenly awoke to the sound of a door slamming. The winds of early spring rushed down the mountainside and through the spruce trees, competing with the sound of the river's white waters. The door to the shed outside unlatched and slammed shut again. Michael was sound asleep, unaffected by the noise. Sophia quietly dressed and threw a blanket around her shoulders. She took a flashlight and walked outside to latch the door.

Before she came back inside the cabin, she looked up at the skies filled with sparkling starlight. She shut off the flashlight and laid back in a comfortable chaise lounge, wrapping herself tightly in the blanket while she peered into the cloudless sky. There was no moon that night, leaving the heavens to blaze with crystal reflections. She marveled at the Milky Way arching directly overhead until its band of stars seemed to disappear beyond the surrounding mountain peaks.

Sophia believed that the galactic starlight traveled millions of miles for millennia. Just like her many past lives, many of these cosmic bodies no longer existed, yet their energy remained as the light left behind for her to see. She felt privileged to witness the magnificence of the cosmic order of all things, and possessed a deep desire to understand its mysteries.

She could not help but compare the distant galactic wonder to the memories of her past. She continued to recall her life from thousands of years before as the High Priestess of Akrotiri, the Oracle of Delphi, and as the gifted healers and seers who touched the lives of many who made an enormous impact on human history. Three thousand six hundred years was merely a flash of light in the cosmic picture of time and space, and yet, within that respective point in time, both horrifying and wondrous events occurred, affecting the lives of more than a hundred generations.

She relaxed under the starlit canopy, realizing that she was made of the stuff of stars, emanating from the explosive power of the heavenly bodies that she could see before her in the night sky. Spiritually, and on a quantum level, she was made of the infinite field of possibilities - from the inestimable realm of everything that was not of a physical nature.

Her awareness of all this began with her near-death experience, informing her of life beyond appearances. Sophia finally realized she no longer thought of death as an ending, but rather it was a portal to an ever-expanding life, that of Apeiros, the cause of all unity and measure of all things.

From that point forward, she catapulted into the search for her life's purpose. It left her ever in the quest for understanding God, as Infinite Intelligence, the eternal power of absolute awareness, the consciousness that included love and all its attributes. This was what generated the quest within her to Know Thyself.

From that vast, unbounded expansive nature, her awareness came through to pass on the healing power and all knowledge that she obtained. Her soul would continue to expand - she would be more powerful in the next life - but until then, she had yet to know more of what this life and her past lives had to offer.

Knowing further about the life of Luciana from Genova, Italy, and her association with Nostradamus would be tremendously intriguing. Eventually, Sophia would link Luciana to her descendent, Luciano Delaney, father of Maeve.

She had seen a glimpse of her life as Laurinda, the youngest High Priestess of the Druids in ancient Ireland. Laurinda was an extension of the Oracle tradition. Although there were no written accounts of the Druid people, Sophia's ability to see into Laurinda's history through the golden bowl would fill in details of the early evolution of Ireland's mythic culture.

Sophia was deeply interested in her recall of Maeve, and the life of her daughter, Alannah, during the antebellum days of the Old South leading up to the Civil War. Her recall of their lives would help her to correlate the family history of the plantation house, and the legacy she would eventually inherit.

The most important life to uncover was the unknown life of Sophia's mother, Elizabeth. Going back to query into her mother's childhood would give Sophia insight to the obscurity and secrecy of her life. It would also reveal the mystery about her father, Patrick.

Nevertheless, something was brewing in the near future. She could feel it down to the cellular levels of her body. There was a reason for Sophia to know all that was filtering into her memory. This was partially the meaning to Know Thyself, but none of what she was about to do was hers to do alone. Only with the support of her new association with so many exalted sages, seers, and prophets would she be able to accomplish what she was to do, within her calling.

They were all here in this present time to support her, as she was to be of service to them. Together they would be among the ones to hold the high watch, in high consciousness, for all the earth. Almost nightly, she recalled her past lives as tremendously powerful people and their association with the many sages and teachers of history. None of this was a coincidence. Eventually, what she needed to know would be revealed in due time.

She remembered what her dear friend told her when she had endured great loss: *"I find that the people who have the greatest loss, also have the greatest call."* She knew she had a calling. That was clear to her, but she had no idea of what was yet to come. Sophia knew for herself what she knew for all beings – she was the only one like herself, ever, in perpetuity. The recall of her past lives reminded her of her soul's journey, helping her to realize that never again would there be the same ripe opportunities to utilize, to the fullest, all of her gifts and talents. It was up to her, as her individual self within the nature of God, that she alone could access and bring to fulfillment that which she came *to be* in this lifetime, as was every soul's journey.

Sophia realized she no longer thought of death as an ending, but rather as a continuance – a portal to an ever-expanding, eternal life – that of apeiros.

She leaned back in the still, comfortable night and gazed at the stars until her eyes fluttered and closed...

In her dreams, Sophia shifted into another dynamic past life. She saw herself in Paris, France, as Jocelyn Brewster-Davis during her final weekend abroad after spending over two years in Europe. She had sailed across the Atlantic Ocean for many business opportunities, but most recently, she had traveled as a newlywed with her husband, Henry Davis. Sadly, their marriage was short-lived. Eighteen months earlier, Henry died of influenza during their visit with his family in Pembrokeshire, Wales, where he was born and raised.

Jocelyn came from an ancestry of healthy American stock, as a tenth generation great-granddaughter of William and Mary Brewster, two of the more notable Mayflower passengers. Of the 102 aboard the famed ship, only one-half lived past the first six months of their residence in Plymouth Colony, Massachusetts. William, Mary, and two of their children who came with them on the Mayflower were among the survivors. The Brewsters would later reunite with their remaining children.

They were the only family not stricken by the plague that brought significant death to the colony. William, a natural leader, was later referred to as, "The Patriarch of the Pilgrims." He and Mary were the ancestors of more American descendants, numbering in the thousands, than any of the other original Mayflower passengers.

Following Henry's death, Jocelyn took eighteen months to travel through most of Europe, ending up in the South of France for the winter, but she left for Paris to enjoy its springtime enchantment. There, she was just beginning to feel a new zest for her work as she made the decision to begin her life again in New York. She had a sense to wait a few more months to perhaps travel overseas during the summer, but she had endured such grief and thought that she had best return to the States sooner than later.

War was looming, and she did not want to remain in Europe. Still, she sensed she should not go on this particular voyage. She bypassed her intuitive warnings, thinking it was simply grief holding her back from her return to New York, where she and Henry had their home.

Henry Davis was a successful steel baron and left Jocelyn very well off, leaving her without a financial care. She had achieved distinction of her own before their marriage as a successful Art Nouveau clothing designer, whose fashions sold well in New York, London, Rome, and in Paris, the fashion capital of the world. She believed a woman should be dressed in the highest of standards, to the point of making a statement, but with war on the way, changing lifestyles would naturally alter fashions to accommodate the needs of the general population.

She planned to continue her line of business as a couture designer, creating custom clothing designs for her elite patrons. However, a new concept in shopping for pleasure at the department store made way for ready-to-wear clothing, offering off-the-rack fashions for the shopper. What emerged for Jocelyn was an expanded vision for her career - to begin her life again in New York as one of the world's first clothing designers to mass-produce affordable, yet stylishly beautiful garments for the modern-day woman. In the mid 19th century, mass production in New York began out of necessity for the making of thousands of Civil War military uniforms for Union soldiers. It was fifty years later, and Jocelyn believed she could revolutionize the fashion trade, projecting that she could provide jobs for hundreds of people in America and in Europe. She would take New York's Garment District and make it hers.

In celebration of her vision for a new life, Jocelyn decided to splurge by traveling over the North Atlantic in style - in a First Class Cabin at the cost of $150.00. Jocelyn was to embark upon a British passenger liner, leaving on Wednesday, April 10, 1912, from Cherbourg, France, destined for New York City. She would be one of the 2,224 passengers and crew on the maiden voyage of the White Star Line's newest and grandest ship, the *RMS Titanic*...

Next up:

AETERNALIS

Continuum Book Two

available in paperback and on
Kindle and other devices
Amazon.com and other online stores

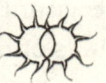

Visit ardyce.org for updated information on the
Continuum Series.

Acknowledgements

While writing is a most solitary endeavor, I could never have accomplished this, my first novel, without the many travelers along my path whom I consider to be my teachers. Some are relations of my bloodline, while others are soul family. We have come together to experience the eternal, whether we have known each other in a brief encounter, or in the continuance of our dance into other lifetimes. We have journeyed together, both in challenge and in triumph. From these experiences, I write. I thank you for the dance.

To those who lived before me, and to all of history, I humbly and gratefully appreciate your contribution to life. Only through your experience am I here in my humanity to glean bits of wisdom and elements of history, to weave the lives of my characters around that which you brought to the world. I am grateful.

Without the complete support of my husband, my teacher and editor, Kevin, I would not have had the opportunity to take these past three years to write Apeiros. He has not only patiently edited it countless times, but he has brainstormed with me details of the story to take it into the next books of the Continuum series. His excellence, never-ending patience, humor, constant support, and encouragement are the creative atmosphere in which I continue to accomplish this, my dream. For you, my beloved, I am tremendously grateful.

Author's Note

The question most asked of me by my readers is, what inspired me to write the Continuum Series? The reasons are multifaceted.

Many years ago, within a few months of each other, I took a couple of unexpected journeys through two different near-death-experiences, one of which was during a surgical procedure, and the other, from a car accident. While in the next dimension, after witnessing an abundantly beautiful, joyful, and peace-filled existence beyond human description, where it was made known to me that I knew everything there was to know, I then heard what sounded like my intuitive voice clearly ask, "Do you want to stay or go back?" My soul self immediately responded, "Oh no, I must go back. I have too much to do."

It was only upon my return to my earthly existence did I realize there was absolutely nothing of any negativity in the realm from which I just returned. Only Love and all its qualities were everywhere present, as I was left with a portal into the expanded awareness of the eternality of the cosmic universe. After years of pondering my soul's reason for my return - while in the question of *Just what was it that I returned to do?* - I began to put pen to paper.

I now write the best way I am able to convey, from my human perspective, what I witnessed while in the timeless realm of the Divine without the veils of my earthly existence. Everything I experienced "there" is here. The eternal *is* here, around us, within us, always and in all ways. It is in every moment - in each timeless moment of now. We experience it in the smallest moments - a tender gaze into the eyes of another as a gentle exchange of the heart, in the laughter of children, and when we take notice of nature's beauty. Each heart-filled experience adds on to the next, creating the sacred way of Love's eternal exchange, which beckons us on to the next moment of grace. We have access to the entire universe, which exists within each of us, and it is up to us to say yes to this magnificence within our own potential. From that place of knowing, we then take positive steps, which lead to giant leaps within the celestial enfoldment - the eternality of our lives.

Each of us is of importance, as in the metaphor of the big cosmic jigsaw puzzle. Each elemental being is an individual piece of the puzzle, shaped differently, in varied colors and textures - all fitting together perfectly to make the grand picture we know as our greater selves - as One. No piece is more important than another, and yet each is crucial in the importance of their individuality and to the whole.

The characters in the Continuum Series are everyday heroes, who face real life challenges while living in their individual part of the world, raising the vibratory frequency, both as individuals, and as a collective body of thirteen. They are wisdom keepers, oracles, light workers, sages, and shamans, some who have joined yet again in this lifetime as they all hold the high watch for the world - and for the universe as a whole. As we journey through each character's life story and witness his or her human challenges, it is my intention to illustrate that no one is without significance or value.

As a lover of history, I wanted to find a way to research and write about historic events and people of interest who have made a profound impact in the metaphysical (beyond the physical) nature of the world. Although I personally believe in past lives, it is not my intention for my readers to do so. I chose to tell the story of Sophia, the main character throughout the series, through her past lives so I could incorporate endless historic accounts for this ongoing tale, while weaving the sacred way of Love's qualities throughout the series. Those same attributes are the basis for the Order of Apeiros, enabling the thirteen to remember their individual soul's journey as they hold fast the highest consciousness for the world.

I have experienced many rich and diverse lifetimes in this singular life, at times through the dark night of the soul. I am so very grateful, for my life has rarely been boring. I live a life of great fortune, for I do what I love, and love what I do, through my writing, my art, and as a spiritual practitioner, life coach, and speaker. Each day I am ever more aware of how blessed I am to have people of tremendous value surrounding me. Everyone I meet is a sacred soul upon this precious planet. This is why I returned - to help people remember who they came here to be, so they can embrace and express their utmost potential, using their individual gifts and talents, which already exist within them.

With my highest intentions, I reach out through the written word, through my illustrations, and my photography, to create stories that bring to the reader joy, peace, hope, harmony, grace, compassion - all wrapped in love... sometimes with a bit of added intrigue and mystery as well.

Knowing for you that love lights your way,

~Ardyce West

About the Author

Ardyce West is an optimum blend of spirituality and transformation. She is a Licensed Practitioner for United Centers for Spiritual Living in Colorado, as well as a certified Life Mastery Consultant and DreamBuilder Coach. Ardyce has expertly chaired large retreats and facilitated transformative healing workshops, assisting others in living a full spectrum wholehearted life through the brilliant guidance and intuition she provides for individuals and groups. Also an extremely accomplished artist, Ardyce has conducted many art and jewelry workshops.

Through captivating storytelling, Ardyce presents an empowering workshop featuring her two near-death experiences, which have resulted in her fascinating life, living through the grace of the Eternal Now.

She is the author of the metaphysical Continuum historical fiction series, including *Apeiros - Continuum Book One, Aeternalis - Continuum Book Two, Síoraí - Continuum Book Three, and Ouroboros - Continuum Book Four,* as well as the beautifully written poignant non-fiction book, *I Never Heard You Cry - A Compassionate Journey Through Abortion,* written to give a voice to the many who are affected by abortion, either through personal experience or through that of a loved one. With *Réalta - Continuum Book Five* in the works, Ardyce also wrote and illustrated her first children's book, *There Once Was a Kitty Name Digit.*

Visit ardyce.org for updated information.

Praise for

I Never Heard You Cry -

A Compassionate Journey Through Abortion

"I Never Heard You Cry . . . never approaches political edict or social commentary regarding abortion. Ardyce West focuses rather on the substantial number of people who do struggle with complex and deeply emotional post-abortion issues." - *Publisher*

"For me, a great book is one that leaves me moved and tingling when I complete its final passages. Ardyce West's book, *'I Never Heard You Cry'*, did precisely that for me. Not only will you be supported and inspired, you will find numerous springs of healing in this book. It is poignant as well as practical, offering compassion and insight in a controversial and troubled arena. Read this book and let your heart be touched." - *Dr. Roger W. Teel, Senior Minister and Spiritual Director, Mile Hi Church, Lakewood, Colorado*

"Ardyce West courageously shares her vulnerability in exposing her soul's journey of healing after her experience of abortion. Her insights give us all strength in moving forward after irreplaceable loss into greater awareness. *'I Never Heard You Cry'* is a significant and much needed work that will heal lives." - *Rev. Christian Sorensen, D.D., Seaside Center for Spiritual Living, Encinitas, CA*

"This is a book that will support healing and transform the way people look at abortion if they are willing to suspend fearful concepts. I highly encourage you to read this book and share it with your family, friends and even counseling clients. It will make a difference in how they view the experience of abortion and hopefully encourage them to open their hearts." - *Cynthia James, Author, What Will Set You Free, Revealing Your Extraordinary Essence*

"This extraordinary book isn't about pro-life, pro-choice, politics or religion. It's about people - the vast majority of us who understand that abortion is not a black-and-white issue that can only be addressed in absolutes. While it is an essential book for those who are struggling with unexpected and unattended post-abortion grief, it's also an excellent book for parents to share with their kids to help them learn about consequences and accountability." *- Kevin Cahill, Author, Sand Creek, Letters to a Rose, The Last Cafe, Knights of Harvest*

What reviewers are saying on Amazon.com:

"Few know how to heal the emotional wounds that accompany abortion. We don't talk about it much. This book is a good place to begin. It speaks with compassion, and offers signposts to acceptance, forgiveness, and healing." - *T. Nash*

"This book attempts to sort it out without all the screaming, finger-pointing and useless drama. I applaud this author for bringing some peace to all the pain on both sides of this serious and divisive issue." - *Jane*

"It has been written with such care and compassion while elevating us beyond the false oversimplification of this being a matter merely of either pro-life or pro-choice." - *Bruce*

"It was like finding Spring water in the desert of judgment that surrounds abortion and other such life decisions that many face in this complicated world." - *Suzanne*

"This book should be given to anyone considering or has been through an abortion." - *Susan*

"The book is about so much more than the journey through abortion, it speaks to me on many different levels about my own experiences in life." - *Frannie*

"I would highly recommend *"I Never Heard You Cry"* for anyone facing a healing process or anyone who works in an area of healing or spiritual counseling." - *Carol*

I Never Heard You Cry -
a Compassionate Journey Through Abortion
by Ardyce West

Available in paperback
and e-book at Amazon.com,
BarnesAndNoble.com,
and other online book stores